THE
INDIA
FAN

By Victoria Holt

THE INDIA FAN

THE SILK VENDETTA

SECRET FOR A NIGHTINGALE

THE ROAD TO PARADISE ISLAND

THE LANDOWER LEGACY

THE TIME OF THE HUNTER'S MOON

THE DEMON LOVER

THE JUDAS KISS

THE MASK OF THE ENCHANTRESS

THE SPRING OF THE TIGER

MY ENEMY THE QUEEN

THE DEVIL ON HORSEBACK

THE PRIDE OF THE PEACOCK

LORD OF THE FAR ISLAND

THE HOUSE OF A THOUSAND LANTERNS

THE CURSE OF THE KINGS

ON THE NIGHT OF THE SEVENTH MOON

THE SHADOW OF THE LYNX

THE SECRET WOMAN

THE SHIVERING SANDS

THE QUEEN'S CONFESSION

THE KING OF THE CASTLE

MENFREYA IN THE MORNING

THE LEGEND OF THE SEVENTH VIRGIN

BRIDE OF PENDORRIC

KIRKLAND REVELS

MISTRESS OF MELLYN

THE INDIA FAN

Victoria Holt

Doubleday

NEW YORK   LONDON   TORONTO   SYDNEY   AUCKLAND

All of the characters in this book
are fictitious, and any resemblance
to actual persons, living or dead,
is purely coincidental.

Published by Doubleday, a division of
Bantam Doubleday Dell Publishing Group, Inc.,
666 Fifth Avenue, New York, New York 10103

Doubleday and the portrayal of an anchor with a dolphin
are trademarks of Doubleday, a division of
Bantam Doubleday Dell Publishing Group, Inc.

Library of Congress Cataloging-in-Publication Data

The India fan / Victoria Holt.
p.   cm.
I. Title.
PR6015.I3I5   1988   87-36497
823'.914—dc19   CIP
ISBN 0-385-24600-5

10 9 8 7 6 5 4 3

BG

Contents

THE
INDIA
FAN

ENGLAND & FRANCE

The Big House

I had always been fascinated by the big house of Framling. Perhaps it had begun when I was two years old and Fabian Framling had kidnapped me and kept me there for two weeks. It was a house full of shadows and mystery, I discovered, when I went in search of the peacock-feather fan. In the long corridors, in the gallery, in the silent rooms, the past seemed to be leering at one from all corners, insidiously imposing itself on the present and almost—though never quite—obliterating it.

For as long as I could remember Lady Harriet Framling had reigned supreme over our village. Farm labourers standing respectfully at the side of the road while the carriage, emblazoned with the majestic Framling arms, drove past, touched their forelocks and the women bobbed their deferential curtsies. She was spoken of in hushed whispers as though those who mentioned her feared they might be taking her name in vain; in my youthful mind she ranked with the Queen and was second only to God. It was small wonder that when her son, Fabian, commanded me to be his slave, I—being only six years old at that time—made no protest. It seemed only natural that we humble folk should serve the Big House in any way that was demanded of us.

The Big House—known to the community as "The House" as though those dwellings which the rest of us occu-

3

pied were something different—was Framling. Not Framling Hall or Framling Manor but simply *Framling*, with the accent on the first syllable which made it sound more impressive. It had been in the possession of the Framlings for four hundred years. Lady Harriet had married into the family most condescendingly, for she was the daughter of an Earl, which, my father told me, meant that she was Lady Harriet instead of simple Lady Framling. One must never forget that, for the fact was that she had married beneath her when she became the wife of a simple baronet. He was dead now, poor man. But I had heard that she never allowed him to forget her higher rank; and although she had come to the village only when she was a bride, ever since she had considered it her duty to rule over us.

The marriage had been unproductive for years—a source of great annoyance to Lady Harriet. I guessed she constantly complained bitterly to the Almighty for such an oversight; but even Heaven could not ignore Lady Harriet forever, and when she was forty years old, fifteen years after her wedding day, she gave birth to Fabian.

Her joy was boundless. She doted on the boy. It was simple logic that *her* son must be perfect. His slightest whim must be obeyed by all underlings; and the Framling servants admitted that Lady Harriet herself would smile indulgently at his infant misdemeanours.

Four years after the birth of Fabian, Lavinia was born. Although, being a girl, she was slightly inferior to her brother, she was Lady Harriet's daughter and therefore far above the rest of the community.

I was always amused to see them come into church and walk down the aisle—Lady Harriet followed by Fabian, followed by Lavinia. They would be watched with awe while they took their places and knelt on the red and black prayer mats embroidered with the letter F; and those behind were able to witness the amazing spectacle of Lady Harriet's kneeling to a Higher Authority—an experience which made up for everything else the service lacked.

I would stare in wonder as I knelt, forgetting that I was in church, until a nudge from Polly Green reminded me and recalled me to my duty.

Framling—the House—dominated the village. It had been

built at the top of a slight incline which made one feel that it
was on the alert, watching for any sins we might commit. Although there had been a house there in the days of the Conqueror, it had been rebuilt over the centuries and there was
hardly anything left of the pre-Tudor building. One passed under a gatehouse with its battlemented towers into a lower
courtyard where plants grew out of the walls, and in iron-
banded tubs shrubs hung over in artistic profusion. There were
seats in the courtyard onto which leaded windows looked
down—dark and mysterious. I always fancied someone was
watching behind those windows—reporting everything to
Lady Harriet.

One went through a heavily studded door into a banquet-
ing hall where several long-dead Framlings hung on the walls
—some fierce, some benign. The ceiling was high and vaulted;
the long polished table smelt of beeswax and turpentine; and
over the great fireplace the family tree stretched out in all di-
rections; at one end of the hall was a staircase leading to the
chapel and at the other end the door to the screens.

During my tender years it seemed to me that all of us in
the village rotated like planets round the glorious blazing sun
that was Framling.

Our own house, right next to the church, was rambling
and draughty. I had often heard it said that it cost a fortune to
heat it. Compared with Framling, of course, it was minute, but
it was true that although there might be a big fire in the drawing room, and the kitchen was warm enough, to ascend to the
upper regions in winter was like going to the arctic circle, I
imagined. My father did not notice. He noticed very little of
practical matters. His heart was in ancient Greece and he was
more familiar with Alexander the Great and Homer than with
his parishioners.

I knew little of my mother because she had died when I
was two months old. Polly Green had come as a substitute; but
that was not until I was just past two years old and had had my
first introduction to the ways of the Framlings. Polly must have
been about twenty-eight when she came. She was a widow who
had always wanted a child, so that just as she took the place of a
mother to me, I was to her the child she never had. It worked
very well. I loved Polly and there was no doubt whatever that

5

Polly loved me. It was to her loving arms that I went in my moments of crisis. When the hot rice pudding dropped into my lap, when I fell and grazed my knees, when I awoke in the night dreaming of goblins and fierce giants, it was to Polly I turned for solace. I could not imagine life without Polly Green.

She came from London—a place in her opinion superior to any other. "Buried myself in the country, all for you," she used to say. When I pointed out to her that to be buried one had to be under the earth in the graveyard, she grimaced and said: "Well, you might as well be." She had contempt for the country. "A lot of fields and nothing to do in them. Give me London." Then she would talk of the streets of the city where something was always "going on," of the markets, lighted by night with naphtha flares, stalls piled high with fruit and vegetables, old clothes and "anything you could think of," and all the costers shouting in their inimitable way. "One of these days I'll take you there and you can see for yourself."

Polly was the only one among us who had little respect for Lady Harriet.

"Who's she when she's out?" she would demand. "No different from the rest of us. All she's got is a handle to her name."

She was fearless. No meek curtsey from Polly. She would not cower against the hedge while the carriage drove past. She would grasp my hand firmly and march on resolutely, looking neither to the right nor the left.

Polly had a sister, who lived in London with her husband. "Poor Eff," Polly would say. "He's not much cop." I never heard Polly refer to him as anything but He or Him. It seemed that he was unworthy of a name. He was lazy and left everything for Eff to do. "I said to her the day she got engaged to him: 'You'll sup sorrow with a long spoon if you take that one, Eff.' But did she take a bit of notice of me?"

I would shake my head solemnly, because I had heard it before and knew the answer.

So in the early days Polly was the centre of my life. Her urban attitudes set her aside from us rural folk. Polly had a way of folding her arms and taking a bellicose stance if anyone showed signs of attacking her. It made her a formidable adversary. She used to say she would "take nothing from nobody" and when I pointed out, having been initiated into the intricacies of English grammar by my governess, Miss York, that two negatives made an affirmative, she merely said: "Here, are you getting at me?"

I loved Polly dearly. She was my ally, mine entirely; she and I stood together against Lady Harriet and the world.

We occupied the top rooms of the rectory. My room was next to hers; it had been from the day she had come and we never wanted to change it. It gave me a nice cosy feeling to have her so close. There was one other room on the attic floor. Here Polly would build up a nice cosy fire and in the winter we would make toast and bake chestnuts. I would stare into the flames while Polly told me stories from London life. I could see the market stalls and Eff and Him, and the little place where Polly had lived with her sailor husband. I saw Polly waiting for him to come home on leave with his baggy trousers and little white hat with *H.M.S. Triumphant* on it and his white bundle on his shoulder. Her voice would quaver a little when she told me of how he had gone down with his ship.

"Nothing left," she said. "No little 'un to remind me of him." I pointed out to her that if she had had a little 'un she wouldn't have wanted me, so I was glad.

There would be tears in her eyes which made her say briskly: "Here. Look at me. You trying to make me soft in me old age?"

But she hugged me just the same.

From our windows we looked down on the churchyard . . . tottery old gravestones, some of them, under which lay those who had long since died. I used to read the inscriptions and wondered what the people who lay there were like. Some of the writing on the stones was almost obliterated, so old were they.

Our rooms were big and wide with windows on either side. Opposite the graveyard, we looked on the village green with its pond and the seats where the old men liked to congregate, sometimes talking, sometimes sitting in silence staring at the water before they shuffled off into the inn to drink a pint of ale. "Death on one side," I pointed out to Polly, "and life on the other."

7

"You're a funny bit of baggage are you," Polly would often reply, for any fanciful remark produced that comment.

Our household consisted of my father, myself, my governess Miss York, Polly, Mrs. Janson the cook-housekeeper, and Daisy and Holly, two lively sisters who shared the housework. I learned later that the governess was there because my mother had brought a little money into the family which had been set aside for my education and I was to have the best possible, no matter what hardship had to be endured to attain this.

I loved my father but he was not as important in my life as Polly was. When I saw him walking across the graveyard from the church to the rectory in his white surplice, prayerbook in hand, fine white hair made untidy by the wind, I felt a great desire to protect him. He seemed so vulnerable, unable to take care of himself, so it was odd to think of him as the guardian of his spiritual flock—particularly when it contained Lady Harriet. He had to be reminded of mealtimes, of when to put on clean clothes, and his spectacles were constantly being lost and found in unexpected places. He would come into a room for something and forget what it was. He was eloquent in the pulpit, but I was sure the villagers at least did not understand his allusions to the classics and the ancient Greeks.

"He'd forget his head if it wasn't fixed on his shoulders," was Polly's comment in the half-affectionate, half-contemptuous tone I knew so well. But she was fond of him and would have defended him with all the rhetoric of her colourful language—sometimes quite different from ours—if the need arose.

It was when I was two years old that I had the adventure of which I could remember so little. I had had the story by hearsay, yet it made me feel I had some connection with the Big House. If Polly had been with me at the time, it would never have happened; and I believe it was due to this that my father realized I must have a nurse who could be trusted.

What happened is an indication of the nature of Fabian Framling and his mother's obsession with him.

Fabian would have been about seven at the time. Lavinia was four years younger and I had been born a year after she was. I had heard details of the story because of the friendship between our servants and those of Framling.

Mrs. Janson, our cook-housekeeper, who worked so well

for us and instilled discipline into the house and kept us all in some order, told me the story.

"It was the strangest thing I ever heard," she said. "It was young Master Fabian. His lordship leads them all a fine dance up at the House . . . always has done. Lady Harriet thinks the sun, moon and stars shine out of his eyes. She won't have him crossed. A little Caesar, that's what he is. He'll have his own way or there'll be ructions. Heaven knows what he'll be like when he's a bit older. Well, his little majesty is tired of playing the old games. He wants something new, so he thinks he'll be a father. If he wants it . . . it's going to be. They tell me up there that he expects everything he wants to be his. And that's no good for anyone, mark my words, Miss Drusilla."

I looked suitably impressed, for I was eager for her to get on with the story.

"You were put in the rectory garden. You could toddle round and that was what you liked to do. They shouldn't have left you. It was that May Higgs, flighty piece, she was. Mind you, she loved little ones . . . but she was courting that Jim Fellings at the time . . . and he came along. Well, there she is giggling with him . . . and didn't see what was happening. Master Fabian was determined to be a father and a father had to have a child. He saw you and thought you would do. So he picked you up and took you to the House. You were his baby and he was going to be your father."

Mrs. Janson put her hands on her hips and looked at me. I laughed. It seemed very funny to me and I liked it. "Go on, Mrs. Janson. What happened then?"

"My goodness, there was a fine how-do-you-do when they found you'd disappeared. They couldn't think where you'd got to. Then Lady Harriet sent for your father. Poor man, he was in a rare flummox. He took May Higgs with him. She was in tears, blaming herself, which was only right that she should do. Do you know, I think that was the start of the rift between her and Jim Fellings. She blamed him. And you know she married Charlie Clay the next year."

"Tell me about when my father went to the House to fetch me."

"Well, talk about a storm! This was one of them tornados. Master Fabian raged and he fumed. He wouldn't give you up.

9

You were his baby. He had found you. He was going to be your father. You could have knocked us all down with feathers when the rector came back without you. I said to him, 'Where's the baby?' and he said, 'She's staying at the Big House, only for a day or so.' I said, shocked-like, 'She's only a baby.' 'Lady Harriet has assured me that she will be well looked after. Miss Lavinia's nurse will take care of her. She will come to no harm. Fabian flew into such a rage when he thought he was going to lose her that Lady Harriet thought he would do himself some harm.' 'You mark my words,' I said, 'that boy—Lady Harriet's son though he may be—will come to a bad end.' I didn't care if it got back to Lady Harriet. I had to say it."

"And so for two weeks I lived in the Big House."

"You surely did. They said it was real comical to see Master Fabian looking after you. He used to wheel you round the gardens in the push chair which had been Miss Lavinia's. He used to feed you and dress you. They said it was really funny to see him. He's always been such a one for rough games . . . and there he was playing the mother. He would have overfed you if it hadn't been for Nancy Cuffley. She put her foot down, took a firm hand for once and he listened. He must have been really fond of you. Goodness knows how long it would have gone on if Lady Milbanke hadn't come to stay with her young Ralph who was a year older than Master Fabian. He laughed at him and told him it was like playing with dolls. It didn't make any difference that this was a live one. It was a girl's game. Nancy Cuffley said Master Fabian was really upset about it. He didn't want you to go away . . . but I suppose he thought it was a slur on his manhood to look after a baby."

I loved the story and asked to have it repeated many times.

It was almost immediately after that incident that Polly came.

Whenever I saw Fabian—usually in the distance—I would look at him furtively, and in my mind's eye see him tenderly caring for me. It was so amusing; it always made me laugh.

I fancied, too, that he looked at me in a rather special way, although he always pretended he did not see me.

Because of our standing in the village—the rector was on a level with the doctor and the solicitor, though of course chasms separated us from the heights on which the Framlings dwelt—

as I began to grow older I was invited to have tea now and then with Miss Lavinia.

Although I did not exactly enjoy these occasions, I was always excited to go into the house. Before those little tea parties I knew very little of it. I had only seen the hall because it had rained once or twice when the garden fête was in progress and we were allowed to shelter from the rain in the House. I shall always remember the thrill of leaving the hall and mounting the stairs, past the suit of armour, which I imagined would be quite terrifying after dark. I was sure it was alive and that when our backs were turned it was laughing at us.

Lavinia was haughty, overbearing, and very beautiful. She reminded me of a tigress. She had tawny hair and golden lights in her green eyes; her upper lip was short and her beautiful white teeth slightly prominent; her nose was small and very slightly turned up at the tip, which gave a piquancy to her face. But her glory was in her wonderful, abundant curly hair. Yes, she was very attractive.

The first time I went to have tea with her stands out in my mind. Miss York accompanied me. Miss Etherton, Lavinia's governess, greeted us and there was an immediate rapport between her and Miss York.

We were taken to tea in the schoolroom, which was large with panelled walls and latticed windows. There were big cupboards there, which I guessed contained slates and pencils and perhaps books. There was a long table at which generations of Framlings must have learned their lessons.

Lavinia and I regarded each other with a certain amount of hostility. Polly had primed me before I left. "Don't forget, you're as good as she is. Better, I reckon." So with Polly's words ringing in my ears, I faced her more as an adversary than as a friend.

"We'll have tea in the schoolroom," said Miss Etherton, "and then you two can get to know each other." She smiled at Miss York in an almost conspiratorial manner. It was clear that those two would like a little respite from their charges.

Lavinia took me to a window seat and we sat down.

"You live in that awful old rectory," she said. "Ugh."

"It's very nice," I told her.

"It's not like this."

"It doesn't have to be nice."

Lavinia looked shocked that I had contradicted her and I felt that ours was not going to be the easy relationship which that between Miss York and Miss Etherton showed signs of becoming.

"What games do you play?" she asked.

"Oh . . . guessing games, with Polly, my nurse, and with Miss York we sometimes imagine we are taking a journey through the world and mention all the places we should pass through."

"What a dull game!"

"It's not."

"Oh yes it *is,*" she affirmed as though that were the last word to be said on the matter.

The tea arrived, brought in by a maid in starched cap and apron. Lavinia dashed to the table.

"Don't forget your guest," said Miss Etherton. "Drusilla, will you sit here?"

There was bread and butter with strawberry jam and little cakes with coloured icing on them.

Miss York was watching me. Bread and butter first. It was impolite to have cakes before that. But Lavinia did not observe the rules. She took one of the cakes. Miss Etherton looked apologetically at Miss York, who pretended not to notice. When I had eaten my piece of bread and butter I was offered one of the cakes. I took one with blue icing on it.

"It's the last of the blue ones," announced Lavinia. "I wanted that."

"Lavinia!" said Miss Etherton.

Lavinia took no notice. She regarded me, expecting me, I knew, to give the cake to her. Remembering Polly, I did not. I deliberated, picked it up from my plate and bit into it.

Miss Etherton lifted her shoulders and looked at Miss York.

It was an uncomfortable teatime.

I believe both Miss York and Miss Etherton were greatly relieved when it was over and we were despatched to play, leaving the two governesses together.

I followed Lavinia, who told me we were going to play hide and seek. She took a penny from her pocket and said:

"We'll toss." I had no idea what she meant. "Choose heads or tails," she said.

I chose heads.

She spun the coin and it landed on the palm of her hands. She held it where I could not see it and said, "I've won. That means I choose. You'll hide and I'll seek. Go on. I'll count to ten . . ."

"Where . . ." I began.

"Anywhere . . ."

"But this house is so big . . . I don't know."

"Course it's big. It's not that silly little rectory." She gave me a push. "You'd better go on. I'm starting to count now."

Of course she was Miss Lavinia of the Big House. She was a year older than I. She seemed very knowledgeable and sophisticated; and I was a guest. Miss York had told me that guests often had to be uncomfortable and do things they would rather not. It was all part of the duty of being a guest.

I went out of the room leaving Lavinia counting ominously. Three, four, five . . . It sounded like the tolling of the funeral bell.

I hurried on. The house seemed to be laughing at me. How could I possibly hide in a house of whose geography I was ignorant?

For a few moments I went blindly on. I came to a door and opened it. I was in a small room. There were some chairs, the seatbacks of which had been worked in blue and yellow needlepoint. It was the ceiling that attracted my attention; it was painted and there were little fat cupids up there seated on clouds. There was another door in this room. I went through it and I was in a passage.

There was no place to hide there. What should I do? I wondered. Perhaps make my way to the schoolroom, find Miss York and tell her I wanted to go home. I wished Polly had come with me. She would never have left me to the mercy of Miss Lavinia.

I must try to retrace my steps. I turned and went, as I thought, back. I came to a door, expecting to see the fat cupids on the ceiling, but this was not so. I was in a long gallery, the walls of which were lined with pictures. There was a dais at one end on which stood a harpsichord and gilded chairs.

I looked fearfully at the portraits. They seemed like real people regarding me severely for having trespassed into their domain.

I felt the house was jeering at me and I wanted Polly. I was getting near to panic. I had the uneasy notion that I was caught and never going to get away. I was going to spend the rest of my life wandering about the house trying to find my way out.

There was a door at one end of the gallery. I went through this and was in another long passage. I was facing a flight of stairs. It was either a matter of going on or going back to the gallery. I mounted the stairs; there was another passage and then . . . a door.

Recklessly I opened this. I was in a small dark room. In spite of mounting fears I was fascinated. There was something foreign about it. The curtains were of heavy brocade and there was a strange smell. I learned afterwards that it was sandal-wood. There were brass ornaments on carved wooden tables. It was an exciting room and for a moment I forgot my fears. There was a fireplace and on the mantel shelf a fan. It was very beautiful, in a lovely shade of blue with big black spots. I knew what it was, because I had seen pictures of peacocks. It was a fan made of peacock feathers. I felt an urge to touch it. I could just reach it by standing on tiptoe. The feathers were very soft.

Then I looked about me. There was a door. I went to it. Perhaps I could find someone who would show me the way back to the schoolroom and Miss York.

I opened the door and looked cautiously in.

A voice said, "Who is there?"

I advanced into the room. I said, "It is Drusilla Delany. I came to tea and I am lost."

I went forward. I saw a high-backed chair and in it an old lady. There was a rug over her knees, which I felt showed she was an invalid. Beside her was a table strewn with papers. They looked like letters.

She peered at me and I looked back boldly. It was not my fault that I was lost. I had not been treated as a guest should be.

"Why do you come to see me, little girl?" she asked in a high-pitched voice. She was very pale and her hands shook. For a moment I thought that she was a ghost.

"I didn't. I'm playing hide and seek and I am lost."

"Come here, child."

I went.

She said, "I have not seen you before."

"I live in the rectory. I came to tea with Lavinia and this is supposed to be a game of hide and seek."

"People don't come to see me."

"I'm sorry."

She shook her head. "I am reading his letters," she said.

"Why do you look at them if they make you cry?" I asked.

"He was so wonderful. It was ill fortune. I destroyed him. It was my fault. I should have known. I was warned . . ."

I thought she was the strangest person I had ever met. I had always sensed that extraordinary things could happen in this house.

I said I should have to go back to the schoolroom. "They will wonder where I am. And it is not very polite for guests to wander about houses, is it?"

She put out a hand which reminded me of a claw and gripped my wrist. I was about to call for help when the door opened and a woman came into the room. Her appearance startled me. She was not English. Her hair was very dark; her eyes deep set and black; she was wearing what I learned later was a sari. It was a deep shade of blue, rather like the fan, and I thought it beautiful. She moved very gracefully, and said in a pleasant sing-song voice: "Oh dearie me. Miss Lucille, what is this? And who are you, little girl?"

I explained who I was and how I came to be here.

"Oh, Miss Lavinia . . . but she is a naughty, naughty girl to treat you so. Hide and seek." She lifted her hands. "And in this house . . . and you find Miss Lucille. People do not come here. Missie Lucille likes to be alone."

"I'm sorry, I didn't mean to."

She patted my shoulder. "Oh no . . . no . . . it is naughty Miss Lavinia. One of these days . . ." She pursed her lips, and putting the palms of her hands together, gazed up at the ceiling for a moment. "But you must go back. I will show you. Come with me."

She took my hand and pressed it reassuringly.

I looked at Miss Lucille. The tears were slowly running down her cheeks.

"This part of the house is for Miss Lucille," I was told. "I live here with her. We are here . . . and not here . . . You understand?"

I didn't, but I nodded.

We went back by way of the gallery and then through parts which I had not seen before and it seemed to me some little time before we reached the schoolroom.

The woman opened the door. Miss York and Miss Etherton were deep in conversation. There was no sign of Lavinia.

They looked startled to see me.

"What happened?" asked Miss Etherton.

"They play hide and seek. This little one . . . in a house she does not know. She was lost and came to Miss Lucille."

"Oh, I *am* sorry," said Miss Etherton. "Miss Lavinia should have taken better care of her guest. Thank you, Ayesha."

I turned to smile at her. I liked her gentle voice and kind black eyes. She returned my smile and went gracefully away.

"I hope Drusilla didn't, er . . ." began Miss York.

"Oh no. Miss Lucille lives apart with her servants. There is another . . . both Indian. She was out there, you know. The family has connections with the East India Company. She is a little . . . strange now."

Both governesses looked at me and I guessed the matter would be discussed further when they were alone.

I turned to Miss York and said, "I want to go home."

She looked uneasy, but Miss Etherton gave her an understanding smile.

"Well," went on Miss York, "I suppose it is about time."

"If you must . . ." replied Miss Etherton. "I wonder where Miss Lavinia is. She should come and say goodbye to her guest."

Lavinia was found before we left.

I said, "Thank you," in a cold voice.

She said, "It was silly of you to get lost. But then you are not used to houses like this, are you?"

Miss Etherton said, "I doubt there is another house like this, Lavinia. Well . . . you must come again."

Miss York and I left. Miss York's lips were pursed together, but she did say to me, "I should not care to be in Miss Etherton's shoes from what she told me . . . and the boy is worse." Then she remembered to whom she was talking and said it had been really quite a pleasant visit.

I could hardly call it that, but at least it had held elements of excitement which I should not easily forget.

Although I was not eager to visit the house again, its fascination for me had increased. Whenever I passed it I used to wonder about the strange old lady and her companion. I was consumed with curiosity, for I was by nature inquisitive; it was a trait I shared with Polly.

I used to go down to my father's study on some days when he was not busy. It was always just after tea. I almost felt I was one of those things like his spectacles which he forgot about from time to time; it was when he needed his spectacles that he looked for them and when a sense of duty came over him he remembered me.

There was something lovable about his forgetfulness. He was always gentle with me and I was sure that if he had not been so concerned about the Trojan Wars he would have remembered me more often.

It was quite a little game talking with him, the object being for him to get onto some classical subject and for me to steer him away from it.

He always asked how I was getting on with my lessons and whether I was happy with Miss York. I thought I was doing quite well and told him that Miss York seemed satisfied.

He would nod, smiling.

"She thinks you are a little impulsive," he said. "Otherwise she has a good opinion of you."

"Perhaps she thinks I am impulsive because she is not."

"That could be so. But you must learn not to be rash. Remember Phaeton."

I was not quite sure who Phaeton was, but if I asked he would take possession of the conversation, and Phaeton could lead to some other character from those old days when people were turned into laurels and all sorts of plants, and gods became swans and bulls to go courting mortals. It seemed to me such an odd way of going on and in any case I did not believe it.

"Father," I said, "do you know anything about Miss Lucille Framling?"

A vague look came into his eyes. He reached for his spectacles as though they might help him to see the lady.

"I did hear Lady Harriet say something once . . . Someone in India, I think."

"There was an Indian servant with her. I saw her. I got lost playing hide and seek and I found her. The Indian took me back to Miss York. It was rather exciting."

"I did know that the Framlings were somehow connected with India. The East India Company, I suppose."

"I wonder why she is shut off like that in a wing of the house."

"She lost her lover, I think I heard. That can be very sad. Remember Orpheus who went down to the underworld to search for Eurydice."

I was so preoccupied with the mystery of Miss Lucille Framling that I allowed my father to win that session and the rest of the time was taken up by Orpheus and his trip to the underworld to find the wife who had been snatched from him on their wedding day.

In spite of that unfortunate beginning, my acquaintance with Lavinia progressed and, though there was always a certain antipathy between us, I was attracted by her and perhaps most of all by the house, in which anything might happen; and I never entered it without that feeling that I was embarking on an adventure.

I had told Polly about the game of hide and seek and how I had met the old lady.

"Tut tut," she said. "There's a nice little madam for you. Don't know how to treat her guests, that's for certain. Calls herself a lady."

"She said the rectory was small."

"I'd like to get her carrying coal up them stairs."

I laughed at the thought.

Polly was good for me. She said: "You're a sight more of a little lady than she is. That's for sure. So you just stand up to

18

her. Tell her a thing or two and if she don't like it, well, there's no harm done, is there? I reckon you could enjoy yourself somewhere nice with me . . . more than that old house. Time for it to go to the knacker's yard if you was to ask me."

"Oh, Polly, it's the most marvellous house!"

"Pity it's got them living in it that don't know their manners."

I used to think of Polly when I went into the house. I was as good as they were, I reminded myself. I was better at my lessons. That had slipped out. I had heard Mrs. Janson say that that Miss Lavinia led Miss Etherton a nice dance and refused to learn when she didn't feel like it, so that that young lady was at least a couple of years behind some people. I knew who "some people" implied and I felt rather proud. It was a useful piece of knowledge to be remembered when I was in the presence of Lavinia. Moreover I knew how to behave better than she did, but perhaps she knew and refused to act as she had been taught. I had been in Lavinia's company long enough to know that she was a rebel.

Then there was Polly's admonition to give her as good as I got, so I did not feel quite so vulnerable as I had on that first occasion.

My father constantly said that all knowledge was good and one could not have too much of it. Miss York agreed with him. But there was one piece of knowledge that I could have been happier without.

Lady Harriet had smiled on my friendship with Lavinia and therefore it must persist. Lavinia was learning to ride and Lady Harriet had said that I might share her lessons. My father was delighted, and so I went riding with Lavinia. We used to go round and round the paddock under the watchful eyes of Joe Cricks, the head groom.

Lavinia enjoyed riding and therefore she did it well. She took a great delight in showing how much more proficient she was than I. She was reckless and did not obey orders as I did. Poor Joe Cricks used to get really scared when she disregarded his instructions and she was very soon ordering him to take her off the leading rein.

"If you want to feel good on your mount," said Joe Cricks,

"don't be afraid of him. Let him see that you are the master. On the other hand . . . there's dangers."

Lavinia tossed her tawny hair. She was fond of the gesture. Her hair was really magnificent and this called attention to it.

"I know what I am doing, Cricks," she said.

"I didn't say as how you didn't, Miss Lavinia. All I says is . . . you have to consider the horse as well as yourself. You may know what you're doing but horses is nervous creatures. They get it into their heads to do something you might not be expecting."

Lavinia continued to go her own way; and her very boldness and assurance that she knew better than anyone else carried her through.

"She's going to be a good horsewoman," was Joe Cricks's comment. "That's if she don't take too many risks. Now, Miss Drusilla, she's a more steady party. She'll come to it in time . . . then she'll be real good."

I loved the lessons, trotting round the paddock, the excitement of the first canter, the thrill of the first gallop.

It was one afternoon. We had had our lessons and had taken the horses back to the stables. Lavinia dismounted and threw her reins to the groom. I always liked to stay behind for a few minutes to pat the horse and talk to him, which was what Joe had taught us to do. "Never forget," he said. "Treat your horse well and the chances are he'll treat you well. Horses is like people. You have to remember that."

I came out of the stables and started across the lawn to the house. There I was to join Lavinia in the schoolroom for tea. Miss York was already there enjoying a tête-à-tête with Miss Etherton.

There were visitors in the house. There often were, but they did not concern us. We hardly ever saw Lady Harriet—a fact for which I was extremely grateful.

I had to pass the drawing-room, which was open, and I caught a glimpse of a parlourmaid serving tea to several people. I went hurriedly past, averting my eyes. Then I paused to look up at that part of the house which I thought must be Miss Lucille's quarters.

As I did so I heard a voice from the drawing room. "Who is that *plain* child, Harriet?"

"Oh . . . you mean the rector's daughter. She is here quite frequently. She comes to keep Lavinia company."

"Such a contrast to Lavinia! But then Lavinia is so beautiful."

"Oh yes . . . You see, there are so few people. I gather she is quite a pleasant child. The governess thinks so . . . and it is good for Lavinia to have the occasional companion. There aren't so many people here, you know. We have to make do with what we can get."

I stared ahead of me. *I* was the plain child. *I* was here because they couldn't get anyone else. I was stunned. I knew that my hair was a nondescript brown, that it was straight and unmanageable . . . so different from Lavinia's tawny locks; my eyes were no colour at all. They were like water, and if I wore blue they were blueish, green, greenish . . . and brown . . . just no colour at all. I knew I had a big mouth and an ordinary sort of nose. So that was plain.

And of course Lavinia was beautiful.

My first thought was to go into the schoolroom and demand to be taken home at once. I was very upset. There was a hard lump in my throat. I did not cry. Crying for me was for lighter emotions. Something within me was deeply hurt and I believed that the wound would be with me forever.

"You're late," Lavinia greeted me.

I did not explain. I knew what her reaction would be.

I looked at her afresh. No wonder she could behave badly. She was so beautiful that people did not mind.

Polly, of course, noticed my preoccupation.

"Here, don't you think you'd better tell me?"

"Tell you what, Polly?"

"Why you look about as happy as if you've lost a sovereign and found a farthing."

I could not hold out against Polly, so I told her. "I'm plain, Polly. That means ugly. And I go to the House only because there is no one better here."

"I never heard such a load of nonsense. You're not plain. You're what they call interesting, and that's a lot better in the long run. And if you don't want to go to that house, I'll see you don't. I'll go to the rector and tell him it's got to stop. From what I hear you'd be no worse without them."

"How plain am I, Polly?"

"About as plain as Dundee cake and Christmas pudding."
That made me smile.

"You've got what they call one of them faces that make
people stop and take a second look. As for that Lavinia . . . or
whatever she calls herself . . . *I* don't call her all that pretty
when she scowls . . . and my goodness, she does a good bit of
that. I'll tell you what. She'll have crows' feet round her eyes
and railway lines all over her face the way she goes on. And I'll
tell you something else. When you smile your face all lights up.
Well, then you're a real beauty, you are."

Polly raised my spirits and after a while I began to forget
about being plain, and as the House always fascinated me, I
tried not to remember that I was only chosen because there was
no one better available.

I had caught glimpses of Fabian, though not often. Whenever I did see him I thought of the time when he had made me
his baby. He must remember, surely, because he would have
been seven when it happened.

He was away at school most of the time and often he did
not come home for holidays, but spent them with some school
friend. His school friends came to the House sometimes, but
they took little notice of us.

On this occasion—it was Easter time, I think—Fabian was
home for the holidays. Soon after Miss York and I arrived at the
House it began to rain. We had tea and Lavinia and I left the
governesses together for their usual chat. We were wondering
what to do when the door opened and Fabian came in.

He was rather like Lavinia, only much taller and very
grown up. He was four years older than Lavinia and that
seemed a great deal, particularly to me, who was a year
younger than Lavinia. He must therefore have been twelve,
and as I was not yet seven, he seemed very mature.

Lavinia went to him and hung on his arm as though to say,
this is my brother. You can go back to Miss York. I shan't need
you now.

He was looking at me oddly—remembering, I knew. I was
the child whom he had thought was his. Surely such an episode

must have left an impression, even on someone as worldly as Fabian.

"Will you stay with me?" pleaded Lavinia. "Will you tell me what we can do? Drusilla has such silly ideas. She likes what she thinks are clever games. Miss Etherton says she knows more than I do . . . about history and things like that."

"She wouldn't have to know much to know more than you do," said Fabian—a remark which, coming from anyone else, would have thrown Lavinia into a temper, but because Fabian had said it, she giggled happily. It was quite a revelation to me that there was one person of whom Lavinia stood in awe—not counting Lady Harriet, of course, of whom everyone was in awe.

He said, "History . . . I like history, Romans and all that. They had slaves. We'll have a game."

"Oh, Fabian . . . really?"

"Yes. I am a Roman, Caesar, I think."

"Which one?" I asked.

He considered. "Julius . . . or perhaps Tiberius."

"He was very cruel to the Christians."

"You need not be a Christian slave. I shall be Caesar. You are my slaves and I shall test you."

"I'll be your queen . . . or whatever Caesars have," announced Lavinia. "Drusilla can be our slave."

"You'll be a slave, too," said Fabian, to my delight and Lavinia's dismay.

"I shall give you tasks . . . which seem to you impossible. It is to prove you and see whether you are worthy to be my slaves. I shall say, 'Bring me the golden apples of Hesperides' . . . or something like that."

"How could we get them?" I asked. "They are in the Greek legends. My father is always talking about them. They are not real."

Lavinia was getting impatient, as I, the plain outsider, was talking too much.

"I shall give you the tasks to perform and you must carry them out or suffer my anger."

"Not if it means going down to the underworld and bringing out people who are dead and that sort of thing," I said.

"I shall not command you to do *that*. The tasks will be difficult . . . but possible."

He folded his arms across his chest and shut his eyes as though deep in thought. Then he spoke, as though he were the Oracle of whom my father talked now and then. "Lavinia, you will bring me the silver chalice. It must be a certain chalice. It has acanthus leaves engraved on it."

"I can't," said Lavinia. "It's in the haunted room."

I had never seen Lavinia so stricken, and what astonished me was that her brother had the power to drive the rebellion out of her.

He turned to me. "You will bring me a fan of peacock feathers. And when my slaves return to me, the chalice shall be filled with wine and while I drink it my slave shall fan me with the peacock-feather fan."

My task did not seem so difficult. I knew where there was a peacock-feather fan. I was better acquainted with the house than I had once been and I could find my way easily to Miss Lucille's apartments. I could slip into the room where I knew the fan to be, take it and bring it to Fabian. I should do it so quickly that he would commend me for my speed, while poor Lavinia was screwing up courage to go to the haunted room.

I sped on my way. A feeling of intense excitement gripped me. The presence of Fabian thrilled me because I kept thinking of the way in which he had kidnapped me, and there I had been, living in the house for two weeks just as though I were a member of the family. I wanted to astonish him with the speed with which I carried out my task.

I reached the room. What if the Indian were there? What would I say to her? "Please may I have the fan? We are playing a game and I am a slave."

She would smile, I guessed, and say "Dearie dearie me," in that sing-song voice of hers. I was sure she would be amused and amenable, though I wondered about the old lady. But she would be in the adjoining room, sitting in the chair with the rug over her knees, crying because of the past which came back to her with the letters.

I had opened the door cautiously. I smelt the pungent sandalwood. All was quiet. And there on the mantel shelf was the fan.

I stood on tiptoe and reached it. I took it down and then ran out of the room back to Fabian.

He stared at me in amazement.

"You've found it already?" He laughed. "I never thought you would. How did you know where it was?"

"I'd seen it before. It was when I was playing hide and seek with Lavinia. I went into that room by accident. I was lost."

"Did you see my great-aunt Lucille?"

I nodded. He continued to stare at me.

"Well done, slave," he said. "Now you may fan me while I await my chalice of wine."

"Do you want to be fanned? It's rather cold in here."

He looked towards the window from which came a faint draught. Raindrops trickled down the panes.

"Are you questioning my orders, slave?" he asked.

As it was a game I replied, "No, my lord."

"Then do my bidding."

It was soon after that when Lavinia returned with the chalice. She gave me a venomous look because I had succeeded in my task before she had. I found I was enjoying the game.

Wine had to be found and the chalice filled. Fabian stretched himself out on a sofa. I stood behind him wielding the peacock-feather fan. Lavinia was kneeling proffering the chalice.

It was not long before trouble started. We heard raised voices and running footsteps. I recognized that of Ayesha.

Miss Etherton, followed by Miss York, burst into the room.

There was a dramatic moment. Others whom I had not seen before were there and they were all staring at me. There was a moment's deep silence and then Miss York rushed at me.

"What have you done?" she cried.

Ayesha saw me and gave a little cry. "You have it," she said. "It is you. Dearie dearie me . . . so it is you."

I realized then that they were referring to the fan.

"How could you?" said Miss York. I looked bewildered and she went on, "You took the fan. Why?"

"It . . . it was a game," I stammered.

"A game!" said Miss Etherton. "The fan . . ." Her voice was shaking with emotion.

"I'm sorry," I began.

Then Lady Harriet came in. She looked like an avenging goddess and my knees suddenly felt as though they would not hold me.

Fabian had risen from the sofa. "What a fuss!" he said. "She was my slave. *I* commanded her to bring me the fan."

I saw the relief in Miss Etherton's face and I felt a spurt of laughter bubbling up. It might have been mildly hysterical, but it was laughter all the same.

Lady Harriet's face had softened. "Oh, Fabian!" she murmured.

Ayesha said, "But the fan . . . Miss Lucille's fan . . ."

"I commanded her," repeated Fabian. "She had no alternative but to obey. She is my slave."

Lady Harriet began to laugh. "Well, now you understand, Ayesha. Take the fan back to Miss Lucille. No harm has been done to it and that is an end to the matter." She turned to Fabian. "Lady Goodman has written asking if you would care to visit Adrian for part of the summer holiday. How do you feel?"

Fabian shrugged his shoulders nonchalantly.

"Shall we talk about it? Come along, dear boy. I think we should give a prompt reply."

Fabian, casting a rather scornful look at the company which had been so concerned over such a trivial matter as the borrowing of a fan, left with his mother.

The incident was, I thought, over. They had been so concerned and it seemed to me that there was something important about the fan, but Lady Harriet and Fabian between them had reduced it to a matter of no importance.

Ayesha had gone, carrying the fan as though it were very precious, and the two governesses had followed her. Lavinia and I were alone.

"I have to take the chalice back before they find we had that, too. I wonder they didn't notice, but there was such a fuss over the fan. You'll have to come with me."

I was still feeling shocked, because I had been the one to take the fan, which was clearly a very important article since it had caused such a disturbance. I wondered what would have happened if Fabian had not been there to exonerate me from blame. I should probably have been banned from the house forevermore. I should have hated that, although I never felt welcome there. Still, the fascination was strong. All the people in it interested me . . . even Lavinia, who was frequently rude and certainly never hospitable.

I thought how noble Fabian had looked pouring scorn on them all and taking the responsibility. Of course, it *was* his responsibility, and it was only right that he should take the blame. But he had made it seem that there was no blame, and that they were all rather foolish to make such a fuss.

Meekly I followed Lavinia to another part of the house, which I had never seen before.

"Great-Aunt Lucille is in the west wing. This is the east," she told me. "We are going to the Nun's room. You had better watch out. The Nun doesn't like strangers. I'm all right. I'm one of the family."

"Well, why are you frightened to go alone?"

"I'm not frightened. I just thought you'd like to see it. You haven't got any ghosts in that old rectory, have you?"

"Who wants ghosts anyway? What good do they do?"

"A great house always has them. They warn people."

"Then if the Nun wouldn't want me, I'll leave you to go on your own."

"No, no. You've got to come, too."

"Suppose I won't."

"Then I'll never let you come to this house again."

"I wouldn't mind. You're not very nice . . . any of you."

"Oh, how dare you! You are only the rector's daughter and he owes the living to us."

I was afraid there might be something in that. Perhaps Lady Harriet could turn us out if she were displeased with me. I understood Lavinia. She wanted me with her because she was afraid to go to the Nun's room alone.

We went along a corridor. She turned and took my hand. "Come on," she whispered. "It's just along here."

She opened a door. We were in a small room that looked like a nun's cell. Its walls were bare and there was a crucifix hanging over a narrow bed. There was just one table and chair. The atmosphere was one of austerity.

She put the chalice on the table and in great haste ran out of the room, followed by me. We sped along the corridors and then she turned to regard me with satisfaction. Her natural arrogance and composure had returned. She led the way back to the room where, a short time before, Fabian had sprawled on a sofa and I had fanned him with the peacock-feather fan.

"You see," said Lavinia, "we have a lot of history in our family. We came over with the Conqueror. I reckon your family were serfs."

"Oh no, we were not."

"Yes, you were. Well, the Nun was one of our ancestresses. She fell in love with an unsuitable man . . . I believe he was a curate or a rector. Those sort of people do not marry into families like ours."

"They would have been better educated than your people, I dare say."

"*We* don't have to worry about education. It is only people like you who have to do that. Miss Etherton says you know more than I do, though you're a year younger. I don't care. *I* don't have to be educated."

"Education is the greatest boon you can have," I said, quoting my father. "Tell me about the Nun."

"He was so far below her that she couldn't marry him. Her father forbade it and she went into a convent. But she couldn't live without him, so she escaped and went to him. Her brother went after them and killed the lover. She was brought home and put in that room, which was like a cell. It has never been changed. She drank poison from the chalice and she is supposed to come back to that room and haunt it."

"Do you believe that?"

"Of course I do."

"You must have been very frightened when you came in for the chalice."

"It's what you have to do when you're playing Fabian's games. I thought that since Fabian had sent me the ghost wouldn't hurt me."

"You seem to think your brother is some sort of god."

"He is," she replied.

It did seem that he was regarded as such in that household.

When we walked home, Miss York said, "My goodness, what a to-do about a fan. There would have been real trouble if Mr. Fabian hadn't been behind it."

I was more and more fascinated by the House. I often thought of the nun who had drunk from the chalice and killed herself for love. I talked of this to Miss York, who had discovered from Miss Etherton that Miss Lucille had become quite ill when she discovered that the peacock-feather fan had been taken away.

"No wonder," she said, "that there was all that fuss about it. Mr. Fabian should never have told you to take it. There was no way that you could know. Sheer mischief, I call it."

"Why should a fan be so important?"

"Oh, there is something about peacocks' feathers. I have heard they are unlucky."

I wondered whether this theory might have something to do with Greek mythology and if it did my father would certainly know about it. I decided to risk a lecture session with him and ask.

"Father," I said, "Miss Lucille at the House had a fan made of peacock's feathers. There is something special about it. Is there any reason why there should be anything important about peacocks' feathers?"

"Well, Hera put the eyes of Argus into the peacock's tail. Of course, you know the story."

Of course I did not, but I asked to hear it.

It turned out to be another of those about Zeus courting someone. This time it was the daughter of the King of Argos and Zeus's wife, Hera, discovered this.

"She shouldn't have been surprised," I said. "He was always courting someone he shouldn't."

"That's true. He turned the fair maiden into a white cow."

"That was a change. He usually transformed himself."

"On this occasion it was otherwise. Hera was jealous."

"I'm not surprised . . . with such a husband. But she should have grown used to his ways."

"She set the monster Argus who had one hundred eyes to watch. Knowing this, Zeus sent Hermes to lull him to sleep with his lyre and when he was asleep to kill him. Hera was angry when she learned what had happened and placed the eyes of the dead monster in the tails of the peacocks."

"Is that why the feathers are unlucky?"

"Are they? When I come to think of it, I fancy I have heard something of that nature."

So he could not tell me more than that. I thought to myself: It is because of the eyes. They are watching all the time . . . as Argus failed to do. Why should Miss Lucille worry so much because the eyes are not there to watch for her?

The mystery deepened. What an amazing house it was, having a ghost in the form of a long-dead nun as well as a magic fan with eyes to watch out for its owner. Did it, I wondered, warn of impending disaster?

I felt that anything could happen in that house; there was so much to discover and, in spite of the fact that I was plain and only asked because there was no one else to be a companion to Lavinia, I wanted to go on visiting the house.

It was a week or so after the incident of the fan that I discovered I was being watched. When I rode in the paddock I was aware of an irresistible urge to look up at a certain window high in the wall and it was from this one that I felt I was being observed. A shadow at the window was there for a moment and then disappeared. Several times I thought I saw someone there. It was quite uncanny.

I said to Miss Etherton, "Which part of the house is it that looks over the paddock?"

"That is the west wing. It is not used very much. Miss Lucille is there. They always think of it as her part of the house."

I had guessed that might be so and now I was sure.

One day when I took my horse to the stable, Lavinia ran on ahead and, as I was about to return to the house, I saw Ayesha. She came swiftly towards me and, taking my hand, looked into my face.

She said, "Miss Drusilla, I have waited to find you alone. Miss Lucille wants very much to speak to you."

"What?" I cried. "Now?"

"Yes," she answered. "This moment."

"Lavinia will be waiting for me."

"Never mind that one now."

I followed her into the house and up the staircase, along corridors to the room in the west wing where Miss Lucille was waiting for me.

She was seated in a chair near the window that looked down on the paddock and from which she had watched me.

"Come here, child," she said.

I went to her. She took my hand and looked searchingly into my face. "Bring a chair, Ayesha," she said.

Ayesha brought one and it was placed very near Miss Lucille.

Ayesha then withdrew and I was alone with the old lady.

"Tell me what made you do it," she said. "What made you steal the fan?"

I explained that Fabian was a great Roman and that Lavinia and I were his slaves. He was testing us and giving us difficult tasks. Mine was to bring a peacock fan to him, and I knew there was one in that room, so I came and took it.

"So Fabian is involved in this. There are two of you. But you were the one who took it and that means that for a while it was in your possession . . . *yours*. That will be remembered."

"Who will remember?"

"Fate, my dear child. I am sorry you took the fan. Anything else you might have taken for your game and no harm done, but there is something about a peacock's feathers . . . something mystic . . . and menacing."

I shivered and looked around me. "Are they unlucky?" I asked.

She looked mournful. "You are a nice little girl and I am sorry you touched it. You will have to be on your guard now."

"Why?" I asked excitedly.

"Because that fan brings tragedy."

"How can it?"

"I do not know *how*. I only know it does."

"If you think that, why do you keep it?"

"Because I have paid for my possession."

"How do you pay?"

"I paid with my life's happiness."

"Shouldn't you throw the fan away?"

She shook her head. "No. One must never do that. To do so is to pass on the curse."

"The curse!" This was getting more and more fantastic. It seemed even wilder than my father's version of the maiden being turned into a white cow.

"Why?" I asked.

"Because it is written."

"Who wrote it?"

She shook her head and I went on, "How can a feather fan be unlucky? It is, after all, only a fan, and who could harm the one who had it? The peacock whose feathers it was must be dead a long time ago."

"You have not been in India, my child. Strange things happen there. I have seen men in bazaars charm poisonous snakes and make them docile. I have seen what is called the Rope Trick when a seer will make a rope stand on end without support and a little boy climb it. If you were in India you would believe these things. Here people are too materialistic; they are not in tune with the mystic. If I had never had that fan I should be a happy wife and mother."

"Why do you watch me? Why do you send for me and tell me all this?"

"Because you have had the fan in your possession. You have been its owner. The ill luck could touch you. I want you to take care."

"I never thought for an instant that it was mine. I just took it for a while because Fabian commanded me to take it. That was all. It was just a game."

I thought: She is mad. How can a fan be evil? How could someone turn a woman into a white cow? My father seemed to believe this though, which was extraordinary. At least he talked as though he believed it. But then the Greeks were more real to him than his own household.

"How can you be sure that the fan is unlucky?" I asked.

"Because of what happened to me." She turned to me and fixed her tragic eyes on me, but they seemed to be staring past me as though she were seeing something which was not in this room.

"I was so happy," she said. "Perhaps it is a mistake to be so happy. It is tempting the fates. Gerald was wonderful. I met him in Delhi. Our families have interests there. They thought it would be good for me to go out for a while. There is a good social life among the English and the members of the Company . . . that is, the East India Company, and we were involved in that. So were Gerald and his family. That was why he was out there. He was so handsome and so charming . . . there could never have been anyone like him. We were in love with each other from the first day we met."

She turned to smile at me. "You are too young to understand, my child. It was . . . perfect. His family were pleased . . . so were mine. There was no reason why we should not be married. Everyone was delighted when we announced our engagement. My family gave a ball to celebrate the occasion. It was really glittering. I wish I could describe India to you, my dear. It was a wonderful life we had. Who would have guessed that there was a tragedy waiting to spring up on us? It came suddenly . . . like a thief in the night, as it says in the Bible, I believe. So it came to me."

"Was it because of the fan?" I asked tremulously.

"Oh, the fan. How young we were! How innocent of life! We went to the bazaar together, for when we were officially engaged that was allowed. It was wonderful. Bazaars are so fascinating, though I was always a little afraid of them, though not with Gerald, of course. It was thrilling . . . the snake charmers . . . the streets . . . the strange music . . . the pungent smell that is India. Goods to sell . . . beautiful silks and ivory . . . and strange things to eat. It was exciting. And as we went along we saw the man selling fans. I was instantly struck by them. 'How lovely they are!' I cried. Gerald said, 'They are very pretty. You must have one.' I remember the man who sold them. He was badly crippled. He could not stand up. He sat on a mat. I remember the way he smiled at us. I did not notice it then, but afterwards it came back to me. It was . . . evil. Gerald unfurled the fan and I took it. It was doubly precious to me because he had given it to me. Gerald laughed at my delight in it. He held my arm tightly. People looked at us as we passed along. I suppose it was because we looked happy. Back in my room I opened the fan. I put it on a table so that I could see it all the time. When my Indian servant came in, she stared at it in horror. She said, 'Peacock-feather fan . . . Oh no, no, Missie Lucille . . . they bring evil . . . You must not keep it here.' I answered, 'Don't be silly. My fiancé gave it to me and I shall always treasure it for that reason. It is his first gift to me.' She shook her head and covered her face with her hands as though to shut out the sight of it. Then she said, 'I will take it back to the man who sold it to you . . . though now it has been yours . . . the evil is there . . . but perhaps a small evil.' I thought she was crazy and I wouldn't let her touch it."

She stopped speaking and the tears began to run down her cheeks.

"I loved the fan," she went on after a while. "It was the first thing he gave me after our engagement. When I awoke in the morning it was the first thing I saw. Always, I told myself, I will remember that moment in the bazaar when he bought it for me. He laughed at my obsession with it. I did not know it then, but I do now. It had already cast its spell on me. 'It is only a fan,' said Gerald. 'Why do you care so much for it?' I told him why and he went on, 'Then I will make it more worthy of your regard. I shall have something precious put in it, and every time you see it you will be reminded of how much I care for you.'

"He said he would take it to a jeweller he knew in Delhi. The man was a craftsman. When I received the fan back it would indeed be something to be proud of. I was delighted and so happy. I ought to have known happiness like that does not last. He took the fan and went into the centre of the town. I have never forgotten that day. Every second of it it is engraved on my memory forever. He went into the jeweller's shop. He was there quite a long time. And when he came out . . . they were waiting for him. There was often trouble. The Company kept it under control, but there were always the mad ones. They didn't see what good we were bringing to their country. They wanted us out. Gerald's family was important in the country . . . as my family was. He was well known among them. When he came out of the jeweller's they shot him. He died there in the street."

"What a sad story. I am so sorry, Miss Lucille," I said.

"My dear child, I see you are. You are a good child. I am sorry you took the fan."

"You believe all that was due to the fan?"

"It was because of the fan that he was in that spot. I shall never forget the look in my servant's eyes. Somehow those people have a wisdom we lack. How I wish I had never seen that fan . . . never gone into the bazaar that morning. How blithe and gay I had been . . . and my foolish impulse had taken his life and ruined mine."

"It could have happened somewhere else."

"No, it was the fan. You see, he had taken it into the jeweller's shop. They must have followed him and waited for him outside."

"I think it could have happened without the fan."

She shook her head. "In time it came back to me. I will show you what was done." She sat there for a few moments with the tears coursing down her cheeks. Ayesha came in.

"There, there," she said. "You shouldn't have brought it all back to yourself. Dearie me, dearie me, it is not good, little mistress . . . not good."

"Ayesha," she said. "Bring the fan to me."

Ayesha said, "No . . . forget it . . . Do not distress yourself."

"Bring it, please, Ayesha."

So she brought it.

"See, child, this is what he did for me. One has to know how to move this panel. You see. There is a little catch here. The jeweller was a great craftsman." She pulled back the panel on the mount of the fan to disclose a brilliant emerald surrounded by smaller diamonds. I caught my breath. It was so beautiful.

"It is worth a small fortune, they tell me, as if to console me. As if anything could. But it was his gift to me. That is why the fan is precious."

"But if it is going to bring you bad luck . . ."

"It has done that. It can bring me no more. Ayesha, put it back. There. I have told you because, briefly, the fan was yours. You must walk more carefully than most. You are a good child. There. Go and rejoin Lavinia now. I have done my duty. Be on your guard . . . with Fabian. You see, he will take some of the blame. Perhaps because you were in possession of it for such a short time it will pass over you. And he, too, would not be considered free of blame . . ."

Ayesha said, "It is time to leave now."

She took me to the door and walked with me along the corridors.

"You must not take too much notice of what she says," she told me. "She is very sad and her mind wanders. It was the terrible shock, you understand. Do not worry about what you have heard. Perhaps I should not have brought you to her, but she wanted it. She could not rest until she had talked to you. It is off her mind now. You understand?"

"Yes, I understand."

And I said to myself: What happened made her mad.

And the thought of the ghostly nun in the east wing and the mad woman in the west made the house seem more and more fascinating to me.

As time passed I ceased to think about the peacock-feather fan and to wonder what terrible things might befall me because it had once been in my possession. I still visited the House; the governesses remained friendly; and my relationship with Lavinia had changed a little. I might still be plain and invited because I was the only girl in the neighbourhood of Lavinia's age and my station in life was not too lowly for me to be dismissed entirely, but I was gaining a little superiority over Lavinia because, while she was exceptionally pretty, I was more clever. Miss York boasted a little to Miss Etherton and on one occasion when Miss Etherton was ill, Miss York went over to the House to take her place until she recovered; and then the gap between myself and Lavinia was exposed. That did a lot for me and was not without its effect on Lavinia.

I was growing up. I was no longer to be put upon. I even threatened not to go to the House if Lavinia did not mend her ways; and it was obvious that that was something she did not want. We had become closer—even allies, when the occasion warranted it. I might be plain, but I was clever. She might be beautiful, but she could not think and invent as I could; and she relied on me—though she would not admit it—to take the lead.

Occasionally I saw Fabian. He came home for holidays and sometimes brought friends with him. They always ignored us, but I began to notice that Fabian was not so oblivious of my presence as he would have us believe. Sometimes I caught his furtive glance on me. I supposed it was due to that adventure long ago when I was a baby and he had kidnapped me.

It was whispered now that Miss Lucille was mad. Mrs. Janson was very friendly with the cook at the House, so, as she said, she had it "straight from the horse's mouth." Polly was like a jackdaw. She seized on every bit of dazzling gossip and stored it up so that she could, as she said, "piece things together a treat."

We used to talk about the House often, for Polly seemed as fascinated about it as I was.

"The old lady's mad," she said. "Not a doubt of it. Never been right in her head since she lost her lover out in India. People must expect trouble if they go to these outlandish places. It turned Miss Lucille's head, all right. Mrs. Bright says she's taken to wandering about the House now . . . ordering them around like they was black servants. It all comes of going to India. Why people can't stay at home, I don't know. She thinks she's still in India. It's all that Ayesha can do to look after her. And she's got another black servant there."

"That's Imam. He comes from India too. I think she brought him with her when she came home . . . with Ayesha, of course."

"Gives me the creeps. Them outlandish clothes and black eyes and talking a sort of gibberish."

"It's not gibberish, Polly. It's their own language."

"Why didn't she have a nice British couple to look after her? Then there's that haunted room and something about a nun. Love trouble there, too. I don't know. I think love's something to keep away from, if you ask me."

"You didn't feel like that when you had Tom."

"You can't find men like my Tom two a penny, I can tell you."

"But everyone hopes you can. That's why they fall in love."

"You're getting too clever, my girl. Look at our Eff."

"Is he still as bad?"

Polly just clicked her tongue.

Oddly enough, after that conversation, there was news of

Him. Apparently he had been suffering, as Polly said, from "Chest" for some time. I remember the day when news came that he was dead.

Polly was deeply shocked. She wasn't sure what this was going to mean to Eff.

"I'll have to go up for the funeral," she said. "After all, you've got to show a bit of respect."

"You didn't have much for him when he was alive," I pointed out.

"It's different when people are dead."

"Why?"

"Oh, you and your 'whys' and 'whats.' It just is . . . that's all."

"Polly," I said. "Why can't I come to the funeral with you?"

She stared at me in amazement.

"You! Eff wouldn't expect that."

"Well, let's surprise her."

Polly was silent. I could see she was turning the idea over in her mind.

"Well," she said at length, "it would show respect."

I learned that respect was a very necessary part of funerals.

"We'd have to ask your father," she announced at length.

"He wouldn't notice whether I had gone or not."

"Now that's not the way to speak about your father."

"Why not, if it's the truth? And I like it that way. I wouldn't want him taking a real interest. I'll tell him."

He did look a little startled when I mentioned it.

He put his hands up to his spectacles, which he expected to have on his head. They weren't there, and he looked helpless, as though he couldn't possibly deal with the matter until he found them. They were, fortunately, on his desk, and I promptly brought them to him.

"It's Polly's sister and it shows respect," I told him.

"I hope this does not mean she will want to leave us."

"Leave us!" The idea had not occurred to me. "Of course she won't want to leave us."

"She might want to live with her sister."

"Oh no," I cried. "But I think I ought to go to this funeral."

"It could be a morbid affair. The working classes make a great deal of them . . . spending money they can ill afford."

"I want to go, Father. I want to see her sister. She's always talking about her."

He nodded. "Well, then you should go."

"We shall be there for a few days."

"I daresay that will be all right. You will have Polly with you."

Polly was delighted that I was going with her. She said Eff would be pleased.

So I shared in the funeral rites, and very illuminating I found it.

I was surprised by the size of Eff's house. It faced a common, round which the four-storied houses stood like sentinels. "Eff always liked a bit of green," Polly told me. "And she's got it there. A little bit of the country and the horses clopping by to let her know she's not right out in the wilds."

"It's what you call the best of both worlds," I said.

"Well, I won't quarrel with that," agreed Polly.

Eff was about four years older than Polly but looked more. When I mentioned this Polly replied, "It's the life she's led." She did not mention Him because he was dead, and when people died, I realized, their sins were washed away by the all-important respect; but I knew it was life with Him that had aged Eff beyond her years. I was surprised, for she did not seem to be the sort of woman who could be easily cowed, even by Him. She was like Polly in many ways; she had the same shrewd outlook on life and the sort of confidence that declared that none was going to get the better of her before anyone had attempted to do so. During my brief stay I recognized the same outlook in others. It was what is referred to as the cockney spirit; and it certainly seemed to be a product of the streets of London.

That visit was a great revelation to me. I felt I had entered a different world. It excited me. Polly was part of it and I wanted to know more of it.

Eff was a little nervous of me at first. She kept apologizing for things. "Not what you're used to, I'm sure," until Polly said, "Don't you worry about Drusilla, Eff. Me and her get on like a house afire, don't we?" I assured Eff that we did.

Every now and then Polly and Eff would laugh and then remember Him lying in state in the front parlour.

"He makes a lovely corpse," said Eff. "Mrs. Brown came in to lay him out and she's done a good job on him."

We sat in the kitchen and talked about him. I did not recognize him as the monster of the past; I was about to remind Polly of this, but when I attempted to, she gave me a little kick under the table to remind me in time of the respect owed to the dead.

I shared a room with Polly. We lay in bed that first night and talked about funerals and how they hadn't known how ill He had been until He had been "took sudden." I was comforted in this strange house to be close to Polly, because below us in the parlour lay "the corpse."

The great day came. Vaguely I remember now those solemn undertakers in their top hats and black coats, the plumed horses, the coffin, "genuine oak with real brass fittings," as Eff proudly explained.

It was piled with flowers. Eff had given him "The Gates of Heaven Ajar," which I thought a little optimistic for one of his reputation—before death, that was. Polly and I had hurried to the flower shop and bought a wreath in the shape of a harp which seemed hardly suitable either. But I was learning that death changed everything.

There was a solemn service, with Eff being supported on one side by Polly and on the other by Mr. Branley, to whom she let rooms in the house. She drooped and kept touching her eyes with a black-bordered handkerchief. I began to think that Polly had not told me the truth about Him.

There were ham sandwiches and sherry, which were taken in the parlour—blinds now drawn up and looking quite different without the coffin—a little prim and unlived-in, but without the funereal gloom.

I learned that there was a great bond between Polly and Eff, though they might be a little critical of each other—Polly of Eff for marrying Him and Eff of Polly because she had "gone into service." Father, Eff hinted, would never have approved of that. Mind you, Eff conceded, it was a special sort of service and Polly was almost one of the family, with that rector who never seemed to know whether he was standing on his head or his heels, and Eff admitted that I was "a nice little thing."

I gathered that Eff was in no financial difficulties. Polly told me that it was Eff who had kept things going in the house on the common. *He* hadn't worked for years because of his Chest. Eff had taken lodgers. The Branleys had been with her for two years and they were more like friends than tenants. One day, of course, when the little nipper grew up they would have to consider getting a place of their own with a garden, but just now the Branleys were safe.

I realized that Eff's fondness for the Branleys was largely due to "the nipper." The nipper was six months old and he dribbled and bawled without reason. Eff allowed them to keep his perambulator in the hall—a great concession of which Father would never have approved—and Mrs. Branley would bring him down so that he could have his airing in the garden. Eff liked that; and I gathered so did Polly. When he lay in his pram Eff would find some excuse to go into the garden and gaze at him. If he were crying—which was often—they would babble nonsense at him: "Didums want his Mumums then?" or something like that, which sounded so strange on their lips, as they were both what Mrs. Janson would have called "sharp tongued." They were completely changed by this baby.

It occurred to me that the great lack in the lives of both Polly and Eff was a baby of their own. Babies seemed to be very desirable creatures—even Fabian had wanted one.

I remember very well an occasion two days after the funeral. Polly and I were going back to the rectory the next day. Polly had been making the most of our last day and she had taken me "up West," which meant the west end of London.

We were in the kitchen. I was seated by the fire and I was so sleepy that I dozed off.

Vaguely I heard Polly say, "Look at Drusilla. She's half asleep already. Well, we did a bit of traipsing about, I can tell you." Then I really did doze.

I awoke suddenly. Eff and Polly were at the table, a big brown earthenware teapot between them.

Eff was saying, "I reckon I could take two more people in here."

"I don't know what Father would have said, you taking in lodgers."

"They call them paying guests . . . in the sort of place I'll have. Did you know, Poll, the Martins next door are going and I reckon I could take on that place."

"Whatever for?"

"More paying guests, of course. I reckon I could make a real business out of this, Poll."

"I reckon you could."

"Mind you—I'd need help."

"What'll you do . . . get someone to come in with you?"

"I'd want somebody I know. Somebody I could trust."

"Nice business."

"What about you, Poll?"

There was a long silence. I was quite wide awake now.

"The two of us would make a regular go of this," said Eff. "It would be a nice little venture. You in service . . . well, you know Father would never have liked that."

"I wouldn't leave Drusilla. She means a lot to me, that child."

"Nice little thing. No beauty . . . but she's sharp and I reckon she's got a way with her."

"Sh!" said Polly.

She looked in my direction and I immediately closed my eyes.

"Well, that won't go on forever, Poll. I reckon sisters ought to stick together."

"Well, if it wasn't for her I'd be with you like a shot, Eff."

"You like the sound of it, do you?"

"I'd like to be here. The country's dead dull. I like a bit of life."

"Don't I know that. Always did, always will. That's you, Poll."

"While she wants me I'll be there."

"You think about it, that's all. You don't want to be at the beck and call of others all your life. You was never one for that."

"Oh, there's not much of the beck and call there, Eff. He's soft . . . and she's like my own."

"Well, it would be a good life. The two of us working together."

"It's nice to know you're there, Eff."

So a new fear had come into my life. There would come a day when I would lose Polly.

"Polly," I said to her that night when we had retired. "You won't go away from me, will you?"

"What you talking about?"

"You might go in with Eff."

"Here! Who's been listening to what she wasn't meant to? Pretending to be asleep. I know. I rumbled you."

"But you won't, will you, Polly?"

"No. I'll be there as long as I'm wanted."

I hugged her, holding her tightly for fear she would escape from me.

It would be a long time before I forgot Eff's holding out the bait of freedom to Polly.

The French Affair

The years passed and I was fourteen years old, doing much the same as I had always done. Miss York was still with me and Polly was my guide, comforter and mentor. I still paid my periodic visits to the House, but I was no longer so subservient to Lavinia. I only had to hint that I would refuse to come and she changed her hectoring ways. She had a faint respect for me—though she would never admit it. I had helped her through one or two scrapes and that gave me an advantage.

Polly and I were closer together. We had paid several visits to Eff, who now had the house next door and was doing well with her paying guests. She seemed to have grown in importance and presided over her two houses in a very gracious and genteel manner. Polly had to admit that Father would have had very little to complain of. The Branleys had gone and been replaced by the Paxtons. "Much better," commented Eff. "Mrs. Paxton always wraps her rubbish before putting it in the dustbin. Mrs. Branley never did. Though I must say I miss the nipper." So, apart from the loss of the baby, the change really was for the better.

"Eff'll do well," said Polly. "All this is right up her street."

I knew that, but for me, Polly would have been with Eff, keeping all those paying guests in order and secretly laughing with Eff over their little foibles. But Polly had sworn never to leave me while I wanted her, and I trusted Polly.

Then life started to change. An architect came to the House because there was something wrong with the structure of the east wing and it had to be put right by an expert who would know how to restore it in a suitable manner. This was Mr. Rimmel, and he and Miss Etherton became very friendly. Lady Harriet was unaware of this until it had gone too far and Miss Etherton announced her engagement to Mr. Rimmel and gave notice to Lady Harriet that she would be leaving in a month to prepare for her wedding.

Lady Harriet was incensed. Apparently there had been a succession of governesses before Miss Etherton's arrival and she had been the only one who had stayed. "People are so inconsiderate," said Lady Harriet. "Where is their gratitude? All these years she has had a good home here."

But Miss Etherton, secure in the love of Mr. Rimmel, was by no means dismayed. She was beyond Lady Harriet's disapproval now.

In due course she went. Two governesses came, but neither of them stayed more than two months.

Lady Harriet then declared that it was rather absurd to employ two governesses when there were two girls virtually of the same age living so close. She had been impressed by Miss York's efficiency and she saw no reason why the young woman should not teach Lavinia and me at the same time.

My father hesitated and said he would have to consult Miss York, which in due course he did. Miss York, like the two governesses whose stay at the House was brief, was not eager to undertake the education of Lavinia; but in due course, attracted by the offer of a larger salary and no doubt overwhelmed by the dominating personality of Lady Harriet, she agreed; and as a result Lavinia sometimes came to the rectory and I sometimes went to the House, where we took lessons together. Miss York, buoyed up by the knowledge that she could to some extent make her own terms, refused to take up residence at the House and insisted on regarding the rector as her employer.

So Lavinia and I did our lessons together.

I was not displeased, for the schoolroom was the scene of my triumphs. Miss York was constantly shocked by Lavinia's ignorance, and though Lavinia often copied my work, and I helped her on many occasions, she was very much my inferior in the schoolroom.

I was at heart quite fond of Lavinia, though I could not understand why. Perhaps it was a feeling of familiarity, for we had known each other for so many years. She was arrogant, selfish and domineering; but I took that as a sort of challenge. I was rather flattered to find that she secretly relied on me. I think I knew her better than anyone else did; thus I became aware of a trait in her character which, without doubt, was the reason why certain things happened to her.

She was governed by a deep sensuality and she had matured early. She was a woman at fifteen, whereas I, in spite of my superior knowledge, was physically a child. She had a small waist and was always at great pains to accentuate her figure, which was showing signs of nubility. She had always been excessively proud of her gorgeous hair. She had perfect white teeth and was fond of displaying them; she would bestow her smiles right and left so that people might see and admire them, which gave a false impression of affability.

Because she had failed academically she had decided that learning was for those who lacked physical charms.

It dawned on me that Lavinia had a perpetual love affair with the opposite sex. She blossomed when men were near. She smiled and sparkled—showing her teeth and tossing her hair—and was an entirely different person.

I saw Fabian now and then. He had been away, first at school, then at the university. Sometimes he came home, almost always bringing a friend with him. I would see him riding out or perhaps in the house when I was having a lesson there.

When Lavinia talked of the young men who came to the House with her brother her eyes would sparkle and she would giggle a good deal. Fabian took no notice of me, and I supposed he had forgotten that time when he had looked after me and made such a fuss when they wanted to take me away. Although it was just a child's game, I had liked to think it had made a special bond between us.

A few days after my fifteenth birthday I met Dougal Carruthers. I was taking the shortcut across the churchyard to the rectory when I noticed the door of the church was open, and as I came nearer I heard the sound of footsteps on the flagstones. I thought perhaps my father was there and that he should be making his way home, as Mrs. Janson would be displeased if he were not at the table punctually for lunch. One had constantly to remind him of such matters.

I stepped into the church and saw a young man standing there gazing up at the roof.

He turned as I entered and smiled at me.

"Hello," he said. "I was just admiring the church. It's very attractive, isn't it?"

"I believe it is one of the oldest in the country."

"Norman obviously. And excellently preserved. It is wonderful how these old places stand up to time. Do you know the history of the place?"

"No. But my father does. He is the rector."

"Oh . . . I see."

"He would be only too delighted to tell you anything you wanted to know."

"How kind!"

I was debating with myself. If I took him home to meet my father we would have to invite him for lunch, and Mrs. Janson did not welcome unexpected guests at mealtimes. On the other hand, if we did not ask him to lunch my father would keep him talking and miss his. In either case we would invoke Mrs. Janson's displeasure.

I said, "Why don't you come and see my father sometime? He will be free this afternoon. Are you staying near here?"

"Yes," he said, waving his arm, "here." I thought he was indicating the local inn, where I believed they occasionally put up paying guests.

I left him in the church and went home. Over lunch I told my father that I had met a man in the church, and he was interested in the architecture and history of the place.

My father brightened, sensing an encounter with someone who shared his enthusiasm.

"He's coming this afternoon. I said you'd see him."

I waited for the young man to arrive, for I feared that if I did not my father would have forgotten he was to see him and I felt I was needed to make the introduction.

In due course he arrived and my father received him delightedly. To my surprise, he told us that he was staying at Framling. I left my father with him and went over to ride.

Lavinia and I were good horsewomen, but we were not allowed to ride without a groom in attendance. Reuben Curry, who had succeeded Joe Cricks as head groom, usually accompanied us. He was a taciturn man, quite immune from Lavinia's wiles, and he kept a firm hand on us. He was an interesting man, very religious. His wife, I had heard from Polly or Mrs. Janson, had "gone astray" when a gypsy encampment rested nearby. Apparently there was one among the gypsies who was "a fascinating fellow. All white teeth and gold earrings and he could play the fiddle a treat. All the maids were in a twitter about him and as he was up to no good a certain amount of harm was done. Goodness knew what went on." Mrs. Janson wouldn't have put anything past him. And Reuben's wife . . . well, she got carried away by the fellow and the truth was he took advantage of her; and when the gypsies went off at the end of the summer, they left a little something behind. The "little something" was Joshua Curry—a bundle of mischief from the day he was born. Another such as his father, it was reckoned, and one for the maids to beware of.

Having heard of Joshua's colourful beginnings, I was interested in him. He had black curly hair and sparkling dark eyes which were always smiling and alert—for what, I could only guess. He was so dark—brown-skinned, lithe and unlike anyone else I knew.

On this occasion, when Lavinia and I arrived at the stables Joshua was there alone. He grinned at us as we entered. I noticed the change in Lavinia at once, for, though he was only a servant, he was a member of the opposite sex. She dimpled and her eyes shone.

Joshua touched his forelock, but not in the way most of them did. He gave the impression that he was doing it as a kind of joke and it did not really mean respect.

"Are our horses saddled?" asked Lavinia haughtily.

Joshua bowed. "Oh yes, my lady. All waiting for you."

"And where is Reuben?"

"He's working. I'm here, though. I reckon I could be your escort today."

"It is usually Reuben or one of the older men," said Lavinia, but I could see that she was secretly pleased.

"Well, today it's yours truly . . . that's if you young ladies will have me."

"I suppose we must," said Lavinia languidly.

We went to the horses. I mounted, using the mounting block. I looked back at Lavinia. Joshua was helping her into the saddle. It seemed to take quite a little time. I saw his face close to hers and noticed how his hand rested on her thigh. I thought she might be angry at the familiarity, but she was by no means so. The colour had heightened in her cheeks and her eyes were sparkling.

"Thank you, Joshua," she said.

"I answer to the name of Jos," he told her. "More friendly, don't you think?"

"I hadn't thought about it," said Lavinia, "but I suppose it is."

I saw his hand on her arm.

"Well then, Jos it is."

"All right," she said. "Jos."

We rode out of the stables and soon we were cantering along. Lavinia let me go ahead so that she was behind with Jos. I heard her laughing, and I thought how strange that was. She was usually so haughty with the servants.

She was more inattentive than ever at her lessons. She was continually studying her face in a looking glass, combing her hair, pulling out little tendrils and letting them spring back, smiling to herself as though she were hoarding some secret.

"I despair of teaching that girl anything," sighed Miss York. "For two pins I would go to Lady Harriet and tell her it's a hopeless task. Really she gets worse than ever." Lavinia did not care. A smugness had settled on her. She was content with life. Something had happened. I was sorry I was the one to discover what.

Dougal Carruthers had formed a firm friendship with my father and during his stay at Framling he came several times to see us and once to lunch.

He told us he was staying for three weeks at the House and that his father had been a great friend of Sir William Framling; they were connected with the East India Company and he would shortly be leaving the country. He confessed to my father that he would rather have studied medieval art and architecture. He shrugged his shoulders, adding that it was a tradition that sons of the family should go into the Company, just as Fabian Framling would eventually do.

Mrs. Janson was not displeased. She reckoned she could put on as good a lunch as Mrs. Bright of the House. All she wanted was notice, and this time she had it.

I liked Dougal. He was very charming to me and did not treat me as Fabian and his friends had—not unkindly or rudely, but simply as though I did not exist.

Dougal had a pleasant habit of glancing my way when he was talking, thus giving the impression that he included me in the conversation, and when, occasionally, I offered a comment, he would listen with attention.

I wished that I had paid more attention when my father talked of the antiquity of our Norman church, so that I could have contributed more.

Once Fabian came to the rectory with him. They sat in the garden and took wine with my father. Dougal and my father were soon deep in conversation and that left me to talk to Fabian.

I saw that he was studying me with a certain interest and I said, "Do you remember when you kidnapped me?"

He smiled. "Yes, I remember. I thought if I wanted a baby all I had to do was find one."

We laughed.

"And you found me," I said.

"I think you must have been a very tolerant baby," he went on.

"I don't remember anything of it. I was rather flattered when I heard of it. Flattered to have been chosen, I mean. But I suppose any baby would have done."

"You seemed to me a suitable subject for adoption."

"I believe there was a great fuss."

"People always make fusses if something unconventional happens."

"Well, you wouldn't have expected my family to let me go without a word, would you?"

"No. But I kept you for two weeks."

"I have heard the story often. I wish I had been aware at the time."

"You would probably have protested if you had known what it was all about. As it was you took it very calmly."

I was very pleased, because it seemed that in talking of the matter, we had broken through some barrier. I imagined that he felt the same and that our relationship would be easier from now on.

We suddenly became involved in the general conversation and after a while Dougal and he left. Dougal was leaving Framling the next day and at the end of the week Fabian would be gone, too.

I could not resist telling Lavinia that they had called.

"Well, they didn't come to see *you*," was her comment.

"I know that, but they came and I was there to talk to them both."

"Dougal is *lovely*, but he's only interested in old things." She grimaced. I imagined she had flaunted her flaming hair before him and had expected him to be overcome by admiration. I was rather pleased that, presumably, he had not been.

I said, "Fabian talked about that time he abducted me."

"Oh, that," she said. "That's all rather boring."

But I could see that my meeting with Dougal rankled. She was quite annoyed when we rode out that afternoon.

Jos was with us. I think he contrived to be our guardian whenever he could; and the fact that he accompanied us rather than Reuben usually put Lavinia in a good mood.

She was very wayward that afternoon. She was both haughty and familiar with Jos; he said little and just smirked at her.

We came to a field across which we always galloped, and it was a competition between Lavinia and me to see who reached the other side first.

I set off and was well ahead. When I came to the edge of the field I pulled up and looked round. I was alone.

Amazed, I called out, "Lavinia, where are you?"

There was no answer. I cantered back to the other side of the field. When I had started off on my gallop they could not have accompanied me.

I rode around looking for them, but after half an hour I

went back to the stables. There was no sign of them. I did not want to go back to the House alone, for there might be a fuss. We were not supposed to ride without a groom. It was at least half an hour before they returned.

Lavinia looked flushed and excited. She assumed an annoyed expression.

"Wherever did you get to?" she demanded. "We've been looking for you everywhere."

"I thought you were galloping across the field after me."

"What field?"

"You know, where we always gallop."

"I can't think what happened," said Lavinia. She smirked and I was quick enough to see the exchanged glances between her and Jos.

I suppose, had I been wiser and more experienced in the ways of the world, I should have guessed what was going on. It would have been obvious to an older person. But I really believed there had been a misunderstanding and that they had not realized I had broken into a gallop.

Polly was in close conversation with Mrs. Janson and Mrs. Janson was saying, "I've warned her time and time again. But does she take any notice? That Holly was always a flighty piece . . . and now I believe she's taken leave of her senses."

"You know what girls are," soothed Polly.

"Well, that girl's courting trouble, that's what. And a nice thing that'll be."

When I was alone with Polly I said, "What's Holly doing?"

"Oh . . . just being silly."

"It sounded as if it was rather dangerous."

"Oh, it's dangerous all right . . . with one like that."

"Who . . . like Holly?"

"No . . . him."

"Tell me about it."

"You've been listening again. Little pitchers have long ears."

"Polly. I'm quite a sizeable pitcher and my ears are normal size, but they work as well as anyone else's. Stop treating me like a child."

Polly folded her arms and looked at me intently.

"Growing up fast," she said, with a hint of sadness.

"I'm not going to be a child forever, Polly. It's time I learned something about the world."

She regarded me shrewdly. "There might be some truth in that," she said. "Young girls have to watch out. Not that I'm worried about you. You're sensible. Been brought up right, you have. I've seen to that. It's that Jos . . . He's one of that kind . . ."

"What kind?"

"He's got a way with him. He'll always have girls after him, and it seems to me that's about all he thinks of. Perhaps that's why he gets what he wants."

I was thinking of the way he looked at Lavinia and how she accepted familiarities from him which, I am sure, as Lady Harriet's daughter, she should not have done.

"And Holly?" I asked.

"She's being silly over him."

"Do you mean he's courting Holly?"

"Courting her! Courting her for one thing . . . and that won't involve a wedding ring. I reckon the silly girl has given what he's after already . . . and that's no clever thing for any girl to do, I can tell you."

"What are you going to do about it?"

Polly shrugged her shoulders. "Me! What can I do? I could speak to the rector. Might just as well speak to a brick wall as speak to him. Mrs. Janson's done her best. Well, we shall see. Perhaps she'll find him out before it's too late."

Ignorant as I was, I did not realize the implications of the situation. Holly might dally with Jos as Jos's mother had with the gypsy and there could be a similar result.

But Jos was not a wandering gypsy; he could hardly wander off and shirk his responsibilities.

I wished I had not been the one to find them.

The grounds surrounding the House were large and in some places wild and uncultivated. Beyond the shrubbery was a part that was somewhat isolated. There was an old summer house there, which I had discovered by accident. When I asked Lavinia about it she had said, "Nobody goes there nowadays. It's locked. There's a key somewhere. One day I'll find it." But that was a long time ago and she had never done anything about it.

On this particular day I went over to join Lavinia. It was early afternoon—a rest period for Miss York—and I knew that Mrs. Janson "put her feet up for an hour" at that time; I suspect Mrs. Bright of the House did the same.

A somnolent atmosphere hung over the house. It was very quiet. Lavinia was nowhere about. She should have met me at the stables, but she was not there. Her horse was, so I knew she had not gone without me.

I thought she must be somewhere in the gardens, so I decided to look round before going into the House.

I could not find her and my steps eventually led me to the shrubbery. Thus it was that I came on the old summer house. The place had always attracted me in a morbid way. I believe it was said to be haunted and that was why people did not go there often.

I paused at the door and thought I heard a sound within. It was a long, low chuckle which made me shiver. It sounded ghostly. I turned the handle of the door and to my surprise it opened. Then I saw who was there. It was no ghost. It was Jos and Lavinia. They were laying on the floor together.

I did not want to notice details. I felt myself get very hot. I shut the door and ran and did not stop running until I reached the rectory. I felt sick. I glanced at my face in a mirror. It was scarlet.

I could not believe what I had seen. Lavinia . . . proud, haughty Lavinia . . . doing *that* with a servant!

I sat down on my bed. What should I do? Lavinia may have seen me. She would have heard the door open. What ought I to do? How could I tell anyone—and yet how could I not?

The door opened and Polly came in.

"Heard you running up . . ." She stopped and stared at me. "Why, what is it? What's the matter?"

She came and sat on the bed beside me and put an arm round me.

"You're upset," she said. "You'd better tell old Polly about it."

"I don't know, Polly. I can't believe it. I don't know whether she saw me or not. It was awful."

"Come on. Tell me."

"I think I ought not to tell anyone . . . ever."

"You can tell me, as it's as good as if you'd kept it to your-self . . . only better because I know what's best to do. Don't I always?"

"Yes, you do. Only swear you won't do anything . . . without telling me."

"Cross my heart."

"Swear it, Polly."

"Here." She licked her finger and rubbed it dry. "See me finger's wet, see me finger's dry, Cross my heart and never tell a lie," she finished with a dramatic gesture.

I had heard Polly swear that before and I knew she would keep her word.

"I couldn't find Lavinia," I said. "I went to look for her. You know that old summer house . . . the haunted one . . . someone killed herself in it years ago . . ."

Polly nodded.

"She was in there . . . with Jos. They were . . . on the floor together . . . and . . ."

"No!" cried Polly, aghast.

I nodded. "I saw them clearly."

Polly rocked gently back and forth. "This is a nice sort of how-di-do. I can believe anything of them two. A regular pair. I'd like to see her ladyship's face when she hears of this."

"You mustn't tell her, Polly."

"What! Let them go on till he leaves his signature on the family tree! That wouldn't be one for the drawing over the fireplace, I can tell you."

"She'd know that I told. I can't tell tales."

Polly sat quietly thinking. "Nor can you let this go on. And I wonder how far it *has* gone. She's a little . . . er . . . madam . . . that one. As for him, I reckon he's his father all over again and no girl would be safe from him . . . unless she had her head screwed on right, of course. I reckon it's got to be stopped. There could be big trouble . . . and I wouldn't like even Lady Harriet to have that foisted on her."

"Perhaps I should speak to Lavinia."

"Not you. You keep out of it. You'd make her worse. I

know her kind. We've got to do something, though. You leave it to me."

"Polly, you won't tell I saw them, will you?"

She shook her head. "I've given you my promise, haven't I?"

"Yes, but . . ."

"Don't you worry, my love. I'll find some way and you can bet your life I'll see that you are not mixed up in this."

Polly was most inventive. She found the way.

It was a few days later. I went over to the House as usual. Lavinia was not to be found, nor was Jos. I hurried back to the rectory and told Polly, who was waiting to hear.

She told me to go to my room and read because she wanted me out of the way.

I heard what happened later.

Polly let Holly know that her lover was in the Framling haunted summer house with another woman. Holly wouldn't believe her at first, but after a while she went to investigate. Polly's assumption had been right. Holly came upon Jos and Lavinia, as Lavinia told me later, *flagrante delicto*. Poor Holly, she had been deceived by her lover, and finding him in such a position with another woman—even though she was Miss Lavinia—aroused her unbridled fury.

She shouted at him, cursing him and Miss Lavinia. He could not escape, because he was not fully dressed, and it was the same with Lavinia.

Holly's shouting was heard and several of the servants came hurrying, thinking a burglar had been caught.

It was disastrous, for it became a matter that could not be hidden from Lady Harriet herself.

Lavinia and Jos had been caught in the act.

There was certain to be a big storm.

I did not see Lavinia for some days. Polly told me what had happened and she had it from the horse's mouth via Mrs. Janson, who had had it from Mrs. Bright. Lavinia was confined to her room and something big was about to take place.

Jos could hardly be dismissed, as he was known as Reuben's son although he wasn't—so he would have to stay in the stables, because Reuben was too useful to be dispensed with and it was not fair that the sins of the children should be visited on their elders, even though it was the other way round in the Bible. If he had been caught with any of the servants it would have been a venial sin—but Miss Lavinia!

"I always knew what she was," commented Polly. "Plain as the nose on your face. You can be sure your sins will find you out . . . and Madam Lavinia's have surely done that."

We waited to see what would happen and we did not have to wait long.

Lady Harriet sent for my father and they were in conference for a long time before he returned home. As soon as he came back he asked me to go to him.

"As you know," he said, "you were always intended to go away to school. Your mother and I used to plan for you before you were born. It mattered not whether you turned out to be a boy or a girl, we both believed absolutely in the necessity of education and your mother wanted the best for our child. As you have heard, there is some money—not a great deal, but perhaps adequate—and that has been set aside for your schooling. Miss York is a very good governess and Lady Harriet will do all in her power to find her another place, and with such a recommendation it should not be difficult. Polly . . . well, she has always known that she could not be with you permanently and I believe she has a sister whom she can join . . ."

I stared at him. It was not the thought of school that appalled me. I could only think of the loss of Polly.

"Lavinia will accompany you. Lady Harriet approves of the school and the two of you will be together."

Then I understood. Lady Harriet had decreed that Lavinia must go away. There must be an end to this disastrous affair with Jos. Separation was the only answer—and I was to go with her. Lady Harriet ruled our lives.

I said, "I don't want to go away to school, Father. I am sure Miss York is a wonderful teacher and I can do just as well with her."

"It is what your mother wanted for you," he said sadly. I thought: And it is what Lady Harriet wants!

I went straight to Polly. I flung my arms round her and clung to her.

"Polly, I can't leave you."

"Better tell me," she said.

"I'm going to school. Lavinia and I are going."

"I see. I see. This is because of madam's little prank, eh? I shouldn't think school is going to stop that one. So you are going away to school, eh?"

"I won't go, Polly."

"It might be good for you."

"What about you?"

"Well, I've always known this would come to an end one day or another. That was certain sure. I'll go to Eff. She's always on at me to come. There's nothing to fret about, lovey. You and me . . . we'll always be friends. You'll know where I'll be and I'll know where you'll be. Don't be so downhearted. School will suit you, and then when you have your holidays you can come and stay with me and Eff. Eff would be so proud. So . . . look on the bright side, there's a love. Life goes on, you know. It never stands still and you can't be Polly's baby forever."

It was getting better already.

Miss York took the news philosophically. She had been expecting it, she said. The rector had always told her that one day I should have to go away to school. She would find another post and the rector had said she must stay at the rectory until she did. Lady Harriet had promised to help her find another situation, so she was as good as fixed up.

It was about a week after Lavinia's exposure that I saw her.

She was smoulderingly resentful. She looked more like a tigress than a spoiled kitten. Her eyes were slightly red, so I knew she had been crying.

"What a fuss!" she said. "It was that awful girl Holly."

"Holly wasn't any different from you. Jos had made fools of you both."

"Don't you dare call me a fool, Drusilla Delany."

"I shall call you what I like. And you are a fool to do what you did, with a groom at that."

"You don't understand."

"Well, everybody else does, and it is why you are being sent away."

"You are being sent as well."

"That is only because you are going. I have to be with you."

She snorted. "I don't want you."

"I daresay my father could send me to another school."

"My mother would not allow that."

"We are not your mother's slaves, you know. We have freedom to do what we want to. If you are going to be objectionable I shall ask my father to send me away without you."

She looked a little alarmed at that.

"They treat me like a child," she said.

"Jos didn't."

She began to laugh. "He is a rogue," she said.

"That's what they all say."

"Oh . . . but it was so exciting."

"You should be careful."

"I was . . . if that woman hadn't come and found us in the summer house . . ."

I turned away. I wondered what she would say if she knew what had led up to her discovery.

"He said I was the most beautiful girl he had ever seen."

"I think they all say that. They think it will get them what they want more quickly."

"They don't. And what do you know about it?"

"I've heard . . ."

"Shut up," said Lavinia, and seemed near to tears.

We made a sort of truce. We were both going into a strange place and the only familiar things there would be each other. We were both a little pleased that we should not be alone.

We talked a good deal about school.

We spent two years at Meridian House. I fitted in quite well. I was immediately noticed as a bright child, and as such attracted the attention of the teachers. Lavinia was backward for her age, and showed no inclination to change that state. Moreover, she was arrogant and moody, which did not make her popular, and the fact of her exalted parentage—which she was apt to stress at first—was a deterrent rather than an asset. She had always expected those about her to fit in with her ways and it never occurred to her that she must adapt to others.

There was a boys' school close by and occasionally we saw

the boys playing games on the green near the school. This caused a certain amount of excitement among a section of the girls, particularly on Sundays when we went to the village church for the morning service and the boys occupied the pews immediately opposite us. Of course, Lavinia was to the fore among these girls who had a marked interest in the boys. Notes were smuggled across the aisle, and Sunday morning church was the high spot of the week for some girls, for a reason which would not have pleased the vicar or our formidable headmistress, Miss Gentian.

It was during our second year at Meridian House that Lavinia experienced her second disaster, and it was inevitable that it was of a nature similar to the first.

She ignored me for a good deal of the time, remembering me only when she needed help with her work. She had her own little community and they were known as "the fast set." They regarded themselves as adult and worldly; they were very daring and knowledgeable of the facts of life. Lavinia was queen of this little band, for though most of them could only theorize on the topic nearest their hearts, Lavinia had had practical experience.

When she was very angry with me she would sometimes refer to me in a tone of complete contempt as "You . . . *virgin!*"

I often thought that if Lavinia had been one of that despised sect I might be at home cosily doing my lessons with Miss York and with dear Polly to run to when an emergency arose.

Polly wrote to me in a rather laborious hand. She had learned to write when Tom had gone away to sea so that she could keep in close touch with him. Her words were often misspelt, but the warmth of her feeling came through to comfort me.

I often thought of her and Eff during that time, and in the summer holidays I did go to see them. I stayed a week and it was wonderful to be with Polly. She and Eff were doing well. Both had an aptitude for business. Polly was soon on friendly terms with the paying guests and Eff supplied the essential dignity which was part of keeping everyone in order.

"We're what Father would have called a good team," Eff

told me. She was particularly pleased at that time, for "Downstairs No. 32" (which was what she called the tenants of the lower floor in the most recently acquired house) had brought a nipper with them. They were very content and had the garden for the pram, which was a very comfortable arrangement, and Eff and Polly could pop in at any time and gurgle over the child. Eff always referred to her tenants as "Top Floor 30," "First Floor 32" and so on.

They were wonderful days while Polly listened to my news about school and I learned the backgrounds and idiosyncrasies of Top Floor to Basement Room.

For instance, Top Floor left the tap running and First Floor wouldn't do her part of the stairs properly; even Downstairs No. 32 hadn't really come out of the top drawer, but of course they were forgiven a great deal because they had brought the nipper.

"He's a regular little fellow, he is. You should see the smile I get from him when I go out there." So I gathered that, as previously in the case of the Branleys, the nipper made up for his parents' shortcomings.

Going "up West" with Polly, looking at the big shops, walking through the market on a Saturday night when the flares were lighted and the faces of the costers gleamed scarlet in their light, looking at the rosy apples piled onto the stalls, listening to the cries of "fresh herring, cockles and mussels," past the old quack who swore his remedies would cure falling hair, rheumatic pains and all the ailments that the flesh was heir to . . . it was the greatest excitement and I loved it.

Polly made me feel that I was the most important person in the world to her and it was comforting, even when we parted, that I felt I had not lost her forever.

She loved me to talk about my life. I told her about Miss Gentian, the absolute ruler of us all. "A real tartar that one," commented Polly, chuckling, and when I imitated Mademoiselle the French mistress, she rolled about with glee and murmured, "Them foreigners. They're real cautions. I reckon you have a real lark with her." It all seemed incredibly amusing— much more funny than it was in reality.

When I left Eff said, "Mind you come again."

"Think of it as your home, love," said Polly. "I'll tell you this: Where I am . . . that will always be your home."

What a comfort that was! I should remember it always.

During the last term I spent at Meridian House, Lavinia and two other girls were caught coming in late at night. They had bribed one of the maids to let them in and were caught in the act by a mistress who, having a toothache, had come down to the medical stores to get something to soothe it. Her arrival in the hall had coincided with the surreptitious opening of the door and the conspirators were caught red-handed.

There was a terrible scene. Lavinia crept up to the bedroom she shared with me and another girl. We had to be in the secret, of course, for it was not the first time it had happened.

Lavinia was shaken. "There'll be trouble over this," she said. "That sly Miss Spence. She caught us coming in."

"Did Annie let you in?" I asked. Annie was the maid.

Lavinia nodded.

"She'll be dismissed," I said.

"Yes, I suppose so," said Lavinia carelessly. "I reckon we'll be for it tomorrow. You wait until old Gentian hears."

"You shouldn't have involved Annie."

"How would we have got in otherwise?"

"You should not have used her."

"Don't be idiotic," snapped Lavinia; but she was very worried.

And with good reason. The reverberations were greater than we had feared. Poor Annie was dismissed immediately. Miss Gentian had the girls involved brought to her and, according to Lavinia, had gone on and on about how ashamed she was that girls from her school should have behaved in such a cheap and common manner. They were finally sent to their rooms after being told that this was not the end of the matter.

The term was almost over, and the day before we returned Lady Harriet received a letter stating that Miss Gentian was of the opinion that Lavinia would be happier at another school and she regretted there would be no place for her at Meridian House next term or in the foreseeable future.

Lady Harriet was furious that a school should have refused to take *her* daughter. She would not allow that to pass. Lady Harriet and Miss Gentian were like two commanders going into battle. Lady Harriet began by writing to Miss Gentian suggesting that perhaps her letter had been a little unconsidered. She, Lady Harriet, was not without influence and she had wished her daughter to remain at Meridian House for at least another year. Miss Gentian replied that she was sure Lavinia would be happier elsewhere in such a manner that she implied that she herself would also be happier in that event.

Lady Harriet suggested that Miss Gentian come and see her that they might talk the matter over in a friendly fashion. Miss Gentian replied that she had many commitments, but if Lady Harriet cared to come to see her that might be arranged. However, she thought she ought to point out that she had given much thought to the problem and in her mind Lavinia was not suited to Meridian House and the matter was settled.

Lady Harriet came to the rectory to see what report Miss Gentian had given me.

"Drusilla has worked well. Her mathematics leave much to be desired, but she is improving in this field. She is making good progress generally." It was clear that I was not included in the edict of excommunication. I had enjoyed the school. I was interested in my studies, and the feeling of competition, which I had missed at home, spurred me on to do better. True, I was not very much interested in sport, but Miss Gentian herself was not either. I fancied I had now and then caught a gleam of approval in her eyes when they rested on me. Moreover, I had not been caught illegally consorting with members of the boys' school. Lady Harriet was more concerned than ever to find that I was making a success of my scholastic career.

She took the unprecedented step of going to see Miss Gentian, but she came back defeated. I think she must have learned about the escapade and this made her feel deflated. Her fears that her daughter might be turning into a nymphomaniac were being confirmed. If it had been possible for me to feel sorry for such an exalted being, I should have done so.

But she did not hesitate long before taking action. She sent for my father. I was not present at the interview, but I heard of it later.

She told my father that what girls needed was a finishing school. She had been enquiring among her friends and she knew of a good one in France. The Duchess of Mentover had sent her daughter there and, knowing the Duchess, one knew also that she would never send her daughter to a school which was not everything it should be.

Meridian House had been a bad choice. That Miss Gentian was far too domineering. What girls wanted to learn if they were to do well in later life was social grace.

My father feebly protested that it was a good education that he and his late wife had wanted for me and he believed that I was getting that at Meridian House. I had, according to my reports, been doing very well. Miss Gentian had written to him personally.

"Foolish woman!" said Lady Harriet. "She is evidently eager to keep one of the girls I sent to her."

"I thought that if Drusilla stayed on another two years, say . . ."

"Quite wrong, rector. Girls need a good finishing school. They must go to this one in France recommended by the Duchess."

"I fear it will be beyond my means, Lady Harriet."

"Nonsense. I will pay the extra. I would like Drusilla to be with Lavinia. They have been *such* friends over many years. It will be a good thing for them both to go together."

After a good deal of hesitation, my father gave in. My mother had been concerned solely with education. "Polish" was not something which had come into her mind. Erudition was one thing; social graces another. Presumably Lavinia would have a season in London when she emerged with a sufficiently high gloss upon her; then she would be presented at Court. No such future was envisaged for me.

I see now that my father wanted me to be prepared to look after myself when he died. There would be a little money—a very little—just enough for me perhaps to live in a very modest fashion. I wondered whether he was aware that I was plain and might never marry. Lady Harriet had evidently assured him that, though my circumstances were very different from those of Lavinia, I should be better equipped to face the world with that veneer which could only be obtained at one of the schools to which she was suggesting I should go; and as she was prepared to pay what would be extra to the cost of Meridian House, it was finally decided that I should accompany Lavinia.

The chosen establishment was the Château Lamason, the very name of which excited me, and in spite of the fact that I should be beholden to Lady Harriet, I could not help being thrilled at the prospect of being there.

Jos had been spirited away. He had gone, Lavinia told me with a grimace, to the stables of a friend of Lady Harriet. But Lavinia and I could talk of little but the prospect before us. For the first time we were going abroad.

"It is not like an ordinary school," she explained. "It's for people who will be coming out. There won't be stupid lessons and that sort of thing."

"No, I know. We are going to be polished."

"Prepared to go into society. That won't be for you, of course. They will all be aristocracy over there."

"Perhaps I should be better at Meridian House."

I only had to suggest that I might not accompany her for Lavinia to become placating. I knew how to deal with her now and she was so easy to read that I often had the upper hand.

The last thing I wanted was to miss this tremendous adventure. I was as excited about Château Lamason as Lavinia was.

I went to stay a few days with Polly before I left. We laughed about the polish. Eff thought it was "ever so nice" and told everyone that I was staying with them before I went off to my finishing school. She particularly enjoyed talking of me to Second Floor No. 32, who "fancied herself" and was always explaining that she had "known better days."

The summer holidays were coming to an end and we were leaving in September. A day before our departure I was summoned to Lady Harriet's presence. She received me in her sitting room. She was seated in a high chair rather like a throne and I felt I ought to curtsey.

I stood uncertainly on the threshold of the room.

"Come in, Drusilla," she said. "You may sit down." Graciously she indicated a chair and I took it.

She said, "You will shortly be leaving us for the Château Lamason. It is one of the best finishing schools in Europe. I have chosen it very carefully. You are very fortunate. I hope you realize that."

Now that I was growing up Lady Harriet's divinity had

decreased a little. I was seeing her as a woman who created a
sense of power which people accepted because she was so determined that they should. My feelings for her would never be the
same as they had been before the battle with Miss Gentian.
Miss Gentian had clearly shown that Lady Harriet was not the
mighty figure she had made herself out to be, and Miss Gentian
had won the war between them. It was like the case of Napo-
leon and Wellington, and it had taught me that Lady Harriet
was not invincible.

"Well, Lady Harriet," I said. "I was very happy at Meridian House and Miss Gentian thought I would do well there. I
would have liked to stay."

Lady Harriet looked astonished. "That is nonsense, my
child. It was an ill choice."

I raised my eyebrows. An admission of failure? It was
Lady Harriet who had chosen Meridian.

She was ever so slightly disconcerted, and laughed dismis-
sively. "My dear *child*, you are going to be so grateful that you
had a chance of going to Lamason. That Gentian woman has
no sense of the needs of society. Her great ambition was to stuff
her pupils' head with facts which would be no use to them after
their schooldays." She waved a hand as though to dismiss Miss
Gentian. "You and Lavinia will be far from home. You are a
sensible girl and er . . ." She did not say "plain," but she
meant it. "I want you, my dear, to keep an eye on Lavinia."

"I am afraid, Lady Harriet, that she will not take any notice of what I say."

"There you are wrong. She thinks very highly of you."
She paused and added: "And so do I. Lavinia, you know, is very
beautiful. People flock about her because of that . . . and who
she is. She is a little . . . impulsive. "I shall rely on you, my
dear, to"—she gave me a little smile—"to look after her." She
laughed lightly. "Your father is delighted that you are to have
this opportunity and I know you are very grateful. Girls need
polish." I felt myself laughing inwardly. I must remember every word of this interview and store it up so that I could give
Polly an accurate account when we met. I pictured myself taking the rôle of Lady Harriet. I would tell Polly that I expected
to feel like the Cromwellian table in the Framling Hall after an
application of beeswax and turpentine.

I felt a little triumphant to discover so much about Lady Harriet. She was uneasy about her daughter and she found it humiliating to admit to the rector's plain little daughter that her own daughter was less than perfect. Polly had said that both Lavinia and Fabian Framling would have to pay for all the coddling they had had in their childhood, and all that "Lord God Almighty stuff" would have to be knocked out of them. "Who are they when they're out?" she demanded. "No different from the rest of us. That's not the way to bring up children. They want loving, but brought up sharp now and then. They want cuddles too . . . not coddling." Poor Lady Harriet, so sublimely aware of her superiority and making the most fearful mistakes with her offspring!

"You will find a spell at the Château Lamason will be a great asset to you in later life. Your father understands and that is why he is so eager to accept my offer for you. I want you to keep an eye on Lavinia. She is too . . . warmhearted and inclined to make unsuitable friends. You are more thoughtful, more serious. It is only natural that you should be. Just be a good friend to her. There now, you may go."

I took a ready leave of Lady Harriet and joined Lavinia.

"What did Mama want?" she demanded.

"She was just saying that you were warmhearted and inclined to make the wrong friends."

She grimaced. "Don't tell me she was asking you to be my nursemaid. What nonsense!"

I agreed that it was.

We left England with four other girls who were going to the Château Lamason in the charge of Miss Ellmore, one of the mistresses.

Miss Ellmore was middle-aged, very genteel, the daughter of a professor. When she was no longer young she had found herself without means and had been forced to earn her own living. She was employed at the Château, not because of her academic qualities, I learned later, but because she was a lady.

She was rather a sad person, and somewhat harassed by her task of looking after six girls in their mid-teens.

For us it was an exciting adventure. We all met at Dover, to which port Lavinia and I had been taken by the Framling coachman and head groom, and we were delivered safely into the custody of Miss Ellmore.

At the Paquet Hotel, the grooms departed and we were introduced by Miss Ellmore to our travelling companions. They were Elfrida Lazenby, Julia Simons, Melanie Summers and Janine Fellows.

I was immediately interested in Janine Fellows, because she was quite unlike the other three. Elfrida, Julia and Melanie resembled so many of the girls I had already met at Meridian House—nice and ordinary, with their separate identities of course, but with a similarity among them. Right from the first, though, I noticed the difference in Janine.

She was of small stature and very slim, with reddish hair and light sandy lashes; her skin was milky white and faintly freckled. I felt I should have to wait, to know whether I was going to like Janine or not.

It was clear from the start that they were all very interested in Lavinia. They could not stop looking at her. I had already noticed that most people turned to have a second glance at her when passing . . . particularly men. Lavinia was aware of this and it always put her into a good mood.

We crossed the Channel. Miss Ellmore told us what we must do and what not.

"We must all keep together, girls. It would be disastrous if one of us were lost."

The crossing was smooth and my excitement increased when I saw the coastline of France looming up.

It was a long journey across France and by the time we reached the Château Lamason, I felt I knew my travelling companions well . . . except Janine.

Château Lamason was right in the heart of Dordogne country. We left the station and drove through what seemed like miles of beautiful country to reach it, past forest land, streams and fields.

And there was the *château*. I could hardly believe we were going to live in such a place. It was so impressive and so romantic. Close by were the forest and steep hills down which little waterfalls tumbled. The great stone *château* looked ancient and formidable with its pepper-pot towers at either end and its thick stone bastions.

I caught my breath in amazement. It was like stepping into another age. Miss Ellmore was clearly pleased by my obvious awe, and as we drove under an arch and into a courtyard she said, "The *château* was owned by Madame's family for hundreds of years. They lost a great deal during the Revolution, but this one was left alone, and she decided to turn it into a school for young ladies."

We alighted and were taken into a great hall where numbers of girls were assembling for the opening of the term. Many of them apparently knew each other well. There were several middle-aged ladies, rather like Miss Ellmore. They had an air of doing something not quite natural to them because they had come down in the world.

Mademoiselle Dubreau showed us the rooms that had been alloted to us. There were to be four in a room. Lavinia and I were to share with a French girl whose name was Françoise and a German girl, Gerda.

Miss Ellmore had said, "You two are together as you are friends, but Madame likes to mix nationalities. It is an excellent way of improving your understanding of languages."

Françoise was about seventeen and pretty. I saw Lavinia examining her with some intenseness, which almost immediately turned to complacency. The French girl might be pretty, but she could not compare with Lavinia's flamboyant tawny beauty. The German girl, Gerda, was plump and had no pretensions to good looks.

"Two plain, two purl," I commented inwardly and thought, as I often did: I'll tell that to Polly.

We unpacked and chose our beds. Françoise was not a newcomer to the *château* so she was able to tell us a little about it.

"Madame," she said, "is one fierce lady. The rules . . . oh so many . . . You wait and see. But we have our fun, yes? You understand?"

I understood and translated for Lavinia. "What sort of fun?" she wanted to know.

Françoise raised her eyes to the ceiling. "Oh . . . there is fun. In the town. It is near. We take coffee at the café. It is good."

Lavinia's eyes sparkled and the German asked in stilted French what the food was like.

Françoise grimaced, which I suppose was not very flattering to the chef. Gerda was a little dismayed, so I guessed the reason for her somewhat full figure.

I quickly realized that life at the *château* would be far from dull. To be in such surroundings in itself was exciting to me. The *château* dated back to the fourteenth century and many of its old features remained. There were turrets, and winding spiral staircases which led to various dark passages. The hall had obviously once been the centre of life in the château, and though there was a huge fireplace, one could see where the original one had been, right in the centre of the hall, with a vent above to let out the smoke. There was even an *oubliette*, from which, it was said, strange noises could be heard at certain times from the ghosts of those who had been incarcerated there to be forgotten. But it was the people who attracted me most.

Madame du Clos reigned over the *château* like some medieval queen. As soon as I saw her I recognized her as one of those formidable women cast in the same mould as Lady Harriet and Miss Gentian. Known simply as Madame, she was by no means tall but she gave an impression of grandeur. Clad in black—I never saw her in any other colour—her person glittered with jet, which hung from her ears and rose and fell over her impressive bosom. She had small hands and feet and sailed rather than walked, her voluminous skirts making a gentle swishing noise as she moved. Her small dark eyes darted everywhere, and she missed little, as we were to discover. Her dark hair, piled high on her head, was always immaculate; her nose was long and patrician; she bore a striking resemblance to many of the portraits which were in various parts of the *château*. They were undoubtedly members of the great family of du Clos, a certain branch of which had managed to survive the Revolution. Her grandfather, we were soon to discover, had been an intimate friend of Louis XVI and Marie Antoinette. They had lost their estates—apart from this *château*—in the debacle, but some of them had contrived to retain their heads. Madame had decided to turn the *château* into an exclusive finishing school, thereby bestowing a great privilege on those who were fortunate enough to gain admission to her establishment, and at the same time restoring her own fortunes sufficiently to enable her to live among the remains of her onetime glory.

On the first day we were all assembled in the great hall, where we were addressed by Madame and reminded of our great good fortune in being here. We should be instructed in the art of social grace; we should be ladies taught by ladies; and by the time we left Château Lamason we should be prepared to enter any society with ease. All doors would be open to us. Lamason was synonymous with good breeding. The greatest sin was vulgarity, and Madame du Clos would make aristocrats of us all.

The majority of the girls were French; next came the English, followed by Italian and German. We were to be given certain tuition which would enable us to make light conversation in French, English and Italian. Beside Madame on a dais sat three mistresses: Mademoiselle Le Brun, Signorina Lortoni and our own Miss Ellmore. They would lead the girls in appropriate conversation and, as they were all well bred, their speech would be that which was spoken in the highest circles of society. We were also instructed by Signor Paradetti, who taught us singing and the pianoforte, and Monsieur Dubois, the dancing master.

We learned a great deal from Françoise. She was eighteen years old, almost a year older than Lavinia. This was to be her last term and she was leaving to marry the man of her parent's choice. He was thirty years older than Françoise and very rich. It was for this reason that the marriage had been arranged, and he was eager for it, for in spite of his money he was not of a noble family. Françoise explained that he would become ennobled, and her impoverished aristocratic family would benefit from his wealth.

Gerda said she thought it was a mercenary arrangement.

Françoise shrugged her shoulders. "It makes sense," she said. "He marries into a noble family; I marry into a wealthy one. I am tired of being poor. It is terrible. Always there is talk of money . . . money for the roof . . . damp coming in the bedrooms . . . spoiling the Fragonard and the Boucher in the music room. Alphonse will change all that. I hope never to hear talk of money any more. I only want to *spend* it."

Françoise was philosophical and realistic. Gerda was different. I supposed there was plenty of money in the iron works and it seemed possible that she would be allied with another giant in industry.

It was interesting listening to it all. We used to talk at night. Those nights remain vividly in my memory . . . lying there in the darkness with perhaps only the light of the stars to give our room with its high ceiling and panelled walls an eerie look. I remember the comfort of those four beds in each corner of the room and the knowledge that we were not alone.

I felt very much the odd one. They were all rich. What was the daughter of a country rector doing here? I knew the answer. I was here to look after Lavinia and I owed the experience to her waywardness. I had my duty to do. Yet when I saw her casting interested looks at Monsieur Dubois I wondered how I should be able to protect her from future follies. It was, of course, what I was here to do. I should never have been given the opportunity to be in this exalted place but for the fact that Lady Harriet had selected me for this purpose.

Françoise and Lavinia talked together quite a lot. They discussed men, a subject dear to the hearts of both. I would see them whispering together. I believed that Lavinia had told Françoise about her experiences with Jos. It was the reason why she had been sent away really, although of course she had first gone to Meridian House; but from there she had been expelled for going out with boys.

In the darkness of our dormitory Lavinia would tell of her adventures, stopping short at certain points and saying, "No, I can't go on . . . not in front of Drusilla. She is too young yet." She did not mention Gerda, whose deep breathing and occasional snore indicated that she was asleep. It was her way of denigrating me.

Françoise told us all that several girls had grown rather romantic about Monsieur Dubois.

"He's really quite good looking," commented Françoise. "Some of the girls are quite mad about him."

I was quite interested in Monsieur Dubois—not that I felt that fascination which some of the girls seemed to. He was just a rather slight little Frenchman with very smooth dark hair and a jaunty mustachio. He wore very ornate waistcoats and a signet ring on his little finger, which he always looked at with affection when he beat time with his hands.

"One . . . two . . . three . . . the lady turns . . . four . . . five . . . six . . . she faces her partner . . . Come, ladies, that will *not* do. Ah, Gerda, you have the feet of lead."

Poor Gerda! She was not very good at it. Perhaps that was not very important, as the iron master might not be all that concerned with dancing. In Françoise's case it was different. In the noble *châteaux* of France she would be expected to lead the dance.

Some of us had to take the part of men in the dance. Gerda was usually assigned to that role. She disliked the ritual in any case and lumbered round on reluctant feet.

Lavinia had always danced well and had done it with a sensuous abandonment. Monsieur Dubois was quick to notice this and when he was demonstrating he invariably chose Lavinia to partner him.

She would move close to him sinuously and meaningfully. I wondered whether in my role of guardian I should speak to her about it. She was showing too clearly how she felt about Monsieur Dubois.

He was quite tender to her, always implying that he liked her very much. But he was like that with all the girls. He had a way of letting his hand rest on one's shoulders or even round one's waist. Monsieur Dubois seemed to like all girls so much that it was difficult to know whether he liked any one in particular. But it did seem that he paid Lavinia just a little more attention.

Françoise said, "He only comes to school to teach. I expect he's got a wife and six children somewhere."

"I think he is very attractive," said Lavinia. "He told me I was the most beautiful girl in the school."

"He tells others that," said Françoise.

"I don't believe it," retorted Lavinia. "He looked really sincere."

"Don't fall in love with him," warned Françoise. "It is all on the top . . . how you say it?"

"On the surface," I supplied. "He doesn't mean anything. He is just being polite to the girls who throw themselves at him."

73

Lavinia scowled at me.

But the affair did not progress, much to Lavinia's chagrin and my relief.

Françoise was right when she said that Monsieur Dubois would be too much afraid of losing his job to take any of his little flirtations to a logical conclusion.

Because of the distance from home we were only to return once a year. At first the time went very slowly, but then it began to fly past.

I enjoyed the life; so did Lavinia. It was more or less up to ourselves to learn if we wanted too. I was very eager to improve my languages, so I soon became fluent in French and had quite a smattering of Italian. I enjoyed the dancing and singing lessons and I was doing quite well at the piano.

There was a good deal of freedom.

Sometimes in the afternoons we would go into the little town of Perradot. One of the mistresses would take us in the wagon, which would hold about twelve of us, and the wagon would be left in the square while we wandered round. It was a lovely little town with a river running through it, over which was a small but attractive bridge. There were shops, including a café where delicious cakes were sold, and in the hot weather we would sit under the gaily coloured sunshades and watch the people pass by. On Fridays there was a market in the square and so there was always a number who wanted to go on that day. One could buy clothes at the stalls, or shoes, sweets, cakes, eggs, vegetables and cheeses. The place always seemed to be permeated by the smell of hot crusty bread, which the *boulanger* used to rake out of his cave-like oven to sell to the waiting customers.

What we liked best was to go into the *pâtisserie*, choose our cake and then bring it out and sit at one of the little tables under the coloured sunshade, and drink a cup of coffee and watch the people go by.

We became acquainted with many of the tradespeople and market-stall holders and we were known throughout the town as *les jeunes filles du château*.

Life formed itself into patterns: language classes, which were more or less optional; dancing and music, which were essential, as were deportment and conversation. There was a *thé dansant* once a week, at which Madame herself presided.

Time was passing. We had arrived at Lamason in September and it was not until the beginning of the following July that we returned to England for the summer holidays, escorted by Miss Ellmore. We were to return in September for another year and then we should be ready to take our place in the highest society.

I was rather shocked by the sight of my father. He looked rather wan and had aged more than a year warranted.

Mrs. Janson told me that he had been ailing during the winter, and there was talk of getting a curate to help him.

"He's had some funny turns," she said. "I haven't liked the look of him at times."

I talked to my father. He assured me that all was well. I said that perhaps I should not go too far away, but he would not hear of that. He was pleased about the languages and music, but he thought some medieval French history might have been included in the curriculum.

Lady Harriet was delighted by the change she saw in Lavinia. I was sent for and took tea with her and Lavinia. Fabian was at home, but he did not join us. Lady Harriet asked me a number of questions about the school and she sat listening with obvious approval. I was glad, for I should have hated it if she had decided that we were not to return.

I learned through Mrs. Janson that Miss Lucille was madder than ever. She was more or less shut up now in her part of her house. Some of the staff had seen her wandering around looking like a ghost. They said she had lost all sense of time and was often heard calling for her lover.

I also resumed my acquaintance with Dougal Carruthers, who was very affable when he saw me. I was now seventeen years of age—adult, one might say—and I was learning what a difference that made to one's relationships. Dougal's attitude towards me had changed subtly. I quite enjoyed the change.

He came to see my father and talked a great deal about Norman architecture, Norman customs and so on. My father was delighted to have met a kindred spirit and was more animated than he had been for a long time.

Fabian, too, had changed towards me. He took more notice of me and asked questions about the *château*.

The four of us went riding together and I could see that Lavinia was annoyed because Dougal talked more to me than to her. It was the first time any young man had shown interest in me, and that rankled with Lavinia.

"He's only being polite," she said. When we rode out she would endeavour to get beside him, which left me with Fabian. I always felt that he was a little embarrassed with me because of that long-ago time when he kidnapped me—and he was a little ashamed of it.

I was glad to have a week with Polly. She pretended to be blinded by the sight of me, which was because of the old joke about polish.

"My word, someone's been rubbing you up a bit. I can't see nothing for shine."

Everything was going well with the two houses. Polly and Eff were, as Polly told me, quite well-to-do in the neighbourhood—ladies of substance. The houses were full of good payers and Eff had her eyes on another house in the same row.

" 'Expansion,' that's what she calls it. Father always said Eff had a head for business." Downstairs No. 32 had left some months before and it had been a bit of a wrench because of the loss of the nipper. But they had found a good replacement in Mr. and Mrs. Collett, a good steady couple, too old for nippers alas, but you had to count your blessings.

There was the usual round of markets and "up West" and everything we had done before; and it was good to be with Polly, and wonderfully comforting to know that the bond between us was as strong as ever.

I said a sad farewell, knowing that it would be a year before I saw her again.

In September we returned to Lamason.

There were changes. Françoise had left, and must be married to her rich, elderly husband by now. In her place in our dormitory was Janine Fellows.

I did not know whether I was pleased or repelled by this, for I was still not sure whether or not I liked Janine. Françoise had been a good companion; she had been entertaining and her knowledge about the *château* had helped us along in our first days. Her nonchalant acceptance of her fate, her philosophical views of life, her realism and lack of sentiment had intrigued me. I felt I had learned a good deal from Françoise. Gerda, of course, was not the most interesting of roommates. Her preoccupation with food had always bored me a little; she was too phlegmatic and intent on her creature comforts, but she was never malicious and was fundamentally good hearted. Lavinia, of course, was my familiar; and now there was Janine.

Her presence had changed the atmosphere of our dormitory. It had been cosy and rather exciting with Françoise; now I felt there was something malevolent there.

In the first place, she and Lavinia seemed to take an instant dislike to each other, and what made it a little sinister was that Janine rarely showed this. It was only now and then that it came out in certain flashes of temper with Lavinia and sly sarcasm from Janine.

Janine was plain, and that gave her something in common with me. Her reddish hair was fine and straight, hardly ever tidy; her eyes were small, very light blue, and her fine eyebrows made her look perpetually surprised.

She seemed to turn more to me for friendship. Gerda was interested mainly in herself, and her eyes would become glazed and vague when other subjects were raised. She never made trouble; neither did she contribute anything to companionship.

So naturally Janine talked to me more than any of the others, simply because Lavinia, like Gerda, was not interested in anything but her own desires, Gerda's for food and Lavinia's for admiration.

Lavinia had renewed her admiration for Monsieur Dubois, perhaps because there was no other male available. Janine noticed this and her lips always twitched with amusement every time he was mentioned.

Lavinia was an excellent dancer and Monsieur Dubois still chose her when he wished to demonstrate how a step should be danced. Lavinia revelled in this, twirling round, swaying from side to side, pressing closer than was necessary to Monsieur Dubois, raising her beautiful eyes to his face and then allowing the lids to fall over them, showing her long curling lashes, which alone would have made a beauty of her.

"Monsieur Dubois is a born flirt," said Janine. "It's part of his trade. Of course he knows what girls he can flirt with. He wouldn't dare with some. You can't see him trying it on with the Princess, can you?"

The Princess belonged to the ruling house of some obscure middle European country and Madame was especially proud of her title.

"I should hardly think he would want to," said Lavinia.

"My dear, he doesn't want to with any of us. It's just his way of keeping us happy. If he sees a girl wants to flirt, he flirts. It's what he has been paid to do."

Lavinia was not subtle in conversation and Janine was too clever for her. She nearly always lost in these verbal battles. But she continued with her wooing of the dancing master.

She was the best dancer and the most outstanding beauty of the school—or certainly the most flamboyant one. She was now at the zenith of her youth. Eighteen years old, full-hipped, full-bosomed, with the tiniest of waists. Sometimes she wore her hair hanging down her back, caught back by a bow of ribbon; sometimes she piled it high on her head with little tendrils nestling against her white neck. Hardly anyone could stop taking a second glance at Lavinia.

One day Janine came in bursting with excitement. She waited until Lavinia was with us until she spoke of what was amusing her.

She had followed Monsieur Dubois to his home. She had waited for him and kept a safe distance. She saw his home, his wife and four children; she overheard the greeting between him and his wife, for Janine spoke fluent French. They embraced, she said, like lovers who had been separated for months. "How was it today, Henri?" "Oh, not bad . . . not bad at all, my cabbage." "How many silly girls were chasing you today?" "Oh . . . the usual. It is always so. Such a bore. You must bear with it, my angel. I must keep the little girls happy. It is a nothing . . . all in the matter of the work, eh."

"I don't believe it," said Lavinia hotly.

Janine shrugged her shoulders, as though it were immaterial to her whether Lavinia believed her or not.

Janine sought me out.

"You're different from the others," she said. "They are

78

silly frivolous nonentities, most of them. As for your friend
Lavinia, I don't know how you endure her."

"I've known her all my life."

"Far too long," commented Janine.

"Her mother pays some of my fees. My father couldn't
afford to send me here. You are right in saying I am different
from the others. I am, I am not rich and destined for a grand
marriage."

"Thank your lucky stars for that."

Janine had a way of ferretting our secrets. I was often
amazed at myself for being so frank with her. She was an avid
listener—rare among self-centred girls. I was soon giving her a
picture of Lady Harriet and our village.

"Spoilt brat," she commented of Lavinia.

"Lady Harriet sees herself and everything connected with
her as perfect, and that includes her daughter."

"She must be mentally blind. Lavinia hasn't much above
the neck beyond her curly hair and her pretty face."

"I suppose that makes up for a good deal."

"She is too . . . *physical* for her own good. It wouldn't surprise me if she got herself into some mess sooner or later. She's
so blatant about men. Look at the way she throws herself at
Monsieur Dubois."

"She didn't like what you said about him and his wife. Was
it true?"

She looked at me and laughed. "In a way," she said.

"So you made it up!"

"I'm sure it goes something like that. I've seen them in the
market together. They are very devoted. He must be bored
with silly romantic girls throwing themselves at him; and she
must be grateful to have such a desirable husband."

Janine confided to me about herself. I was not sure
whether I believed her. The story, according to her, was quite
romantic. She was the illegitimate offspring of two people in
very high places. She hinted at royalty.

"They couldn't marry, you see. He . . . my father . . .
was to make a very grand marriage for political reasons. That is
how it is with the royals. My mother was a lady of the Queen's
Bedchamber. She, too, was to marry into high circles. However, I happened. I was born in a clinic run by the woman

whom I call Aunt Emily. She is not my aunt at all, but I was brought up there and always called her Aunt Emily. I was to have the best education. It was paid for by my parents, but I was meant to believe that I owed everything to Aunt Emily. Aunt Emily has close connections with the Court. She is known to be discreet. People come to her . . . if they don't want it known . . ."

I said it was very interesting, while only half believing it. I could not imagine why, but I felt sorry for her. I fancied she was always trying to prove something to herself. She was not very popular with the other girls, and as, after all, she was one of the quartet that shared our room, I seemed to be with her more than anyone else.

It was a week or so after our return to Lamason . . . a lovely golden September afternoon. We had gone into the town on the wagon and then dispersed, going our various ways. We were at the *pâtisserie*. There were myself, Janine, Lavinia and a girl called Marie Dallon. We had chosen our cakes and had seated ourselves under one of the sunshades. Charles, the garçon, had brought our coffee.

We were laughing together when a man strolled by. He paused to look at us. He half smiled. Lavinia immediately responded, for, a little mature, he was very good looking in a dark, rather Italianate way. I noticed how his eyes rested on Lavinia; but there was nothing unusual in that.

"Good afternoon," he said. "Forgive me. I was so enchanted. I heard your laughter and I saw you all sitting there . . . looking so happy. It is unforgivable of me . . . but please forgive me."

"You are forgiven," said Lavinia, flashing a smile at him.

"Then I am indeed happy."

I thought he would bow and pass on, but he did not. He was still looking at Lavinia.

"Tell me," he went on, "are you not the young ladies from the *château?*"

"You are right," cried Lavinia.

"I have seen girls from the *château* in the past. Today I have just arrived here . . . on my way to Paris. And I see that it is just the same. I rejoice. There are still young ladies from the *château* and . . . they grow more enchanting than ever. I would make a request."

We looked at him enquiringly.

"It is that I may be allowed to stay here . . . just for a little moment . . . so that I may continue to look at you . . . and perhaps talk a little."

Janine, Marie and I looked at each other a trifle uneasily. Heaven knew what would be the result if we were discovered in conversation with a strange man. It would be disastrous, quite outside the laws of Lamason; and the mistress who had brought us might appear at any moment.

But Lavinia was saying, "If you can become invisible when our dragon of a mistress comes into sight, do. You will have to stop talking to us if she comes along. Then we can say you are just someone who sat here after we had been served with our coffee, so we could not move away."

"How delightfully devious!" He sat down. The garçon came and he ordered coffee.

"I think we are safe," said Lavinia, leaning her arms on the table and studying him intently. Her very attitude was inviting.

"I shall be watchful and at the first appearance of the dragon I shall summon my magical powers and become invisible."

Lavinia laughed, throwing back her head and displaying perfect teeth.

"Now you must tell me about the Château Lamason. Are the rules there very strict?"

"In a way . . . but not as bad as school," said Lavinia.

"For which you are very grateful?"

"Oh yes," I said. "It enables us to come into the town like this."

"And meet interesting people," added Lavinia, smiling at him.

We talked. He asked a good many questions about us and the school, and in return he told us that he was the Comte de Borgasson. His *château* was some fifty miles from here. It was one of those which had escaped the Revolution.

"Like Lamason," I put in.

"Yes . . . that is so." He gave me a grave smile, but he could not for long keep his eyes from Lavinia.

During that first encounter he established himself as an aristocrat with a castle some fifty miles away, a large estate which included vineyards. He was young, unmarried; his father had just died and he had inherited the title and large estates.

"My student days are over," he said. "I have to be serious now."

It was quite an adventure. I was sure Lavinia had enjoyed it, particularly as he had shown so clearly that she was the one among us who held his attention.

When we saw Mademoiselle coming towards us we all rose innocently, murmured goodbye to our handsome companion and joined the others at the wagon.

I saw Lavinia look around as I clambered in. I saw the Comte lift his hand. Lavinia was smiling secretly as we drove back to the *château*.

We saw the Comte the next time we went into town, and he took coffee with us in the same way as he had before. There was a great deal of lighthearted chatter. This time he sat next to Lavinia.

Perhaps because I knew her so well I guessed she had a secret. She often disappeared and we were not sure where she was. She was very absentminded and seemed no longer aware of the charms of Monsieur Dubois. She danced with a kind of abandon, but she never sought to make him choose her, as she had in the past, by moving a little forward and flicking back the hair from her face.

I did not see the Comte again, and I forgot about him until one day I met him near the *château*. He smiled at me in a rather absentminded way, as though he were trying to remember who I was. I was not surprised, for during our encounters he had had eyes for no one but Lavinia.

She continued in a kind of euphoric mood. She was less querulous, and would often sit twirling a lock of her hair, staring into space and smiling.

I asked her one day what was happening.

She gave me a rather contemptuous look.

"Oh, *you* wouldn't understand."

"If it is so very profound I wonder you do."

"This isn't silly old schoolwork. This is life."

"Oh . . . that," I retorted. "Has Monsieur Dubois discovered that he no longer loves his wife and four children and dreams only of you?"

"Don't be silly. Monsieur Dubois! That little dancing master! Do you think he is a real man? Oh, you might . . . knowing so little about them."

"Of course, *you* know a great deal."

She smiled secretly.

"So it is something to do with men," I said.

"Hush," she replied, quite good temperedly.

I should have been prepared.

One day when we all went to the town she did not come. She said she had a headache. I should not have believed her. She looked quite radiant on that occasion.

When we returned she was not in our room and it was some time before she came in. She was very flushed. I cannot understand now why I was so blind. After all, I had seen it all before with Jos.

Christmas had come. It was celebrated in the traditional manner at Lamason, and most of the girls remained at the *château*, because it was too far to go home, so it was a merry time.

Janine told me that she had seen the Comte again. He was quite near the *château*. He had not seemed to recognize her. Janine said, "He looked a little purposeful."

A few days later I was alone with Lavinia and I told her that Janine had seen him.

She smirked a little and said: "Can you keep a secret?"

"Of course. What is it?"

"I'm going to be married."

"Married? Of course you will be. When Lady Harriet has found a husband for you."

She shook her head. "Did you think I couldn't find one for myself?"

"You certainly give the impression that you are on the lookout."

"I didn't have to wait very long, did I?"

"What do you mean?"

"I am going to marry the Comte."

"The Comte! Do you mean that man who spoke to us in the town?"

She nodded gleefully.

"But what of your mother?"

"She will be delighted."

"Have you told her?"

"No, Jean-Pierre thinks it better not . . . just yet. Not until we have decided how to break the news."

"Jean-Pierre?"

"The Comte, of course, silly. Just think of it. I shall be the Comtesse de Borgasson, and I shall live in a wonderful *château*. He is very rich. He will go to England and see Mama. He noticed me at once . . . that first afternoon, and he knew that I was for him. Isn't it wonderful?"

"Well, it sounds as if . . ."

"As if what? Are you jealous, Drusilla?"

"Of course not."

"You must be. Everyone will be jealous of me."

"Well, you hardly know him."

She looked very wise. "In these matters it is not how long you know people. It is how deeply you know them. Don't tell anyone yet . . . especially Janine."

"Why do you have to keep it secret?" I asked.

"It's only for a while. I shouldn't have told *you*, but you know how I seem to tell you things."

She was certainly ecstatically happy. She was more pleasant to me. She did not come on the wagon in the afternoons and I guessed she was keeping some secret rendezvous with the Comte. I wondered where. Perhaps he had his carriage, which would wait for her in a secret place and carry her off . . . to where? I felt a twinge of uneasiness.

Janine said, "What's happened to Lavinia? She's changed."

"Has she?" I asked innocently.

"Don't tell me you haven't noticed."

"Well, you never know what mood she will be in."

"Something has happened," said the all-seeing Janine. There were suspicions in her eyes. Her overweening curiosity had been aroused; and when Lavinia's mood changed once more she was the first to notice.

Lavinia looked a little pale. She was absentminded; sometimes when one spoke to her she did not seem to hear.

I thought something must have gone wrong with the romance and was making up my mind to ask her when she told me she wanted to speak to me . . . urgently.

"Come into the garden," she said. "It's easier there."

As it was February, the weather was cold. We had discovered that although the summers here were hotter than in England, the winters could be far colder. In season the gardens were quite glorious, with bougainvillaea and oleander and many coloured plants. But this was, after all, winter. In the gardens during the month of February, we were less likely to be interrupted than anywhere else.

I met her there. "Well, what is it?" I asked.

"It's the Comte," she replied.

"I can see it is not good news. Has he called off the engagement?"

"No. I just haven't seen him."

"He's probably been called away on important business . . . that large estate and all that."

"He would have let me know. He was supposed to meet me."

"Where?"

"At that little hut place. You know it . . . about half a mile away in the forest."

"That broken-down old shed! That was where your meetings took place, then?"

"Nobody goes there."

I was becoming uneasy. It was getting to look like the Jos affair.

"So he didn't arrive . . ."

She shook her head. I could see she was trying to hold back the tears.

"How long is it since you've seen him?"

"It's three weeks."

"That is a long time. I have no doubt someone else will turn up. If not you will have to give your attention to Monsieur Dubois."

"You don't understand." She looked at me steadily and burst out, "I think I am going to have a baby."

I stared at her in horror. My first thoughts were of Lady Harriet. Her shock . . . her reproaches. Lavinia had been sent away to escape that sort of thing; and I had been sent with her to protect her.

I said, "You must marry him . . . at once."

"I don't know where he is."

"We must get a *message* to that *château* of his."

"It is three weeks since I saw him. Oh, Drusilla, what am I going to do?"

I was immediately sorry for her. All her arrogance had been wiped away. There was only fear; and I was flattered that she had turned to me for help. She looked at me wheedlingly as though I could certainly find the solution. I was pleased that she held me in such esteem.

"We must find him," I said.

"He loved me so much, Drusilla. More than anyone he has ever known. He said I was the most beautiful woman he had ever seen."

"I think they all say that to everyone." I thought of a sharp retort, but I spoke gently, for there is something more than ordinarily pathetic about the arrogant when they are brought low. I was looking at a very frightened girl, as well she might be.

"Drusilla," she begged, "you will help me?"

I did not see how, but it was gratifying that the normally overbearing Lavinia should turn to me with that innocent belief in my ability to solve her problem.

"We have to think about it," I said. "We have to give our minds to it."

She clung to me desperately. "I don't know what to do. I've got to do something. You will help, won't you? You're so clever."

I said, "I'll do all I can."

"Oh thank you, Drusilla, thank you."

My mind was occupied with her problem. I thought: The first thing to do is to find the Comte.

I went into the town on the wagon with the girls that afternoon. Lavinia stayed behind, pleading a headache. Perhaps it was a real one on this occasion.

I chose my cake and when Charles came out with the coffee I seized the opportunity to talk to him.

"Do you know Borgasson?" I asked.

"Oh yes, Mademoiselle. It's some fifty miles from here. Did you think of taking an excursion? It is hardly worth a visit."

"There is an old *château* there . . . owned by the Comte de Borgasson . . ."

"Oh no, Mademoiselle, there is no *château* . . . just a few little farms and some small houses. Just a village . . . No, not worth a visit."

"Do you mean to say that there is no Château de Borgasson?"

"Certainly there is not. I know the place well. My uncle lives there."

Then I began to see clearly what had happened. Lavinia had been duped by the bogus Comte; and the significance of her position was borne home to me.

I had to tell her. I said, "Charles, the garçon, says there is no *château* in Borgasson; there is no Comte. He knows because his uncle lives there. You have been deceived."

"I don't believe it."

"He would know. And where is the Comte? You'd better face up to the truth, Lavinia. He was pretending all the time. He merely wanted you to do . . . what you did. And that is why he talked of marriage and all that."

"He couldn't have . . . not the Comte."

"Lavinia, the sooner you face the facts the better . . . for the easier it will be for us. We have to look at this as it really is and not as you would like it to be."

"Oh, Drusilla, I am so frightened."

I thought: I'm not surprised at that. She was relying on me. I would have to do something. But what?

People began to notice the change in her. She was looking pale and there were shadows under her eyes.

Miss Ellmore said to me, "I think Lavinia is unwell. Perhaps I should have a word with Madame. There is a good doctor here . . . a friend of Madame . . ."

When I told Lavinia this she fell into a panic.

"Don't worry," I said. "Pull yourself together. It would be fatal if she sent for the doctor. They would all *know.*"

She tried, but she was still pale and wan.

I told Miss Ellmore that she was considerably better.

"Girls do go through these phases," said Miss Ellmore; and I felt we had got over that fence.

It was inevitable that Janine should notice.

"What's wrong with our forlorn maiden?" she asked. "Has the noble Comte deserted her? Are we witnessing the symptoms of a broken heart?"

It suddenly occurred to me that the worldly Janine might be able to help us and I asked Lavinia if I might tell her.

"She hates me," said Lavinia. "She would never help me."

"She would. She hated you because you were more attractive than she was. Now that you are in deep trouble she wouldn't hate you so much. People are like that. They don't hate people half as much when they fail. And she might be able to help."

"All right, tell her. But make her swear not to tell anyone else."

"Leave it to me," I said.

I went to Janine. "Will you swear not to divulge it to a soul if I tell you something?"

Her eyes glistened at the prospect of sharing a secret. "I promise," she said.

"Lavinia is in deep trouble."

I must say I did not like the light of pleasure that came into Janine's eyes.

"Yes . . . yes . . ." she urged.

"The Comte has gone."

"I always knew he was false. All that talk about the title and the estates . . . at the first meeting. Go on."

"She is going to have a baby."

"What?"

"I'm afraid so."

"My goodness. What a story! Well, well. It serves her right. She was anybody's for the taking. All that attraction she is supposed to have for the opposite sex. What is it? Just . . . I'm easy. Smile at me and I'm willing."

"What are we going to do?"

"We?"

"We've got to help her."

"Why should we? She has never been particularly pleasant to us."

"It's just her way. She's different now."

"Of course she is." Janine was thoughtful. "What could we do? We can't have the baby for her."

"There'll be a terrible scandal. You can't imagine what her mother is like. There is already a mad aunt in the house who believes peacocks' feathers are unlucky."

"What's that got to do with it?"

"It just means it will be awful for her if she has to go home and tell them she is with child."

"Being biblical about it may sound very fine, but it doesn't alter anything."

"I persuaded her to let me tell you because I thought you might help."

I could see that that had flattered Janine.

She began to laugh. "I'm just thinking of the fuss there'd be. It just serves Madame Lavinia right. When you think how arrogant she has always been, lording it over us all . . . and now this. 'Pride goeth before a fall.' I reckon this will put an end to that grand marriage her mama has in mind for her. Wealthy gentlemen do like to think they are getting a virgin."

"Janine . . . please . . . try to help."

"What can I do?"

I used the tactics Lavinia employed with me. "You're clever. You know something about the world. You might think of something."

"Well," she said grudgingly, "I might."

Janine did give her mind to the matter. She talked with Lavinia, discovered when the baby was likely to appear, and when Lavinia calculated that it might be in August, Janine said with an air of wisdom: "Well, it will be in the holidays. That's something to be thankful for."

We looked at her eagerly.

"You see," she explained, "it gives you a chance to have the child and no one know."

"How?" pleaded the newly humble Lavinia.

"If you could leave here at the beginning of July when the terms ends . . . My goodness, it will be eight months. Can we hide it so long?"

"We'll have to," I said.

"I will. I will," said Lavinia, like a drowning woman clutching a life belt which has just been handed to her.

"There is my Aunt Emily," went on Janine.

I turned excitedly to Lavinia. "Janine's aunt runs a clinic where people go to have babies . . . among other things."

Lavinia clasped her hands as though in prayer.

"Aunt Emily is very discreet," said Janine.

"Where is it?" asked Lavinia.

"Near the New Forest." Janine's eyes were sparkling. "Listen. We'll go there. You must tell your people that you have been invited to stay . . . you might say at the Princess's place."

"That would please Lady Harriet," I said.

"And you are to go there from Lamason when the term breaks up."

Lavinia nodded excitedly.

"I will write to my aunt and see if she will have you. If she will, you must write to your people and tell them that you will be staying at the Princess's mansion in . . . wherever it is. It is very remote, I know. I had never heard of the place. When we leave here we will go together to my aunt's clinic, and there you will have your baby."

"It is wonderful," cried Lavinia. "Thank you, Janine."

I said, "And when the baby is born?"

Lavinia's face fell.

"Adoptions are arranged," said Janine. "You might have to pay . . ."

"I would manage," said Lavinia. I knew she was already compiling a letter for her mother. She was going to stay with a noble Princess; she needed new clothes—French clothes—and they were rather expensive. Lady Harriet would be delighted at the thought of her daughter's visiting royalty, however remote.

It seemed that we were getting somewhere with the help of Janine. That took us up one step. But perhaps what was more important was what we were going to do with the baby afterwards.

Then I had a brilliant idea. My thoughts went back to that tall house opposite the common. I saw Polly and Eff with the "nippers." Polly would do anything to help me; she had always said so. But she would not be so ready to do anything for Lavinia, whom she had always disliked; and I fancied that she might not be displeased to see Lavinia in that spot of trouble which she had prophecied for her. But if *I* asked her she would surely help.

I mentioned this. Lavinia was overcome with relief. She said what good friends we were to her and she did not know what she would have done without us.

It was amazing to see her in this humble mood.

And from then on we became the three conspirators.

I must say that Lavinia played her part well, which could not have been easy. There was a certain anxiety about her health, but fortunately the true state of affairs had not occurred to anyone in authority.

I was on tenterhooks lest they should guess. We bought a voluminous skirt in the marketplace. It was very concealing. Spring came; we were all three deeply involved in the enterprise and Lavinia was able to sit outside the *pâtisserie* without being overcome by bitter memories.

We were to leave at the end of that term, having completed our allotted span. The three of us could scarcely wait, so eager were we to put our plan into action.

Janine had had a reply from her Aunt Emily, who said that it was not the first time this sort of thing had overtaken an unwary girl like Lavinia, and we could rely on her.

Polly wrote back. She and Eff would, of course, take in the little baby when it was born. Eff was really good with little babies and ought to have had some of her own, but there had been Him to look after. It seemed that He, being sometime dead, had lost a good deal of that sanctity which had descended on him when he was recently expired. However, the news was good. Polly and Eff would take the child in. It was only later that it occurred to me that the reason Polly was so quick to offer help was because she thought the child was mine.

So the plans were laid. It was pathetic to see the way in which Lavinia relied on us. Both Janine and I enjoyed that.

The weeks were passing. In a short time we should be on our way to put the first part of our venture into practice. The full skirt was becoming inadequate. Several of the girls told Lavinia she was putting on weight. Sometimes I wondered whether Madame was aware. It seemed to me that she discreetly shielded Lavinia from exposure. She would want no scandal attached to the most impeccable of institutions.

I was relieved when the day came to say goodbye to our fellow students. We exchanged addresses and promised to write and to see each other if we ever found ourselves in close vicinity.

We travelled with Miss Ellmore to England. I did see her glance once or twice at Lavinia, and we held our breath in case she had noticed, but, like Madame, Miss Ellmore wanted no complications while we were in her care.

She had been told that we were going to stay for a brief visit with Janine, and it was left at that.

When she had put us on the train we were almost hysterical with relief. We laughed and laughed and could scarcely stop ourselves. Lavinia was in good spirits. We had successfully eluded disaster, which had at times seemed imminent, and she owed it to us.

In due course we arrived at Candown, close to the New Forest. The Firs was a large white building set among trees. Aunt Emily received us graciously, but her eyes immediately went to Lavinia.

"We will get you to your room," she said. "You, Miss Delany, can share with Miss Framling. Janine will show you, and then I must have a talk with Miss Framling. But first we will get you settled in nice and comfy."

She was a large woman with a breezy yet soothing manner, which I thought from the first did not quite match the rest of her. She was slightly unctuous. She had light sandy hair and piercing eyes, which were between green and blue. As soon as I saw her I thought that was how Janine would look in thirty years' time, and I could not believe that there was not some blood relationship between them. In spite of her attempt to create what she would call "a comfy atmosphere," there was a

92

certain sharpness about her, a certain coldness in her eyes, and an aggressive point to her nose gave a look of alertness to her face. She reminded me of some kind of bird—a crow or, I thought with a certain uneasiness, a vulture.

But we had successfully completed what seemed to us the most hazardous part of the adventure and must rejoice.

Janine took us to our room. It had blue curtains and the furniture was of light wood. It was a pleasant room and there were two beds in it.

"I am glad you are sharing with me," said the newly humble Lavinia.

Janine said, "You'll be all right now. You've just got to wait until your time comes."

"It's another month . . . at least I think so," replied Lavinia.

"You can't be sure," Janine told her. "Aunt Emily will soon find out. She'll get Dr. Ramsay to have a look at you."

Lavinia shivered slightly.

I said soothingly, "It will be all right. I know it will."

Lavinia swallowed and nodded. Now that the difficulties of getting her here had been successfully accomplished she was beginning to brood on the ordeal before her.

A tray of food was sent up to us. Janine brought it and shared the food with us.

When we had eaten, she told Lavinia, "Aunt Emily wants to see you as soon as we've finished. She just wants to discuss a few things."

In due course she took Lavinia off to see Aunt Emily. I was left alone in the room. I went to the window and looked out on a garden. There was a seat there among the shrubs and two people sat on it. One was a very old man. Although seated, he leaned forward on a stick, and I could see that his hand was shaking; every now and then his head gave a little jerk. Beside him was a girl of about Lavinia's age; she was obviously pregnant. They did not speak together; they just sat staring into space. They looked as though they were bewildered.

A shiver ran through me. I had a sudden feeling that the walls were closing round me. From the moment I had entered I had had a premonition of evil . . . and that had not been soothed by the breezy presence of Aunt Emily.

In a few weeks, I reminded myself, it will be over. The baby will be with Polly and we shall all go home. Lavinia was away for the best part of an hour and when she came back she looked a little frightened.

I said, "Well?"

"It's going to cost a great deal. I hadn't thought of that."

"But we haven't got the money."

"I don't have to pay it all at once. She'll give me time. I've got to give her some money now . . . to start with. It's almost all I've got."

"I didn't think about the money," I said. "Janine didn't say how much it would cost."

"I'll have to find it somehow."

"Perhaps you should tell your mother."

"No!"

"What about your brother?"

"I couldn't tell him I'd got myself into this mess. I shall have to pay for your bed and board, too."

"I could go home."

"Oh, no, no. Promise you won't go."

"Well, if it is going to cost money we haven't got."

"I can pay. She'll give me time. I told her what I'd got and she said she would open an account. I shall have to send her something every month. Oh, Drusilla, why did I ever get myself into this?"

"Ask yourself. You knew how it was with Jos."

"Oh, Jos!" She smiled faintly. "He was only a stable boy, but . . ."

"Not quite so dangerous as a bogus French aristocrat."

"I don't know how I could have been so taken in."

"I do," I said. "You are bemused by flattery. After this, you'll have to be more sensible."

"I know. Oh, Drusilla, you are my best friend."

"You didn't seem to think so before this happened."

"I always did. But it is things like this which test friendship."

"Well, you only have to wait now for the baby and then we'll leave. You'll have to pay Polly something, too. You can't just have children and send them off for someone else to keep."

"Polly was always so fond of you."

"But she wasn't so fond of you. You were always rather arrogant with her."

"I didn't know."

"Well, she didn't like you."

"She's only helping because *you* asked her. Oh, Drusilla, what would I do without you?"

"Or Janine," I reminded her.

"I know. You have both been . . . wonderful."

"Don't get emotional. Remember the baby."

She smiled at me gratefully.

Those few weeks I spent at Aunt Emily's clinic were the strangest I had ever known up to that time.

I was not sure whether I was aware of the sinister atmosphere at that time or whether I built it up afterwards.

There were twelve patients staying there and there was nothing ordinary about any of them. There were four other young women expecting babies. They were always called by their Christian names, which in itself was significant. They were under a cloud and their identity was a secret known only to themselves. But I learned a little about them during our stay at The Firs.

I remember Agatha, a bold beauty, mistress of a wealthy merchant. Much to her chagrin, she had conceived his child. She had a rather curious cockney voice and a loud laugh. She was the only one who was not particularly reticent about her life. She told me she had had numerous lovers, but the father of the child was the best; he was oldish and grateful for her favours and in exchange for them was ready to lavish his wealth upon her. "Suits me, suits him," she said, giving me a wink. And in her presence it seemed to me that normality returned; and because I wanted to rid myself of that feeling of unreality I used to meet her in the gardens and we would sit on a seat while she did most of the talking. She knew I was merely accompanying Lavinia, who had been the victim of a little miscalculation, as she said with another of her winks.

"Bound to have happened to her sooner or later," she said. "She'll have to watch out and get the wedding ring soon. These little bastards can be most inconvenient."

She had successfully summed up Lavinia's character.

Another of the pregnant ladies was Emmeline, sweet-faced and gentle, no longer very young—about thirty, I supposed. I discovered a little about her, too. She was nurse to a querulous invalid lady, and she had fallen in love with the lady's husband and he with her. She had been genteelly brought up and I could see that she regarded her present position as a sin. Her lover came to see her. I was rather touched. It was clear to me that there was a genuine affection between them. They used to sit in the garden holding hands; he was very tender towards her.

I fervently hoped that the querulous wife would die and they would be able to marry and live in respectable happiness ever after.

There was one young girl who was expecting a baby. She had been raped and used to cry out at night; she was terrified at the sight of men. Her name was Jenny and she was only twelve years old.

Then there was Miriam. I think in time I grew to know Miriam better than any of the others. There was something intense about her. She was reticent and did not want to know anyone. She was locked in with her own tragedy.

I found the days long and strange. Lavinia rested a good deal. Janine had certain duties which Aunt Emily expected her to perform; but I was there more as an onlooker. I could not help feeling that I was in some way in a world of shades, among people who would one day escape from it and resume their normal personalities. At the moment they were unreal . . . lost souls in a kind of Hades, fearing Hell and hoping for a sight of Heaven.

Miriam used to sit in the garden quite often, alone and brooding. At first she did not encourage me to sit with her, but it might have been that she sensed my sympathy and the temptation to talk to someone was too strong to resist.

Gradually I learned her story. She was passionately in love with her husband. He was a sailor. They had longed for a child and that blessing had been denied them. It was a sadness, but not a great one, because they had each other. She loved him deeply; she lived through one separation after another, waiting for the reunion. Her cousin had said she must not stay at home and brood during his absences, but go out a little. She had had no great desire to, but finally she had been persuaded.

She looked at me with tragic eyes. "That is what makes it all so stupid . . . so pointless."

Tears coursed down her cheeks. "To think that I have done this to him."

I said, "Don't talk of it if you'd rather not."

She shook her head. "Sometimes I feel better for talking. Sometimes I think I'm dreaming and this is a terrible nightmare. What am I doing in this place? If only I hadn't gone . . . if only . . ."

"That is what so many people say."

"I couldn't bear him to know. It would kill him. It would be the end of everything we had."

"Wouldn't it be better to tell him? What if he should find out?"

"He never will." She became fierce suddenly. "I'd kill myself rather."

"This baby . . ."

"It came about in the most silly way. I didn't know the man. They had given me too much to drink. I wasn't used to it. I told him about Jack—that's my husband—and he said his name was Jack. I don't know what happened. He took me somewhere. I woke up next morning with him beside me. I nearly died. I dressed . . . I ran out. I wanted to wash everything out of my mind. I didn't want to remember that night. I wanted to pretend it hadn't happened. And when I found I was pregnant because of it I just wanted to die."

I put my hand over hers. She was trembling. I said, "Why don't you tell him? He would understand. You love him so much and he loves you. Surely he would forgive you."

"I could never face him. You see it was perfect . . . and now . . ."

I said, "You wanted a child."

"*His* child."

"This is your child."

"I would hate it. It would always be a reproach."

"You were innocent. They gave you too much to drink. You weren't used to it and that happened. I am sure that if your husband really loved you he would understand."

"He would not. He could not. We were everything to each other."

"And what of the baby?"

"I shall get someone to adopt it."

"Poor little baby!" I said. "It will never know its mother."

"You are too young to understand what was between Jack and me. No child could ever mean more to me than he does . . . not even his. I have thought and thought. I have to do it this way."

"But it is making you very unhappy."

"I don't expect ever to be happy again."

"You should try, I am sure. It was one little moment when you were off guard. It wasn't as though you took a lover."

"It would seem like that."

"Not if you told him."

"He would never understand."

"Why don't you try? That poor little baby . . . to be born unwanted. That is the most terrible tragedy of all."

"I know. My sin is heavy on me. I have thought of taking my life."

"Please don't talk like that."

"If I did it would break Jack's heart and if he knew of this it could never be the same between us. He would never believe me entirely. He is passionate and jealous. He so much wanted a child . . . and to think that another man gave me what he couldn't . . . I know Jack. You don't. You're too young to understand these things."

And so she talked to me and again and again she went over her problems. I tried to advise her but, as she said, I was too young to understand.

I thought a great deal about those children who would be born in Aunt Emily's clinic—the unwanted ones—and I thought of my own parents, who had planned my education while they were waiting for me. I thought of Lady Harriet, who had long upbraided the Almighty for denying her offspring, and who had rejoiced so wholeheartedly when her prayers had been answered that she spoiled her children to such an extent that Lavinia had come to this pass.

There were other patients besides the women who were expecting babies. There was the poor old man whom I had seen from my bedroom window sitting on the seat, on the first day I had come. I learned that he had been a great scientist in his day, but he had had a seizure which had robbed him of his mind; and he was at this place because he was unwanted by his family and had been put here to await death because it was the most convenient way of disposing of him. There was one woman who lived in a world of her own. Her manner was haughty and she believed she was reigning over a large household of servants. She was known as the Duchess. There was George Thomson, who was always laying fires in cupboards. He caused a great deal of anxiety and had to be watched. He had never attempted to light the fires, but there was always the fear that he might.

They were like people from a shadow world.

I often wondered about Janine, who had been brought up in this place by an aunt whose relationship to her she denied. The house was bright. There were blue curtains and white furniture everywhere, and yet somehow it seemed a dark and mysterious place, and I never felt at ease in it. I would wake in the night sometimes and start up in fear. I would gaze to that other bed where Lavinia lay, her beautiful hair spread out on the pillow. Her sleep was often troubled. I wondered how often she thought of her lover, swaggering up to us outside that *pâtisserie* with his tales of grandeur, his sole motive being the seduction of gullible girls. And those weeks of pleasure had led to this. What a lesson! I wondered if Lavinia would ever learn it.

She had been seen by Dr. Ramsay—a small man with dark, rather frizzy hair, some of which grew out of his nose and ears. He had examined her, declared her to be in good health and had said that all was going reasonably well and that we could expect the baby during the second week of August. This was good news. We had thought it would be two weeks later.

I told myself: Soon we shall be out of this strange place. Here I felt shut away from the real world. It would be good to be back in the natural world, for the idea struck me that anything could happen here. Yet Aunt Emily seemed determined to create a homely atmosphere. She was always bright and breezy and wanting to know if we were "comfy." If only she had not those sharp blue-green eyes, which seemed to betray something to me that I would rather not know.

The days seemed normal enough; it was during the night when I heard strange noises. The little girl would suddenly cry out in terror, and the scientist would wander about tapping his stick, murmuring to himself that there was something wrong in the laboratory. The Duchess sometimes walked in her sleep, and we would hear her giving orders to the bust of George IV in the hall, thinking it was her butler.

It was a house of contrasts; the robust Agatha with her accent of the streets of London, gentle Emmeline awaiting the visits of her lover. Yes, it was a mysterious world and, while I found it of absorbing interest in a morbid sort of way, I longed to escape from it.

I knew that tremendous problems awaited us—or at least Lavinia—when we were out of here. I guessed that all the people here were paying Aunt Emily a considerable sum of money for her services; and even though Lavinia was to be allowed to pay over a period of time, it would not be easy for her.

There was something strange about most of the people here. It was the sort of nursing home where people who had something to hide went . . . except those like the Duchess and the old man, whose people sent them here to get them out of the way. It was very pathetic and I could not get out of my mind the thought that it was also sinister.

I did not greatly like the doctor. There was something secretive about him. He looked to me like a man who had something to hide.

Janine was different here. She had to help her aunt and was often sent to look after the patients. There was one young man who was made her special charge. He was the Honourable Clarence Coldry and was quite clearly mentally deficient. He had a beaming smile and was delighted if anyone spoke to him. He himself had difficulty in speaking; his tongue seemed too large for his mouth. There was something doglike about him.

I had an idea that Janine was not very happy. She did not seem like the same girl who had been to school with us. I sensed a scheming nature behind Aunt Emily's smiles and she was very watchful of Janine.

I was longing to get away. It seemed as though we had

been here for months. We took little walks, Janine and I. Lavinia had become quite cumbersome in the last weeks and she
could not accompany us.

"Soon you'll be gone," Janine said to me once. "It can't be
long now. Lavinia is almost ready to deliver the goods."

I winced. I was more fond of that yet-to-be-born baby than
any of them. I did not like to hear it referred to as "the goods."
"And I shall still be here," she said with a little grimace.

"Well, it is your home," I reminded her.

She nodded grimly. "Aunt Emily has plans for me."

"Not the Honourable Clarence!"

"Afraid so."

"Oh, Janine . . . you couldn't!"

"Perhaps. After all, he is an Hon."

"He wouldn't want to marry."

"I have to make him rely on me."

"Janine, why do you stay here?"

"It's where I was born. I have lived here all my life . . .
except when I was at school."

"Your aunt must have been fond of you to send you to
Lamason."

"She is not my aunt. It's my real family who pay."

"They would not want you to marry Clarence."

"It's Aunt Emily who has the say."

"She seems very powerful. I hope she will give Lavinia
time to pay."

"She will. Although if there was any delay in the pay-
ments she might decide to approach Mama."

"She mustn't do that. I don't think Lavinia realized it was
going to be so costly."

"Mistakes always are . . . in one way or another. After
all, she was in a real mess. We got her out of it . . . you and I.
What would she have done if we hadn't brought her here?
There will be the baby's keep too. Mind you, she's been lucky.
Can't expect any more than she's got."

"At least we have come so far," I said.

And I thought again: It can't be long now.

It was soon after that when Lavinia awoke one night to
find her pains had started.

The doctor and Aunt Emily came to her room. I had hastily put on some clothes and was sent to arouse one of the maids, who knew something about childbirth and had assisted before.

It was not a difficult birth. Lavinia was young and healthy and the next day her little girl was born. A cradle had been set up in our room.

"We are rather full at the moment," explained Aunt Emily apologetically to me. I did not mind sharing the room, which had become a nursery. I was fascinated by the baby.

Lavinia was greatly relieved to have come through her ordeal. During the first day she sat up in bed, smiling and marvelling with the rest of us at the baby.

She had many visitors—Emmeline, Agatha and the Duchess; the latter mistook Lavinia for her daughter and kept calling the baby Paul. Miriam did not come.

There was to be a short respite for Lavinia before we moved on. I was conscious of an immense relief. Lavinia had come through safely. I had heard tell of many things which could go wrong in childbirth and I had had some anxious moments wondering what action we could take if anything of that nature happened to Lavinia. But there was no longer need to worry on that score. She was perfectly well and the baby appeared to be flourishing. Moreover the end of our stay in the house was certainly at hand.

For the first few days we gave ourselves up to marvelling at the baby. It was like a miracle to me that such an enchanting creature could have come out of that sordid little affair. Even Lavinia succumbed to her charm and looked rather proud and almost happy to have produced her. I loved her red wrinkled face, her screwed-up eyes and the tufts of dark hair, her little hands and feet all equipped with delicate pink-tinted nails.

"She has to have a name," I said. "She is like a little flower."

"We'll call her Flower and as she is half French she shall be Fleur."

"Fleur," I repeated. "It seems to suit her."

So Fleur she became.

I had written to Polly to tell her that the baby was born and that it was a little girl named Fleur. Polly wrote back that they couldn't wait to get the baby. Eff was so excited; she had everything ready . . . cradle, bottles and nappies. Eff was very knowledgeable about babies' needs. She did think the name was a bit outlandish and would have liked Rose or Lily or perhaps Effie.

"You're on your own, now," said Janine. "I've got your address. I'll write."

Aunt Emily took a cosy farewell and at the same time presented Lavinia with the outstanding account, which depressed Lavinia every time she looked at it.

She and I were to take the baby to London. Polly would meet us at the station. Eff would be at home preparing the welcome.

In due course we arrived. I was carrying the baby. I was less awkward with her than Lavinia was. And so Polly saw us. She cried out, "Drusilla!" Then she was beside me, her eyes brimming over with love and hugging me and the baby at the same time.

"So here you are with that little love. And you . . . Let's have a look at you. You're looking well."

"And you, too, Polly. It's wonderful to see you."

"You bet," said Polly. "And wait until Eff sees the nipper."

Her greeting to Lavinia was less warm. I was glad that Lavinia was suitably subdued and did seem to be aware of what she owed to Polly and her sister.

Polly had a cab already waiting for us and we all got in and drove to the house on the common, where Eff was waiting for us.

Eff had changed. She was quite stately now. They had taken the house across the road and now had three houses, which they let very profitably. It took me some little time to learn who the tenants were because there were now the various floors One, Two and Three, and so on.

Their joy over the baby eclipsed all else. Eff took charge. I could see that Polly was a little baffled. She kept looking at me intently. Of course, the presence of Lavinia was a mystery to them and it put a certain restraint on them. Lady Harriet's invisible presence seemed to brood over us; and I supposed even Polly was not quite immune from that. Eff apologized for everything to Lavinia, for she was far more aware of the grades of society than Polly would admit to being, and however much they disliked Lavinia, she was still Lady Harriet's daughter.

We stayed only a few days. I wrote to my father from London and Lavinia wrote to Lady Harriet. We said we had now returned from Lindenstein and were breaking the journey in London. We should be home within a few days.

Murder in
Fiddler's Green

I was further shocked to see the deterioration in my father. He now walked with a stick, but he said he was still capable of carrying on. He had many good workers in the village who were of inestimable help of him.

He wanted to hear about Lindenstein; he believed the *Schloss* was very ancient, Gothic in fact. And was there any evidence of the Goths in the neighbourhood?

"It must have been fascinating for you, my dear. A great opportunity. You were wise not to miss it."

I parried his questions about the place and told myself I must find a book on it if that were possible, and learn something about it. I upbraided myself for my folly in not trying to do this earlier. But, of course, we had had too much to contend with.

Mrs. Janson said he had been ailing last winter and she dreaded the one to come. She was glad I was home. "You ought to be here," she added significantly. "I was a bit worried when I heard you wasn't coming straight home, but were going gadding about with foreign princesses."

"There was only one princess, Mrs. Janson," I reminded her.

"One's enough. You ought to have come straight home. I don't mind telling you, I'm glad school's done with. How was Polly?"

"Very well."

"I reckon she was glad to see you."

I said she was.

So, I was finished with school now. I was the polished article. What difference it had made to me I was not sure, except that I knew I was no longer the innocent girl who had gone to France.

That night as I lay in my familiar bed I had muddled dreams.

Faces seemed to swim in and out of my mind. The Duchess . . . the scientist . . . the man with his fires . . . all waiting for Death . . . and so many of the women for a new life to begin. I pictured Agatha's cheerful grin, Emmeline's wistful looks and Miriam's tortured face. I was aware of Aunt Emily's secret smile as she smiled at me as though she were saying: You'll never escape . . . you will be here forever . . . cosy . . . cosy . . .

I awoke crying out, "No, no."

Then I realized I was in my own familiar bed and it was only a dream. I was free.

Lavinia came over the next day.

"Let's ride," she said, and we rode out together, for being finished young ladies we could ride—as long as there were two of us—without a groom in attendance.

She said, "It's the only way I can really feel safe to talk. There are so many people around. I feel they might be listening. My mother is talking about a London season."

"She doesn't guess anything?"

"Of course not. Why should she?"

"My father asks awkward questions about Lindenstein."

"Oh, it's too far away for people to know about. A London season, think of that!"

"Do you want it?"

"Of course I want it. I want to marry a rich man so that I can pay off Aunt Emily. The woman's a shark."

"You didn't think that when you went to her."

"I didn't know it was going to cost so much."

"How long is it going to take you to pay?"

"More than a year . . . unless I can get Mama to top up my allowance."

"Why don't you ask Fabian?"

"I couldn't tell him what I wanted it for and he'd want to know."

"Couldn't you tell him it's a secret?"

"You don't understand Fabian. He wants to know everything. That's how he has always been. No. I'll have to pay it out of my own allowance until I find a rich husband."

I looked at her wonderingly that she could talk so. Did she never think of little Fleur? Did she not want to be with her baby sometimes?

I asked her.

"Oh yes," she replied, "but I can't, can I? Those two will look after her. They love her already."

"I shall go down and see them soon. I want to see Fleur, too."

"Oh good! You can let me know how she is."

I marvelled at how rapidly she was regaining her old assurance. The submissive, fearful Lavinia was fast disappearing. She had overcome her misfortune and was, I could see, ready for adventure again.

She could think of little but the coming season. How she would revel in it. She was already regaining her healthy looks; she was even preening herself, certain that she would become the debutante of the season.

I went once or twice to Framling. I saw Lady Harriet, who was gracious in a detached sort of way. I was no longer of importance in her scheme of things. I had served my purpose as Lavinia's steadying companion over the school years and was now relegated to my proper position—the rather plain rector's daughter.

Lavinia's excitement grew. Such plans there were. Lady Harriet was having her schooled in certain accomplishments. She would soon be leaving with Lavinia for their London residence and there Lavinia would be put through her paces, learning how to curtsey, how to dance the new fashionable dances and certain matters of deportment; and of course she must visit the Court dressmakers. She was to be presented at Easter time.

All through the winter I saw little of Lavinia. I had written several letters to Polly and she reported the progress of Fleur. The child was flourishing. There wasn't a baby like her on the common. She and Eff took it in turns to wheel her out; and they had that nice bit of garden at the back where she could be in her pram.

She already knew them, and did she kick up a fuss when she wanted a bit of a cuddle!

I imagined there would be plenty of "bits of cuddle" for Fleur, and I rejoiced, as I had throughout my life, for the good fortune which had brought Polly into my life.

Christmas came—always a busy time for us at the rectory. There were the usual services—midnight mass on Christmas eve, the carol service—and before that the decorating of the church, organized by church workers, but my father had to be present, of course. We had friends from the neighbourhood to dinner on Christmas Day. They were the doctor, his family, and the solicitor and his wife.

There was a good deal of entertaining at Framling. Fabian was home. I saw him once or twice. He would call a greeting and give me that somewhat cryptic smile, which I had come to expect from him.

"Hello, Drusilla," he said. "Finished school now?"

"Yes," I told him.

"Now you are really a grown-up young lady."

What was there to say? He smiled as though it were a great joke that I had grown up.

He did not stay long at Framling. I heard from Mrs. Janson, who had it from the Framling cook, that he would be going to India soon; and that he was in London most of the time, in the offices there, learning about the East India Company, with which the Framling family had been concerned ever since it came into existence.

I wrote to Polly and sent Christmas presents to them, among them a little jacket for Fleur. Polly wrote back, but her letters were full of how the baby was getting on, how she smiled at Polly first, only Eff wouldn't have it, that that was not a smile. It was only a bit of wind, said Eff, determined to be the first to win recognition from the baby. In February, Lavinia and Lady Harriet went to London. The weather was extremely cold and my father caught a chill, which turned to bronchitis. He was quite ill and most of my time was spent nursing him.

A curate came to help out. He was Colin Brady, a fresh-faced, earnest young man who was quickly popular with the household. Mrs. Janson cossetted him and the others followed her lead. He was very much liked in the neighbourhood.

I was pleased that he had come, for willingly he took all the onerous tasks from my father's shoulders; he very quickly became part of the household.

He and I got along well together. We both enjoyed reading and discussing what we had read. There was an air of innocence about him which I found refreshing. He would discuss his sermons with me and he always listened to my ideas. I seemed to take more part in church affairs than I had when my father was in charge.

My father's health was improving, but, as Mrs. Janson said, he had to take care. We never allowed him to go out if the wind was cold; it was really quite touching to see how Colin Brady was always there when there was a question of my father's doing something which would be too much for him, and doing it himself in an unostentatious way.

I was very grateful to him and very glad that he was there, until I began to notice the surreptitious looks that came to us, not only from Mrs. Janson, but from the servants and certain of the parishioners. They had decided that the ideal solution was for me to marry Colin and that he should take over completely, thus solving the future of my father, Colin and myself in one swoop.

The result was that they had spoilt my pleasant relationship with the curate. I liked him very much, but the thought of what was in people's mind concerning us made me less comfortable in his presence.

With the coming of the spring my father was almost back to normal.

"He's a marvel," said Mrs. Janson. "They say creaking doors go on for a long time."

Fabian came to Framling and with him was Dougal Carruthers. Lady Harriet and Lavinia were still in London. I was writing regularly to Polly and received news of the baby. I told Polly that I wanted to come and see them, but in view of my father's health I had not been able to do so before. But now that he was better I wanted to arrange a visit. Polly wrote back that the baby was a little love, bright as a button, and did she know how to get her own way! I was not to worry about *her* and when I did come I could be sure of a big welcome.

Dear, dear Polly! What would I have done without her? What would Lavinia have done? I imagined her now being presented to the Queen, going to balls and parties; she would have completely forgotten the bogus Comte just as she had Jos. But could she have forgotten Fleur? I could not believe even Lavinia would do that.

I decided that I would go to London during the following week.

Dougal called to see my father. He stayed to tea and my father greatly enjoyed his visit. I was pleased to see him so animated, looking as well as he had before the winter.

When Dougal left I conducted him to the hall and thanked him for calling.

"But it was a pleasure," he said.

"It has done my father so much good. He has been rather ill and that makes him low in spirit."

"I hope I may come again."

"Please do. My father will be delighted to see you at any time."

"You too, I hope."

I did not expect him to come again so soon, but the next afternoon he presented himself. It was another pleasant teatime and my father said, "Do come and dine with us. There is so much we have to talk about."

"I should greatly enjoy that," replied Dougal, "but I am a guest at Framling. I could hardly leave my host."

"Bring him too," said my father rashly.

"May I? I am sure he would be delighted to come."

Mrs. Janson was slightly less than delighted. She did not like the idea of entertaining "them up at the House," and of course Sir Fabian would be our guest.

I said, "Don't worry. Just forget who he is."

"The trouble with them Framlings is they never let you forget who they are."

And so Fabian came to dine.

He took my hands and held them for a few moments in a warm grip.

"Thank you for letting me come," he said, somewhat insincerely, I thought, for I was sure he was not in the least grateful to be invited to our humble dwelling.

"Mr. Carruthers suggested it," I told him.

He raised his eyebrows as though he were amused. In fact I was beginning to feel that most of the time he regarded me with amusement.

"The Rector has an astonishing knowledge of ancient Greece," said Dougal. "He has some quite unusual ideas."

"How fascinating!" said Fabian, continuing to smile at me.

I took them to the drawing room, where my father was seated in his chair. Colin Brady was with him.

"I think you all know each other," I said.

"I don't think we have met," said Fabian, eyeing Colin closely.

"Mr. Brady came to help my father when he was ill and we are hoping he is going to stay with us."

"That must be useful," said Fabian.

"And Mr. Brady . . . this is Sir Fabian Framling."

Colin was a little in awe of Fabian. He knew he came from the influential family that ruled the village.

Soon we were seated at table. Mrs. Janson had excelled herself and the maids had been given detailed instructions as to how they were to behave.

Dougal was in conversation with my father, with Colin Brady now and then throwing in a remark. Fabian turned to me.

"Did you enjoy Lamason?" he asked.

"It was a most interesting experience," I told him.

"I think my sister found it so, too."

"I am sure she did."

"And now you are back . . . what shall you do?"

"I suppose . . . I just go on living here."

He nodded.

My father was talking about the ancient civilizations that flourished for a while and then passed away.

"It is a pattern," said Dougal. "Empires rise and fall. I suppose the most significant fall was that of the Roman Empire. All over Europe you can see the remains of that civilization . . . in spite of the fact that its fall was followed by the Dark Ages."

Then I heard my father say, "Drusilla was at Lindenstein only recently."

"Lindenstein," said Dougal. "Now that is a very interesting spot. You remember it, Fabian." He turned to me. "Fabian and I did a kind of grand tour. We visited all the conventional places, didn't we, Fabian? But we did stray from the beaten track now and then. Actually we were quite near Lindenstein."

I felt myself flushing a little. I was always uncomfortable when there was reference to our deceit. I wanted to change the conversation quickly.

"Tell us what you think of Florence, Mr. Carruthers," I said. "I have always felt it must be the most fascinating city in the world."

"There are many who would agree with you," replied Dougal.

My father said, "How I should love to stroll along the Arno where Dante met Beatrice."

"What do you think of Lindenstein, Miss Delany?" asked Fabian.

"Oh . . . very interesting."

"That medieval *Schloss* . . ."

"That is where Drusilla stayed, isn't it, Drusilla?" said my father. "The Princess was at school with Drusilla and Lavinia. She invited them. It was a great experience."

"Yes," I said with feeling. "We had a great experience."

My father had turned the conversation back to Dante, and Colin and Dougal joined in.

Fabian said quietly to me, "An amazing little country, Lindenstein. Those mountains . . . stark and grim . . . don't you think?"

"Oh yes," I said.

"And the *Schloss*. Extraordinary architecture . . . all those towers . . ."

I nodded.

"It must have been very interesting to stay in such a place."

I nodded again.

He was regarding me intently. I wondered if Lavinia could have confided in him after all; and I felt suddenly angry that I should have been burdened with her secret.

When I left the men with the port I went to my room. Fabian Framling always disconcerted me. It was the way in which he looked at me, as though he were trying to remind me how vulnerable I was.

When they were taking their departure my father said, "This has been a pleasant evening. I rarely meet people who are interested in my hobbies. Do please come again."

"You must dine at Framling," said Fabian.

"Thank you," I said, "but my father should not be out in the evening." I was looking at Dougal. "It is better for you to come here."

"That I shall certainly do . . . when I am asked."

"I hope you will be here for a little while yet," said my father.

"I think so," answered Fabian. "I doubt we shall be leaving the country until the end of next year."

"Next week . . . it is next week, is it not, my dear? . . . Drusilla is going to London."

"Oh?" said Fabian, his gaze on me.

"It is to stay with her old nurse," explained my father. "You know how strong these ties are."

"Yes," said Fabian. "Then perhaps we may come when Miss Drusilla returns."

"There is no reason why you should not come when I am away," I said. "Mrs. Janson will take care of things, and my father would enjoy your company."

"I shall invite you," said my father.

Then they took their leave.

My father said what a delightful evening it had been and Colin Brady agreed with him. Mrs. Janson was not displeased. Her verdict was that the Framlings were just like anybody else and she wasn't afraid of *him*. As for the other one, he was a perfect gent and no one could take objection to him.

I felt I had come through the evening tolerably well, although I had had certain qualms when they began to talk about Lindenstein.

I was growing excited about my coming visit to London. The prospect of seeing Polly again always filled me with joy, and now there was the baby as well as Eff. I went down to the town, which was about a mile out of the village. I had a pleasant morning shopping and bought a little jacket and bonnet and a pair of bootees for Fleur and a pair of bellows for Polly and Eff, because I could see they had had some difficulty in getting the kitchen fire to draw up.

As I was coming out of the shop a carriage drove by. I knew it was from Framling, because I had seen Fabian driving it around. It was drawn by two spirited grey horses and he liked to go at great speed.

I saw Fabian in the driver's seat and to my surprise he pulled up.

"Miss Delany."

"Oh . . . hello," I said.

"You have been shopping, I see."

"Oh yes."

"I'll drive you back."

"Oh, that is not necessary."

"Of course I'll take you back."

He had leaped down from the seat and taken from me the bag that contained my purchases. As he did so the contents fell out, and there on the pavement were the bellows, the baby's jacket, the bonnet and the bootees.

"Oh dear," he said, stooping to pick them up. "I hope no harm is done."

I flushed hotly. He stood there with the bootees in his hand.

"Very pretty," he commented, "and they are all safe."

"Really," I stammered, "there's no need to take me home."

"But I insist. I like to show off my horses, you know. They really are a superb pair. You can sit beside me. Then you can see the road better. You'll enjoy it."

He carefully put my purchases in the carriage and helped me up.

"Now," he said. "Off we go. I shall not take you directly home."

"Oh, but . . ."

"Again I insist. You'll be home just as soon as you would if you had walked. And you will have the pleasure of seeing Castor and Pollux in action."

"The heavenly twins . . ." I murmured.

"They are as like each other as twins only to look at. Pollux has a bit of a temper and Castor is inclined to be lazy. But they know the master's touch."

The horses broke into a gallop and he laughed as we gathered speed.

"Just cling to me if you're scared," he said.

"Thanks," I replied. "But I'm not."

"And thank you for the compliment. It is well deserved in fact. I know how to manage my horses. By the way, I haven't seen you riding lately."

"Not since I returned."

"Why not?"

"We don't have a stable at the rectory."

"But you used to ride regularly."

"That was when Lavinia was at home."

"My dear Miss Delany, you don't have to ask permission to use a horse from the Framling stables. I thought you understood that."

"It was different when Lavinia was here. I rode with her."

"There is no difference at all. Please, whenever you wish, ride the horse you have always had."

"Thank you. That is very good of you."

"Oh no. After all, you are a great friend of my sister. Do you envy her, preening in London?"

"I don't think I should greatly care for the process."

"No, I dare say not. But please ride when you want to."

"You are very kind."

He gave me a sideways, rather sardonic smile.

"Tell me about Lamason," he said.

"Oh, it is supposed to be a very fine school."

"Where they turn hoydens into young ladies."

"I think that is the idea."

"And do you think they have done a satisfactory job on you and Lavinia?"

"I cannot speak for Lavinia. You should ask her."

"But yourself?"

"That is for others to judge."

"Do you want to hear my judgement?"

"Not particularly. It could not be a true one because you scarcely know me."

"I feel I know you very well."

115

"I can't think why. I have so rarely seen you."

"There have been significant moments. Do you remember when you took the peacock fan?"

"On your orders, yes. Tell me, how is your Aunt Lucille?"

"She has grown very feeble. She is lost to this world and exists only in her own."

"Does she still have the Indian servants?"

"She does. They would never leave her, and she would be completely lost without them."

"I'm sorry," I said.

There was a brief silence; then he said, "You will be going to London soon."

The carriage lurched and I fell against him, clutching his coat.

He laughed. "All's well. I told you you were safe with me."

"I really think I should be home. I have a great deal to do."

"You have to prepare for your visit to London."

"Yes, that and other things."

"How long shall you stay?"

"Oh . . . about a week."

"You are very fond of your old nurse."

"She is not really old. Polly is one of those people who never will be."

"Your loyalty does you credit."

"Is it so very creditable to express one's true feelings?"

"No, of course not. There. You see how docile I am. I'll have you at the rectory door in three minutes."

"Thank you."

He pulled up sharply at the grey stone house, leaped down and helped me out. He took my hands and smiled at me.

"I hope the gifts are acceptable."

"What gifts?"

"The bellows and the baby's clothes."

To my annoyance I flushed again.

I took the bag he handed me, said "Thank you," and went into the house.

I was disturbed. He had always disturbed me. It was a pity he had seen my purchases. I felt he had looked at them cryptically. I was wondering what he had thought.

My father asked if it were wise of me to travel to London alone.

"My dear Father," I replied, "what harm could befall me? I shall get on the train under the eyes of Mr. Hanson, the stationmaster, and Mr. Briggs, the porter. Polly will be waiting for me at the other end. I am grown up now, you know."

"Still . . ." said my father.

"I shall be all right."

At last he agreed that I could come to no harm and I set out, with my case containing the gifts and the little bit of luggage I was taking with me.

I sat in the carriage by the window and closed my eyes while I contemplated the pleasure of a reunion with Polly and seeing Eff and the baby again.

The door opened. Fabian was getting into the carriage.

He grinned at me. "I had to go to London unexpectedly. This is fun. We can travel together. Why, you don't look very pleased to see me."

"I hadn't expected to . . ."

"Surprises are pleasant, don't you think?"

"Sometimes."

He sat opposite me and folded his arms.

"I am sure your father would be pleased. I believe he is a little anxious about your travelling alone. Young ladies don't usually, do they?"

"I am of the opinion that we are not so fragile as some try to pretend."

"I wonder why?"

"Oh, it is a masculine idea . . . meant to show the superiority of men."

"Do you really believe that?"

The train was beginning to move out of the station.

"Believe what?" I asked.

"In masculine superiority."

"Certainly not."

"They are inferior then?"

"I did not say that."

"That is gracious of you."

"No . . . just common sense. The sexes are meant to complement one another."

"Doesn't it say that in the Bible? But I believe there are some occasions when the subservient role of the female is expressed. St. Paul . . ."

"Oh, St. Paul! Wasn't he one of those who found women a temptation and blamed them for being that?"

"Did he? I think your Biblical knowledge is greater than mine. It all comes of being such a polished young lady."

"Thank you."

"How long shall you be staying in London?"

"A week, I think. I do not like leaving my father longer."

"He was very ill in the winter, I believe. I understand your anxiety. The curate is a very worthy young man, I gather."

"He is very helpful and popular with the parishioners, which is very important."

"It is important for us all to be popular."

"But particularly with someone in his position. For instance, I don't suppose you care very much whether you are popular or not."

"I do . . . where some people are concerned." He smiled at me in the quizzical manner with which I was familiar.

He sat back, still smiling. "This is really a pleasant way of travelling. Usually I regret the time spent on it."

"You will be doing a good deal of travelling, I daresay."

"Oh, you mean India, where I shall be going at some time."

"Soon, I suppose."

"Probably at the end of the year. Carruthers will go, too. You see, our families are connected with the East India Company."

"I had heard."

"From Carruthers, I suppose. I know he is a frequent visitor at the rectory."

"He gets on well with my father. They have shared interests."

"We have been brought up with the idea that we shall eventually go into the Company. My uncle . . . my father's brother . . . has offices in London. I go there now and then . . . gleaning experience, you might say."

"It must be interesting."

"The Company . . . oh yes. It is part of history, of course. It goes back years and years. As you know, trading with India started when Vasco de Gama discovered the eastern passage and cast anchor off Calicut. But the Portuguese never started a trading company; they left that to us. Did you know that Queen Elizabeth granted us a charter to trade? It was on the very last day of the sixteenth century. So, you see, we have our roots in the past and it is obligatory in the family to carry on."

"You must be very proud of your ancestors."

"We do have our share of sinners."

"All families have that."

"Some more than most. Now I imagine yours is very worthy . . . just the occasional peccadillo perhaps."

"It might be better not to enquire."

"I am sure you are right, but with a family like ours it all seems to be recorded. We know that an ancestor was one of those who founded the Company and we know something of the lives of those who followed him. People are unexpected, don't you agree? Those who appear so virtuous often have their secrets and the villains often a grain of goodness."

I said, "Tell me about the merchandise. What commodities do you deal in?"

"We send out bullion, woollens, hardware and such things to India and we bring back silks, diamonds, tea, porcelain, pepper, calico, drugs and so on."

"I see. You are traders."

"Exactly. But we have become very powerful. You see, we were not content with trading. We wanted to rule, and we have taken part in quarrels between Indian princes, supporting one against another. We have gained power, and some would say that the East India Company is the true ruler of India."

"Do the Indians resent this?"

"Naturally, some of them do. Others see the advantages we have brought them. The French had an East India Company, too. That is the reason for the trouble between our two countries."

"It seems to me that this ambition for power causes a great deal of trouble."

He nodded. "You see why, do you not, that it is a family tradition."

"Yes, I do," I said, "with a family like yours."

"Well, enough of the Company and my family. What of you? What do you propose to do now you are home?"

"Do? What could I do?"

"You tell me."

"At the moment I am helping to run the rectory and look after my father. There are a great many duties that fall to the rector's family. I suppose that is what I shall continue to do."

"You have no plan . . . no ambition? To travel perhaps? You have already been to France . . . and Lindenstein."

I replied hurriedly, "I suppose one waits to see what happens."

"Some of us are impatient and prod fate. Are you one of those?"

"That is something I have to find out. Up to now I have never done any prodding. Have you?"

He leaned towards me. "I am continually doing it. If I want something I make an effort to get it."

"It is all that ambition and lust for power. It is because you belong to the Framlings and the East India Company."

"Not entirely. It is my pushing nature."

I laughed and he said, "How different you are when you laugh. Did you know that you look a little severe in repose?"

"I did not know I was particularly so."

"Perhaps it is only when you see me."

"I can't think why you should induce solemnity."

"Perhaps because you disapprove of me?"

"Why should I?"

"I can think of a few reasons."

"Then I don't know them."

"Don't look expectant. I am not going to tell you. I should not be so foolish as to increase your disapproval."

"The disapproval is entirely of your imaginings. How could one disapprove of someone one did not know?"

"Perhaps through ill repute."

"I know nothing of that."

"There! Now you are severe again. I feel we are getting to know each other well on this journey."

"Why should being in a train do that which all the years living as neighbours has failed to do?"

"There is something very intimate about trains."

"Is there?"

"Don't you feel it?"

"I suppose we have talked together more than we ever did before."

"There you are, you see. You can't get away from me."

"Nor you from me."

"Oh, but I don't want to."

I laughed. "I think we must be near our destination."

"Five more minutes," he said. "Alas! What a short journey it has seemed. Most enlivening. How fortunate that we had a carriage to ourselves. I will tell you something. It wasn't luck. I had the foresight to tip the guard."

"Why?"

"Obvious reasons. I thought it would be interesting to get to know each other. People would have spoilt our little tête-à-tête."

"I can't understand why you took the trouble."

"I take a lot of trouble to do what I want. Didn't I tell you that I'm a prodder?"

I was a little startled and faintly alarmed. I did not know what was in his mind. It seemed to me that he might be preparing to indulge in a little light flirtation. No doubt he thought that I was an innocent maiden ready to fall into the arms of the all-powerful lord of the manor. If Lavinia had learned little from her experience, I had learned a great deal.

I said coolly, "I can't imagine why you should wish to do so."

"I'll tell you later."

"In the meantime, here we are."

He took my case.

"I can manage, you know," I said.

"I wouldn't think of allowing you to carry it."

It seemed to me that he was taking a proprietorial attitude already.

I should have to be wary of him. He was the type of person who thought he only had to beckon to a girl and she would come running. He was Sir Fabian, rich and powerful, and his mother had made him feel—as they used to say—the little Caesar.

I tried to take my case from him, but he resisted, smiling. We walked along the platform and there was Polly waiting for me.

She stared in amazement to see me with a man, and her amazement turned to dismay when she recognized him.

I ran to her and she embraced me. "Oh, Polly," I cried, "how wonderful to see you."

"Well, it's not like a smack in the chops to me neither."

She was restrained because he was there.

"It's Sir Fabian, Polly. He kindly carried my bag."

He bowed to Polly. "Miss Delany and I met on the train."

"Did you now?" said Polly, very faintly bellicose. She had never approved of the Framlings. I knew she was thinking, Who were they when they were out? Or on trains and carrying people's bags. Up to no good, shouldn't reckon. I knew her so well that I was aware of her thoughts.

"Well, thank you, Sir Fabian," I said. "It was good of you."

"We'll get a cab and be home in a tick," said Polly.

"I shall see you home," he said. "I shall get the cab."

"There is no need . . ." I began.

"But I insist." He spoke as though his word was law. It was faintly irritating. I felt an urge to snatch my case from him and tell him we did not need his help. But if I did that might betray something that I ought to hide.

I was aware of the imperious manner in which he hailed the cab and in a very short time we were on our way to the common.

I tried to chat to Polly as I should have done if he had not been there. I asked about Eff. Eff was flourishing. Doing very well. Might even take on No. 10 Maccleston if the old man living there moved out. Eff had always had her eyes open.

Neither of us mentioned the baby, but I knew Polly was longing to talk of her, as I was.

I was glad when the journey was over. He alighted and carried my bag to the door. Eff was waiting to open it. She cried out with pleasure when she saw me and then stepped back at the sight of Fabian.

He raised his hat and bowed.

"This is Sir Fabian Framling, a neighbour of mine," I explained. "I saw him on the train and he has been very helpful."

I could see she was wondering whether he should be asked in for a cup of tea and a piece of the special sultana cake she had baked for the occasion; her only hesitation was because of his title and perhaps his undeniable presence.

I said quickly, "It was kind of you, Sir Fabian. Thank you so much." With that I turned away, and he, with another bow, went back to the waiting cab.

We went inside.

"Well, I never," said Polly. "You could have knocked me down with half a feather when I saw who he was."

She shook her head; she was bothered. I would tell her as soon as I had an opportunity that there was no need for alarm.

Eff said, "I know who you'll be wanting to see. I'd have her here, but she's having her nap, and I don't want to disturb her, else there'll be ructions, eh, Poll?"

"You bet," said Polly.

"Well, what about a nice cup of tea first. I've got some muffins."

As we sat over tea and muffins I heard of the increasing prosperity of the business and how the baby grew more beautiful every day.

At length she was brought down by Eff and I held her in my arms while she gazed at me wonderingly, her little hands curled round my finger and what could have been a smile of contentment on her pinkish face. She had changed a good deal from the day when Lavinia and I had brought her here. She was getting on for nine months old—quite a personage. I had always been distressed by unwanted babies, but this one, at least, thanks to Polly and Eff, was overwhelmed with love.

Fleur had vivid blue eyes and the almost black hair she had been born with had lightened considerably. It was dark brown with tawny lights in it—inherited, no doubt, from Lavinia. She was clearly a contented baby, and that was something to be happy about.

Being with Fleur made me wonder about the other babies who had been born round about the same time. What had happened to Emmeline? Her child would have had a happy home, I was sure. And the poor little girl who had been raped? Surely

123

her family would look after her child. And Agatha? She would know what to do. She was warmhearted and would never desert her child. Mostly I thought of Miriam, who would have to give up hers for the sake of not disturbing her marriage. That seemed the saddest case of all.

But I was delighted to see Fleur here. She would not miss her parents, because she could not have two more devoted people to care for her than Polly and Eff.

The bellows were seized on with joy. "That kitchen fire never did draw like it ought," said Eff.

The bonnet was immediately tried on and Fleur was very interested in the bootees.

"Nice for her afternoon nap," said Polly. "She's starting to toddle now. I reckon she thinks she's done enough shooting round on her hands and knees."

"Don't you think she's a little angel?" said Eff.

I said I did.

"Eff spoils her really," said Polly.

"I like that!" retorted Eff. "Talk about the pot calling the kettle black!"

It was all so comforting, so much what I had expected from them. Polly was still the anchor in my life.

She was uneasy though. I sensed that. When she came to my room that night, after Eff had retired, she talked very seriously to me.

She said, "I've been worried about you, Drusilla. I didn't like to think of you in that foreign place. I didn't know what was happening. Fleur . . . she's Lavinia's. I know that now. At first I thought she was yours."

"Oh, Polly!"

"Well, that's why we took her in so prompt. I said to Eff, 'This is my girl and she's in trouble. We're going to help her all we know how and if that means having the baby here, well then we'll have the baby here.' "

"I thought of you immediately. I remember how you and Eff always liked babies."

"We do. But having one of your own is something that has to be thought about."

"You didn't hesitate."

"No . . . As I told you, I thought it was yours."

"You've always been wonderful to me, Polly . . . always."

"I know now she's that Lavinia's. That saucy baggage. Just like her. Gets into trouble and gets someone else to sort it out for her."

"Lady Harriet took over a big part of my school bills. I was there to be with Lavinia."

"I know. That sort think they own the world and everyone in it. Now there's that Fabian . . . or whatever he calls himself."

"Everyone else calls him Fabian. It's his name."

"*Sir* Fabian, if you please."

"He inherited the title from his father. He's been a sir ever since his father died."

"Silly way of going on . . . Little children getting airs. No wonder they grow up thinking they are Lord God Almighty."

"Do you think he does?"

"Clear as daylight."

"That's not always very clear."

"Now you're being clever and I want to talk serious-like. It's about Fleur."

"Oh, Polly, hasn't Lavinia sent you any money?"

"It's not money we're after. What I wanted to say was that Fleur . . . well, she is one of them Framlings when all's said and done. She's all right now. Wouldn't know the difference between Buckingham Palace and the rookeries . . . as long as we're there to look after her and give her a kiss and a cuddle . . . she's all right. But when she grows up a bit, is this place going to be good enough for her?"

"It will be good enough if you and Eff are there. She loves you both. Look how contented she is when you're there."

"Oh, she's a loving little thing. No bones about that. But there'll come a time when she'll have to be told who she is and something done about her education and all that."

"Let's leave it at that, Polly. When I get a chance I'll talk to Lavinia."

"And there's you."

"What about me?"

"What are you going to do?"

"What do you mean, Polly?"

"You know what I mean. Rector's not well, is he? How long can he go on working? I reckon this Colin Brady will take over. Do you like him?"

"You are not trying to do a little matchmaking, are you, Polly?"

"People have to be serious about these things. I'd like to see you settled, I would. You'd be happy with some little ones. Oh, I know. I've seen you with Fleur. There's some who are natural mothers and you are one of them."

"You are going too fast, Polly."

"Well, you like him, don't you, this Colin Brady?"

"Yes."

"And he's a good man."

"I daresay he is."

"You don't want to let some people pick up when they think they will and like as not drop you when they get a little tired."

"To whom are you referring?"

"That *Sir* Fabian."

"Oh, there is no question of his picking me up. He just happened to be on the train."

"Some people have a way of making things happen when they want them to."

I thought of what he had said about prodding, and he had certainly contrived the meeting. I felt rather pleased and excited that he had bothered to do so. It ought to have irritated me, but it didn't.

Gradually she wormed the story of Lavinia's betrayal and downfall from me.

"That one had trouble coming to her if ever anyone had. Perhaps this will be a lesson to her. Could be . . . though I doubt it. She's got mischief written all over her, that one. She'll be in trouble again sooner or later. And to think that Sir Fabian is our Fleur's uncle and doesn't know it!"

"Of course, he doesn't know there *is* a Fleur."

"Bit of a shock to him if he did. I'm not surprised that Lavinia went to all them lengths to keep her little secret. I've always been sorry for girls in trouble, but I can't say I'm getting out my sackcloth and ashes for her."

And so we talked, and it was as comforting to me as it used

to be in the old days when we sat in the room at the rectory with the churchyard on one side and the village green on the other.

Polly and I had our trips "up West"; I bought some clothes and some gloves for Polly and a scarf for Eff. I had my allowance, which came from the money my mother had left. It was not very much, but at least I was not penniless. I told Polly I was going to send her half of what I had to help with Fleur, but she was indignant. "You'll do no such thing! If you attempt to do that I'll send it right back . . . pronto . . . and Eff and me 'ull be most put out."

She told me how they loved having the baby. It was important . . . particularly to Eff. Eff loved the business, but she often said she'd missed something. She had put up with Him for years and she would have forgiven him all his little ways if he had given her a baby. But it seemed he wasn't any good . . . even at that. Polly, too, had been disappointed in that respect.

"But now we've got Fleur," she said, "and if that Lavinia ever wanted her back she wouldn't get her. I'd fight to the death for Fleur . . . so would Eff . . . and Eff always wins . . . always has and always will. Father used to say that."

I often thought of Lavinia and wondered what she was doing and if she ever gave a thought to the child. I doubted it. She had recklessly conceived the child for her own gratification and as casually cast her off without seeming to realize how fortunate she had been to find people to take the burden from her shoulders.

During that week, I would wheel the baby out on the common. I used to sit on a seat and think of everything that had happened over the last two years. Often in my mind I went back to the little town, choosing my pastry and bringing it out on a plate to sit under the sunshade and wait for Charles to bring the coffee. I could recall with vividness the day the so-called Comte had strolled up to us. I could see Lavinia smiling provocatively at the handsome intruder in her secretive manner. I remembered so well that inner satisfaction of hers. I should have guessed that the Comte was false and all he wanted was a brief love affair.

While I was dreaming thus and Fleur was dozing in her pram, I was suddenly aware that someone had sat down on the seat beside me. I turned and with a mingling of exhilaration and consternation I saw that it was Fabian.

"Sir Fabian . . ." I stammered.

"Oh please," he said, "not so formal. I'm simply Fabian to my friends."

"What . . . what are you doing here?"

"Rejoicing in this happy turn of fortune. How are you faring? You look well. Such a rosy colour in your cheeks. Is that due to the London air or to reunion with your devoted nurse?"

I did not answer and he went on, "What a pretty child! Whose is it?"

"She has been adopted by Polly."

"She is an unusual woman, your Polly. The bonnet suits her." He looked at me rather roguishly. "It was a good choice."

"Yes, it was."

"And the little socks."

"She is really too old for those, so it wasn't such a good choice. She crawls and totters and needs shoes for that."

"You should have thought of that. How enterprising those two are! They have their own houses and they take it upon themselves to adopt a child. Most unusual! Tell me, have they acquired Number 10 Maccleston yet?"

"No, but it will come. Are you on business down here?"

He looked at me with a half-amused smile. "I see you suspect me of playing truant. I happened to be in the neighbourhood and when I came across the common I remembered you were staying here. Luckily I saw you. I was surprised. First the baby carriage disconcerted me. I thought it must be some young mother . . . and then I realized that no one could look quite as you did . . . and I rejoiced. When are you returning? I believe you said you would stay for a week. Friday would be a week exactly."

"Yes. I expect it will be then."

"I hope you are having a rewarding week."

"Extremely so."

Fleur had awakened and, after regarding us gravely for a few moments, decided that she had been ignored long enough and started to whimper. I took her out of her pram and she was immediately smiling. I bounced her up and down a little, which she obviously enjoyed. She showed great interest in

Fabian and, stretching out towards him, took hold of one of the buttons on his coat. She looked up at him, staring intently into his face.

"Is that an expression of disapproval?" he asked.

"I am not sure, but it is certainly one of interest."

Fleur laughed as though she found him amusing.

"She will soon be talking," I said. "She wants to say something to you, but she just cannot get the words."

"She's a nice creature."

"I think so, and so do Polly and Eff."

"Eff?"

"Short for Effie."

At the mention of Eff, Fleur began to mumble, "Eff, Eff . . . Eff."

"You see," I said, "she is already beginning to speak."

"It did not sound like speech to me."

"Oh, you have to listen carefully. She is saying Eff."

"Effeff . . . eff," said Fleur.

"What is her name?" he asked.

"Fleur."

"A little French flower. Is she French?"

"Polly did not say."

"But they gave her a French name."

"I think she may have had that before she came to them."

I tried to persuade her to relinquish the button, but she refused to do so, and when at length she did her hand shot out and gripped his ear.

"She clearly likes you," I said.

"I wish she would find another way of expressing her fondness."

"Come, Fleur," I said. "It is time we went home. Polly will be waiting for you and so will Eff. They will be cross if I keep you out too long."

"I have an idea," he said. "Take the baby back and let me give you luncheon."

"It is kind of you," I replied, "but I have such a short time left. I must be with Polly."

"Because you will soon be leaving. All right. We'll travel back together."

I did not answer. I put a mildly protesting Fleur back into

the pram and turned to him. He stood there hat in hand, bow-
ing.

"Goodbye," I said.

"*Au revoir,*" he replied meaningfully.

I did not tell Polly I had met him on the common. I knew
it would disturb her.

It was the following morning. Polly and I were breakfast-
ing. Eff took hers very early, which often meant that Polly and
I could talk, as we loved to do. I think Eff knew this and was
glad to make herself scarce and give us the opportunity.

Polly had been glancing through the paper and she cried as
soon as I appeared, "Here, what do you think of this?"

I sat down expectantly.

"There's been a big fire at the place . . . that Firs. Nursing home it calls it . . . in the New Forest."

She started to read: " 'Firs Nursing Home. Terrible fire,
believed to have been started by one of the patients. The fire
was well under way before it was discovered. Mrs. Fletcher,
the proprietoress, lost her life. It is not yet known how many
died, but the fire was very intense and it is feared that several
lives were lost. Many of the inmates were suffering some infirmities . . .' "

I sat staring ahead. Had Janine been one of the victims? I
wondered how many women awaiting their babies had perished. I thought of the Duchess and the young man whom
Aunt Emily had intended for Janine. I imagined that one day
George had lighted one of those fires he had laid so many times
in cupboards and such places.

I told Polly about George.

"Thank goodness it didn't happen when you were there,"
she said.

All that day I could not stop thinking of The Firs and
Aunt Emily, Janine and the people I had known.

It might so easily have happened while we were there.

I scoured the papers later that day and all those I could
find on the next. I supposed it was not considered of enough
interest to be given more than the initial space.

The day for my departure arrived.

An hour before the train was due to leave, Fabian appeared

at the door with a cab to take us to the station in time to catch the three o'clock train. It was the only one that afternoon, so he knew I would be taking it.

Eff opened the door when he knocked. Her surprise was obvious; she was greatly impressed. She liked distinguished people to come to the house. As she said, it went down well with the neighbours.

There was nothing to be done but to accept his offer with a good grace. Polly came with us to the station, but of course his presence prevented intimate conversation between us.

He was very affable to her. When we arrived he insisted that the cabdriver should take her back and he paid for the journey.

Polly said, "There's no need for that."

But he waved aside her protests and even Polly had to fall in with the arrangement, though she resented it and I knew was disturbed to see me sitting with him in the carriage.

He seemed very pleased with his manoeuvering.

"It was a pleasant visit," he said, as we moved out of London.

"I always enjoy being with them."

"A most unusual pair of ladies, and there is the baby, too. I could see how much you liked her. A pleasant child. I fancy she looked a little French."

"Oh, did you think so?" I forced myself to say.

"Oh yes. And the name Fleur. I don't know whether it is used much in France, but it is certainly charming, don't you think?"

"Yes, I do."

"It makes one wonder who could abandon such a child. I should like to know the story behind her birth. A liaison, I imagine . . . with both participants realizing that they had made a mistake."

"Perhaps."

"Most certainly, I would say. Did you hear how those two worthy ladies undertook the adoption?"

"I don't know how such things are done."

I looked out of the window.

"You find the view interesting," he said.

"The home counties are very pleasant," I replied.

131

"They are indeed. There is an air of peaceful prosperity about them. Nothing rugged . . . all neat and pleasant. It always seems to me that even the trees submit to conventions. How different from Lindenstein!"

I felt sick with apprehension. He had guessed something and he was determined to bait me. He was teasing me as a cat teases a mouse before the final death stroke.

"Oh . . . Lindenstein," I murmured, trying to sound nonchalant.

"Rather flat, I thought when I saw it. Stark, in fact. Rather surprising when you consider its position. Not quite what one would have expected."

He was trying to trap me. I remembered snatches of that conversation when he had visited us and there had been mention of the mountainous country.

I was growing very uncomfortable under his scrutiny.

I turned from the window and met his gaze. There was a faint amusement in his eyes. Was he telling me that he knew I had never been to Lindenstein? I could see that he was working things out. Lavinia and I had left school at the end of term; we had said we were visiting the Princess; we had been away for two months; and there was a mysterious baby—French—who had been taken in by my devoted nurse.

I imagined he was fitting things together and thinking he had the solution. The inference would seem obvious to him. I felt indignant. I wanted to tell him to stop his insolent probing and ask his sister for the explanation.

I said coldly, "I suppose everywhere is different from what we expect it to be. Perhaps it is not wise to compare."

"Odious, aren't they . . . comparisons? . . . Or is it odorous?"

"It depends in which source you are consulting."

"That is true, of course, but in either case it means they are rather obnoxious."

He continued to regard me with amusement. Surely he must consider Lavinia's involvement in this. Knowing her—as he must—he could not believe that she would be ready to make any sacrifice for a friend. If I had been the one who was forced to hide, she would never have gone to such lengths to help me.

I wanted to shout at him, "You Framlings take up such an

attitude of superiority when you are the ones who cause all the trouble."

He must have seen that I was shaken, and when he spoke it was rather tenderly. "I hope there is an improvement in your father's health when you return."

"I hope so. Of course, his duties are considerably lightened by the coming of Colin Brady."

"Oh, the curate. I hear he is quite a success."

"That's true, and it is very fortunate that he is there. There are some days when my father is unable to work and that distresses him. But Mr. Brady takes on all the duties and it is a great load off my father's shoulders."

"I suppose he will want a living of his own one day."

"He certainly will."

He nodded and again he was giving me that probing look.

"I daresay you have a great deal in common."

I raised my eyebrows.

"Both in Holy Orders, so to speak. You by accident of birth and he by choice."

"I suppose you could say that."

"And you are obviously good friends."

"One could not be anything else with Mr. Brady. He is so friendly with everyone."

"An admirable young man."

Again the almost derisive smile. I was annoyed with him. First he had decided that I had had a liaison in France and that Fleur was the result and now he was contemplating marrying me off to Colin Brady. It was really quite impertinent . . . assuming the role of lord of the manor taking care of the underlings.

I wanted to tell him that I had not sought his company and that I did not care for his assumptions, but of course I did nothing of the sort, and in due course he changed the subject.

He talked about India, a subject which clearly fascinated him, the scenery and the people. He had not yet seen it, he told me, but he was learning so much about it that he felt he was beginning to know it.

I was interested to hear about the people, the caste system, the power of the company, the markets and the exotic goods which could be bought there. I was quite beguiled, but I could not forget our previous conversation, and the implication that Fleur was the result of an indiscretion on my part; and, of course, I could not tell him that it was his sister and not I who was at the centre of that sordid tragedy.

In due course the train steamed into our station. One of the grooms from Framling had brought the carriage and Fabian drove me to the rectory.

He took my hand and smiled at me as he said goodbye. It had been a most interesting and illuminating visit, he told me, with double-edge meaning.

I felt very uneasy, and I could not get out of my mind that thought of the fire at The Firs. I wondered which of the strange people I had known had been its victims. Had Janine been one of them?

Mrs. Janson told me that all had been as well as could be expected at the rectory during my absence. The rector had had one rather bad turn but she hadn't thought it necessary to interrupt my holiday. That Mr. Carruthers had been over once or twice and his visits seemed to do the rector a power of good. There they had been, huddled over some old maps and things that Mr. Carruthers brought, and it was like a tonic for the rector. And, of course, Mr. Brady was there to look after everything, so she could say it had all gone off rather well.

During the next week or so my friendship with both Dougal Carruthers and Colin Brady seemed to take a new turn.

Dougal came often and my father was eager for me to join them in their discussions.

"You will find it all so interesting," he said. "Of course, Mr. Carruthers' forte is the Anglo-Saxons . . . a little late for me, but I am finding it all absorbing. He has a good knowledge of early European history, which is very necessary to the period, of course. You will find his conversation quite fascinating."

I was rather surprised that this was so. He brought books for me to read and I was glad of the diversion, for I had been more upset than I had realized by those encounters with Fabian. I could not stop thinking about him and his insinuations. When Lavinia returned I would tell her that she must explain to her brother what my part had been in the adventure.

It was clear that he had pieced things together and come up with what he thought was the right solution. I did not want him to think that first I could have been involved in such a sordid affair and secondly that I should abandon my child . . . even to a trusted nurse. Lavinia would *have* to explain.

I wished I could stop thinking of Fabian. He intruded constantly into my thoughts. I was not sure of my feelings towards him and sometimes they came close to dislike. I dreaded meeting him, which was always possible as we lived so close to each other; on the other hand, I hoped I would.

He made me feel alive, on the defensive as no other had ever done before. It was rather alarming because of Fleur; on the other hand, our meetings had been an exhilarating experience.

I wished I could stop thinking of the fire at The Firs. Janine was constantly in my mind. What had become of her? She knew where we were, so perhaps she would get in touch. I believed her aunt had amassed a fortune and surely she would have left Janine well provided for. I wished there had been more news in the papers.

My friendship with Dougal was developing and I began to think that he came to the rectory to see me as well as my father.

The interest of probing into the past took hold of me for a time; it was because I needed to keep my mind from dwelling on Fabian and what he might be thinking about me—if he gave me another thought. Perhaps it was presumptuous of me to think that he would, but he had seemed deeply interested at the time, which might be because of his sister's involvement. Moreover, I had muddled dreams in which The Firs featured. I was back in that half world, surrounded by strange people. I saw George laying his fires and in the middle of the night creeping out and lighting one. I dreamed of waking up, suffocating smoke in my lungs. How dreadful for those poor people caught in such a place!

Colin's attitude was changing towards me, too. Church matters brought us together. He would always discuss them with me—what hymns should be chosen for special services, who should have which stall at the annual bazaar, and when the Framlings should be asked when we might make use of their grounds.

I imagined I could see plans forming in Colin's mind. It was only natural that they should. He was a young curate in search of promotion. This would seem the perfect parish for him. Parsons needed wives; promotion was easier for them if they had the right one. The rector's daughter would be considered highly acceptable, and the likelihood was that, married to me, the living would be his.

I thought, as most girls do, of marriage; but I had learned in the Framling garden that I was plain and I knew that plain girls did not attract husbands as readily as pretty ones. I had told myself that if no one wanted to marry me I did not care. I would be my own mistress and not have to consider the vagaries of any man.

My chances, if any, would be few and, as Polly would say, no sensible girl would turn them away without consideration; but I had made up my mind that I would prefer not to be married at all than because it was a convenient solution for Colin Brady.

I had to admit at the same time that I had been thinking just a little romantically of Dougal Carruthers. He was moderately good looking, gentle and courteous to everyone. Mrs. Janson was always delighted if he stayed to lunch. She was also very fond of Colin Brady, but I believed she had a special admiration for Dougal Carruthers.

I was becoming very interested in history and he brought books for me to read, which we discussed. One day he suggested that we ride to Grosham Castle, which was about eight miles away. It would be a day's outing and Mrs. Janson could give us a picnic lunch to take with us. She was delighted to do this. Leave it to her, she said. She knew just what was wanted.

So early in the morning we set out from the Framling stables. It was a lovely summer's day, not too hot, with a gentle breeze; and we made our leisurely way to the castle.

Dougal did not want to hurry. He liked to savour the countryside. He was interested in wildlife. We walked our horses side by side so that it was easier to talk. He told me that he was not looking forward to going to India. He would rather stay at home. He would have liked to be attached to some university and pursue his studies.

We reached the castle at about noon. The sun was getting

warm and as we had made an early start we decided to take a quick look at the ruins and after that refresh ourselves with what Mrs. Janson had prepared for us. After that we could explore more thoroughly.

Grosham was a shell, although the walls were intact and, riding up to it, one would have no idea that the interior had been destroyed.

We picked our way over the jutting stones—part of an inner wall—past broken columns, over grass which was growing where once there had been a tiled hall.

Dougal's indignation was great, for it was not natural age and decay which had ruined Grosham, but Cromwell's soldiers.

In the shadow of the castle we opened the picnic basket to find legs of roasted chicken with salad and crusty bread with a pot of butter. There was fruit to follow, and a bottle of Mrs. Janson's homemade elderberry wine.

We were hungry and the meal tasted especially delicious.

I did enjoy talking with Dougal and as I had been reading a great deal more since I had known him I was able to talk with confidence.

I had rarely seem him so indignant. "To think that castle might be in perfect condition today but for that . . . vandal."

"You are referring to the self-righteous Oliver, of course."

"I hate to see beautiful things spoilt."

"But he thought they were sinful."

"Then he must have been a fool."

"I think he is not generally regarded as such."

"People can be wise in some ways and foolish in others."

"That's true. Cromwell did raise an army and taught peasants how to fight. He did win a war and governed the country for a time."

"He destroyed beautiful things and that is unforgivable."

"He made war and destroyed people, which is worse. But he believed he was right, that he had God on his side. Can people be blamed for doing what they think right?"

"It is arrogant to think one is right when so many people have different views."

"It is difficult to understand whether he was right or not. Some historians agree, others take the completely opposite view. It is not easy to form a judgement on such a man. About people like Nero and Caligula there are no possible doubts. But your opinion on Oliver Cromwell must be your own."

"He destroyed beautiful things," insisted Dougal, "and that is something for which I cannot forgive him. When people kill in the name of God I feel more strongly against them than I would if they were openly cruel. That castle is just one example. When you think of what he did all over the country."

"I know. But the point is that he *thought* he was right and that he was doing the best for the people."

"I suppose you have a point. I love beauty so passionately. I cannot bear to see it destroyed."

"I believe that beautiful things mean more to you than they do to most people. Cromwell saw them as sinful because people worshipped them more than they did God."

He became animated in discussion. There was a faint colour in his pale, rather aesthetic face. I thought: I believe I could be very fond of him. He is the sort of person who becomes more interesting as one knows him. I could picture myself taking up his interests and making them mine. It would be a rich and rewarding way of living. Already he had opened up new ideas in my mind. He was a man of intellect, a lover of humanity—except those who vandalized beautiful things. I had never seem him show such indignation towards a living person as he did towards Oliver Cromwell.

He seemed to follow my thoughts. He said, "It has been a great pleasure to me to know you and your father."

"It has been a great pleasure to us to know you."

"Miss Delany . . . it seems absurd to address you so formally when there is such friendship between us. Perhaps I shall call you Drusilla."

"It seems a good idea," I replied, smiling.

"What an excellent picnic this is."

"I shall tell Mrs. Janson what you say. She will be delighted."

"Drusilla . . ."

I never knew what he intended saying, for just at that moment we heard the sound of a horse's hoofs approaching and as Dougal paused in surprise, Fabian rode up.

"Hello," he called. "I knew you were coming here so I

thought I'd join the party. Food! What an excellent idea!" He dismounted and tied up his horse with ours. "Are you going to invite me to join you?"

I felt a faint annoyance. I had been serenely contented listening to Dougal and now this man had arrived to put me on the alert, to destroy that serenity.

I could not help saying, "It seems you have invited yourself, Sir Fabian."

"I guessed you wouldn't mind my joining you. Is that chicken?" He stretched out a hand and took a leg. "The bread looks delicious," he added.

"It was made by Mrs. Janson."

"An admirable cook, Mrs. Janson, as I learned when I had the pleasure of dining at the rectory. How good it tastes! I am so glad I came along."

"How did you know where we had gone?" asked Dougal.

"Ha. Devious methods. I shall not tell you. I might want to use the same again. It's a wonderful old ruin, is it not? I am not surprised it aroused your interest. Outside perfect and inside . . . not quite what you would expect. It is like some people, who present an innocent face to the world and hide secrets."

He was looking straight at me.

I said, "We were discussing Oliver Cromwell."

"An unpleasant fellow, I always thought."

"There is one who would agree with you, Dougal," I said.

"Drusilla had a good word to say for him."

I read his thoughts. Drusilla? Dougal? He had noticed the use of Christian names and was considering the significance of this. He looked faintly displeased.

"And so . . . Drusilla . . . admired the man?"

I replied, "He believed he was right in doing what he did and that has to be taken in consideration when assessing people."

"You are very fairminded. I, of course, have to be grateful to him for leaving us Framling intact."

"He was a strongminded man with firm views."

"It is a necessity for a ruler. Is that wine? I wonder if I might partake."

I poured a little into a small tumbler which Mrs. Janson had thoughtfully provided. "I am afraid it is one I have used," I told him. "Mrs. Janson naturally believed there would be only two of us."

"I am delighted to share your glass," he said, smiling at me. He sipped the wine. "Nectar of the gods," he murmured. "Your Mrs. Janson is a most excellent provider."

"I will pass on your compliments. I am sure she will be gratified."

"How delightful this is! We should do more of it. Alfresco picnics! What an excellent idea. Whose was it? Yours, Dougal's or Drusilla's, eh?"

"Mrs. Janson naturally provided some food, since we would not be returning to luncheon."

"A most thoughtful lady! Yes, certainly we should do more of this. You and Drusilla will be able to tell me of the antiquities we should explore. I confess being something of an ignoramus in these matters. But I am always ready for instruction."

Since he had come he dominated the conversation. The pleasant intimacy had gone. When we had packed up the remains of the meal and were exploring the castle it seemed different. *He* was there, making me uneasy now and then and casting his amused glance on me from time to time. It seemed to be a speculative glance and it both irritated and disturbed me.

The magic had gone out of the afternoon and he had a way of making our comments about the castle sound pretentious.

We curtailed the exploration considerably and thus returned to the Framling stables an hour or so earlier than we had expected to.

Two days later, Dougal came to the rectory. My father expressed his great pleasure and Mrs. Janson brought out wine and her special wine-biscuits into the drawing room, where we were.

She purred rather like a cat to show her pleasure. She liked distinguished visitors to come to the rectory and Dougal was certainly one of those.

As soon as she had gone I poured out the wine.

Dougal said, "I have come to tell you that I shall be leaving tomorrow."

"I hope you will be coming back soon," replied my father.

"I hope to. This is a matter of trouble in my family. My cousin has had a fall from his horse and is rather badly injured. I must go to see him."

"Is he far from here?" I asked.

"About sixty miles. It's a place called Tenleigh."

"I have heard of it," said my father. "Some Roman remains were discovered nearby . . . on the Earl of Tenleigh's land, I believe."

"Yes, that is so."

"Very interesting. Fine mosaic pavings and baths. What a wonderful race the Romans were. They brought benefits to the lands they occupied, which is, of course, what a conqueror should do. It was a great tragedy that they should have become decadent and their empire fade away."

"It is the fate of many civilizations," Dougal commented. "It is almost like a pattern."

"One day there might be one to break free of the pattern," I suggested.

"That may well be," agreed Dougal.

"We shall miss your visits," my father told him.

Dougal smiled from my father to me. "I shall miss them, too," he said.

I was a little sad that he was going away. I went to the door with him to say goodbye. He took my hands and held them firmly.

"I am sorry to have to go just now," he said. "I was so enjoying our meetings. I was planning some more excursions like those to the castle. There are so many interesting places all over England. It has been such a pleasure."

"Well, perhaps when you have seen your cousin . . ."

"I shall be back. You may be assured of that. I shall insist on being invited."

"I daresay my father would be pleased if you stayed with us. We can't offer you the grandeur of Framling, of course."

"I should so much enjoy that, but wouldn't it be putting you out?"

"Not in the least. There is plenty of room at the rectory and Mrs. Janson would enjoy cooking special meals for you."

"It would not be the food I came for. Food for the mind is another matter."

"Well, think about it." He looked at me earnestly and went on, "Drusilla . . ." He stopped and I looked enquiringly at him. Then he went on, "Yes, I should so much like to stay here. I'll just get over this matter and then . . . we'll talk."

"I should like that," I said.

He leaned towards me and kissed me lightly on the cheek. Then he had gone.

I felt a sudden contentment. The relationship between us had deepened and that gave me a feeling of great serenity.

The future seemed suddenly promising.

I thought a good deal about Dougal during the days that followed. I believed that in time he would ask me to marry him. Dougal was a thoughtful person. He was seriousminded; he would not make hasty decisions. That he was attracted to me, I knew; yet our friendship had grown steadily and I felt that was the best way it should grow. Ever since I had overheard that comment in the Framling gardens I had recognized the fact that I was plain and that no man was going to fall violently in love with me on account of my beauty, for I had none. But relationships were formed in other ways, and I believed that one founded on mutual understanding would be firmer than a blinding passion for a beauty.

Dougal had been away for a week. Fabian was in London, a fact for which I was glad. I could well do without his disturbing presence. I was becoming obsessed by the thought of Janine and my dreams about The Firs kept recurring. I had an idea that if I went to the New Forest and saw the place for myself, I might discover something from the local people. Janine had been so close to us during those anxious months and had done so much to help us, I just could not forget her.

I was in constant communication with Polly, who kept me informed of Fleur's progress, and I wrote to her and told her of my concern about Janine and how I could not forget the fire at The Firs and the terrible tragedy that had overtaken all those people among whom for a short time I had lived.

Polly had an idea. What if I came to London? She and I could take a trip to the place. Eff would be in sole charge of Fleur, which would please her. And so it was arranged.

I left the rectory and this time travelled alone to London.

Polly was at the station to meet me and there was the usual affectionate greeting.

Then there was the joy of seeing Fleur and Eff again. Fleur had grown amazingly; she now toddled and could even say something that sounded like Eff . . . Poll . . . yes . . . no—quite emphatically this last. She was enchanting and seemed very satisfied with life.

Eff and Polly vied for her affection and she gave it with regal unconcern; and it was quite clear to me that no mother could give a child more love than did those two dear people.

Polly had made plans for our visit. She suggested we go the next day and spend the night at one of the inns nearby. She had discovered through Third Floor Back in one of the houses—who most fortuitously knew the district—that The Feathers was the best one and she had taken the precaution of booking two rooms for the night.

This was progress and Polly and I in due course set out on our voyage of discovery.

We arrived in the late afternoon and decided that on the following morning we would visit the site.

In the meantime we were able to have a little conversation. First of all we talked to the chambermaid. She was a middle-aged woman who had worked at The Feathers when she was a girl, and now that her children were off her hands she came in the afternoons. She lived only a few yards from the hotel.

"So," I said, "you know the district well."

"Like the palm of my hand, Madam."

"You must remember the fire."

"At The Firs?"

"Yes."

"Oh, that wasn't so long ago. My goodness, what a blaze that was! It happened in the night."

"We read about it in the paper," said Polly. "It was quite a piece of news, that."

"It was a strange place. Used to give me the horrors every time I passed by."

"Why?" I asked.

"I dunno. That Mrs. Fletcher . . . As a matter of fact, before I came back here . . . just when my youngest was old enough not to need me at her heels all the time . . . I worked there for a bit."

"Oh," I said faintly, fearing suddenly that she might have seen Lavinia and me.

"Best part of five years ago, that was."

I was relieved.

"Why did it give you the creeps?" asked Polly.

"I can't rightly say. There was something about it. It was all them old people. You get the feeling that they are all there waiting for death to come along and take them. It gives you the shivers in a way. People used to say they were put there because their families did not want them. And a funny lot they was . . . and there'd always be one or two who had come there to have a baby . . . on the quiet, if you know what I mean?"

I certainly knew what she meant.

"And the fire?" I prompted.

"Lit up the whole place. I was in bed and I said to my old man, 'Jacob, something's going on.' He said, 'Go to sleep,' and then he realized there was a funny smell and a sort of light in the room. 'Snakes alive,' he said, and he was out of that bed in a flash. He was out there helping them. The whole village seemed to be out there. Oh, it was a night, I can tell you."

"There were a lot of casualties, were there not?" I asked.

"Oh yes. Well, you see, this batty old man had started fires in one of the downstairs cupboards and the whole of the ground floor was well on the way to being destroyed before it spread about. They were all burned to death . . . Mrs. Fletcher herself among them."

"All?" I asked. "Everyone?"

"Everyone in the place. It was too late to rescue them. Nobody knew the place was on fire until it was well on the way."

"What a terrible tragedy."

I did not sleep that night. I kept on thinking of Janine and how easily it might have been the end for Fleur, Lavinia and me.

The next day Polly and I made our way to The Firs. The gate, with "The Firs" on it in brass letters, was open. Memories rushed back as I went up the drive. The walls were surprisingly still standing in some parts. I looked through the windows onto the scorched pile.

Polly said, "It makes you think. I'll tell Eff we've got to be specially careful. Make sure all the fires are out before we go to bed. Watch out for candles. Them paraffin lamps could turn over as soon as you could say Jack Robinson . . . and then it would be a case of God help you."

It was difficult to recognize the place. I tried to work out which room would have been Lavinia's and mine, which Mrs. Fletcher's sanctum on the first floor and Janine's room . . . and that of Emmeline and the others.

It was impossible, and Polly thought we should not try to mount the remains of the staircase.

"You'd only have to take a look at that and it would collapse."

I was thoughtful and sad, remembering so much.

Polly said, "Here. Let's go. We've had enough of this."

It was as I stood with Polly among the debris that I heard quick footsteps coming along the drive. A middle-aged woman came into sight. I saw her before she saw us. Her face was pale and her eyes tragic. She stood for a few moments looking up at the grim remains. Then she saw us.

"Good morning," I said.

"Oh . . . er . . . good morning."

"Like us, you are looking at the burnt-out house."

She nodded. She looked as though she were fighting to conceal her emotion.

Then she said, "Did you have . . . someone . . . someone who perished?"

"I don't know," I replied. "There was a girl I used to know at school. Mrs. Fletcher was her aunt."

She nodded. "It was my daughter who was here. We didn't know she was. It wouldn't have mattered. She could have told me. She was so bright . . . a lovely girl . . . to go like that."

I guessed the story. It was similar to others. The daughter was going to have a baby and she had come here in secret and here she had died.

"Such a tragedy," said the woman. "It should never have happened."

"It doesn't really help us to come here," I replied.

She shook her head. "I have to. When I found out she was here and died in the fire . . . I would have done anything . . ."

Polly said, "Things like that happen sometimes. It's hard to know why. Makes you bitter. I *know*."

The woman looked enquiringly at her.

"My husband was lost at sea."

It is amazing how someone else's tragedy can make one's own seem lighter. The woman certainly looked a little comforted.

"Have you been here before?" I asked.

She nodded. "I can't seem to keep away. I just had to come."

"Do you know anything about the people who died?"

"Only what I've heard from others."

"There was a young girl with whom I was at school. I wonder if you knew whether she was saved."

"I wouldn't know. I only know that my daughter was there and it happened to her . . . my girl."

We left her there contemplating the ruins as if by doing so she could bring her daughter back.

We walked slowly to The Feathers. There was a bench on a stretch of grass in front of a pond and on this sat two old men. They were not talking . . . just staring into space.

Polly and I sat down on the seat and they regarded us with interest.

"Staying there?" said one of the men, taking his pipe from his lips and jerking it towards The Feathers.

"Yes," I replied.

"Nice place, eh?"

"Very nice."

"Used to do pretty well before the fire."

"That must have been terrifying."

One of the old men nodded. "Reckon it was the vengeance of the Lord," he said. "The lot they had up there. Sodom and Gomorrah . . . that's what it was. They got their just deserts."

"I heard there were several old people there."

The old man fiercely tapped his head. "Not right up there. Offended against the Lord in some way. It was the punishment

146

of the Lord, that's what I reckon. Her . . . she was a queer one . . . and all them women . . . no better than they should be."

I was in no mood to enter into a theological discussion. I said, "Did you hear if there were any survivors?"

The two old men looked at each other. The religious fanatic said with satisfaction, "All burnt to a cinder . . . taste of hell fire that's waiting for 'em."

Polly said ironically, "You're destined for the heavenly choir, I reckon."

"That's so, Missus. Good churchgoer all me life. Regular every Sunday . . . night and morning."

"My goodness," said Polly. "You must have a good record. Wasn't there any time you did a bit of sinning?"

"I was brought up in the shadow of the Lord."

"Oh, I reckon the recording angel would have looked the other way when you got up to your little bits of mischief."

I could feel a real antagonism building up between them and I guessed that if I were going to get any information from them this was not the way to do it.

"So everyone there died," I said.

"Here," put in the other. "Wasn't there some niece or something, Abel?"

I said eagerly, "Her name was Janine Fletcher. Do you know what became of her?"

"Oh, I remember," said the man to Abel. "You know that young woman . . . wasn't she out of the place on a visit or something? That's right. She was the only one who didn't die."

"It was God's will," said Abel.

I was excited. I turned to his companion. "So she didn't die?"

"No . . . that's it. She came back. There was some sort of to-do about insurance and that sort of thing."

"It wasn't insured," said Abel. "They was like the foolish virgins unprepared when the bridegroom came."

"Doesn't sound much like a wedding to me," commented Polly.

"Do you know where she went?" I asked.

"Can't tell you that, Miss."

I could see that that was all the information we could get. I rose as Abel began reminding me about the rewards of evil. I said, "We must get back."

Polly agreed. "I reckon," she said, as we walked away, "that that Abel's got a nasty surprise waiting for him when he gets to Heaven."

I felt our journey had not been wasted. We had not discovered where Janine was, but we knew she was still alive.

I had not been back at the rectory for more than two days when, to my surprise, Fabian called.

In all the years he had not called before, except with Dougal, and I was surprised to see him.

I must have shown my surprise.

"I heard that you had been to London," he said. "I came to assure myself of your safe return."

I raised my eyebrows. "That was extraordinarily kind of you."

"I was concerned. Had you told me I should have made my visit coincide with yours."

"The journey is not long and I was met at the other end."

"By the inestimable Polly, I guess. And how is her sister and that enchanting ward of theirs?"

"Very well."

"That is good. I have news of a friend of yours."

"Really?"

"Dougal Carruthers."

"What news?"

"He has become an exalted gentleman overnight."

"What do you mean?"

"You were aware that his cousin had an accident. Alas, the cousin died from his injuries."

"Were they close friends?"

"Relations." He smiled sardonically. "That is quite a different thing. They say that one chooses one's friends, but one's relations are thrust upon one."

"There is often a stronger bond between relations than friends."

"The proverbial blood being thicker than the proverbial water."

"Exactly."

"Well, I don't think the cousin . . . or to give him his full name, the Earl of Tenleigh . . . had very much in common with our friend Dougal. He was the hunting man—more at home on a horse than on his own two legs. Athletic, all physical activity and a brain that hardly ever got any consideration and had begun to pine away from neglect. Ah, I'm speaking ill of the dead and perhaps shocking your conventional heart just a little."

I smiled. "Not in the least," I said. "But how has Mr. Carruthers become an exalted gentleman?"

"By the death of the cousin. You see, the Earl was the son of Dougal's father's elder brother, so he got the title and the family estates. Dougal's father was just a younger son. I gathered from Dougal that he was rather pleased about that. Like his son, he was the studious type. I am not sure what his obsession was. The Byzantine Empire, I fancy. Dougal takes after him with his Anglo-Saxons and Normans. Alas for Dougal. The present has impinged itself on the past. He will have to tear himself away from Hengist and Horsa and Boadicea, most likely, and think a little about his obligations to the present."

"I daresay he will enjoy it. He will probably have the money to continue with his research in the way he wanted it."

"Great estates are demanding and he may not find it so easy. In any case I thought I ought to warn you that we shall doubtless see little of him from now on. These things change people, you know."

"I do not believe they will change him."

"He's too wise, you think?"

"I do think that. He would never be arrogant."

I looked at him and he smiled. "As some people are," he murmured.

"Yes, as some people are."

"Well, we shall see. But it will mean that he will not be here to enjoy those little picnics in ruined places. I thought I should warn you."

"Thank you."

"It is a pity that the picnics cannot continue."

"There was only one . . . in which you shared."

"Into which I forced myself. It would be rather pleasant

not to have to do that. Why do we not have a picnic of our own
. . . you and I?"

"It would be quite impossible."

"Whenever I hear that word I am always challenged to
disprove it."

"You are not interested in ruins."

"You could teach me."

I laughed at him. "I don't think you would relish the idea
of being taught anything."

"You are mistaken. I am avid for knowledge . . . particularly the kind which you can supply."

"I don't quite know what that means."

"Now you are looking like a teacher . . . a little severe
. . . rather displeased with the bad boy and wondering
whether to give him a hundred lines or make him stand in the
corner with the dunce's cap on his head."

"I am sure I implied nothing of the sort."

"I shall see if I can discover a ruin you have never seen
. . . and tempt you."

"Don't bother. I am sure I should not be able to come with
you."

"I shall never give up hope," he said and added, "teacher."

"If you will excuse me I have several things to do."

"Let me help you."

"You could not really. They are parish matters."

"Which you perform with Mr. Brady?"

"Oh, no . . . he has his own affairs. You have no idea
what has to be done in a rectory . . . and with my father not
so well we are very busy."

"Then I must detain you no longer. I will see you very
soon. *Au revoir.*"

When he had gone I could not get him out of my thoughts.
It made me forget Dougal's elevation to high rank and fortune.
Then I began to consider that and to wonder what difference it
would make to him and to our relationship, which was just
beginning to flower into something deeper.

Colin Brady said to me, "We should be thinking about the
summer *fête.*"

"Everyone knows it is to be on the first Saturday in August. It always has been. Most of them have been working for months getting things together for the stalls."

"The rector was saying that it is the custom to ask permission of the Framlings to hold it in the grounds and if it is wet to use the hall. I suppose it's big enough."

"Oh, yes. It's vast. There have only been a few occasions in my memory when we have had to go inside. The Framlings know about it. It's a tradition and Lady Harriet has always granted permission most graciously."

"Yes, but your father says it has to be asked for. That is also a part of the tradition."

"Yes, I suppose so."

"Well, Lady Harriet is in London with her daughter. We shall have to make the request to Sir Fabian."

"I should hardly think that was necessary."

"But he should be asked."

"It would be different if Lady Harriet were there. She is a stickler for convention."

"I think it would be wise to ask Sir Fabian . . . just as a gesture. Perhaps you would go and get his formal consent."

"If you are passing . . . it would only be a matter of looking in."

"Well, I have to go and see Mrs. Brines today. She has been confined to her bed for several weeks and is asking to see me. Also I have a good deal to sort out . . . so if you could see your way . . ."

There was no reason why I should not do it, except that I felt uneasy about approaching Fabian. But I could not refuse without explaining, so I thought I would go over, quickly make the request and get it over.

Sir Fabian was at home, I was told. I asked if they would tell him that I had merely come to ask his permission for the *fête* to be held in the grounds if the weather was fine and in the hall if it was wet. I would not take up much of his time.

I was hoping the maid would come back and say that permission was granted so that I could be on my way. Instead she came back with the news that Sir Fabian was in his study and would be pleased to see me there.

I was ushered across the great hall to the staircase. His study was on the second floor.

He rose as I entered and came towards me, smiling. He took both my hands.

"Miss Delany! How nice to see you. You've come about the *fête*, they tell me."

The maid went out, shutting the door, and that feeling of mingling excitement and apprehension was with me.

"Do please sit down."

"I shan't stop," I said. "It's a formality really. Lady Harriet usually grants permission for the grounds to be used, and if it is wet, the hall."

"Oh, my mother always deals with that sort of thing, doesn't she?"

"There is nothing to be dealt with really. Framling has always been used for the *fête*. I just want to get formal permission, so I will say 'thank you' and 'goodbye.' "

"But you haven't got my permission yet."

"It is really taken for granted."

"Nothing should ever be taken for granted. I should like to discuss this with you."

"But there is nothing to discuss. It is the same every year. So I may take it as granted . . . ?"

He had risen and I immediately did the same. He came close to me.

"Tell me," he said, "why are you afraid of me?"

"Afraid? Of you?"

He nodded. "You look like a frightened fawn who has heard the approach of a tiger."

"I do not feel in the least like a frightened fawn. Nor do you strike me as being tigerish."

"Then a bird of prey perhaps . . . a rapacious eagle, ready to swoop on a helpless creature. You know, you should not be frightened of me, for I am very fond of you and the more I see you the fonder I grow."

"That is good of you," I said coolly. "But I must go."

"It is not good of me. It is an involuntary emotion and one for which I cannot personally take credit."

I laughed with an attempt at lightness.

"Well," I said, "I take it we can go ahead with plans for the *fête*."

He put his hands on my shoulders and drew me towards him.

"Sir Fabian?" I said in surprise, drawing back.

"You know how I feel about you," he said. "Isn't it obvious?"

"I have no idea."

"Aren't you curious to know?"

"It is not really of great interest to me."

"You don't give that impression."

"Then I am sorry if I misled you."

"You haven't misled me in the least, for I know a good deal about you, my dear Drusilla. After all, we have been acquainted all our lives."

"In spite of that I would say we hardly know each other."

"Then we must remedy that."

He drew me towards him with a strength I could not resist and kissed me on the lips.

I flushed and encouraged the anger that arose in me. I said, "How dare you!"

He smiled mockingly. "Because I am a very daring person."

"Then please keep your daring displays for others."

"But I want to show them to you. I want us to be good friends. I am sure that could be very pleasant for both of us."

"It would not be so for me."

"I promise you it will."

"I do not believe in your promises. Goodbye."

"Not yet," he said, taking my arm and holding it fast. "I think you like me just a little."

"Then that assumption must be due to your good opinion of yourself."

"Perhaps," he said. "But you are not indifferent to my undeniable charm."

"I do not wish to be treated in this flippant manner."

"I am not in the least flippant. I am in deadly earnest. I am very fond of you, Drusilla. You have always interested me. You are different . . . so serious . . . so dedicated to learning. You make me feel humble and that is such a new experience with me that I find it exciting. It is growing more and more impossible for me to hide my feelings."

153

"Goodbye," I said. "I shall tell the church committee that permission has been granted in the usual way."

"Stay a while," he pleaded.

"I do not wish to. I will not be treated like this."

"Your maidenly modesty is most affecting." He paused and raised his eyebrows. "But . . ."

I felt myself flushing. I read the suggestions in his eyes.

I wrenched myself free and walked to the door, but he was there before me, standing with his back to it, mocking me.

"I could detain you," he said.

"You could do no such thing."

"Why not? This is my house. You came here willingly. Why should I not keep you here? Who would stop me?"

"You seem to think you are living in the Middle Ages. Is this some idea of *droit de seigneur?*"

"What an excellent notion! Why not?"

"You had better step out of the past, Sir Fabian. You and your family may have the idea that we in this place are your serfs, but that is not the case and if you attempt to detain me as you suggest I shall . . . I shall . . ."

"Bring in the law?" he asked. "Would that be wise? They probe, you know."

"What do you mean?"

He looked at me slyly and I knew he had been planning something like this. He had only been waiting for the opportunity and I, foolishly, had given it to him. He thought he had discovered a secret in my past and he was going to use it against me. I wanted to shout at him, "Fleur is not my child. She is your sister's." I almost did; but even at such a time I could not bring myself to break my promise to Lavinia.

He was so gratified at my discomfiture that he released his hold. I dashed past him out of the room and hurried down the staircase into the hall and out of the house. I did not stop running until I reached my room at the top of the rectory. I flung myself on the bed. My heart was beating furiously. I was very deeply disturbed.

I was so angry. I hated him. It was a sort of blackmail: I have discovered your secret. As you are the sort of girl who can have a love affair before you are out of the schoolroom, why are you so outraged when I make certain suggestions to you?

It was too humiliating.

I heard the news from Mrs. Janson. Lavinia and Lady Harriet had come home.

Lavinia sent a message over. "You must come at once. I want to talk to you. Meet me in the garden where we can get right away from people."

I sensed an urgency in her message. She would not be so anxious to see me if she did not want something from me. Perhaps, I told myself, it was merely because she wanted to boast of her successes in London. But had her season been so successful? There was no news of an engagement to a duke or a marquess. I was sure Lady Harriet would aim for the highest stakes.

I was chary of going to Framling after that encounter with Fabian, and I was therefore glad that she suggested a meeting in the garden.

She was waiting for me. There was a change in her, or perhaps I had forgotten how beautiful she was. Her skin was milk-white; her catlike eyes with the dark lashes were arresting, but it was her magnificent hair that was her crowning glory. She wore it high on her head and little tendrils escaped from the mass on her forehead and in the nape of her neck. She was wearing a green gown which was most becoming to her colouring. She was, in fact, the most beautiful girl I had ever seen.

"Oh, hello, Drusilla," she said. "I've got so much to tell you."

"You have had a successful season?"

She grimaced. "One or two proposals, but no one Mama thought good enough."

"Lady Harriet would set high standards. None but the highest in the land for her beautiful daughter. Did you see the Queen?"

"When I was presented, and once at the opera and once at a ball for charity. She danced with Albert. Drusilla, that fire . . ."

"You mean at The Firs?"

155

"I was so relieved."

"Lavinia! A lot of people died!"

"Those people . . . well, life wasn't much for them, was it?"

"They might have thought so, and there were people there who were going to have babies, as you were. I met the mother of one of them when I went down."

"You went there?"

"I wanted to see what had happened. Polly came with me."

"All those demands for payment . . ."

"Well, it was what you owed. What would you have done without her?"

"I know . . . but it cost a lot and *I* had to find the money."

"It was your affair."

"I know, I know. But it's Janine."

"Janine? I gathered she wasn't there on the night of the fire."

"I wish she had been."

"Oh . . . Lavinia!"

"You haven't heard what I'm going to tell you. It's Janine I'm worried about. I have seen her."

"So she is all right?"

"It's far from all right. There was I thinking I was free of all that and then Janine turns up."

"Did she come to see you?"

"She certainly did. There were pieces in the paper about the debutantes and I was mentioned. They called me 'the beautiful Miss Framling.' Every time they mentioned me they called me that. She must have seen it. Oh, Drusilla . . . it was awful."

"How? What do you mean?"

"She's asked for money."

"Why?"

"Because she says she is very poor and I've got to help her or else . . ."

"Oh no!"

"But yes. She said if I didn't, she would put a piece in the paper about Fleur."

"She couldn't."

"She could. I never liked her."

"She got you out of your trouble."

"She just took us to that dreadful place . . . that awful aunt of hers who kept demanding money."

"You can't do what you did and get away without paying for it."

"I know. Well, Janine is living in London. She's got some miserable place. It's all she can afford. She said how lucky I was and she wanted me to give her fifty pounds, and then she would say nothing of what she knew about me."

"It's blackmail."

"Of course it's blackmail. You are not supposed to submit to that sort of thing, but what could I do? Mama would have been furious."

"I daresay she would have known how to deal with Janine."

"I knew how to deal with her. I had to give her fifty pounds to keep her quiet. I did . . . and I haven't heard any more of her."

"It is terrible to think of Janine's stooping to that."

"It was awful. I had to pretend I was going to the dressmaker and I went to this place where she lives. It's in a little house in a place called Fiddler's Green. It's in a row of little houses. She's got rooms there. She says it's all she can afford. She said she wouldn't have asked if she hadn't been desperate. You see, the fire burned down the house that belonged to her aunt and all the contents of the place, too. Her aunt hadn't insured the place. She had only just succeeded in buying the house and all she had was tied up in it . . . so there was nothing much for Janine. She said fifty pounds would set her on her feet. I found it hard to get the money together, but I did. And that's the end of it."

"I hope so," I said.

"Of course it will be."

"Blackmailers have a habit of coming back and asking for more."

"I shan't give her any more."

"You should never have given her anything in the first place. What you should have done was confessed to your

157

mother. It is always unwise to submit to blackmail. I've heard that said many times."

"By people who are not being blackmailed, I suppose."

"Perhaps."

"Well, it was worth it to me to shut her up. She said she was going to marry that Hon. . . . whatever his name was . . . and she would have been set up for life, for he was quite rich. But he died in the fire. It was just good luck for Janine that she was away that night."

I was thoughtful. "Lavinia," I said, "you will have to confess."

"Confess? Why ever should I?"

"Because it's got to come out. There's Fleur."

"She's all right. She's happy with those two nice old women."

"For the moment. But she will have to be educated. Polly and Eff will have to be paid for keeping her. Why don't you tell your mother?"

"Tell my mother! I don't think you know my mother."

"I assure you that everyone around here knows Lady Harriet very well."

"I just can't think what she would do."

"She would be horrified, but she would certainly do something, and something has to be done."

"I could never tell her."

"Your brother has seen Fleur."

"What?"

"I went to London and he was on the train. He saw where I was staying. He came there one day when I was taking Fleur out in her pram."

She had turned pale.

"He was suspicious," I said. "I want you to tell him the truth, because he suspects the baby is mine."

She tried to disguise the look of relief that came onto her face.

I went on, "You must tell him. He can't go on with this half-truth."

"*You* didn't tell him!"

"Of course not. But I do object to his sly references, and I think you ought to tell him the truth right away."

"I couldn't possibly tell him."

"Why not? I don't suppose he has led a blameless life."

"It's all right for men. It is girls who have to be so pure."

"Obviously there are some who are not. I don't suppose you are the only one who has indulged in premarital adventures."

"Oh, Drusilla, I do rely on you."

"Far too much. I am not going to be insulted by your brother."

"He wouldn't *insult* you."

"He would and he has . . . and I want him to know the truth."

"I . . . I'll think about it."

"If you don't tell him, I might be tempted to."

"Oh, Drusilla . . . first Janine and now you . . ."

"This is quite different. I'm not blackmailing you. I am merely asking you to tell the truth."

"Give time. Just give me time. Oh, Drusilla, you have always been my best friend. Promise you won't say anything . . . yet."

"I wouldn't say anything without telling you first, but I won't have your brother hinting . . . at things."

"However did you let him guess there was a baby!"

"I told you . . . he followed me."

"But why should he follow *you?* It could only be that he suspected something like this. It's not as though . . ."

"I am the sort of girl men follow?" I finished for her. "Nobody could be interested in *me*, of course."

"Well," she began.

"Don't feel you have to wriggle out of that," I said. "I know I'm not the beauty you are."

"Well, there is that Mr. Brady. Mama thinks it would be most suitable."

"Do thank her for her concern," I said.

"She likes everything to run smoothly in the neighbourhood."

"I am sure she does. But I don't propose to be someone's neat ending to a problem."

"Oh . . . look who's coming."

I looked and saw Dougal approaching us.

"Mama invited him," went on Lavinia. "Do you know, he is an earl now. Mama insisted that he come and stay."

I was pleased to see him. My friendship with him had been so refreshing and promising. His regard for me restored my faith in myself.

"Oh . . . Drusilla . . . Lavinia," he said. He was smiling at us. Lavinia was standing a little apart. The faint wind ruffled the tendrils and as she put up a hand to her hair the green material of her loose, rather Grecian-style gown flapped round her, clinging to her figure.

Dougal could not take his eyes from her. I saw the light in them and I remembered his adoration of beautiful objects.

He looked rather startled, as though he were seeing something for the first time. It was the new Lavinia, in her studiedly simple gown with her escaping curls and her tigerish eyes.

I knew in that moment that he had fallen in love with her or that he was on the brink of doing so.

The moment passed. He was smiling his gentle smile at me, asking how my father was, telling me that he would be soon coming to see us if he might.

I said my father would be delighted.

"I have discovered two new books on the Conquest," he said. "I must bring them over."

I was not thinking so much of the Norman Conquest as of Lavinia's.

I did not go into the house with them. I excused myself. "There is so much to do at the rectory."

"Even now you have that nice curate," said Lavinia a little roguishly. "I hear you and he get on very well together."

"He is very efficient," I said.

"I am so glad you came and that he is so nice," said Lavinia. "Well, see you soon, Drusilla. Drusilla and I are the greatest friends," she went on, turning to Dougal. "We always have been." Some spirit of mischief seemed to take hold of her. I think she knew of my feelings for Dougal. She was also aware that he had just been blinded by her great beauty. A few moments before she had been terrified that her secret might be revealed, but now she had forgotten the past and was revelling in the present. Admiration always stimulated her. "Drusilla and I were at school together. It was in France."

"I know," Dougal told her.

"That sort of thing draws people together," went on Lavinia. "We had some exciting times there, didn't we, Drusilla?"

She was laughing at me, triumphing over the spell she had cast on Dougal. She would have heard rumours of his attachment to the rectory and its inhabitants; she was savouring her triumph to such an extent that she forgot to be anxious about Janine.

I felt angry, humiliated and hurt. I went back sombrely to the rectory.

Mrs. Janson said, "That Lady Harriet is making a dead set at that Mr. Carruthers . . . oh, beg his pardon, the Earl of Tenleigh if you please. Well, it stands to reason. That Miss Lavinia goes up to London. The most beautiful debutante, they say . . . the Debutante of the Season. All very well, but where's this duke that Lady Harriet thinks she's going to get? All that season and not one in sight. I reckon that won't please her ladyship. An earl will have to do, and what's she doing going up to London when she's got one right on her own doorstep? I can tell you, there are some goings-on up at the House. Lady Harriet says he must come. She insists . . . and earl as he is, he can't refuse Lady Harriet. I reckon something will come of this. Lady Harriet will see to it."

That was what I overheard, and when I appeared she was silent. I was sure that long ago they had paired me off with Dougal as a first and Colin Brady as a second.

Mrs. Janson liked Dougal and he had been a frequent visitor. They were sure he was, as they said, "sweet on me." But now Lady Harriet was making a rare fuss of Dougal. Mrs. Janson had it from the maids there. "Now that he's got this title and money it's been a leg up for him. Before, he was just a friend of Sir Fabian's . . . treated just like one of them young boys from the school. Now it's a different matter. We didn't see him so much then . . . Why, there was a time when he seemed to make the rectory his home."

He did come over to bring the books he had spoken of. My father was delighted to see him and they had long discussions together. I went in and joined them. I did fancy he was a little subdued with me. He made a special effort to include me in the conversation, whereas previously it had been done without effort. I remembered how we had talked just before he left, when I had been foolish enough to think that he was on the point of making a declaration.

It was a bitter blow to my pride rather than to my deep emotions. I was not sure what I really felt about Dougal, except that he was a very pleasant and interesting friend. I had allowed myself to envisage a future with him and I had believed it could be very rewarding. How foolish I had been! Of course, he liked to talk to me about things that interested him, and he would never be able to talk to Lavinia in that way. But that was not love. It was not what people married for. The beauty of Lavinia had suddenly struck him and he could not help but marvel at it.

I did not go over to the stables for I would not avail myself of Fabian's offer. I wanted to take nothing from him. Moreover, I avoided Framling, for fear of meeting him.

I was in the rectory garden one day when he came riding by.

"Drusilla," he called. "It is such a long time since I saw you."

I merely replied, "Good morning," and turned to go into the house.

"I trust you are well. And your father?"

"Thank you, yes."

"You know, of course, that Dougal is here."

"He has been to see my father."

"And you too, I daresay. I know what good friends you are."

I did not answer.

"I hope you are not still put out with me. I think I rather allowed my feeling to get the better of my good manners."

Still I did not answer.

"I am sorry," he went on humbly. "You must forgive me."

"It is of no importance. Please forget it."

"You are very generous."

"I must go in now."

"There is so much to do at the rectory." He spoke mockingly, finishing my sentence for me.

"That is true," I retorted sharply.

"There is quite a flutter of excitement at the House," he went on.

In spite of myself I waited to hear what had caused this.

"We are expecting them to announce it shortly."

I felt the blood rushing to my head.

"Lavinia and Dougal," he added. "My mother is delighted."

I looked at him steadily, my eyebrows raised.

He nodded, smiling—was it maliciously? "My mother says there is no need to delay . . . long. Why should they? It is not as though they were strangers. They have known each other for a long time. They have suddenly realized how they feel. People do, you know. My mother is all for an early wedding. I am sure you will be pleased for them, for you know them both so well."

"It is most . . . suitable."

"That's what my mother thinks."

I thought angrily: Yes, since Dougal acquired a title and a fortune and the London season did not produce anyone of higher rank.

"I daresay Lavinia will be coming over to tell you the good news. Dougal too, perhaps. They will want you to give them your blessing."

I felt a great need to get away from his probing eyes. I knew what he was telling me. You have lost Dougal. My mother will never let him slip out of her hands now. It was different before he came into this glory.

He raised his hand, inclined his head and, murmuring *"Au revoir,"* rode off.

A month after the arrival of Dougal at Framling the engagement was announced between the Earl of Tenleigh and the beautiful Miss Lavinia Framling, the debutante of the season.

I did not go to Framling to congratulate Lavinia. She came to me. I could see at once that she was disturbed.

"What's the matter?" I asked. "You don't look like the happy betrothed."

"It's that woman . . . Janine. She wants more money."

"I told you how it is with blackmailers. You should never submit in the first place."

"Why should this have happened to me?"

"You have to pay for your sins."

"I only did what a lot of people do." She was aggrieved and I felt a sudden anger sweep over me. She had had so much and now she had taken Dougal. I had analysed my feelings for him and I was desperately hurt. But I was honest enough to admit to myself that it was mainly my pride that had been wounded. It had been hard for me to realize that at first, for I had enjoyed his friendship and I had thought of eventual marriage as a pleasant prospect. It would have been a wonderful experience to be loved by a man whom I could trust.

But could I have trusted him if our close relationship, which might have developed into a serious commitment, could have been shattered by the appearance of a girl just because she happened to be outstandingly beautiful?

I whipped up my anger against Lavinia. These Framlings seemed to think the whole world was made for them. Lavinia believed she could commit the greatest indiscretion, have a child even and everyone should cover up for her and leave her to sail happily on. As for her brother, he had thought he could insult me and then come along and behave as though nothing untoward had happened.

I was tired of the Framlings.

"And," Lavinia was saying, "I haven't come here to be quoted at from the Bible. I suppose that is in the Bible. You, Miss Know-all, would be aware of that."

"I'm sorry, Lavinia. You must get yourself out of your own troubles."

"Oh, Drusilla." She had run to me and flung her arms round my neck. "Help me, *please*. I know you can. I didn't mean to say those silly things. I'm at the end of my tether. I am really. If Mama or Dougal found out . . . I'd just kill myself . . . I've thought about jumping out of my window."

"You'd land on the furze bush, which would be very uncomfortable."

"Oh, help me, *please*, Drusilla."

"How can I?"

"I thought you might see her."

"I? What good would that do?"

"She likes you. She thinks you're interesting. She told me you were worth a dozen of me. I know she's right."

"Thanks. I'll remember that. But talking to her would do no good."

"It might . . . if *you* did."

"What could I say?"

"You could tell her how good I've been so far and if she would wait a little time . . . until I'm married . . . I'll be very rich and I'll do something for her then. I will. I promise."

"I don't think she would believe in your promises, Lavinia."

"You promise for me. Tell her you'll be a sort of witness and you'll make sure she gets the money. It is only a matter of waiting."

"I think you should go to your mother or your brother or Dougal and tell the truth."

"How could I? Dougal might refuse to marry me."

"I believe he is a very understanding young man."

"He wouldn't understand. He'd be furious. He believes in perfection."

"He has a shock waiting for him when he marries you."

"I am going to try to be a good wife to him."

What a fool he is! I thought. He wants to marry Lavinia without knowing her. Even the village idiot would know better than that; and Dougal is supposed to be clever! Well, he would discover, I thought, with a certain satisfaction—and Lavinia was not the sort to change just because she was married to the indulgent husband he would probably be.

Lavinia went on pleadingly, "We've been such good friends . . . ever since we met."

"I remember the time well. You were not the most charming of hostesses. It is rather unwise of you to recall that occasion if you are trying to show the loving nature of our relationship."

"Stop being clever, Drusilla. You are too clever and always showing off. Men don't like it. I never do that."

"You are showing off, as you call it, all the time."

"Yes, but only in the right way. Drusilla, stop beating about the bush. Do say you'll help me. I know you will in the long run. You are just making me suffer."

165

"But what can I *do?*"

"I told you. Go and see Janine. Explain to her."

"Why don't you?"

"How could I go to London? You could . . . easily. You can just say you have gone to see Polly."

I hesitated. I always felt better after a visit to Polly. She would understand how I felt about Dougal's engagement. I had no need to go into explanations with Polly. I could talk to her as I could to myself. I could see Fleur. The child was beginning to get a hold on me. She could pronounce her version of my name. Polly had written, "You should hear Eff go on at her. 'Who's got a nice Aunty Drusilla, eh? Whose Aunty Drusilla is coming to see her soon?' That's how she goes on." Yes, it would be wonderful to be with Polly, Eff and Fleur. Moreover, I had a raging curiosity to see Janine.

Lavinia could see that I was wavering.

"You love Fleur," she said. "She's a little darling."

"How do you know? You never see her."

"I'm going to . . . when I get this sorted out. When I know Dougal better I'll tell him. I will, really. I know he'll say I can have her with me."

"That would be the last thing Fleur would want. Don't you understand that children are not pieces to be moved round a board as people want to for their convenience?"

"You're being the governess again."

"Somebody has to try to teach you a few facts of life."

"I know. I'm wicked. But I can't help it. I'm trying to be good. Once I'm married to Dougal I shall settle down. Oh please . . . *please,* Drusilla."

"Where does she live?"

"I've written it down. I went there to take the fifty pounds. I'll tell you how to get there. It's not so very far from Polly's place."

I took the address. "Fiddler's Green, Number 20," said Lavinia. "It's easy to find."

"Did you take a cab?"

"Yes, I did. The driver looked surprised, but I made him wait for me to come back. I didn't want anyone to know where I was. It was awful . . . and then . . . her. She sneered at me. She kept calling me the Countess. Then she told me I had to find the money, for if I didn't come with it she was going to let the world know what I had done. She said I had deserted my child and a lot of other unpleasant things. I said I hadn't. I'd found a good home for the child. She said, 'Drusilla found that. You would probably have left her on someone's doorstep so that you could go on with your life.' I told her she was wrong. I did care about Fleur and when I was married I was going to take her. I know it will be all right once I am married."

"I shall not come to your wedding, Lavinia. It's such a mockery really. Have you thought how you are deceiving Dougal? You will be standing there in virginal white . . ."

"Oh, shut up. Are you going to help me or not? Can't you see how miserable I am?"

"I can't do anything. *I* haven't any money."

"I'm not saying give her money. I just know if you talked to her she'd listen to reason."

"No, she wouldn't."

"She would. She has always admired you. I know you can persuade her. Please, Drusilla, go to London. You know how you like to see Polly and Fleur. Please, Drusilla."

And then I knew I had to go.

I considered what I should say. It gave me something to think about. The wedding plans were going ahead, as Lady Harriet did not see why there should be any delay. I might not be exactly in love with Dougal, but I did not want to hear about them.

I said to my father, "I think I will go and see Polly."

"I know." He smiled. "You want to go and see that child they have adopted. You are very fond of her, are you not?"

"Well, yes . . . and I am very fond of Polly."

"A good woman," he said. "Somewhat forthright, but good at heart."

I went, and as usual Polly was delighted to see me. I did not tell her where I intended to go, for I felt she would try to dissuade me. She would think I should not involve myself further in Lavinia's affairs. I had done so once and that had brought them Fleur and she could not regret that; but, as she would have said, once is enough.

I took a cab to Fiddler's Green. The driver looked at me in

surprise but did not comment. I asked him to wait for me—not outside the house, but a little distance away.

He looked at me as though he thought I was on some nefarious mission. I wondered whether Lavinia had had the same experience.

I found my way to No. 20 Fiddler's Green. It was a tall house showing signs of what must have been an attempt at grandeur; but now the stucco was broken away and what should have been white was a dirty grey. Four steps leading to the front door were broken away; two mangy-looking stone lions stood on guard. Lavinia had told me to knock three times, which meant that I wanted Janine, who was on the third floor.

I did so and waited. It seemed a long time before Janine appeared.

She stared at me for a few seconds in amazement. Then she cried, "Drusilla! Whatever made you come here?" She lifted her shoulders. "You'd better come in," she added.

I was in a dingy passage with a staircase facing me. The carpet on the stairs was showing signs of wear and was threadbare in places.

We went up three flights and the carpet grew shabbier as we rose. She threw open a door to disclose a fairly large room, sparsely furnished. She turned to me, grimacing. "Now you see how the poor and needy live."

"Oh, Janine," I said, "I'm so sorry."

"Just my luck. Everything went wrong for me."

"I've wanted to know what happened since I heard of the fire."

"Everything lost . . . Aunt Emily dead . . . and all those people with her. That stupid George. It was his fault, you know. I told her how dangerous he was and that we should all be burned in our beds one night."

"Yes, he was certainly dangerous."

"Dangerous! He destroyed everything for Aunt Emily . . . and for me, too. I was going to marry Clarence . . . Oh, I know he was simple, but he adored me. He would have given me anything . . . anything I asked. And then he died . . . killed by that stupid George."

"He didn't know what he was doing. Oh, Janine, what a blessing that you weren't there on that night."

"Sometimes I've almost wished I had been."

"Don't say that."

"I do say it. How would you like to live in a place like this?"

"Do you have to?"

"What do you mean . . . do I have to? Do you think I would if I didn't have to?"

"Surely there is something you can do? People of education usually become governesses."

"Well, I don't intend to."

"What will you do then?"

"I'm planning. It made me mad when I saw all that fuss over Lavinia Framling. When you think of her . . . and that child . . . and there she is queening it over everyone. It's not fair."

"One has to make up one's mind that life never is fair."

"I intend to get something out of it anyway."

"She told me you had asked her for money."

"She would! And why shouldn't she give me something? I helped her. Where would she have been without me? I reckon the noble Earl would not be so keen if he knew he was getting soiled goods."

"Don't be bitter, Janine."

"It's not so much bitterness as sound thinking. She has everything. I have nothing. Well, then, I think it is about time I took a share."

"You will regret this, Janine."

"I am sure I shall not. I want to start a business. I could, I am sure. Making hats. I think I'm quite clever at it. I know someone who has a little shop. If I could find the money I could go in with her. I have to have the money and I don't see why Miss Lavinia Framling should not provide me with some of it."

"You'll need more than fifty pounds."

She looked cunning. "I intend to have it."

"It's blackmail, you know, and that is a crime."

"Would she take me to court? That would be nice, wouldn't it? Miss Lavinia Framling bringing a charge against someone who knew she had an illegitimate child whose existence she was keeping secret. I can see her doing that, can't you?"

"Janine, it is not the way."

"You tell me another."

"I should think you could work . . . work and save. You'd be happier that way."

"I certainly should not. In some ways you are a simpleton, Drusilla. The way you've worked to keep that little matter a secret . . . and all for her. She's thoroughly selfish. Do you think she would have helped you in the same way?"

"No."

"Then why bother? Let her pay up or take what's coming to her."

She looked fierce and very angry, and I knew there was nothing I could say to divert her.

I looked round the room and she noticed my glance.

"Grim, isn't it?" she said. "You can see why I want to get out of it."

"I do, of course, and I am very sorry. Where were you that night?"

"You remember the Duchess?"

"Yes, I do."

"Her family decided they would take her back. They might have been ashamed of themselves dumping her on Aunt Emily like that—but I think perhaps it was something to do with money. They wanted to have her under their noses so that she couldn't make a will leaving it all to someone else. They didn't trust Aunt Emily. They weren't far wrong on that one. I had to take her home. There was no one else. It was too long a journey to make in one day, so I was to stay the night at the family's stately home. It was a bit different from this, I can tell you."

I nodded.

"So, you see, that's what happened. Everything gone in the fire. The house would have been mine. That was worth something. I could have started some business. But I wouldn't have had to because I would have married Clarence. I'd have been set up for life and now . . . nothing. The place wasn't insured. How could Aunt Emily have been so foolish with madmen like George about!"

"But you were lucky not to be there."

"If you can call it luck."

170

"I've come to ask you to think again."

She shook her head. "No, she's got to pay. She has to give me some of what she's got."

"She doesn't have a large allowance."

"Then I want a share of what she's got, and when she marries her noble lord . . ."

"Do you mean you will go on demanding money? You told her that the fifty pounds she gave you would be all."

"Well, it's not. I'm desperate, Drusilla. I'm not going to let a chance like this go by."

"You won't do it, Janine, I know you won't. You'll stop it. Whatever you feel—and I do understand your bitterness—it is wrong."

"It's right for me. It's time someone taught Lavinia Framling a lesson. She always thought she was superior to the rest of us because of that red hair."

"Oh, Janine! Listen. I shall come to see you again. I could take you back with me to the rectory. You could have a holiday with us. We might be able to find some work for you to do. We know a number of people, and if you were recommended by a rector it would be a help. You could stay with us until you found work. Leave this place . . ."

She shook her head. "You are good, Drusilla," she said rather gently. "You are worth twenty of Lavinia."

I smiled. "My value has gone up. You told Lavinia twelve."

"I overestimated her. Actually she's not worth anything at all. I'm sorry for this earl. He's going to have a nice dance with her. She's one who can't leave the men alone. I've seen one or two of those in my time."

"I think she may settle down when she marries."

"I know you were top of the class, Drusilla, but you are a babe in arms when it comes to the facts of life."

"Do listen to me."

"I have."

"So you are going on with this . . . blackmail."

"I'm going on getting money until I set myself up."

"It's a mistake."

"I'll be judge of that. Did you keep a cab waiting?"

"Yes."

"You'd better go then. He might not wait. He wouldn't

believe anyone who came here would be able to pay him. He'll think you've made off."

"He didn't seem to think so and he said he would wait."

"I appreciate what you have done."

"If I hear of anything I shall come along and let you know."

She smiled at me and shook her head.

And that was all I could do at the time with Janine Fletcher, but I did not give up hope.

I avoided telling Polly where I had been. I knew she would have disapproved and told me to keep away. But I was sorry for Janine. I think in a way I always had been. She had had such a strange life; there appeared to have been little affection from Aunt Emily. Janine had been sent to an expensive school because Aunt Emily had had plans for a rich marriage and she must have intended to select one of her clients for her. Poor Clarence had been an ideal young man for the case. Oblivious of what was going on, affectionate to anyone who showed him kindness and rich into the bargain. He was like a puppet to be manipulated, and Aunt Emily had performed the manipulation with skill. And now . . . instead of making a desirable marriage, poor Janine was alone and penniless; so she had taken to that most despicable of crimes: blackmail.

I wrote to Lavinia and told her that I had made little headway with Janine. She was adamant.

I could image Lavinia's dismay on reading that letter. She would rage against Janine and perhaps against me for failing to perform the mission satisfactorily. But she had to know the truth.

Polly said, "Is anything wrong, love?"

"No. Why should there be?"

"You seem . . . thoughtful. You can tell me, you know. That Dougal . . . he seems a bit of a fool to me . . . to be taken in by that Lavinia. I like a real man, I must say, one who can see what's what and is not going to make a fool of himself. I think you were a little bit fond of him."

"He is a very charming man, Polly, and clever."

She sniffed. "Bit of a jackass, if you ask me."

"Lots of men fall in love with beauty. Lavinia is really

lovely. Going to Court has done a great deal for her and she has some exquisite clothes."

"Men don't marry clothes-horses . . . not if they've got any sense."

"Polly, I was not in love with Dougal Carruthers and he did not throw me aside to marry Lavinia. He had never asked *me* to marry him."

"I thought . . ."

"Then you thought wrongly. Lavinia will be a countess. Can you see me as one?"

"Why not? I reckon you could be Queen of England if you wanted to."

"I don't think Prince Albert would think so. And I shouldn't fancy him either . . . even if Her Majesty was willing to abdicate in my favour."

"Oh, you!" she said, smiling. "But you know there's nothing you can't tell me."

I tried to forget Lavinia's affairs. I concentrated on Fleur, who was more enchanting than ever. I used to sit by the kitchen fire in the evenings and neither Polly nor Eff omitted to mention every day how well the fire drew nowadays, throwing a glance at the bellows which had pride of place nearby. I listened to their cosy talk while they heated the poker and put it red hot into the stout; and then I felt a certain peace. Somewhere at the back of my mind was the fact that I should always find a home where I would be loved and cherished. I had Polly, Eff and Fleur. In my most despondent moments I should never forget that.

One day Eff said, "Second Floor 32 says her relation is the Honourable Mrs. Somebody."

"Honourable my foot," said Polly. "That one's always going on about her high-class relations."

"She's got breeding," said Eff. "I know about these things."

On such matters Polly had to bow to Eff's superior knowledge. "Well, what about her?" she added, conceding the point by implication.

"This cousin . . . or somebody's going abroad. Oh, hoity toity, she is . . . connected with the highest in the land. This cousin, or whatever she is, is looking for a companion to take abroad with her . . . have to be a lady and know how to manage things."

I had been in a soporific mood, watching the leaping flames and seeing pictures in them, when suddenly I was alert. A companion to travel . . . to get right away. Janine, I said to myself.

"It sounds like a good post," I said aloud.

"Good post!" retorted Eff. "It's one in a million. Now if I had been young . . . before I met Him . . . it's just the sort of thing I would have jumped at."

"Why, you always hated foreigners, Eff," said Polly with a little laugh.

"They're all right in their own country and that's where I'd be seeing them."

I was still thinking of Janine.

I said excitedly, "One of my old schoolfellows is rather hard up. She is looking for a post. I was with her the other day."

"You didn't say," said Polly. "Did you run into her somewhere?"

"Yes. I know she needs work. I wonder if . . ."

"I tell you what," said Eff. "You find out if she'd like the job and I'll have a word with Second Floor 32. Perhaps we could arrange a meeting."

"I should like to do that."

"Do you know where she lives?"

"Yes, I have her address. I might write."

"It would be a feather in Second Floor 32's cap if she found this educated young woman and she turned out to be just what they was looking for."

I asked a few questions about Second Floor 32, who was, according to Eff, "the genuine article, a lady who had come down in the world."

If I wrote to Janine she would tear the letter up, I guessed. If I talked to her it might just possibly be different. Perhaps I flattered myself, but I did imagine I had made some impression on her.

The next day I took a cab and did the same as before. I was deposited in the same spot and made my way to No. 20 Fiddler's Green. I walked quickly, making up my mind what I would say to Janine as I went along.

As I came into the street I noticed a group of people standing near No. 20. They looked at me curiously as I approached. I mounted the broken steps and knocked three times on the door.

It was opened by a man. He said, "What do you want?"

"I have come to see my friend Miss Janine Fletcher," I told him.

His expression became alert. "You'd better come in," he said.

I went in. A woman opened a door and looked at me.

"Better wait here," said the man.

He went up the stairs. It was very strange. I could not understand what it meant. The woman was looking at me. "Terrible, ain't it?" she murmured. "A young woman like that."

"What happened?"

"She must have been up to something. It's not good for the house."

I was getting very worried. I knew something awful had happened to Janine.

I heard the sound of a carriage drawing up at the door.

"That's them," said the woman. "They've come to take her away."

"I don't understand," I said.

There was a knocking on the door. As the woman went to open it the man who had let me in appeared on the stairs.

There were two men at the door carrying a stretcher.

"It's all right," said the man on the stairs. "Come up."

They went up the stairs carrying the stretcher. The woman had retreated into her room, but she left the door open. I was still standing in the hall.

There was a movement from upstairs. The men emerged with the stretcher; they were carrying someone on it this time —a body covered with a sheet. As they passed me I caught a glimpse of sandy-coloured hair. It was matted with blood.

I knew that under that sheet lay Janine.

A man followed the stretcher bearers down the stairs. He came to me and said, "I am a police officer. I am here to investi-

175

gate the death of Miss Janine Fletcher. What are you doing here?"

"I came to see her."

"You are a friend of hers?"

I felt sick. I tried to suppress the thought that persisted in my mind. I was telling myself that Lavinia had done this. She would never get away with it . . . never.

"I was at school with her," I heard myself say.

"Do you visit her often?"

"No. I came once before."

"When?"

"Three days ago."

"And she was all right then? Did she seem frightened? Worried?"

I shook my head.

"Where do you live?"

I gave him the rectory address.

"You have come some way to visit Miss Fletcher."

"I am staying with my old nurse for a few days."

A younger man had joined us and the first said to him, "Take the lady's address. We shall be wanting to ask you a few questions as we shall be visiting you at some time. Please remain in London."

"Well, I have to go back . . ."

"We must ask you to stay. You may have something important to tell us. It is necessary."

I murmured, "I'll stay."

My legs were trembling and I felt myself sway a little. I wanted to run away from this macabre scene. There was so much I wanted to know. How had this happened? Who had done it? Whom did they suspect? I kept saying to myself: You would never do this, Lavinia. You always left others to do your dirty work.

The man turned to the other who had joined us. "Oh, Smithson," he said, "take the young lady to the cab she is alleged to have waiting for her." And to me, "One of our men will be wanting to ask you a few questions about your relationship with the deceased. It's just a formality."

I was only too glad to escape. I noticed the man who was

accompanying me was very young and he looked a little nervous.

"Bit of a shock," he said as we walked away.

"I feel . . . shaky."

"I'm a bit nervous myself," he admitted. "It's my first murder."

Murder! It was a word that set me shivering. I could not believe it. Janine! To think that we had all been to school together and now . . . in a short time Lavinia had become a mother and Janine . . . a corpse. I tried to shut out the idea that these two facts were in some way connected.

As we moved away a young man approached us. He took off his hat and bowed.

"May I ask you if you are a friend of the young lady?" he asked.

I thought he was another policeman and I said, "Yes."

"Would you tell me your name?"

I told him and he produced a notebook from his pocket.

"Do you live near here?"

"No . . . in the country. I'm just staying here."

"Interesting. Did you know the young lady well?"

"We were at school together. I have just told your people this."

"Just a few questions. We have to get this right, you see." He went on, "Where abouts in the country?"

I gave him the address of the rectory.

"So you are the rector's daughter?"

I nodded.

"And you were at school together. Have you any idea why anyone would want to kill your friend?"

"No," I said emphatically.

My escort nudged me. "You're talking to the press," he whispered.

"You needn't worry about that, Miss," the other assured me. "Just a few questions, that's all."

I stammered, "I thought you were connected with the police."

He smiled disarmingly. "There is a sort of connection," he said.

"I don't want to say anything more. I know nothing about this."

He nodded, smiling, lifted his hat and walked away.

I felt I had behaved in a very indiscreet manner.

The young man walked with me to where the cab was waiting. He came with me back to the house.

"You should never talk to the press," he said. "We don't like it. We like to give them the information we want them to have."

"Why didn't you tell me sooner?"

He blushed. He did not like to admit that the identity of the reporter had not immediately dawned on him.

His parting words struck a note of doom. "I reckon you'll be hearing from us soon," he said. "They'll have to check up and all that."

Polly and Eff were in the hall wondering what had happened.

"Here," said Polly, "what's all this? Who was that young man with you?"

"A policeman," I said.

Polly turned pale.

Eff said, "Police here. What's police doing with respectable people? What are the neighbours going to think?"

Polly interrupted her. "Get a drop of brandy. Can't you see how upset she is?"

I was lying on my bed and Polly was seated beside me. I had told her everything that had happened.

"My goodness," she murmured. "This is something. Murder, eh? That Janine, she was a nasty piece of work if you was to ask me, going round blackmailing people."

"I feel sure her death has something to do with that, Polly."

"Shouldn't be surprised. Do you reckon that Lavinia had a hand in this?"

I shook my head. "I can't believe that."

"I'd believe anything of that piece of goods . . . and this will put paid to her and her great romance if it's true. I reckon not even the mighty Framlings would be able to hush this up."

"Oh, Polly, it's terrible."

"I only hope to God you can keep out of it. What a pity you went there. Don't want to be mixed up in this sort of thing."

"I'm afraid I am involved now, Polly."

"That Lavinia . . . she spells trouble. I think there's a very good chance she has had a hand in this."

"I can't believe it, Polly. She would lie if necessary . . . but I am sure she could not commit murder. She could never bring herself to do it. Where would she get a gun?"

"They'd have guns at Framling. That wouldn't be hard for her. I reckon she's capable of doing anything to save her own skin. I'm not telling Eff any of this. She'd go stark raving mad if she thought we'd be having the police here."

"Perhaps I'd better go back to the rectory."

"It would be worse still there. No, I'm keeping you here till this blows over."

I just clung to her. I was bewildered and frightened. I could not get out of my mind the thought of Janine lying under that sheet . . . dead.

The police came. They asked more questions. What did I know of Janine's life? What friends had she? I told them I knew nothing of her friends. I had met her only a few days ago for the first time since we left school.

"She was the daughter of a Miss Fletcher, who ran a nursing home."

"That was her aunt," I said.

The two policemen exchanged glances.

I thought: They discover everything. They will learn who Fleur is. This is going to be terrible for Lavinia . . . and just when she was about to get married.

I was so relieved when they went, but there was worse to come. Polly saw it first in the morning paper and she knew then that it was no use trying to keep it from Eff.

She read it to me in a shaky voice: " 'Who was Janine Fletcher? Why should someone take this young girl's life? I had the opportunity of speaking with an old school friend of hers. This was Miss Drusilla Delany who is at present staying with her onetime nurse.' They've given this address." Polly went on: "She is the daughter of the rector of Framling and was on a

179

visit to her school friend when she found her lying on a stretcher being conducted out of her lodgings. Janine had been shot through the head. Miss Delany said she knew of no one who would want to kill her friend. Janine was the daughter of Miss Emily Fletcher, who ran an exclusive nursing home for the well-to-do in the New Forest. Police at the moment are saying nothing, but it is rumoured that they have hopes of an early arrest."

Polly finished reading and looked at me in dismay.

"Oh, Polly," I said, "it's terrible."

"I wonder if they'll find out about Fleur. Police has noses for sniffing out nasty tit-bits."

"It would be terrible, just as the wedding is about to take place. I do hope Lavinia is not involved in this. I am sure she isn't, but all sort of things could come out."

"It might be better for that earl or whatever he is to know something about the girl he's marrying before the ceremony. He'll find out quite enough after, I shouldn't wonder."

"Oh, Polly . . . I'm frightened."

"Nothing for you to be frightened of. If anything comes out you've got to stand up and tell the truth. Never mind covering up for Madam Lavinia. It's time she came out in the open."

It was comforting to be with her, but I felt I should return to the rectory, for I knew how concerned Eff was for the respectability of the house. Polly was, too, but her love for me overcame her desire for respectability.

It was the day after we read that piece in the paper when Fabian appeared at the house. I heard the knock and I had an uneasy feeling that it might be the police. I went to open it and there was Fabian.

"Good afternoon," he said, stepping into the hall without invitation. "I want to talk to you."

"But . . ." I began.

"Where can we go?" he asked.

I took him into the parlour, that prim little room with the straight velvet-backed chairs and the sofa to match, the whatnot with the precious ornaments on it—dusted only by Eff—the marble mantelpiece, the aspidistra in the big brown pot on the table standing by the window and the paper flowers in the vase in the fireplace. It was the unlived-in room, the sanctum of respectability used for callers, interviewing would-be tenants and, sometimes, on very special occasions, Sunday afternoon tea.

"What has brought you here?" I asked.

"Need you ask? I've seen the paper. This girl . . . Janine . . . what has she to do with you?"

"If you read the paper you would know that we were at school together."

"The girl's been murdered . . . and you were there at the time."

"I arrived after she was dead."

"After she was murdered," he said. "Good God! What does it mean?"

"I think that is what the police are deciding."

"But you have been mentioned in regard to this case."

"I happened to be there. I was questioned."

"The police don't question just to be sociable, you know. The fact that they questioned you means they think you know something."

"I did know her. I was going to call on her."

"For what purpose?"

"Purpose? She was an old school friend."

"Just renewing acquaintance? I want to know the truth. Do you hear me? You can't go on lying forever. You'd better tell me. I insist on knowing."

At that moment the door burst open and Polly stood there. She told me afterwards that she had heard him come in and had been listening at the door.

She stood there, her cheeks aflame, her arms akimbo.

"Now, Sir High and Mighty Whatever Your Name Is, I'm going to tell you a few things. I'll not have you coming here and upsetting my girl. She's worth the lot of you all tied up in a bundle, and I wouldn't give you tuppence for it either."

He was taken aback, but I saw the amused look in his eyes.

"Polly!" I said reproachfully.

"No. You let me have my say. I've had enough of this, if you haven't. I'm going to tell these Framlings a thing or two.

Coming here . . . upsetting you. He's going to have the truth."

"Nothing would please me more," said Fabian.

"Oh! You won't be so pleased when you hear it, I can tell you, and if them policemen come here trying to trap Drusilla into saying what they want, I'll tell them, too. Drusilla's done a lot for your sister. Whose child do you think it is we've got here? Your sister's, that's whose. Drusilla tried to help her and gets insulted for it. Who was it went away with her to that home? Pretending they were at Princess something or other's place? Who was it brought the baby to me? It was plain to me when they come here that your sister didn't know the difference between a baby and a pound of butter—and cared just about as much. So I am not having you here bullying Drusilla. You go back and bully your sister. She's the cause of the trouble."

He said, "Thank you for telling me." He turned to me. "This is true, I suppose?"

"Of course it's true," cried Polly. "Are you calling me a liar?"

"No, Madam, but I thought a little corroboration might be in order."

"Now we're in this bother and it's all along of your sister. So don't you start accusing Drusilla of nothing, because I won't have that, either."

"You are quite right," he said, "and I am indebted to you. It is an unpleasant situation and I want to do all I can to help."

"H'm," said Polly, slightly mollified. "It's about time, too."

"Yes. Once more you are right. Do you think I might have a little talk with Miss Delany?"

"That's for her to say."

"Yes, certainly," I said.

I was trembling slightly. Polly's revelations had staggered me, but I was glad that he knew, and that I was not the one who had betrayed Lavinia.

Polly said, "Well, I'll take myself off." She looked at me. "Will you be all right?"

"Yes, Polly, thank you."

The door shut on us.

"A redoubtable lady," he said. "So now I have the truth. I

think you should tell me more about this. You see, I am deeply involved through my sister. It happened in France, did it?"

"Yes."

"A Frenchman?"

I nodded.

"You knew him?"

"I saw him once or twice."

"I see. And my foolish sister asked for your help."

"Janine Fletcher was a girl at school. She had an aunt."

"So you lied about going to Lindenstein. I knew you hadn't been there, of course."

"Yes. You tried to trap me. And you had some idea of what really happened."

"When I saw the child . . ."

"And you thought that I . . ."

"It seemed hard to believe."

"Yet you did."

He did not answer. Then he said, "This girl . . . Janine . . . what do you think happened?"

"I don't know."

"You came along just after. Why?"

"I was trying to talk to her."

"About Lavinia. Was she blackmailing Lavinia?"

I was silent. I did not want to betray her, but of course Polly had already done that.

He was serious now. "My God!" he said. "But she wasn't here. She was at Framling. It must have been . . . someone else."

"You mean . . ."

"Did that woman have other girls there in the same position?"

"There were some."

"What a mess! It is a pity you were seen there. I am glad I know. I shall keep in touch. I shall be in London. I'll give you the address of my place in town. Get a message to me if anything develops."

He looked really anxious. I imagined he was thinking of the scandal if anything came out about Lavinia's staying at the nursing home and for what reason. That would be headline news. I only rated a mention and a short paragraph. Lavinia's reputation would be in ruins. I could see that her brother was prepared to prevent that at all costs.

I felt a certain relief. I had great confidence in his powers to help. He would be strong and resourceful. Of course, he was only concerned about protecting his sister, but in doing so he would look after me at the same time.

He said he would go now. He took my hands and smiled at me; it was almost like an apology for his behaviour in the past. I was glad that at last he knew the truth and I had not been the one to tell him.

There was no news of the case—just brief references. The police were pursuing their enquiries. There was no more visits from them.

Fabian called at the house. Eff let him in. She was not at all displeased.

"Eff's a rare one for a title," Polly explained. "You'll hear her going on to Second Floor about *Sir* Fabian calling. She thinks it's good for the house. He looks the part too. I hope he's behaving right."

"Oh yes," I assured her.

"Don't you put up with any old truck from him."

"No, I won't."

He wanted to talk to me about the child, he told me. Those two women had looked after her from birth, had they? I told him they had.

I knew by his attitude that he had a respect for Polly. I think he quite enjoyed her manner of dealing with him, although what she had to impart had been unpalatable. He had seemed faintly amused to contemplate the rector's daughter having stepped out of line; it was not quite so amusing for his own sister.

"It's a little girl, isn't it?"

"Yes. You should meet your niece. Apart from that one encounter on the green you have not seen her."

"I want to meet her. And those two have looked after her, fed her . . . clothed her . . ."

"They have also loved her," I said.

"Poor child! What would she have done without them . . . and you?"

"Lavinia would have had to make some arrangements, but none could have been so good for Fleur as Polly and her sister."

"I want to make sure that they are compensated for what they have done."

"You mean . . . money?"

"I did mean that. They cannot be wealthy enough to take care of other people's children. It must be a costly business."

"They are, as they would say, comfortably off. They let rooms and Eff is a good businesswoman. Polly, too. They work hard and enjoy the fruits of their labours. They might be offended if they thought you believed they were in need of money."

"But they have taken the child!"

"They did that for me, because . . ."

"Because they made the same mistake as I did. You see, I was not such a villain after all if Polly . . . who is so close to you . . . Well, perhaps that sort of thing can happen to anyone."

"Perhaps."

"We all have our unguarded moments." He was smiling at me quizzically. Then he said briskly, "I shall find a way of recompensing these good women. Will you talk to them for me? I am afraid I should never be allowed to state my case. They might listen to you."

I said I would speak to them

They were both rather indignant when I told them.

"Who does he think he is?" demanded Polly. "We don't want his money. We've had Fleur since she was a baby. She's ours . . . If you took money from a man like that you'd have him dictating . . . telling you what you'd got to do. No, we're not having that."

Eff conceded, "It was good of *Sir* Fabian to suggest it." She always made the most of the 'Sir' when talking to Second Floor 32 and fell into the habit with us.

"Look, Polly," I said, "you're all right now . . . but suppose things didn't go so well. You have to think of Fleur and there will be school and all that."

"I wouldn't want her going to one of them foreign places. A lot of good it did to that Lavinia."

But Eff was more practical. I think Polly's emotions dulled

her perception to some extent. She had marked Fabian out as a smooth seducer and she had made up her mind that he had designs on me. She was very wary of him.

However, when Fabian suggested that he should set up an account for them on which they could draw at any time they needed money for Fleur, they at length agreed.

"Not that we'll touch it," said Polly.

"But it's nice to know it's there," added the practical Eff.

During the following week I saw a good deal of him. I had to admit that he was a help and that he comforted me. The fact that he was there and knew the truth took a great weight off my mind.

No one else from the police came to see me. There was little in the papers about the case. It was good to know that if any crisis arose Fabian would be there.

I grew to know a little more of him. He used to visit the house and Eff, with a certain pride, would serve tea in the parlour. I think she was rather proud to show it off. When he was coming, fresh antimacassars were put on the velvet chairs and there was an extra polish on the brass; the ornaments on the what-not were carefully dusted. "We don't want that *Sir* Fabian to think we don't know what's what." I was secretly amused at the thought of his examining the little bits of china on the what-not and assessing the brightness of the brass of the candlesticks. But I liked to see Eff's pleasure in entertaining the titled gentleman and Polly's suspicions of him, which were an indication of her love and concern for me.

He seemed to change a little. He met Fleur, who took quite a liking to him, which surprised me, for he found it difficult to communicate with her and appeared to make no attempt to do so.

"Say hello, *Sir* Fabian," Eff urged; and Fleur did with a halting charm. She put her hands on his knees and gazed up at him with a sort of wonder. It was very amusing. I thought there was a look of the Framlings about Fleur. She had failed to inherit Lavinia's tawny hair, but I thought she would be a beauty like her mother.

"A pleasant-looking child," was Fabian's comment.

"She seemed to sense that she was related to you," I told him.

"Surely not?"

"Who knows? You are her uncle."

Effie brought in tea, which I took alone with Fabian. I guessed Polly was hovering. As she would say, she wouldn't trust him and he might get up to some "hanky panky."

We talked of Lavinia's coming marriage, which would be very soon now. Lavinia would have heard of Janine's death, as it had been reported in the papers. I wondered what she was thinking. If I knew her, she would be mightily relieved on one hand, but on the other she must be wondering what could come out about Janine. I wondered if it occurred to her that if Janine was blackmailing her she might be doing the same to other people. Surely she must be suffering some anxiety.

Fabian would have to return for the wedding.

"I think," he told me, "you would be expected to attend."

"I am not sure whether that is necessary. She will have heard about Janine. I wonder how she is feeling."

"She doesn't let much worry her, but even she must be having some uneasy moments. Thank God she was in Framling when the woman was killed and there can be no question of accusations being brought against her."

"Do you think she will tell Dougal?"

"No, I do not."

"Do you think she should?"

"It is a matter for her to decide."

"Shouldn't he know?"

"I can see you are a stickler for morality."

"Aren't you?"

"I am for good common sense."

"And morality does not always fit in with that?"

"I would not say that. Each situation has to be judged on its own. You cannot generalize about such matters."

"Do you think it is right . . . or even wise . . . for a woman who has a child to marry and not mention that child to her husband?"

"If the woman in question was a virtuous one she would not have had the child in the first place, so you must not expect exemplary conduct from her afterwards. It is a matter for La-vinia to decide."

"And Dougal . . . isn't he being deceived?"

"Yes. But perhaps he would prefer not to know."

"Do you really think so? Would you in similar circum-stances?"

"I find it exceedingly difficult to put myself in Dougal's place. I am not Dougal. I am myself. Dougal is a good, worthy man. I am sure he has lived an exemplary life. I cannot say the same for myself. Therefore I take a different view from the one he would take. I believe that it is better to get through life as easily as one can . . . and if ignorance is more soothing than knowledge, let's remain in the dark."

"What a strange philosophy!"

"I am afraid you disapprove of me."

"I am sure there are very few things you are afraid of and my approval or disapproval is not one of them."

"I would always welcome your good opinion."

I laughed. I was feeling much easier with him. I looked forward to his visits and I was continually warning myself not to become too interested in him. I had had one warning with Dougal. He had seemed the perfect gentleman; Fabian was not that, but I found him, if anything, more interesting. The sub-jects raised by Dougal had fascinated me, but it was Fabian himself who attracted me.

I was on dangerous ground. Polly knew it; that was why she was watchful.

It was evening. Fleur was in bed, and I was sitting with Polly and Eff by the kitchen fire. Eff had just commented on how well it was drawing these days, when there was a knock on the door.

Eff rose in dismay. She never liked anyone to catch her using the kitchen as a living room.

"One of the tenants," she said. "First Floor Back, bet you anything."

She composed herself, putting on the special dignity she reserved for tenants, and went to the door.

Polly followed her with me in the wake.

188

It was not First Floor Back but one of the others, and she was clutching a newspaper.

"I thought you might not have heard the latest," she was saying excitedly. "It's the Janine Fletcher case."

We all went into the parlour. Polly had seized the newspaper and spread it out on the table. We all gathered round. It was on the front page, Stop Press News.

"Startling Developments in the Janine Fletcher Case. Police think they have solution."

That was all.

"Well, well," said Eff. "It was kind of you, Mrs. Tenby."

"Well, I thought you'd want to know. And Miss Delany . . . you'd be interested, seeing as how you knew the poor thing."

"Yes," I agreed.

"Now we have to wait and see what it's all about," said Polly.

Eff, with the utmost dignity, was ushering Mrs. Tenby into the hall.

"Well, thank you for letting us know."

When she had gone we sat in the kitchen asking ourselves what it could mean and we were later than usual going to bed.

I went in to see Fleur, as I always did every night. She was fast asleep, clutching the little doll Eff had bought for her and from which she refused to be parted. I bent and kissed her; she murmured something in her sleep. I felt a great relief because Fabian knew and that meant that her future was assured.

I lay awake for a long time, wondering what new development there had been and whether I should see Fabian next day.

We had the papers early and there it was for us to read. It was a further shock for me and I felt more deeply involved than I had before. Dramas . . . tragedies . . . take place frequently. One reads of them and sometimes they seem unreal because they happen to vague people whom we can only imagine; but when they concern someone we know, that is different.

What I read saddened me greatly, although it must have brought intense relief to Lavinia.

They had found the murderess—not by any great detective

work on the part of the police, but through the confession of the one who had killed Janine.

"Killer of Janine Fletcher confesses."

It was written in flowery prose.

"In a little house on the outskirts of Wanstead near Epping Forest, Jack Everet Masters lay dying of self-inflicted wounds. Beside him was the body of his wife, Miriam Mary Masters. She had been dead some hours.

"They were known as the happiest couple in the neighbourhood. Jack was a seaman. Neighbours tell how his wife used to wait for his return and how each time he came home it was another honeymoon for them. Why should she then have decided to take her life by consuming an overdose of laudanum? It was because she could not face the consequence of a reckless act which took place during one of Jack's absences at sea."

"Double Suicide" was the next headline.

"Miriam could no longer tolerate the situation in which she found herself and decided she could no longer go on living. So, carefully writing two letters—one to Jack and one to the coroner—she confessed to the killing of Janine Fletcher. In that to her husband she gave her reasons for doing so.

"I love you, Jack.

"The letter she wrote to her husband explained what happened. One night when Jack was at sea she had been persuaded by friends to go to a party. She had not wanted to and, little realizing that she was setting out on a path which would lead to misery and finally death, unused to alcohol, she took too much and was unaware of what was happening to her. Some person took advantage of the poor girl's state and seduced her with the result that she became with child. Miriam was desperate. How to tell Jack? Would he understand? She greatly feared that he would not. Her happiness was in ruins. She tried to plan a way out. She had heard of Mrs. Fletcher's Nursing Home in the New Forest. It was expensive, but discreet. She decided there was no alternative but to go there and get the child adopted when it arrived. Janine Fletcher, known as the niece of the owner of the nursing home, was there when Miriam had her baby. Janine knew her secret. The child was born and adopted.

Miriam came home to put the past behind her. And so she did, until Janine Fletcher turned up in her life.

"It is not an unfamiliar story. Janine wanted money to keep quiet. Miriam paid . . . once or twice . . . and then she found she could not go on paying. Greatly she feared the consequences. She could not face telling Jack. She acquired a gun. She went to Janine's rooms and shot her dead. She managed to get away without being seen. But she realized she could not live with such a secret, so she wrote those letters.

"Star-Crossed Lovers.

"They were Romeo and Juliet. He came and found her dead. He read her letter. He was prostrate with grief. He would have understood. He would have forgiven. Perhaps they would have found the child and he would have been a father to it.

"Too Late.

"She had killed Janine Fletcher. She must have realized, while she might have lived on weighed down by the sin of adultery, she could not by that of murder. So the star-crossed lovers died, and the mystery of who killed Janine Fletcher is solved."

Fabian called later in the morning.

"You've heard the news?" he said.

"Yes," I said. "I was deeply touched." I remembered Miriam so well. I remembered her misery and I thought how cruel life had been to her.

"You seem shaken," he said.

"I *knew* her. She was there when we were there. She was such a gentle person. I cannot think of her as a murderess."

"It closes up the case. We can breathe more easily now. Good God! It would have been certain to come out. Lavinia could have been caught up in all this. So could you. I was daily expecting something to be disclosed. And now it's all over."

I said, "She loved her husband . . . deeply. And he must have loved her. He could not contemplate living without her. She made a deep impression on me."

"She must have been an unusual woman . . . to take that gun and shoot her enemy."

"It all seems so unnecessary. If only she had told her husband! If only Janine had tried to work for her living and not turned to blackmail! If only Lavinia had not been carried away by that man!"

"If only the world were a different place and everyone in it perfect, life would be simpler, wouldn't it?" He smiled at me ruefully. "You look for perfection," he went on. "I believe you will have to do with something less. I am going to cheer you up. I am going to suggest that you have luncheon with me. I think we have something to celebrate. The case is over. I can tell you I have had some uneasy moments!"

"For Lavinia," I said.

"For you also."

"I had nothing to fear."

"It is never good to be connected with what is unsavoury. It leaves something behind. People remember . . . vaguely. They forget details . . . who was who . . . what part they played. It is a great relief that it is over."

"I can't stop thinking of Miriam."

"She took what she thought was the best way out of her dilemma."

"And destroyed her life and that of her husband."

"Alas. It was her choice. It is a sad story. I will call for you at twelve-thirty."

Polly was pleased by the news.

"My goodness, it gave me the willies . . . thinking what was going to happen next . . . and now you are going to lunch with *him*." She shook her head. "You want to be careful with that one. I wouldn't trust him as far as I could throw a goose feather."

"That might float in the air for quite a long time, Polly."

"It would come down pretty soon, I reckon. Take care."

"Oh, Polly, I will."

Over luncheon he treated with the utmost deference. He was in good spirits. Naturally, he had never met Miriam, and her tragedy meant little to him except an ending to a situation which could have become dangerous.

"Isn't it strange?" he said. "You and I have been acquainted since you were two years old and it is only now that we know each other. It took this little matter to bring us together. I very much regret that I shall soon be leaving England."

"You are going to India?"

"Yes, by the end of the year or the beginning of next. It is quite a journey."

"Have you ever done it before?"

"No. But I have heard a great deal about it. There are always people at the House connected with the East India Company and they discuss it constantly."

"You will go part of the way by ship, of course."

"One has to decide whether one will take the long haul round the Cape or disembark, say at Alexandria, and take the trek across the desert to Suez, where one can board an East Indiaman."

"Which you will do, I suppose."

"We take that route, yes. It saves time, but I believe crossing the desert can be a little hazardous."

"I am sure it will be of the utmost interest."

"I feel certain of that, too. But in a way I shall be sorry to leave England."

He smiled at me significantly and I felt myself flushing faintly. I could not forget that time when he had, as I believed, made a rather veiled suggestion to me.

"I don't know when your friend Dougal, our bridegroom, will be coming out," he went on. "He was to have done so, but it may be that his new commitments will keep him in England."

"Whereabouts is the ancestral home?"

"Not very far from Framling. I would say some forty or fifty miles." He looked at me intently. "I daresay you will be invited to visit. Perhaps you will enjoy that."

He had a way of insinuating meaning into his conversation. He implied that he knew of my feelings for Dougal and was translating them into aspirations and hopes. I felt indignant. It was a mood I was often verging on with him.

"Of course, the newly married couple may wish to be alone for a while, but doubtless that will pass. Then I am sure you will be an honoured guest."

"Lavinia will have new interests. I daresay she will have little time for me."

"But you and Dougal were so interested in antiquities. It is hardly likely that he will lose his enthusiasm for those after the first delights of marriage are over."

"It remains to be seen."

"As so much does. You are very philosophical."

"I did not know that."

"There is a great deal we do not know about ourselves."

He began to talk about India and the Company. He thought he might be away for several years. "When I come back," he said, "you will have forgotten who I am."

"That's hardly likely. Framling and its inhabitants have dominated the village for as long as I can remember."

"Perhaps you will have married and gone away . . . I wonder."

"It seems hardly likely."

"What seems unlikely today can be inevitable tomorrow." He lifted his glass and said, "To the future . . . yours and mine."

He was disturbing. He was implying that he knew I had cared for Dougal and that I was sad because Lavinia and Lady Harriet had taken him from me. I could not explain to him that, though I liked Dougal and we had been good friends and I had perhaps been a little piqued because he had seemed to forget me when he had been overwhelmed by Lavinia's beauty, I was far from heartbroken.

He leaned forward across the table. "Do you know," he said, "I have always had a special interest in you?"

"Really?"

He nodded. "Ever since I kidnapped you and took you to Framling. Did you ever hear how I cared for you during those two weeks?"

"I did hear of it."

"Don't you think there is some significance in that?"

"The significance is that you were a spoilt child. You had a whim. I was there and I did as well as any other, so you took me to your home and because you had to be indulged you kept me there . . . away from mine."

He laughed. "It shows a purposeful character on my part."

"Rather that you were surrounded by those who allowed you to indulge your whims."

"I can remember it. A little baby. You weren't much more. I enjoyed my part as the father figure . . . and what I am saying is that it gave me a special interest in you. That's natural enough."

"I believe you have a natural interest . . . if a fleeting one . . . in most young women."

He laughed at me. "Whatever you say, I think our little adventure makes a special bond between us."

I shook my head. "Nothing of the sort."

"You disappoint me. Don't you feel it?"

"No," I replied.

"Drusilla, let's be friends . . . good friends."

"One can't make friendship to order."

"One can give it a chance. We live close together. We could see a great deal of each other. This . . . incident . . . has brought us closer together, hasn't it?"

"I hope it has taught you a little about me that you did not know when you jumped to certain conclusions."

"It has taught me a good deal about you and I am eager to learn more."

I thought I knew what he was leading up to . . . not quite so crudely as he had done once before when he came to conclusions about me . . . but it was there all the same.

In my mind's eye I could see Polly's warning face. She did not trust him. Nor did I.

I started to talk about India and he told me more about that country, until I said it was time I left.

I was surprised at myself. I did not want the luncheon to end. Yet I knew Polly was right. I must beware of this man.

When I returned to the house she studied me a little anxiously. I must have shown signs of the elation his company always seemed to inspire in me.

I could not stay with Polly indefinitely. In due course I had to return home.

The wedding day was close.

Lavinia was caught up in a whirl of excitement. I went over to see her and she greeted me with a show of affection and talked excitedly about the wedding and the honeymoon until she was able to get me alone.

"Oh, Drusilla," she burst out, "if you only knew what I went through."

"Others did, too, Lavinia."

"Of course. But I was just going to get married."

"Poor Miriam went through a good deal."

"Fancy her doing that! I couldn't believe it."

"Poor girl. She came to the point when she could endure no more."

"I was terribly worried. What if the police had put my name in the paper! They did have bits about me . . . but in a different way. You know they called me the most beautiful debutante of the year."

"I had heard it."

"Dougal was very proud. He adores me, of course."

"Of course," I said.

"It's going to be such fun. We are going to India."

"So both you and your brother will be there."

She grimaced. "He's been a bit touchy about all this business. Lectured me about Fleur and all that. I told him I'd arranged for her to be well looked after. What else could I do?"

"You might have brought your daughter home and looked after her."

"Don't talk nonsense. How could I?"

"Make a confession, turn over a new leaf and become a devoted mother. Fleur is lovely."

"Is she? Perhaps I'll go and see her one day."

"Polly wouldn't want you to. She'd say it was unsettling the child."

"Unsettle her to see her mother!"

"Certainly, when that mother has left her with others to get her out of the way."

"Oh, shut up. You talk like Fabian. I've had enough of that. It's over. Miriam saw to that."

"She was certainly your benefactress."

"That's a funny way of seeing it."

"It's how you see it. Can you imagine the anguish she suffered?"

"She ought to have told her husband."

"As you have told Dougal?"

"That's different."

"Everything that happens to a Framling is different from that which happens to other people."

"Stop it. I want to talk to you about the wedding. We're going to Italy for our honeymoon. Dougal wants to show me the art treasures." She grimaced.

Poor Dougal! I thought. Then I felt an anger against him. How could he have been so stupid as to marry someone who was so utterly incompatible as Lavinia was?

How self-centred she was! She had hardly spared a thought for Miriam, except to be gratified because she had removed the one who was a threat to herself.

I had daydreams at that time. I dreamed that Dougal realized his mistake, that he came back to the rectory to resume our pleasant friendship, that the relationship between us strengthened.

It was strange that there were three men who were important in my life. There was Colin Brady, who would be prepared to marry me because it would be so convenient and a step towards acquiring the living, with which my father was rapidly becoming too ill to continue; there was Fabian, who had hinted clearly that he would like to indulge in some sort of relationship with me . . . an irregular one, of course. Marriage would not come into it. I had no doubt that Lady Harriet, who had so capably acquired a noble title for her daughter, would have even greater ambitions for her son. He might resist, of course; he would not be so malleable as Lavinia. Lady Harriet must have realized by now that her adored son had as strong a will as her own. That was something I should remember. Just suppose he really did care for me, he would only have to decide to marry me. Lady Harriet, outraged and bitterly disappointed as she would be, would have, nevertheless, to bow to his wishes. It was impossible. He might be sufficiently attracted to me to enjoy a light love affair, but there could be no question of a marriage between the heir of Framling and the humble girl from the rectory. And then there was Dougal. Dougal had the manners of a gentleman and the morals, too. I could have been proud to care for Dougal. I could have shared his interests. But he had seen beauty and succumbed. If I were wise I should agree with Polly and say to myself: I have been

197

lucky. Suppose it had happened later when I had become more deeply involved?

Polly had said before I left, "Men are funny things. There's the good and the bad, the faithful sort and them that can't stop running after women even if they know they're sitting on a keg of gunpowder. It's choosing the right one to start with that's the thing."

"If there is a choice," I reminded her.

"There's a choice whether to or not. That's where it comes in. And there's some I wouldn't touch with a barge pole."

I knew Fabian was one of those; but Dougal hadn't been, and he was soon to be joined in matrimony with Lavinia, who might well be, as Polly had mentioned, one of those who was sitting on a keg of gunpowder. It was almost certain that that marriage would not run smoothly.

The wedding day dawned. It was a great day for the village. My father performed the ceremony. The church was decorated with flowers of all descriptions. These had been sent down from nearby nurseries, which had chosen their best blooms for the purpose. With them had come two ladies to arrange the flowers, much to the disgust of the Misses Glyn and Burrows, who had always previously dealt with the decoration of the church.

It was very impressive. Lavinia was a breathtakingly beautiful bride, Dougal a handsome bridegroom. The guests were numerous.

I sat at the back of the church. I saw Lady Harriet, resplendent in her wedding finery, and Fabian with her, extremely distinguished. I felt like a wren among peacocks.

And so Lavinia was married to Dougal.

Janine was dead. Fleur's future was taken care of. I felt it was the end of an episode.

INDIA

A Perilous Journey
Across the Desert

That happened two years ago. They had been two un-eventful years, and life had taken on a grey monotone. Each day I rose in the morning knowing exactly what the day would bring. There was no light and shadow. The excitement was whether it would be fine for the summer fête or whether the bazaar would make more profit this year than last.

Fabian had left for India earlier than had been expected and went off soon after Lavinia's wedding day.

It was absurd, but it seemed very dull without him. Why it should, when I had seen so little of him and had taken such pains to avoid him, I could not imagine. I should not regret his going. He was, as Polly would have said, a menace.

Although I had often been irritated by Lavinia, I missed her. Framling seemed different without them. I wondered whether Lady Harriet missed them and I was surprised that she had allowed both her darlings to leave her. She gave herself up to the task of ruling the village with more energy than ever. Colin Brady was quite a favourite with her, which I guessed was because he was more conventional than my father had been. He was a subservient young man: "Oh yes, of course, Lady Harriet," "Thank you for telling me, Lady Harriet." I wanted to shout at him, "You don't have to be quite so blatantly humble. I am sure the living will be yours in time."

There was another reason for depression. My father's health was deteriorating. He became tired very easily and I had to be grateful to Colin for his care of him. Colin was to all intent and purposes playing the part of rector. It must be noticed and his reward must come.

I heard Lady Harriet say once, "Such a pleasant young man! The dear rector can be a little odd, you know. All that preoccupation with dead people . . . and those who have been dead so long. He has his own parish to think of. You'd think that would be enough for him."

She called at the rectory now and then, feeling it was her duty to do so. She would cast her probing eyes over me.

I knew her thoughts. She liked everything to be rounded off neatly. My father had been ailing for some time and, like Charles the Second, was an unconscionable long time a-dying. I was his unmarried daughter and there was a young man living in the rectory. The solution was obvious in Lady Harriet's view, and in such circumstances those concerned should realize this and accept what was offered them.

My father had a slight stroke. It did not incapacitate him entirely, but his speech thickened a little and he lost some use of his arm and leg; he had become a semi-invalid.

I nursed him with the help of Mrs. Janson and two of the maids. I could see, though, that I was moving towards some climax.

Dr. Berryman, who had always been a good friend to us, told me he feared my father could have another stroke at any time and that could be fatal.

So I was prepared.

I used to spend a lot of time reading to him. It was what he enjoyed most and this duty certainly increased my knowledge of Greek and Roman history. Each day I woke up and wondered what it would bring, for I knew the existing state of affairs could not last.

Lady Harriet invited me to Framling to take tea with her. I sat in the drawing room while my stately hostess presided behind the lace-covered table, on which was the silver tray with silver teapot, thin bread and butter and a fruit cake.

A parlourmaid took the cup containing the tea that Lady Harriet had poured for me. While the maid remained, conversation was guarded, but I knew it was not simply to take tea that I had been summoned.

She talked of Lavinia and how much she was enjoying India.

"The social life there must be very exciting," she went on. "There are so many people from the Company out there. I believe the natives are so grateful to us. And so they should be. Ingratitude is something I cannot tolerate. The Earl is well and the dear young people are blissfully happy together . . . especially after the birth of little Louise. Dear me. Imagine Lavinia . . . a mother!"

I smiled grimly to myself. Lavinia had been a mother far longer than Lady Harriet realized.

She talked of little Louise and how she at least would have to come home sometime. It would be a little while yet, but children couldn't live in India all their childhood.

I sat listening and agreeing as docilely as Colin Brady might have done.

When we had finished tea and the tray was removed Lady Harriet said, "I am a little anxious about the state of affairs at the rectory."

I raised my eyebrows slightly as though to question why.

She smiled at me benignly. "I have always kept an eye on you, my dear, ever since your mother died. It was so sad. A child left like that. And your father . . . I am very fond of him, but his head is in the clouds . . . just a little. Most men find it difficult to care for a child . . . but he particularly so. So I have watched over you."

I had not noticed the attention and was rather glad that I had not—but, of course, I did not really believe in it.

"Your father is very frail, my dear."

"I am afraid so," I said.

"There comes a time when facts have to be faced . . . however painful. Your father's health is failing. It is time Mr. Brady took over entirely. He is an excellent young man and has my full support. He entertains very warm feelings towards you. If you and he married, it would be a relief to me and such a happy solution to the problems that will inevitably face you. As the rector's daughter you know our ways . . ."

I felt indignant at the manner in which my future was being disposed of.

I said with a certain hauteur, "Lady Harriet, I have no wish to marry." I wanted to add, "And I shall certainly not do so because it is a relief to you."

She smiled indulgently, as though at a wayward child.

"You see, my dear, your father is no longer young. You are of an age to marry. I have spoken of the matter to Mr. Brady."

I could imagine it, and his responses, "Yes, Lady Harriet, if you think I should marry Drusilla, I shall certainly do so."

I felt angry and roused up all the stubbornness in my nature.

"Lady Harriet," I began, but I was saved from giving vent to my anger, which would probably have meant that I should be exiled from Framling forever, by a commotion outside the room.

I heard someone say, "No . . . no, Lady Harriet is in there."

Lady Harriet rose and swept to the door. She flung it open and started back, for standing there was a wild figure whom I recognized at once. Her hair hung down her back in some disarray; she was wearing a loose nightgown and her feet were bare.

"What does this mean?" demanded Lady Harriet.

The woman I had known as Ayesha came hurrying forward, and my memory went back to the first time I had seen Miss Lucille, who had talked to me about the peacock-feather fan.

"I would speak to her," she cried wildly. "She is here. Ah . . ." She was looking at me, stumbling towards me. Ayesha held her back.

"Miss Lucille . . . come to your room. It is better so." I remembered the sing-song voice which had impressed me all those years ago.

Miss Lucille said, "I want to talk to her . . . There is something I must say."

Lady Harriet said briskly, "Take Miss Lucille back to her bedroom. How could this have happened? I have ordered that she should be kept to her own apartments, which is so necessary for her health."

I had risen and the poor demented woman stared at me. Then she smiled rather tenderly. "I want . . . I want . . ." she began.

Ayesha murmured, "Yes, yes . . . later on . . . We shall see. We shall see . . ."

Ayesha took her gently by the hand and led her away; as she went she turned her head and looked at me helplessly.

Lady Harriet was extremely put out.

She said, "I cannot think what happened. She is far from well. I do everything I can to care for her, and that they should have let her come down . . ."

Clearly the scene had shaken her as well as myself. Her thoughts had strayed from me and my affairs. What was happening at Framling was of far more consequence.

"Well, my dear," she said, dismissing me, "you will think about it . . . and you will see what is best."

I was glad to get away and went thoughtfully home.

It was a real problem facing me, and though I would do anything rather than accept Lady Harriet's solution, I had to admit that the future looked rather bleak.

Two days later Colin Brady asked me to marry him.

I did a good deal of walking. I should have liked to ride, but I had no horse of my own, and although Fabian had long ago given me access to the Framling stables, in view of my inability to fall in with Lady Harriet's views, I did not feel I could make use of the offer.

I had come home after a walk and was taking a shortcut across the churchyard when I saw Colin coming out of the church.

"Ah, Drusilla," he said. "I did want to have a word with you."

I guessed what was coming.

I looked at him steadily. He was by no means ill favoured. His face shone with virtue; he was the sort of man who would walk in the paths of righteousness all his life; he would make no enemies, except those who were envious of his virtues; he would bring comfort to the sick and ailing; he would introduce a touch of laboured humour, and many a young woman would be eager to spend a lifetime caring for him. Marriage with him was as much as an impecunious parson's daughter could hope for.

I don't know what I did hope for, but I did feel that I ought to face the world alone rather than with someone who had been more or less ordered to marry me, and whom I had been advised to accept because it was the best thing for me.

"Hello, Colin," I said. "Busy as usual, I see."

"Parish affairs. They can be demanding. The rector was looking less well, I thought, this morning." He shook his head.

"Yes," I answered. "I am afraid he is very weak."

He cleared his throat. "It seems to me a good idea if you and I . . . well, in view of everything . . . it seems a good solution . . ."

Again that irritation arose in me. I did not want marriage to be a solution.

"Well," he went on, "you know this place. And I . . . I have grown to love it . . . and to love you, too, Drusilla."

"I think," I told him, "you have been talking to Lady Harriet. Perhaps I should say she has been talking to you. One doesn't exactly *talk* to Lady Harriet. One listens."

He gave a little titter and coughed.

"What I was really going to say was that you and I could . . . get married."

"And you mean you could take over the rectory."

"Well, I think it would be a successful answer to all our problems."

"I feel one should not undertake marriage as an answer to problems, don't you?"

He looked puzzled. He said, "Lady Harriet has intimated . . ."

"Oh, I know what she intimated, but I wouldn't want to marry just because it is convenient."

"It is not only that . . ." He took my hand and looked earnestly at me. "I am very fond of you, you know."

"I like you, too, Colin. I am sure you will make an excellent job of it all when you take over completely. Well, you really have done that already. As for myself, I am not sure that I want to marry . . . yet."

"My dear girl, you mustn't think like that. Everything will

be all right, I do assure you. I do not want to hurry you. If we could be engaged."

"No, Colin. Not yet."

"I know you have a great deal on your mind. You are worried about your father. Perhaps I have spoken too soon. Lady Harriet . . ."

I wanted to scream at him, "Lady Harriet is not going to govern my life if she governs yours."

"Lady Harriet," I said calmly, "likes to arrange people's lives. Please try to understand, Colin, that I want to manage my own."

He laughed. "She is a very forceful lady . . . but kind at heart, I think, and eager for your welfare. I have spoken too soon. I know you are very anxious about your father. We will speak together later."

I let it go at that, but I wanted to shout at him, "I'll never marry you."

That seemed unkind. He was gentle and goodhearted. I shouldn't let him see how angry I was because he had made himself a tool of Lady Harriet. Perhaps he was wise. He had his way to make in the world and he knew he could not afford to ignore those such as Lady Harriet when they crossed his path, for they could be instrumental in making or breaking his career.

I went to the paddock a good deal. It was in Framling land, but rarely used. I found a certain peace there. I could see the west wing, that which housed Miss Lucille. I thought a great deal about that strange encounter of ours all those years ago. She had remembered, and when she came down to the drawing room where I was having tea with Lady Harriet, she had come to see me.

I brooded on the past and tried to look into the future. It was growing of some concern to me. My father was getting more and more frail. He looked forward to that period of the afternoon when I would read to him for a couple of hours, for his greatest affliction was his failing eyesight, which robbed him of his contact with the world of books. When he dozed off while I was reading I knew he was very weak indeed, for he so much looked forward to these sessions. I would let the book lie in my lap and look at his face, peaceful in repose. I would imagine his coming here with my mother and the hopes they had had and how they had planned for me. And then she had died, leaving him alone, and he had given himself to his books. How different it would have been had she lived!

And now here he was at the end of his life and I should be alone in the world. No, I would have Polly. Polly was like a raft to a drowning person, Polly was the guiding star of my life.

I knew that my father could not live long. I knew that Colin Brady would step into his shoes, and there was no place for me here—where I had lived all my life—unless it was as Colin's wife.

Perhaps some would think the wise thing to do would be to take what was offered to me.

No, no, I said to myself. Why should I feel this revulsion? Colin is a good man. I should be content with him. But I had compared him with others and found him wanting: Dougal, who had made me think our friendship was ripening to something stronger; Fabian, who promised excitement and who had made it clear what sort of relationship there would have to be between us.

It was foolish to think of these two. They were not to be compared with Colin. Colin would never be overwhelmed by beauty as Dougal had been; it would never occur to him to indulge in a less than respectable relationship.

Sometimes I thought I was foolish to turn from Colin. Lady Harriet was right. Marriage with him might well prove not only the best, but the only solution.

While I sat leaning against the hedge of the paddock I often found myself looking up at a certain window and remembering how, years ago, Miss Lucille used to look down on us having our riding lesson.

One day I saw the curtains move. A figure stood at the window looking down at me. Miss Lucille. I lifted a hand and waved. There was no response, and after a while I saw her move away as though she were being led.

I saw her often after that. I usually would be there in the afternoon, and often at the same time. It was like an arrangement between us.

I was getting more and more uneasy about my father. He

talked now and then of my mother, and I felt he was finding great satisfaction in living in the past.

"Everything she was going to do was for you," he told me dreamily when he had nodded off when I was reading and had awakened suddenly to find that I had stopped. "She so much wanted a child. I was glad she lived long enough to see you. I never saw anything more beautiful than her face when she held you in her arms. She wanted everything for you. She wanted you well settled in life. I'm glad Colin Brady is here. He's a good man. I'd trust him as I feel I can trust few others."

"Yes," I agreed, "he has been good."

"He'll take over when I'm gone. It's right that he should. He'll be better at the job than I was."

"You are very much liked here, Father."

"Too forgetful. Not really cut out to be a parson."

"And you think Colin is?"

"To the manner born. He's got it in his blood. His father and grandfather were both in the Church. Drusilla, you could do far worse . . . and you couldn't do better. He's a man I'd trust with you."

"A lot of people seem to think it would be convenient if I married Colin Brady."

"The rectory would always be your home."

"Yes. But does one marry for a home? Did you?"

He was smiling, his mind drifting back to the days when my mother was alive.

"You could do far worse," he murmured.

They were all concerned for my future and the answer seemed obvious to them . . . even to my father.

One day when I was in the paddock Ayesha came to me. I was startled to see her. She smiled at me and said, "You come here often."

"It's so quiet and peaceful."

"Quiet . . . peaceful," she repeated. "My mistress sees you. She looks for you."

"Yes, I have seen her."

"She wishes to speak to you."

"With me?"

She nodded. "She has never forgotten you."

"Oh . . . you mean . . . that time I took the fan."

"Poor soul. She lives much in the past. She is ill, I fear . . . very ill. She talks of joining Gerald . . . He was her lover. It is wonderful to see with what joy she contemplates the reunion. Shall we go? You see, she watches us from the window. Very much she wishes to speak with you."

I followed Ayesha into the house and up the great staircase, hoping that we should not meet Lady Harriet on the way.

Through the long passages we went and came to the door of that room in which I had found the peacock-feather fan. It was still in its place.

Miss Lucille was standing by the window. She was in a dressing gown, her feet in slippers.

"I have her here for you," said Ayesha.

"Welcome, my dear," said Miss Lucille. "How happy I am to see you here. It is a long time since we met face to face. But I have seen you." She waved her hand vaguely in the direction of the window. "Come and talk with me."

"Sit down here," said Ayesha, settling Miss Lucille in her chair and drawing up another for me.

"Tell me, my dear," said Miss Lucille. "Life has not been good . . . ?"

I hesitated. I was not sure. Had it been good? In parts, perhaps.

"Much has happened that is not good?" she persisted.

I nodded slowly. All that trouble with Lavinia . . . the ordeal with the police . . . the sadness of Janine . . . the tragedy of Miriam . . . the disappointment with Dougal . . . the encounters with Fabian.

"You should never have had it in your possession," she went on. "There is the toll . . ."

I realized she was talking about the peacock fan.

"Do you ever think of it?" she asked. "The beauty of those feathers. Do you remember the jewel . . . the good and the evil . . . ? So beautiful . . . but beauty can be evil."

Ayesha was standing by the chair watching her mistress closely. She was frowning a little and I believed that meant she was anxious.

Miss Lucille half closed her eyes and began to tell me the

story of her lover, as she had told me once before, and as she spoke the tears began to run down her cheeks.

"It was the fan . . . If only we had not gone into the bazaar that day. If only he had not bought it for me . . . if only he had not taken it to the jeweller . . . how different everything would have been! And you, my child, you should never have let it cast its spell on you."

"I don't think it cast a spell on me. I only borrowed it for a little while."

"It did. I know. I felt the weight lifted from me."

She closed her eyes and seemed to fall asleep.

I looked questioningly at Ayesha, who lifted her shoulders. "That is how she is," she whispered. "She wanted so much to see you and when you come she forgets what she wanted to say to you. She is content now. She has seen you. She talks of you now and then. She is concerned for you. She makes me tell her about your life at the rectory. She is concerned because your father is so ill."

"I wonder she remembers me."

"It is because she likes you and because of the fan. She is obsessed by the fan."

"Why does she attach such importance to it?"

"She sees it as the source of trouble."

"I am surprised she does not get rid of it."

She shook her head. "No. She believes she cannot do that. It would not get rid of the curse, she says. That goes on forever."

"But if she believes . . ."

"It's an old superstition, and because of what happened after she had the fan, she believes it was because of it that she lost her lover. It has taken possession of her."

"It is very sad. I think I should go now. Lady Harriet would not be pleased to find me here."

"Lady Harriet has gone to London. She is very happy. Her son is coming home . . . for a brief visit. There is some business to which he must attend. It is to be a short stay, but she is delighted that she will see him . . . if only for a little while."

I felt my heart leap and I was alive again. A brief visit! I wondered if I should see him.

"There will be much entertaining. There will be some

grand people here. Invitations go out. It is not good for Miss Lucille. She is always restive when there are people in the house."

I was wondering if his stay in India had changed him.

"I think I should go now," I said.

Ayesha glanced at Miss Lucille. "Yes," she said. "It is a deep sleep now. She sleeps most of the time."

"I have to read to my father. He will be expecting me."

"Yes," she said. "Come. I will take you out."

She led me out through the hall and I went quickly home. I had almost forgotten the visit and the strangeness of Miss Lucille . . . because Fabian was coming home.

That night my father took a turn for the worse. He had had a stroke which left him slightly paralysed and unable to speak clearly. The doctor told us it could not be many weeks before the end.

I was with him most of the time and I could see death coming closer and closer.

Polly wrote. If anything happened I should come to her immediately. We'd talk. There would be a lot to say. I wasn't to rush into anything. Polly was the only one who seemed to think that marriage with Colin Brady was not the most desirable thing that could happen to me.

Fabian arrived at Framling the day my father died. I heard from Mrs. Janson that he was home. I was with my father at the end. He held my hand and I could see that he was at peace.

Colin Brady was very good. He took charge with sympathy and efficiency and if he thought he was a step nearer to his goal he did not show it.

Lady Harriet was displeased that the rector should die just as she was preparing for her son's return. Immersed as she was in parish affairs, the event was, to say the least, inconvenient. I imagined her mentioning the fact somewhat reproachfully in her prayers. There should have been a little more consideration from On High towards one who had always unflinchingly done her duty.

I heard from Mrs. Janson that she had been planning important festivities ever since she had heard that her son was coming home. Lady Geraldine Fitzbrock, with her parents, was coming to stay at Framling and it was an important visit. The Fitzbrocks were of lineage as impeccable as Lady Harriet herself and it was quite clear that she had settled on Geraldine Fitzbrock for Sir Fabian.

I wondered about him now and then, but mostly my thoughts were preoccupied with the past. There was so much in the house to remind me of my father. It seemed oddly quiet, and alien almost, now that he was lying in his coffin behind the drawn blinds of the sitting room. Everywhere there was something to bring back memories . . . his study with the book-lined walls; volumes with bookmarks in his favourite places. I kept thinking of his hunting for his spectacles when he wanted to remind himself of a particularly beloved passage . . . living in another age, halfheartedly trying to tear himself away from it and come back to the affairs of his parish.

I should have been prepared. I could see his furrowed brow when he contemplated me. He had been deeply concerned about my future—as I supposed I should be. In his unworldly heart he had believed I would marry Dougal. How he would have welcomed him as his son-in-law, visualizing long visits when they would delve into the past together. Dougal had been a young man not greatly endowed with worldly goods at that time—a scholar, a man of great gentleness, lacking ambition, a man made in my father's own mould.

Looking back, I realized how disappointed he must have been when it had not turned out as he wished. Not only had he been deprived of a son-in-law whom he would have welcomed, but there was the problem of his daughter's future, which had become an anxiety. Then he had hoped I would marry Colin Brady. That would have been a very sensible conclusion. Colin Brady, true, would have been second best, but very acceptable all the same.

People were thinking that I should take what I could get. Opportunity came rarely in life and when it did must not be lightly turned aside. Lady Harriet had implied that I was foolish. I daresay I was. It was not that I disliked Colin Brady. No one could, really. He was so kind and considerate to all. He would be the perfect priest. But somehow at the back of my mind was the feeling that if I did "the sensible thing" I would regret it, for I would be choosing a way of life that would be so predictable, it would rob me of all the excitement that made up the savour of living.

If I had never known Dougal . . . if I had been a more conventional person . . . perhaps I should have married Colin. But I was myself; and instinctively I rebelled against the suggestion of marriage in such circumstances.

Fabian came over to the rectory to see me. He looked really concerned. "I am so sorry," he said.

"Thank you. It was not unexpected."

"No. But a shock nevertheless."

"It was good of you to call."

"But of course I called."

"I hope your stay in India was successful."

He lifted his shoulders.

"And shall you be here long?" I went on.

"No. Briefly. Very briefly."

"I see."

"And you will be making . . . plans?"

"I shall have to."

"I am sure you will. If there is anything we can do up at Framling . . ."

"Nothing, thank you. Mr. Brady is a great help."

"I was sure he would be. I hear the funeral is tomorrow. I shall be there."

"Thank you."

He smiled at me and soon after left.

I was glad when he went. I did not want him to see how emotional I was. I almost wished that he had not come to see me.

The church was full when my father was buried.

Lady Harriet and Sir Fabian were in the Framling pew. I could think of nothing but my father, and I kept going over all the little things I remembered of him. A feeling of desolation swept over me. I had never felt so lonely in my life.

Colin Brady was brisk and businesslike. He conducted the mourners back to the rectory and we drank mulled wine and ate sandwiches prepared by Mrs. Janson. An air of solemnity enveloped the house.

It was no longer my home. It could be, of course, if I married Colin. I had to think very seriously what I should do.

The will was read. There was little to leave, but what there was was mine. The solicitor told me that it would provide me with a minute income—not enough to live on in any degree of comfort, but something to fall back on if need be. He added that he expected I had already considered the situation, which must be no surprise to me.

I said I was considering.

I was aware of the expectancy around me. Mrs. Janson looked prophetic. I was sure she thought I was going to marry Colin Brady and the household would go on in the way it always had. They knew my ways; they were fond of me; they did not want a stranger in the house.

It seemed inevitable to them, for it was clear that Mr. Brady was willing, and where would I find a more suitable husband? It was high time I settled down and there was the right place just waiting for me.

Colin talked to me on the night of the funeral. I was sitting by the window staring out on the graveyard and an infinite sadness had taken possession of me. I had come to the end of a path and I did not know which way to go. And there was the easy road to take and everyone was pushing me towards it.

"What a sad day," he said. "I know what your father was to you. I was fond of him. He was a wonderfully good man."

I nodded.

"After all these years you have been together, except of course when you were at school."

Ah, there was the point. What had happened then had changed me. If I had stayed all my years in the rectory would I have felt differently? It seemed that I had briefly stepped into a world where people did wild things and paid for them; but it had made me see that there was more to life than being comfortable and living one day after another, quietly, unadventurously, almost like waiting for death.

"It's a great blow to you," he was saying. "Drusilla, won't you let me share it with you?"

"You are doing that," I told him. "You have taken on everything and done it perfectly."

"I would be only too happy to care for you from now on."

I wanted to say that I did not particularly want to be taken care of. I felt capable of looking after myself. I wanted life to be

215

adventurous, exciting . . . I was not looking for comfort, pleasant as it might be.

"There could be an early wedding. Lady Harriet has said that would be best."

"I do not allow Lady Harriet to run my life, Colin."

He laughed at me. "Of course not. But she is important, you know. Her word carries weight." He looked a little anxious. "She is worried about you. We are all worried about you."

"You must not be. You must leave me to plan for myself."

"But you have had a great shock. I don't think you fully realize that. I want you to know you just have to say the word. I won't hurry you. This is your home. It should always be your home."

"Oh, rectories are like tied cottages. They go with the job."

"Yes, that is so." He looked so earnest. I had learned that he was a man who hated indecision; and I knew I could never marry him and that it was only fair to tell him so.

"Colin," I said, "I have to tell you that I shall never marry you."

He looked taken aback.

"I am sorry," I went on. "I am fond of you . . . but differently."

"Drusilla, have you thought . . . ? Just contemplate. Where will you go?"

I said on the spur of the moment, "I shall go to stay with Polly for a while. I shall discuss my future with her. She knows me well. She will advise me."

"I am thinking of what is best for you and what will make a happy solution. It is clear, Drusilla, you must marry me."

"I cannot do it, Colin. You are good and kind and have done a great deal for my father and me. But I cannot marry you."

"Later perhaps . . ."

"No, Colin. Please forget it."

He looked abashed and I added, "I am most sincerely grateful to you for everything and for asking me."

"You are distraught just now."

"No," I said almost angrily, for it seemed he was saying I must be foolish to refuse him. But somehow I managed to convey to him that I meant what I said.

I said, "I want to retire now. It has been a stressful day."

He said he would send one of the maids up with hot milk for me to drink. I tried to protest, but he waved that aside; and later the milk was brought to my room.

I sat by the window looking out. In the distance I could see the lights of Framling. I felt lonely and lost. There would be revelry there. The Lady Geraldine and Fabian would dance together, ride together, talk . . . not today, of course, out of respect for my father, but later. It was Lady Harriet's wish that he should marry her. I wondered if he would. He would be the first to agree that it was suitable.

I told myself angrily that he was the sort of man who would marry *suitably* and indulge his fancies somewhere else . . . with lesser mortals who would be good enough for a light *divertissement* but not for marriage.

I said to myself: I will go to Polly.

The next day I saw Fabian ride by with a young woman whom I presumed was Lady Geraldine. She was tall and handsome. She had rather a loud voice and they were chatting animatedly together. I heard Fabian laugh.

I went into the house and put some things together into a bag. I did not know how long I would stay, but I must make up my mind what I was going to do before I returned.

With Polly I found the comfort I was so sorely in need of.

Fleur was now five years old. She was a sensible child and full of high spirits. "Up to a trick or two," was Eff's fond comment and Polly added that she was as sharp as a "wagon load of monkeys."

She welcomed me. Both Polly and Eff always referred to me in near reverent terms when they spoke of me to her and it had its effect. I spent a lot of time with her. I found some books in a secondhand shop . . . books that I had had as a child . . . and I started to teach her. She was an apt pupil.

I began to think I could make a happy life for myself with Polly and Eff. I had my little income, which would suffice. I could teach Fleur and we could all be happy together.

Polly was worried about me.

"What will you be doing?" she asked.

"I have time to make up my mind, Polly," I replied. "I don't have to rush into anything."

"No. That's a mercy."

"I'd like to stay here for a while. I love being with Fleur. It takes my mind off things."

"Well, for a bit, but it's no life for a young lady as has been educated like you have. Where are you going to meet anyone here?"

"Your mind runs on familiar lines. Are you thinking of getting me married?"

"Well, it's a lottery, they say, but there is a chance of the right number coming up . . . and if it does, well, there's nothing like it."

"I'm sure you're right, Polly."

"It's a pity about that Colin."

"I couldn't marry him just because it provided the good solution."

"Nobody's asking you to."

"Oh yes they are. Lady Harriet for one and Colin Brady for another."

"Oh, *them* . . ."

"I know you're different, Polly, but good solution though it might be, I couldn't do it."

"Then let's go on from there. You're not still thinking of that Dougal. A nice one he'd be . . . leading a girl up the garden path and then liking the flowers in the garden next door."

"Oh, Polly," I laughed, "it wasn't quite like that."

"How else, I'd like to know. There he was coming to see you and the rector and that Lavinia comes along and gives him the glad eye . . . and it's whoops and away."

I couldn't help laughing, which showed how little I minded that it had happened that way.

"He'll rue the day he ever came into his fortune."

"Perhaps not, Polly. She's very beautiful and let's face it . . . I'm not."

"You're as God intended you to be."

"Aren't we all?"

"And you're as good looking as any. There's some men as can't resist that 'come hither' look, and they are the ones to avoid, so thank your lucky stars you fell out of that one. I wouldn't touch that Dougal with a barge pole even if he come crawling back on his hands and knees."

"A spectacle, I assure you, we are unlikely to see."

"He'll soon be seeing he's made a mighty mistake. He'll be wishing he hadn't been so daft. You take my word for it."

"I think Lavinia may have changed now she has a child."

"Leopards don't change their spots, so I've always heard."

"Lavinia is not a leopard."

"She's as likely to change as one of them. Mark my words, he's regretting that hasty step. But it's you we've got to think of."

"I'm happier here than I could be anywhere else, Polly."

"For a while, yes . . . but something has to be done."

"Let's wait, shall we? Let's wait and see."

She nodded.

The days passed. Fleur brought a lot of pleasure. We played games together. Then when she was in bed asleep I would sit with Polly and Eff and listen to their racy talk about the tenants.

"We do see life," said Eff with a chortle.

Polly agreed, but I could see she thought it was not the life I should be leading.

Then the letter came from Lady Harriet. Her family crest was on the envelope and Eff hoped the postman noticed it. She would bring Lady Harriet into the conversation next time she talked to Second Floor No. 32.

I stared at the letter for a few seconds before opening it, wondering what Lady Harriet would have to say to me.

"My dear Drusilla," she had written.

"I have been quite concerned about you. Poor Mr. Brady is most distressed. I only hope you will not regret your hasty decision. The best thing you could have done was to marry him and continue in your rectory home. I am sure in time you will come to regret your stubborn attitude.

"However, I have a proposal to make. Lavinia is very happy in India. She has little Louise, as you know, and I am delighted to tell you that she has just given birth to another—a little boy. Lavinia would like you to go out and help her. I must say she has made me see that this could be quite a good thing. I am sending a nanny out to her. I do not care that my grandchildren should be brought up by foreigners. She has an ayah at the moment, but I want her to have a good English nanny. I have found the right person for the post and I am sending her out almost immediately. Lavinia has expressed a wish that you should go out to be a companion to her and I am of the opinion that this is an excellent idea. It would serve Lavinia's needs and your own. Lavinia wishes the children to be taught in an English manner and she believes that as well as being a companion for her you could instruct the children.

"Lavinia and her husband, the Earl, expect to return to England in two years' time. I am sure you will decide that this will be an excellent opportunity for you. I shall expect an early decision. The nanny will be leaving at the beginning of next month and it would be most convenient if you travelled out together, so there are three weeks for your plans to be made. I shall appreciate an early reply."

I stopped reading the letter. I felt numb with surprise and a certain tingling excitement. To go to India! To be with Lavinia and the children. I would see Dougal and Fabian.

Polly came and saw me staring into space.

"News?" she enquired.

"Polly . . ." I cried. "It's amazing."

"Well?"

"This is from Lady Harriet."

"Interfering again?"

"You could say that . . . but in a rather exciting way. Polly, she is suggesting I go to India."

"What?"

"I would be a sort of governess to Lavinia's children and a companion to her."

Polly stared at me in amazement.

"That Lavinia," she said.

I read the letter to her. I could hear the thrill of excitement in my voice as I did so. It seemed to me that the Framlings had always been a great influence in my life.

Polly said, "When do you have to say?"

"Soon. I would leave in less than a month."

"H'm," said Polly.

We talked it over for hours, but I think I had long before

made up my mind that I would go. Polly came round to the idea very soon.

"It knocked me off my feet at first. India. It's such a long way. But perhaps it would be for the best. It's no life for you here . . . much as we like to have you. A girl of your education . . . she shouldn't be stuck here. Fleur . . . ? We'd been thinking of getting a governess for young Fleur. We want her to be educated, you know. And we can use the money *he* put by for her. I don't see why we shouldn't. After all, he's her uncle. We wouldn't take anything for ourselves, but Fleur's different. She's got to have the best."

Eff agreed with Polly. It was no place for me here. Eff reckoned it was a bit risky going off to foreign places, but Lavinia had gone and she seemed to have survived.

I was going to write to Lady Harriet, but as there was so little time I thought it simpler to return. I had my room in the rectory still and many of my possessions were there, so it was the best place from which to make my arrangements.

Two days after receiving the letter I was on my way back.

I went straight to the rectory. Mrs. Janson had news to impart. Framling was in mourning.

"It's that Miss Lucille. She had a few funny turns and this last one was too much for her. It finished her off. I always say one funeral begets another." She often became biblical in her role as seer. "First the dear rector and then Miss Lucille. Well, it seems this was a happy release for her. We were hoping for a wedding, but I suppose that would be rushing things a bit."

"A wedding?"

"Lady Harriet was all for Fabian marrying Lady Geraldine, but he had to go back to India . . . or somewhere. He had to cut his stay a bit shorter than he thought. I'll tell you what." She was the seer once more. "I reckon there's some understanding. She'll be going out there to him and they'll be joined in holy wedlock, you see."

"Is that so?" I said. "I want to see Lady Harriet immediately. She wrote to me suggesting that I should go to Miss Lavinia in India."

"My goodness gracious me! Indeed . . . indeed! I don't know . . . but I reckon if the Framlings are there . . ."

"I think I should go now. I do need to let her know."

Lady Harriet received me at once.

"My dear Drusilla, I was expecting you."

"It seemed quicker to come than to write."

"And your decision?"

"I want to go, Lady Harriet."

A smile of satisfaction spread across her face.

"Ah. I thought you'd be sensible . . . this time. There will be so many arrangements to be made. Alas, we are now a house of mourning."

"I am so sorry. I heard about Miss Lucille."

"Poor dear creature. It was really a happy release. We shall be concerned with the funeral, but in the meantime we will set our plan in motion. I shall write immediately to Lavinia. I know she will be delighted, and I am sure you will be able to teach Louise. It is a relief to me to *know* who will be in charge of her. Alice Philwright will be coming here for a few days and it would be a good idea for you to get to know her, as you will be travelling together. I think you will be safe with her. She has travelled before and has been looking after children in France. You will go by ship to Alexandria and there travel across country to another ship . . . at Suez, I think. But there will be more details later. In the meantime you will have certain things to prepare . . . your personal things at the rectory and so on. I don't know quite what arrangements you will make . . . but I will leave that to you."

She went on talking, obviously pleased that at last I had fallen in with her decisions and seen the wisdom of following the plans she had made for me. There was little she liked better than arranging the lives of others.

I made my way back to the rectory. Colin was very kind. He was quite pleased with life. He had stepped into my father's shoes and was generally accepted throughout the neighbourhood. My father had been loved more for his foibles than his efficiency. Colin exuded goodwill and bonhomie; he mingled jollity with seriousness, which was very becoming to a man of the cloth. He was ideal for the job.

Moreover, he was already displaying interest in the doctor's daughter, Ellen. She was a few years older than he was, but had all the qualifications a parson's wife should have, plus the approval of Lady Harriet. What could be more suitable, when Colin's only lack to make him an ideal rector was a wife? He was obviously on the way to acquiring one.

He bore me no rancour for refusing his offer. He told me that there was plenty of room in the attics for me to store anything I wished, and after my stay in India I could decide what I wanted to do with it. He would pay me a good price for the furniture in the house, which he was now taking over, and that would save him the trouble of getting his own furniture and at the same time be a help to me.

This all seemed very reasonable and I was grateful to Colin for being so helpful in a practical way. I had to rid myself of all sentimental feeling about my old home and accept the fact that this was the best way.

My excitement grew and as the days passed I realized this was exactly what I needed. I wanted to get right away. My life had come to a dead end. I should experience new scenes, new people.

There was a great deal in the papers at this time about war with Russia. It had been coming to a boiling point for some time and now we were definitely at war.

Despatches were being sent home about the terrible conditions in the Crimea, and a Miss Florence Nightingale had gone out there with a party of nurses. I had read about it and when I was with Polly I had seen soldiers marching through London on the way to the wharf for embarkation. People cheered them and sang patriotic songs, but I am afraid I was so immersed in the dramatic change in my own fortunes that I paid less attention than I would otherwise have done.

I went to the church when Miss Lucille was buried. Colin took the service and I hovered in the background. I was aware that Lady Harriet might think it presumptuous of me to assume the status of a friend.

While the coffin was being lowered into the grave I caught a glimpse of Ayesha, who looked very sad and lost. I went over to speak to her.

She smiled at me and said, "She would be glad you came. She often talked of you."

"I felt I had to come," I said. "Although I saw very little of her, I never forgot her."

"No. And now she is gone. She was glad to go. She believed she would join her lover. I hope she will. I hope she will find happiness again."

The mourners were dispersing and I went slowly back to the rectory.

The next day one of the Framling servants came over to the rectory. Lady Harriet wished to see me at once.

I went over immediately.

"This is rather unexpected," Lady Harriet said. "Miss Lucille has left something to you."

"To me!"

"Yes. Ayesha tells me that you interested her when you came to play with Lavinia."

"I did see her once or twice since then."

"Well, she has requested that one of her possessions should be passed on to you. I have told them to bring it here."

Just at that moment one of the servants came in. She was carrying a case, which she laid on the table.

"This is the object," said Lady Harriet. "There were instructions in her will that it should go to you."

I took the case.

"Open it," said Lady Harriet.

I did so. The sight of the peacock feathers was not really a surprise to me. I knew before I opened it that this would be her bequest to me. I touched the beautiful blue feathers, and as I did so I felt a faint shudder of revulsion.

I could not resist taking out the fan and unfurling it. I touched the little spring in the mount and disclosed the emerald and diamonds I had seen before.

Lady Harriet was beaming at me.

"Worth, I have heard, a small fortune," she said. "Well, you may regard it as your nest-egg."

"Thank you, Lady Harriet," I said.

She inclined her head. "Miss Lucille was a somewhat eccentric lady. A tragedy in her youth affected her deeply. I can comfort myself by the thought that I always had her well looked after to the best of my ability."

So I came back to the rectory carrying the peacock-feather fan.

Ayesha came to see me.

She was very sad. She had spent a great many years looking after Miss Lucille. We walked in the rectory garden, for she
did not wish to come into the house.

I asked her what she would do now.

She told me she would decide later. Miss Lucille had left
her well provided for, so money was not a problem. She might
return to India. She was not sure. Although she had been expecting Miss Lucille's death, it was still a shock to her. She had
permission to stay at Framling until she had decided what she
would do.

She talked about Miss Lucille—her kindness and gentleness and her terrible grief.

"She always said you must have the fan," she said. "She
thought it the best way of disposing of it as you had already
had it in your possession."

"But she thought it brought ill luck."

"She had listened to legends. She was told those stories
after her lover died . . . and in her grief she accepted them.
Perhaps it assuaged her grief to believe that it was to be. You
see, she blamed herself. She had wanted the fan and he had
bought it for her; she had been so attracted by it that he wanted
to embellish it for her, and while he was actually dealing with
this he met his death. It was the only way she could stop blaming herself, to blame the fan . . . which in her eyes represented fate."

"I could never understand why she did not destroy it if she
thought it brought evil."

"It was because she thought it would bring more bad luck
if she did so. It carried the curse. She had suffered; it would
harm her no more. She believed too that you had suffered
through your connection with it. There was gossip at the
House. She heard some of it. She was interested and pleased
when she thought you might marry Mr. Carruthers, who became the Earl. When he became engaged to Miss Lavinia she
was sure this was due to the curse of the fan. It had robbed her
of her lover and now you. She said, 'The curse worked on her,
poor child. She has paid the price. She is young. She has many
years to live. But she has paid the price . . . so she is now free
from its evil.'"

"It doesn't seem to be very logical reasoning."

"Poor lady, she was never reasonable. Her tragedy changed her. It touched her mind."

"It seems a strange legacy . . . to pass on evil."

"She felt it was best. The fan would harm you no more. You had already paid the price. She felt it was best with you." Ayesha touched my hand lightly. "You are no dreamer. You have . . . what is it they say, two feet on the ground. You will see that this is a nonsense. And in the fan is the jewel. It is there when you need it. We never know in this life what will happen to us. Who knows? One day you might be in need of money . . . desperately in need. Then you sell the jewel . . . and when the jewel is gone what is it but a few peacock feathers? You will be wise, as my poor mistress never could be. Remember this. We make our own luck. If you believe in ill luck, it will surely come. Mistress Lucille, she was stricken and she made no attempt to cast off her grief. She nursed it; she nourished it. She told herself that it was the curse of the peacocks' feathers . . . and what did she do? She preserved the fan; she liked to look at it. At times she asked me to bring it to her and she would unfurl it and gaze at it until the tears rolled down her cheeks. You have much sense. You will know that Miss Lavinia's marriage to the Earl was in no way connected with the fan."

"Of course I do. But I was not deeply involved. I suffered from hurt pride, not a broken heart."

"And who knows, it may be in a few years' time you will say, 'That was good for me'—that is, when you find great happiness. Believe this will be so, and it will come. You are going to India. It will seem very strange to you. I shall pray for you . . . that all good may come your way."

After that she talked awhile of India, of the strange sights I would see. She told me of the religion, the conventions, the different castes and the old customs.

"The women . . . ah," she said, "they are the slaves of the men. You will know that the world over the man wants to dominate. It is so here in England . . . but in India doubly so. There was a time when widows burned themselves to death on their husband's funeral pyre. That was the custom of suttee, but it is so no longer. The Governor General Sir William Bentinck made it against the law. But the people do not like their customs changed . . . especially by foreigners."

"It was good to abolish such a custom."

"Yes . . . that and thuggery . . . but there are those who do not care what is good, only that their old laws are being interfered with."

"It is bringing civilization to the land. Surely they want that?"

She looked at me and shook her head, her dark eyes mournful.

"They do not always want what is good. They want what is theirs. Ah, you have much to see and you will understand . . . Miss Lavinia will be glad to see you, I know."

We talked on about my journey and India. I said we must meet again before I left.

I spent a busy time preparing. I was in close touch with Framling and constantly being sent for by Lady Harriet to be grounded in what I must do.

She had already written to Lavinia, who would be getting ready to welcome me, and during one of our meetings she let drop the news that Lady Geraldine, she was sure, would soon be travelling out to India— "for a certain purpose," she added slyly. I felt a little twinge of anger because everything worked out as Lady Harriet wished it to, and even Fabian seemed to consider it imperative to obey her.

We were to stay two nights in London and I would spend those with Polly and Eff. It was what I wanted as I wished to say a proper farewell to them. Lady Harriet had thought it an excellent idea, as we would have to go to London in any case.

About a week before we were due to leave, Alice Philwright came to Framling. I was summoned to meet her.

She was a tall woman about thirty years of age, by no means beautiful, but her face suggested character. She looked a little formidable and extremely efficient. Lady Harriet had interviewed her personally and was pleased with what she had discovered.

First we had tea with Lady Harriet, during which the conversation was predictable, mainly given over to Lady Harriet's views of the upbringing of children. But later, when we were alone together, we came to know each other, which was a pleasure for me and I hoped for Alice.

She told me that she was one of those women who did not care for interference in the nursery, and if it had been Lady Harriet's children she was to care for she would have declined the post without hesitation. "I will not be told what to do in my nursery," she declared. "And I decided that one would not be able to stir outside her ladyship's ideas, which I fear might be a little antiquated in any case."

I laughed and assured her that it would be quite different with the Countess.

"You know her well, I suppose."

"Very well. We were at school together."

"Oh. So the friendship goes right back."

"Oh yes . . . earlier than that. They used to send to the rectory for me to come and play with Lavinia."

"Lavinia is our Countess?"

I nodded. "She was rather a spoilt child, I'm afraid."

"Spoilt! Under that martinet!"

"She thought her children were formed in the same divine mould as herself."

"And this is my new mistress!"

"I am convinced that you will have a free hand in the nursery."

"I believe there is a brother, too."

"Oh yes, Sir Fabian. I doubt he will be aware of us."

"He is going to be married, Lady Harriet tells me."

"I had heard that. A lady of impeccable lineage will be going out to marry him."

"That will be interesting."

"Apparently there was not time to arrange the marriage when he was home, for he was called away on sudden business."

"Connected with the East India Company, I gathered."

"Are you looking forward to going to India?" I asked.

"I always look forward to new children. I've had two families so far and it is a wrench when you leave them. One has to steel oneself not to become emotionally involved with them, and remember all the time that they are not your children, although you're inclined to think of them as such."

"I have never lost touch with my nanny," I told her. "And I never shall. In fact, she is the best friend I have."

I talked often about Polly and Eff and the house.

"She was lucky," said Alice. "She had somewhere to go. Nannies, governesses . . . they spend their lives with other families and never have one they can call their own."

"Unless they marry."

"Then they cease to be nannies and governesses. It's a strange thing. In my profession we understand children . . . we love children . . . we would make the best mothers . . . but we rarely marry. Men are notorious for turning away from the women who would make the best wives and falling in love with some flighty creature because she looks pretty in moonlight . . . and often they regret it later."

"I see you take a cynical outlook on life."

"That comes with increasing years. You wait."

"Oh, you are not so very old."

"Thirty-three. Considered to be most definitely on the shelf. Mind you, there is still a chance . . . a very slight one . . . that someone might see one and take to one. But very, very remote."

She laughed as she made these pronouncements, and I felt we were going to get along very well together.

There was one more session with Lady Harriet. We were given letters for Lavinia, which I was sure were full of admonitions. I went round the neighbourhood saying goodbye to my friends; I took a last leave of Ayesha and then we left.

Polly and Eff were waiting to give us a good welcome.

Alice Philwright was to spend the two days in their house. They had said it would be an easy matter to put her up. I think Polly was secretly pleased to have the opportunity of assessing my companion. I was delighted that they seemed to like each other from the start. Alice was completely at home in the kitchen and even partook of a glass of poker-heated stout.

She talked of her children in France and Italy and confessed that she was finding it hard to imagine what an Anglo-Indian *ménage* might be like.

Polly said, "I'm glad you're going with her." And afterwards to me, "She's a good sensible woman, that one. I was afraid they were going to send you out with some young flighty piece."

I reminded Polly that flighty pieces rarely worked as nannies.

"You find all sorts anywhere these days," was her comment.

I had brought the peacock-feather fan with me. I showed it to Polly.

"It was left to me by Miss Lucille."

"H'm," said Polly. "Pretty."

She opened her eyes and gasped when I showed her the jewels.

"That must be worth a pretty penny."

"I believe so, Polly. Lady Harriet referred to it as a nest-egg."

"Well, that's nice to have, I must say."

"I want you to keep it for me. I didn't know where else to leave it."

"I'll take care of it. I'll put it in a safe place, never fear."

I hesitated. I did not tell her that it was supposed to be unlucky. I knew she would have laughed at the idea in any case; and I think secretly I wanted to forget it.

She said, "I wish I was going with you. Take care of yourself. And look out for that Fabian. I expect you might run into him while you're there."

"I don't suppose I shall see much of him. He'll be engaged on business matters."

"He's the sort who'd bring himself forward and I wouldn't touch him with a barge pole."

"I believe you've said that before."

"Well, I'll say it again. And remember this. We're always here. If they try any hanky panky . . . either of them . . . I never did trust anyone by the name of Framling . . . you just let me know . . . and I'll be waiting for you when the ship comes home."

"That's a comfort, Polly."

"Remember it. There's always a home for you here."

"I will remember it," I said. "Goodbye, Polly, and thank you for coming to the rectory and being there all those years."

"Well, we was made for each other, wasn't we? Now take care and come back soon."

"Two years, Polly. It's not long."

"I'll count the days."

And shortly after that we sailed on the *Oriental Queen* for Alexandria.

Alice and I stood side by side on the deck until the last piece of land that was England was out of sight. Then we went down to the cabin we shared.

It was small and cramped, but, as we realized later, we were lucky to have it to ourselves. But I was too excited to think about such details then. We were on our way to . . . adventure.

I had had very little experience of travelling. True, I had crossed the Channel once or twice on my way to and from Lamason. I was immediately reminded of that secretive journey back to England with Janine and a pregnant Lavinia.

That set me thinking of Lavinia and wondering whether marriage had changed her and what surprises I had waiting for me at my destination. But that seemed a long way off. There was so much to be experienced first.

Within less than an hour of our departure the sea became very rough and continued so all through the Channel and into the Bay of Biscay. We had to curb our inclination to explore for a while, for it was difficult enough to stand upright on the ship.

When we did mingle with our fellow passengers we found them pleasant enough. Many of them knew each other, as they had made the journey several times on the ship; that rather set us apart, and it was quite unusual that two women should be travelling alone, for Alice, although of a more mature age than I, was still comparatively young. I was sure Lady Harriet would not have approved if it had not fitted in so well with her plans to send us out.

However, there we were, and in a few days we did learn a little about the people on board.

There were two girls—of different families—going out to get married. It was a fairly frequent happening, I understood. There was Fiona Macre, a Scottish girl who was going to marry a soldier, and Jane Egmont, whose husband would be one of the officials of what was referred to as the Company.

I kept thinking of Lady Geraldine, who would be coming out on some future voyage to join Fabian. I fell to wondering whether I should see him and what his attitude towards me would be. I wondered whether he would approve of my coming out to be with his sister.

Alice and I were naturally very much together and I learned a little about her. Once she had been engaged to be married. She had not then decided that she would become a nanny. She had lived with her married sister and brother-in-law in Hastings. She had not been very happy; not that her family had not been kind to her, but she had felt an intruder. And then she had met Philip. Philip was an artist. He had come down to Hastings for his health. He had a weak chest and the sea air was said to be good for him.

She met him when he was seated on the shore painting a rough sea. Some of his drawings had blown away and landed right at her feet; she had rescued them and returned them to him.

"There was this howling wind, I remember," she said. "It tore at you. I thought he was crazy to be working in such weather. They were sketches he was making. He was pleased that I'd caught them and we talked and got on well. Then we used to meet every day." Her eyes grew tender and she was like a different woman, soft, gentle and feminine. "We were to have been married. He told me that he was not strong. He had consumption. I planned to nurse him. I was sure I could bring him back to health. He died . . . a month before we were to have been married. Ah, well, that's life. Then I decided I wanted to look after people . . . little ones . . . and I became a nanny. It didn't seem as if I were going to get any children of my own, so I had to make do with other people's."

We did share confidences very quickly. I told her about Colin's proposal and Lady Harriet's conviction that it was the best solution for me and that I was stubborn and foolish not to take it.

She grimaced. "You have to be careful of the Lady Harriets of this world. They are all manipulators. I'd never be manipulated. Good for you that you weren't either."

"I never shall be."

"You were right to refuse him. Marriage lasts a long time and it's got to be the right one. Perhaps you meet that one . . . once in a lifetime. Perhaps he doesn't even notice you. But if he's the one no one else will do."

I did not tell her about Dougal, who had failed me before I had time to fall in love, nor did I mention Fabian, whom I never seemed to be able to get out of my thoughts.

Our first stop was Gibraltar.

It was wonderful to be on dry land. A certain Mr. and Mrs. Carling invited us to go ashore with them. I think they were sorry for two women travelling alone.

We had a very pleasant day inspecting the Rock and the monkeys, and it was exciting to be in a foreign place; but the British flag flew over it, so we still felt we were part of home.

Sailing along the Mediterranean was peaceful. We sat on deck basking in a mild sunshine. It was on one of those occasions that we made the acquaintance of Monsieur Lasseur.

I had noticed him once or twice about the ship. He was of medium height, verging on middle age, with black hair and dark eyes, which seemed to dart everywhere as though he were afraid of missing something.

He had always given me a pleasant smile and bow, with a cheerful "good morning" or whatever time of the day it was. I gathered that he was French.

As we were coming into port at Naples, I was leaning over the rail watching our approach. I was alone. I was not quite sure where Alice was. I became aware of him standing beside me.

"An exciting moment, is it not, Mademoiselle, coming into port?"

"Yes, indeed it is," I answered. "I suppose one feels the excitement because it is all so new."

"I feel it . . . and it is not new to me."

"Do you travel this way frequently?"

"Now and then . . . yes."

"You are going to India?"

"No. I go as far as Suez."

"I believe we have to travel by land from Alexandria."

"That is so. A little . . . lacking in comfort. How will you like that?"

"Everything is so new and exciting to me that I don't think I shall notice the discomfort."

"You are very philosophical, I see. And the . . . older lady . . . your sister perhaps?"

"Oh no."

"Not so? Then . . ."

"We are travelling together. We are both taking up posts in India."

"That is interesting. May I ask . . . ? But I am curious. It is just that on board . . . well, the conventions do not apply in the same way. We are here together . . . we are one family . . . So I can be like the uncle . . . the elder brother *peut-être.*"

"That is a pleasant suggestion."

"You have not made many friends yet."

"So many people seem to know each other already, and married couples drift together. I suppose it is unusual to find two women like us travelling alone."

"Refreshing, shall we say? Refreshing. Now I am going to ask you. Are you going ashore at Naples?"

"Well, I am not sure . . . You see . . ."

"I know. Two ladies alone. Now I am going to be very bold."

I raised my eyebrows.

"I am going to say this. Why do I not conduct you two ladies ashore? Two ladies to go ashore by themselves . . ." He lifted his hands and gravely shook his head. "No . . . no . . . that is not good. These people, they say, 'Here come two ladies . . . we will charge them more.' And perhaps there are other bad things they practise. No, no, ladies should not go ashore without protection. My dear young lady, I offer you that protection."

"That is good of you. I will speak to my friend."

"I shall be at your service," he replied.

At that moment I saw Alice. I called, "Alice, Monsieur Lasseur is kindly offering to escort us ashore."

Alice's eyes widened with pleasure. "What an excellent idea! I was wondering what we were going to do."

"Mademoiselle, the pleasure is mine." He looked at his

watch. "Let us meet say . . . in fifteen minutes. I think we shall be allowed to leave the ship then."

So that day in Naples was spent in the company of the gallant Frenchman. He talked to us a great deal. He was a widower and childless. He had interests in Egypt and would stay in Suez for some time on business.

He contrived to find out a certain amount about us. He had an intent way of listening that made us feel that what we had to say was of the utmost interest to him.

There was about him an air of authority. He shepherded us through the hordes of chattering people, among whom were countless small boys begging or trying to sell us articles. He waved them all aside.

"No, Miss Delany," he said, "I see you are feeling sorry for these piteous waifs, but believe me, they are professional beggars. I have heard that they do very well from gullible visitors."

"There is always a possibility that they may be as poor as they look."

He shook a finger at me. "Trust me," he said. "If you gave to one you would have them all round you like vultures, and you may be sure that while you were concerned with your almsgiving some little fingers would find their way into your pockets."

He hired a little carriage drawn by two small horses and we were driven through the town. Monsieur Lasseur obviously knew the place well, and as we drove under the shadow of the great mountain Vesuvius, he talked interestingly of its menace. We said we wondered why people continued to live so close to it.

"Ah," he replied, "they were born here. Where one's native land is . . . that is where one wants to be . . . except adventurous young ladies who would go to the other end of the earth."

"It is because their work takes them there," pointed out Alice.

"To India . . . land of strange spices and unsolved mysteries."

Then he talked about Vesuvius and the great eruption that had destroyed cities like Pompeii and Herculaneum. He was interesting.

He took us to a restaurant and we sat outside under gaily coloured umbrellas and watched the people passing by. He encouraged us to talk, and I found myself telling him about the rectory and Lady Harriet and how I had been to a finishing school in France. Alice said little about herself and it suddenly occurred to me that he did not prompt her to do so, although he listened avidly to what I told him.

I thought perhaps I was talking too much, and made up my mind to ask Alice when we were alone if this had been so.

Finally it was time to return to the *Oriental Queen*. It had been a most enjoyable day.

I said to Alice when we were alone, "Do you think I talked too much?"

"He certainly encouraged you to."

"I noticed you said little about yourself."

"I thought he did not want to hear. It was you in whom he was interested."

"I wonder . . . if he really is, or whether he was just being polite."

"Oh, there is no doubt that he was very interested in what you said, and yet . . ."

"And yet what?"

"Oh . . . just a thought. I am not sure that I trust him."

"In what way?"

"He seems a little speculative . . ."

"I did not get the idea that he was the least bit . . . flirtatious."

"No. That is what makes it rather odd."

"Oh, Alice, you are being dramatic. I think he is just a lonely man who wants companionship. He travels a great deal. He probably becomes friendly with people for a few weeks and then forgets all about them."

"H'm," said Alice, but she was rather thoughtful.

In due course we arrived at Alexandria, where we left the *Oriental Queen*, boarded a steam barge and sailed up the canal to Cairo.

Monsieur Lasseur had explained to us what would happen. We would spend one night in a hotel—preferably Shepheards —and from Cairo we would make our journey across the desert to Suez in a sort of covered wagon. These wagons were in constant use, carrying people to where they could embark on the next stage of the journey by sea.

It was very exciting to be on dry land after so much time at sea, and we were impressed by the grandeur of the hotel, which was unlike any we had seen. It appeared to be dark and shadowy, and silent-footed men in exotic robes glided about watching us intently with their darting dark eyes.

Monsieur Lasseur told us that there was a constant stream of travellers—mostly going to and from India.

From the moment we entered the hotel, I noticed the man. He was in European dress, and was tall and broad, which made him immediately noticeable. When we came into the hotel after leaving the carriage that had brought us there in the company of the other passengers who were taking the route to India, he seemed to be aware of us. He rose from the chair in which he had been sitting and came close to the desk, where we were being asked our names and informed about our sleeping quarters.

"Miss Philwright and Miss Delany," said the clerk at the desk. "Your room is on the first floor. It is small, but as you see we are very crowded. Here is your key."

The tall man was very close to us then. I wondered what he was doing there, as he was not one of our party. But Alice was pulling at my arm. "Come on," she said. "It's only for one night. We shall be leaving early in the morning."

Excited though I was, I slept well, and I was awakened very early next morning by Alice telling me it was time we got up.

The trip across the desert was to be made in those covered wagons, which were very much as Monsieur Lasseur had described them. They were drawn by four horses and we were told that there were several caravanserais in the desert where we could rest while the horses were changed. Six people rode in each wagon.

Monsieur Lasseur said, "Let us go together. I feel I must keep an eye on you two young ladies. I know from experience how uncomfortable these journeys can be. The drivers are very handy with their whips and their one aim seems to be to get the wagon to the caravanserai as quickly as possible. I am afraid you will find the journey somewhat exhausting."

"As I have already told you, Monsieur Lasseur, it is all so new to us that we are ready to face a little discomfort," I reminded him.

I shall never forget riding through Cairo in the early morning. The buildings looked mysterious in the half light. We passed elegant mosques, one of the palaces of the Khedive, and latticed houses which would have delighted Dougal, who would have seen the Saracen influence in their shadowy walls. Because it was so early the city had not sprung to life, which it would shortly do. I saw just a few donkeys led by small, barefooted boys. There was a hush over the place, but the sun was about to rise, and in the light of dawn Cairo looked like an enchanted city, as though it belonged in the Arabian nights. I could well imagine a loquacious Scheherazade entertaining her sultan behind the doors of some ancient palace.

There were six of us in the wagon: myself, Alice, Monsieur Lasseur, Mr. and Mrs. Carling and, to my surprise, the tall man whom I had noticed in the hotel.

I wondered if he was going to join the steamer that was taking us to India or whether his destination, like that of Monsieur Lasseur, was merely Suez.

Soon the desert closed round us. It was now light enough to see the miles of sand. It was golden in the dawn light. I was fascinated. Then the driver whipped up his horses and we had to concentrate on keeping our seats.

"I told you," said Monsieur Lasseur, "it was hardly a comfortable journey."

We laughed as we were flung against each other. Mrs. Carling said it was a mercy it could not last for long, and Mr. Carling commented that when one undertook such a journey one must be prepared for discomforts. Monsieur Lasseur remarked that there were certain things in life that were wonderful to anticipate and look back on, but less agreeable to experience, and travel often proved to be one of them.

The tall man smiled benignly on us. He seemed to divide his interest between Monsieur Lasseur and me, and whenever I looked up I would find his eyes fixed gravely on one of us.

The horses rattled on.

"What happens if the wagon overturns?" I asked.

"Which," added Mr. Carling, "it might well do if it goes on like this. I don't think our driver realizes what he is putting us through."

"His idea is to get rid of one load, receive his money and then on to the next," explained Monsieur Lasseur.

"But if there is an accident surely that would delay him," I suggested.

"Oh, he is confident that Allah will look after him."

"I wish I shared his confidence," said Alice.

We were all relieved when the horses pulled up. Poor things, they must have been very weary. I knew we all felt considerably battered and we welcomed the short respite before the ordeal started again.

As we alighted I noticed the tall man stayed close to us.

The heat of the desert was intense, for it was round about noon. We had been going for some six hours and were glad of the shelter, although our resting place was like a hut, but the stables adjoining it were extensive.

Beverages were served, and I was glad to see that there was tea. There was food—bread and meat of some indefinable kind, which I declined.

We sat at tables—the six of us who had shared the wagon. I saw no one else from the ship's party and I presumed they would come later, as ours had been one of the first wagons to leave Cairo.

"At least we have come safely through the initial stage of the journey," said Alice.

The tall man replied, "There is still more of the same to come."

"I should not think it could be any worse," went on Alice with a grimace.

The man lifted his shoulders.

"I have heard of frequent breakdowns on the way," put in Monsieur Lasseur.

"How awful," I said. "What would happen then?"

"You wait until the message gets through and they come with another wagon."

"What if we didn't get to Suez in time to catch the ship?"

"They would find some means of getting you there," said the tall man.

"We don't know your name," I told him. "And it does seem as if we are to be fellow passengers on this hazardous journey."

He smiled. He had very white teeth. "It's Tom Keeping," he said.

"So . . . you are English."

"Did you not think so?"

"I wasn't sure."

Monsieur Lasseur said, "I will find out when we are leaving."

He went to the table where a man who was obviously taking charge of the place was sitting.

Tom Keeping said, "I am an interloper. Your party have all come out from England, is that so?"

"Yes, we all sailed together."

"And Monsieur . . . I forget his name . . . the French gentleman."

"Monsieur Lasseur. Yes, he was with us also."

"And all good friends. People quickly become friends when they are travelling, I believe."

"They are thrown very much together," I explained.

"That must be so."

Monsieur Lasseur came back.

"We are leaving in half an hour."

"We had better brace ourselves," said Alice.

The next part of the journey was as hazardous as the first. I noticed that there was a pathway across the desert. Presumably it had been made by the wagons, and if the drivers had kept to this it would have been moderately comfortable, but the frisky horses, maddened no doubt by the frequent applications of the whip, kept straying into the sand, which sent up clouds of it over the wagon.

Several times during the trip to the second caravanserai I thought we were going to be overturned, but by some magic we survived and, after what seemed an interminable journey, we reached the second of the resthouses.

As we were making our way into the caravanserai Monsieur Lasseur slipped his arm through mine and drew me slightly away from the others.

He said, "That was a real shake-up. I feel quite bruised, don't you?"

I told him I did.

"I think," he went on, "I could get a better conveyance for us. Don't say a word. I couldn't take the others . . . only you and Miss Philwright."

As he was talking Tom Keeping came up close behind us.

I said, "How could we leave the Carlings? They should be the ones to travel more comfortably."

"Let me arrange this," went on Monsieur Lasseur. "I'll find a way."

I felt a little uneasy. I wished that I could have asked Alice for her opinion. It was not just the fact of the two of us going off with Monsieur Lasseur. We had travelled with him and knew him well. How could we explain to the Carlings, who were less able to stand up to the journey than we were?

We sat down and refreshments were brought to us.

Tom Keeping said, "I have a bottle of wine here, which I brought with me. Would you care to join me?"

I declined, as did Alice and Mrs. Carling. We preferred tea, although it was not very good. Mr. Carling hesitated and finally said he, too, would take the tea.

That left Monsieur Lasseur and Tom Keeping. The latter went to the end of the room and procured a tray and two glasses, pouring the wine into them.

He brought it back to the table and offered one to Monsieur Lasseur.

"To a successful journey," said Tom Keeping, lifting his glass. "May we all arrive safe and sound at our destinations."

We chatted for a while and then Monsieur Lasseur left us. He looked at me rather conspiratorially as he went. Mr. and Mrs. Carling were so tired that they were dozing off. There was a small room where we could wash and freshen up a little before we began the next phase of our journey. I signed to Alice to accompany me there.

I said to her when the door had closed, "Monsieur Lasseur has plans. He thinks he can get a better carriage for us, but he can't take us all."

"Then he had better take the Carlings. They are elderly and we can stand up to it better than they can."

"I mentioned that, but he wants to take us."

"Why? We have endured the greater part of it."

"He seems to be going to a lot of trouble."

"It would be nice to travel in comfort, but it would be impossible to leave the Carlings. Mr. Keeping will be all right, but I really think Mrs. Carling has had enough."

"Yes, we'll insist that he take them."

"I don't think he'll be eager to do that. He wants to show *you* what a resourceful gentleman he is."

"I think he wants to be more comfortable himself. He said he was going to the stables to arrange it all."

"Well, let's see what happens."

We washed and prepared ourselves for the resumption of the journey.

When we went back to the table Mr. and Mrs. Carling roused themselves and went off to the rest room. There were two of them, naturally, one for men and one for women.

It was some time before Mr. Carling emerged with Tom Keeping, and as soon as I saw them I knew that something was wrong. Tom Keeping came quickly to the table at which Alice and I were sitting.

"I am afraid something has happened to Monsieur Lasseur," he said.

We half rose. "What is it?"

"Oh, don't get alarmed. He is a little unwell. I think it may be something he ate at the last stopping-place. It happens now and then. I am afraid he will be unable to continue with us."

"But . . ." I began.

"Perhaps there is something that we could do," said Alice.

"My dear ladies," said Tom Keeping, "we have to catch the steamer. I believe Monsieur Lasseur's business was in Suez. If he is a day late in arriving that could be of little moment. For us to arrive after the steamer had sailed would be disastrous."

"But what can we do . . . ?"

"He is in good hands. They are used to this sort of calamity here. They will look after him. He will catch a later wagon."

"Where is he now?"

"In the men's rest room. There is a little room there where people can lie down. He has asked me to convey his best wishes to you and tell you not to worry about him."

"Perhaps we could see him . . ." I began.

"Miss Delany, he would not wish that. Moreover the wagon is leaving at any moment now. If you miss it there may not be room on the next."

Mr. Carling said, "This is the most uncomfortable journey I have ever undertaken."

"Never mind, Father," said Mrs. Carling. "We've come so far and this part is nearly over. Only one more lap to do."

Mr. Keeping hurried us to the wagon and we were soon galloping across the desert.

In due course we arrived at Suez, where we spent a day waiting for the rest of the wagons to arrive. To our amazement, Monsieur Lasseur did not come. Alice and I wondered a great deal about him. It was strange. Who would have thought that such a seasoned traveller would have eaten something that did not agree with him. It would have been understandable if it had happened to one of us.

The P. & O. Steamer was waiting for us. We went on board and settled into our small cabin for two, immensely relieved that we had survived the hazardous journey across the desert.

In due course we sailed. Monsieur Lasseur still had not arrived.

We discussed him a great deal during the first days at sea.

"He was very attentive to us," I said to Alice.

"I always felt he had a motive," she said.

"Just friendliness. He liked helping two defenceless females who ought not to have been travelling on their own."

"I could never quite understand him, and his disappearance was most mysterious."

"I wonder how he felt about not being able to get to Suez?"

"He'll only be a few days late, and as he hadn't a ship to catch I don't suppose it mattered all that much."

"It seemed so strange. We were with him most of the time and then . . . he disappeared."

"Tom Keeping seemed to think it was a very ordinary occurrence. The food doesn't always agree with us. I don't suppose standards of hygiene are what they should be. But I thought he would be the sort who would be fully aware of all that and act accordingly."

"I think Tom Keeping did not care very much for him."

"Perhaps the feeling might have been mutual. However, Monsieur Lasseur disappeared, and it is doubtful that we shall ever hear of him again."

We saw Tom Keeping every day. I had a feeling that he was watchful of us and had instituted himself as our protector in place of Monsieur Lasseur.

The seas were calmer and the voyage enjoyable; one day seemed to slip by after another and there was a similarity among them. Many of the passengers who had been on the *Oriental Queen* were still with us, and it seemed just a change of scene, but we had picked up a few passengers at Suez and there were friendly exchanges between us as we sailed down the Red Sea to Aden.

The heat grew great and I remember lazy days when we sat on deck and, as Alice said, recovered from the gruelling time we had endured in the desert.

Tom Keeping often joined us. I noticed that Alice was getting very friendly with him. He was most pleasant to us both, but I detected that while he regarded me more as an object in need of protection he had a great admiration for Alice.

He was an experienced traveller. He told us that he had done the journey from India to England and back many times.

"Most of the people who are going out are in the Army or in the Company; and I think the greater number are in the Company."

"And you," I asked, "are in the Company?"

"Yes, Miss Delany. I am a Company man and I shall be making my way to Delhi as soon as we land."

"We shall be staying in Bombay for a while," Alice told him. "But I believe that our employer may travel round a bit, so we might well find ourselves in Delhi."

"It would please me very much if you did," he said.

He knew, of course, to whom we were going. Fabian, it appeared, was well known to him.

"You must know India well," said Alice.

"My dear Miss Philwright, I don't know anyone who is not a native of the country who knows India well. I often wonder what goes on in the minds of the natives. I don't think anyone can be sure . . . any European, that is."

He talked vividly. He made us want to see the lush, green country, the big houses with their lawns dominated by the spreading banyan trees, the stately pipal and feathery tamarind, but most of all to see the people . . . the mixed races, the several castes, the customs—which were so different from our own.

"I have a feeling that many of them resent our presence," he told us, "although the more sensible of them know that we bring trade and a better style of living. But intruders are never popular."

"How deeply do they resent foreigners?"

"That is something we cannot be sure of. We are dealing with an inscrutable race. Many of them consider themselves to be more civilized than we are and they resent the intrusion of our foreign ways."

"And yet they endure you."

Tom Keeping smiled at me wryly. "I sometimes wonder for how long."

"You mean they might turn you out?"

"They couldn't do that, but they might try."

"That would be dreadful."

"You express it mildly, Miss Delany. But what a topic! India is safe in the hands of the Company."

I shall never forget our time in Aden. It was brief. We were only stopping for a few hours, but Tom Keeping said he would take us for a short drive.

How menacing it seemed as we sailed towards it. The black cliffs rising starkly out of the sea seemed to threaten us.

We were on deck, Alice and I, with Tom Keeping beside us.

"It looks as though we are sailing into the gates of hell," Alice remarked.

"You feel that, do you? Do you know what they say of this place? That Cain—who slew Abel—is buried here, and that since such a notorious murderer was lain here, the atmosphere of the place has changed. It has become evil."

"I could well believe that," I said. "But I imagine it was rather gloomy before."

"No one has left word to tell us so," replied Tom Keeping. "And I think the story got about because it has such a forbidding aspect."

"Oh, I certainly believe legends attach themselves to things and places because they seem to fit," said Alice.

The few hours we spent in Aden were very pleasant. We were under the protection of Tom Keeping and I was glad of it. Alice seemed to be changing. She looked younger. I thought: Can it be that she is falling in love with Tom Keeping?

They talked a great deal together and sometimes I felt like an intruder. It was strange. Alice was the last person, I would have thought, who would have allowed herself to be taken by romantic storm. Perhaps I exaggerated. Just because two people obviously liked each other, that was no reason to conclude that they were contemplating marriage. Alice was far too sensible to take a shipboard friendship seriously, and I was sure Tom Keeping was, too. No. It was just that their personalities were congenial. They struck me as two of the most sensible people I had ever known; quite different from Lavinia and her bogus Comte.

Tom Keeping told us that he would make his way by land from Bombay to Delhi. Travelling was not easy in India. There was no railroad and therefore journeys were tedious and only taken from necessity. Doubtless he would travel by *dâk-ghari*, a sort of carriage drawn by horses; there would be many stops en route, often in places offering inadequate comfort.

"I believe it was you who warned us that travelling was often uncomfortable," I said.

"It is something I have learned through experience."

The sea voyage was coming to an end. There were long, warm, calm days as we crossed the Arabian Sea, and we forgot our cramped cabin, the stormy seas and the ride through the desert when we had rather mysteriously lost Monsieur Lasseur.

I noticed that Alice was growing a little sad as we were nearing our destination and I believed it was at the prospect of saying goodbye to Tom Keeping. He did not seem to be touched by the same melancholy, although I did feel he had enjoyed his friendship with us and particularly with Alice.

He had always given me the impression that he had taken on the role of protector, and I told Alice that I often thought of him as Tom Keeper rather than Tom Keeping. She laughed and said she felt the same.

And then at last we were nearing the end of our long journey.

I was excited by the prospect of seeing Lavinia again . . . and perhaps at some time Fabian. I wondered how I should feel about Dougal. Whichever way I looked at it, I knew it would be far from dull.

"You will be met, I am sure," said Tom Keeping. "So . . . the time has come for us to say our farewells."

"How long will you stay in Bombay?" I asked.

"Only for a day or so. I have to make arrangements to leave for Delhi immediately."

Alice was silent.

There came the last evening. In the morning we would disembark.

As we lay in our bunks that night, I asked Alice how she felt about arriving at our destination.

"Well," she said rather wistfully, *"it*'s really what we set out to do, isn't it?"

"Yes. But the journey was an adventure in itself!"

"Well, it is over now. And here we are. Now we have to begin our duties."

"And remember we are no longer independent."

"Exactly. But work will be good for us."

"I wonder if we shall see Tom Keeping again."

Alice said nothing for a few moments and then, "Delhi is a long way from Bombay. You heard what he said about the difficulties of journeys."

"It is so strange. When you travel with people you get to know them so well . . . and then they are gone."

"I think," said Alice soberly, "that is something you have to accept from the start. Now we should try to sleep. We have a long day ahead of us."

I knew she was afraid of betraying her feelings. Poor Alice. I thought she had begun to care for Tom Keeping. And he might have done for her if they could have remained together. But now he seemed concerned with his business. I thought of Byron's lines:

> Man's love of man's life is a thing apart
> 'Tis woman's whole existence.

The next day we reached Bombay.

The Approaching Storm

There was bustle the next morning. I was accustomed now to these arrivals in port. People seemed to change their personalities and it was almost as though those who had been close friends for weeks now slipped back into the role of strangers. One realized that what had appeared to be a deep friendship was only a pleasant but passing acquaintance.

Poor Alice! She was aware of this, but she was a brave and sensible woman. She would never admit that she had allowed herself to entertain warm feelings towards a man whom she might never see again.

And there we were on that crowded quay.

One of the officials from the dock approached us and asked if we were Miss Delany and Miss Philwright. If so, there was a carriage waiting to take us to our destination. A few paces behind him was a most dignified Indian in a white puggaree and a long blue shirt over baggy white trousers. He ignored the official and bowed low.

"You Missie Delany?" he asked.

"Yes," I replied eagerly.

"I come for you and Missie Nannie."

"Oh yes . . . yes . . ."

"Follow please."

We followed our impressive leader as he shouted orders to two coolies who appeared to be part of his entourage.

"Coolie bring bags . . . Missie follow," we were told.

And we felt that we were well and truly being treated like honoured arrivals.

A carriage was waiting. It was drawn by two grey horses, standing patiently in the care of another coolie.

Tom Keeping left us there, having more or less handed us over. I noticed that he held Alice's hand firmly and seemed reluctant to let it go. I watched her smile at him unflinchingly. I liked Alice more and more as I began to know her better.

We were helped into the carriage by our gracious protector; our hand luggage was passed to us and we understood that our main baggage would be delivered in due course. Such was the outstanding presence of our man that we were confident everything would be in order.

The memory of that drive stays with me still. I suppose it was because it was my first glimpse of India.

The heat beat down on us. There were people everywhere —noisy, colourful. It was quite unlike anything I had ever seen before. Small boys seemed to be darting all over the streets. I thought we would run some of them down, but our driver skilfully avoided them, although on one occasion he shouted something that sounded like a string of curses and the miscreant turned and gave him a look of intense dismay which I was not sure was due to his narrow escape or to the awfulness of the curses.

How colourful were those streets—the buildings white and dazzling and very grand; and in the side streets, of which we had a fleeting glimpse, the contrast of dark little hovels and people squatting on the pavements . . . poor old men who seemed nothing but rags and bones, little children naked save for a loincloth, searching in the gutters . . . for food, I imagined. I was to learn later that, however much I was impressed by the grandeur, there would almost always be the accompanying shadow of appalling poverty.

I wanted to stop and give all I had to the mother with the child in her arms and another pulling at her tattered skirts. Our driver drove furiously on, oblivious of the effect this had on us. I supposed he had seen it all so many times that he accepted it as normal.

There were stalls filled with produce, which I did not always recognize, and people in various styles of costume. I learned afterwards that they belonged to different castes and tribes: the Parsees with their umbrellas, the Brahmins, the Tamils, the Pathans and others. Darting everywhere were the coolies, presumably seeking to beg or earn a little money for some form of labour. I saw women, white-veiled, wrapped up in plain, shapeless robes, and here and there those of lower castes with their beautiful long, black hair hanging down their backs, moving with infinite grace. I thought how much more attractive they were than the purdah women, whose charms, I supposed, were kept for their masters alone.

We said little, as we were both intent on the scene about us and eager to miss nothing. We drove on for some miles and passed several beautiful houses, at length pulling up before one of these.

It was a most impressive residence—dazzlingly white, surrounded by a veranda on which were two white tables and chairs. Over the tables were green-and-white sunshades.

There were steps leading to the veranda.

As we approached, white-clad servants came running out of the house. They surrounded the carriage, chattering excitedly.

Our magnificent driver descended, threw the reins to one of the servants and waved his hand, silencing the chattering servants. He then began to issue orders in a tongue we did not understand. He was immediately obeyed, which did not surprise me at all.

We mounted the steps, he marching ahead of us.

Alice whispered to me, "One feels there should be trumpets . . . not for us, but for him."

I nodded.

We were led from the veranda into the house.

The contrast in temperature was amazing. It was almost cool. The room was large and darkish, the windows being built into recesses. I realized that this was to keep out the heat of the sun. On the wall of the room was a large fan, which I learned after was called a punkah. This was manipulated by a boy in the regulation long white shirt and baggy trousers. I imagined he had been idling, for at our approach he was on his feet, vigorously working the punkah.

The lordly one threw a scathing glance in his direction and I guessed there would be a reprimand at a more suitable moment.

"Missie Nannie go to room . . . in nursery," said our gentleman. "Missie Delany come to Memsahib Lady Countess."

Alice looked surprised, but one of the servants immediately snatched the bag she was carrying and hurried off. Alice followed him. I was left.

"You Missie Delany. You come," I was told.

I was taken up a flight of stairs. Through one of the windows I caught sight of a courtyard. There was a pool on which lotus blossoms floated, and chairs and a table were out there, with a green and white sunshade.

We paused before a door. My guide scratched on it.

"Come in," said a voice I recognized.

"Missie come," said the guide, smiling with the satisfaction of a hero who has triumphantly completed an almost insuperable task. "I bring Missie," he added.

And there was Lavinia standing before me.

"Drusilla!" she cried.

I ran to her and we embraced. I heard the grunt of self-congratulation as the door closed on us.

"You've been so long."

"It is a long journey."

"I'm so glad you've come. Let me look at you. Still the same old Drusilla."

"What did you expect?"

"Just what I see . . . and I'm glad of it. I thought you might have developed into some terrible old bluestocking. You were a little like that."

"I never expected *you* would do such a thing! Now let me look at you."

She took a few steps back, shook out her magnificent hair, which had been loosely tied back with a ribbon, turned her eyes upwards in a saintly manner and posed for me.

She was plumper, but as beautiful as ever. I had forgotten how striking she was. She was clad in a long, loose, lavender-coloured teagown and it suited her . . . in fact, everything always suited Lavinia.

I felt that she had staged our meeting and was acting it as though it were a scene in a play and she was the heroine.

"You haven't changed a bit," I said.

"Well, I hope not. I work on it."

"India suits you."

She smirked. "I'm not sure. We're going home in two years' time. Dougal can't wait. He hates it here. He wants to go home and study some dry old thing. Dougal just doesn't know how to enjoy himself."

"People don't always find enjoyment in the same things."

She raised her eyes to the ceiling—an old habit of hers, I remembered. "Trust Drusilla," she said. "You've been here five minutes and the conversation has already taken a psychological turn."

"That's just a plain, simple fact."

"What's simple to clever you is profound to a numbskull like me. The point is, Dougal can't wait to get home."

"Where is he now?"

"In Delhi. They are always going somewhere. It's the old Company making its demands. I'm sick of the Company. Fabian is there, too."

"In Delhi?"

"It's the headquarters."

"Why aren't you there?"

"Well, we were in Bombay and we're to stay here for a while. I think in time we may be going to Delhi."

"I see."

"Well, tell me about home."

"It's just as it was except that my father died."

"I heard that from Mama, and you were supposed to marry the good Colin Brady and keep up the parsonic tradition. I heard all about it from Mama. You were not very sensible, which meant that you did not do what she had planned for you."

"I see you are well informed in Framling parish matters."

"Mama is a great letter writer. Both Fabian and I get periodic missives from home. One thing . . . she cannot see from there whether her orders are carried out or not . . . which is a mercy."

"She has always arranged everything. It is her mission in life."

"She arranged my marriage." She looked a little sulky.

"You went willingly to the altar."

"It seemed all right then, but I'm a big girl now. *I* decide what I am going to do."

"I'm sorry it didn't work out well."

"Are you? You know, he ought to have married you. You'd have got on well. You would have liked all that talk about olden times. It is just up your street. I can see you getting excited because someone dug up a pot which was used by Alexander the Great. I wouldn't care whether Alexander or Julius Caesar used it. To me it would just be an old pot."

"You're unromantic."

That made her laugh. "I like that. I'm terribly romantic. I'm having quite a good time . . . romantically, as a matter of fact. Oh, I'm so glad you're here, Drusilla. It's like old times. I like to see you look at me disapprovingly. It makes me feel so gloriously wicked."

"I suppose there are . . . admirers?"

"There always have been admirers."

"With disastrous results."

"I have already told you I am a big girl now. I don't get into silly scrapes any more."

"That, at least, is a mercy."

"You're looking prim again. What is it?"

"You haven't asked about Fleur."

"I was coming to that. What about her?"

"She is well and happy."

"Well, what is there to be so disapproving about?"

"Just that you happen to be her mother and are somewhat casual about the relationship."

"I have to remind you, Miss Delany, that I am now your employer."

"If you feel like that I will return to England at the earliest possible moment."

She burst out laughing. "Of course you won't. I'm not letting you go now. You've got to stop here and put up with it all. Besides, you'll always be my old friend Drusilla. We've been through too much together for it to be any other way."

I said, "You didn't see Fleur before you left. In fact, have you seen her at all since Polly took her?"

"The good Polly didn't want me unsettling her. Those were your own words."

"You know that Fabian is aware."

She nodded. "I've been lectured on my folly."

"I hope you didn't think I told."

"He said it was Polly who told, because he had come to conclusions about you. He seemed to be more angry about that than anything else."

"He has been good," I said. "He has deposited a sum of money for Fleur, to be used at Polly's discretion . . . for her education and all that. They are going to have a governess for her. She has to be educated."

"That's fine. What have we got to worry about? And that dreadful Janine was murdered. That worked out very well."

"For you perhaps—hardly for her."

"Blackmailers deserve their fate."

"Have you thought of poor Miriam?"

"I didn't remember her very much. You were the one who was running round getting to know them all while I was in acute discomfort awaiting the birth. It was a horrible place and I'm so glad it's all over."

"Shall you tell Dougal?"

"Good Heavens, no. Why should I?"

"I thought perhaps you might want to see Fleur and have her with you . . . though Polly and Eff would never allow that. Or ease your conscience, perhaps."

"Conscience is something one has to learn to subdue."

"I am sure that is one lesson at which you have excelled."

"There goes Drusilla again. Oh, I mustn't remind you of our respective positions or you'll get huffy and I don't want that. Besides, I like those stern asides. They are pure Drusilla. I'm glad you're here. What about this nanny Mama has sent out with you?"

"She is very good. I like her enormously. She is sensible and, I am sure, absolutely trustworthy."

"Well, that's what I expected, since Mama found her."

"We got on very well." I started to tell her about our journey and the hazardous ride across the desert and the disappearance of Monsieur Lasseur, but I saw that her attention strayed. She kept glancing in the mirror and patting her hair. So I stopped.

I said, "What about the children?"

"The children?"

"Oh, have you forgotten? You have two born in wedlock. We have already discussed and dismissed your illegitimate offspring."

Lavinia threw back her head and laughed.

"Typical Drusillaisms," she said. "I love them. I'm not going to give you the pleasure of being dismissed for impertinence to your mistress, so don't think I am. You have been chosen for me by my determined mama and my overbearing brother approves of the decision . . . so you will have to stay."

"Your brother?"

"Yes, as a matter of fact it was he who suggested it in the first place. He said to me, 'You used to get along well with that girl from the rectory. You went to school with her. I daresay you would be amused to have her here.' When he said that I didn't know why I hadn't thought of it before. I said, 'How would she come?' You know Fabian. He replied, 'By steam to Alexandria and then on from Suez.' I didn't mean that, of course. I said, 'Why? How could she?' 'Well,' he said, 'she's a very erudite young woman. She could teach the children. That's what genteel, well-educated young women of flimsy means do—and the rectory girl is exactly that.'"

She laughed and I felt a foolish elation. *He* had suggested it. It must have been when he had come home and was courting Lady Geraldine that he had spoken to Lady Harriet.

I wanted to ask about Lady Geraldine, but I felt this was not the moment to do so. Lavinia, by no means clever academically, would be an adept at discovering one's feelings towards the opposite sex.

So I just said, "Oh . . . was it like that?"

"Coming from Mama it is like the passing of an Act of Parliament, and the approval of Fabian is like the signature of the Monarch. So, you see, it becomes law."

"You don't always take their advice, I'm sure."

"That is why sin is so enticing to me. If I hadn't such a forceful family it wouldn't be half as much fun. My dear, virtuous Drusilla, so different from your erring friend, I can't tell you what joy it is to have you here. It was delightful that the command from Framling should coincide exactly with my wishes. I'm going to have lots of fun."

"I hope there are not going to be more predicaments like . . ."

She put her finger to her lips. "The subject is closed. I'm out of that one. Seriously, Drusilla, I'll never forget the part you played in it. Then I snatched Dougal from right under your nose."

"He was never mine to snatch."

"He could easily have been. I reckon if he hadn't suddenly become important in Mama's eyes he might still be delving in his books and paying his snail-like courtship to you. He might not have arrived at proposing yet. Speed is not Dougal's greatest strength. But the progress would have been steady . . . and so right for him, really, and it might have been a solution for you. Better than that priggish old Colin Brady, whom you had the good sense to refuse. But then you would always have good sense. At the same time, Dougal would have been happier without his grand title. Poor Dougal! I could feel almost sorry for him. Swept off his snail's path to marry the woman who was the most unsuitable in the world for him. Still, it was Mama's decree and that is like the laws of Medes and the Persians, which you would know of."

I was suddenly very happy to be here. I felt life had been dull too long. I was alive again. Everything was strange, a little mysterious—and Fabian had suggested that I should come.

I wondered why. For the convenience of the Framlings, of course. Lavinia needed a companion, perhaps someone to rescue her from the result of possible peccadilloes, of which there would certainly be many here, where there were more opportunities than there had been in a French finishing school. And I had proved myself very useful once. Fabian would remember that.

Therefore, one of the decrees, which had ordered the marriage of Dougal and Lavinia, was now extending to me. I was to leave everything and report for duty—so here I was.

I was afraid she would see my elation and connect it with Fabian, so I said, "I should like to see the children."

"Drusilla has spoken. I shall indulge her whim, just to show how pleased I am to have her here. I will take you to the nursery."

She led the way from the room up a staircase and we were at the top of the house, where the nurseries were . . . two huge rooms with smallish, shrouded windows set in embrasures. There were heavy drapes, which gave a darkness to the room.

I heard voices and I guessed Alice was already there, making the acquaintance of her charges-to-be.

Lavinia took me to a room where there were two small beds, mosquito-netted, and there was the inevitable punkah on the wall.

The door to the communicating room was opened and a small, dark woman in a sari emerged. With her was Alice.

"This," I said, "is Miss Alice Philwright. Alice, this is the Countess."

"Hello," said Lavinia in a friendly fashion. "I am glad you are here. Are you introducing yourself to the children already?"

"It is the first thing I always do," said Alice.

They went into the room. The slight, dark woman stepped aside to let us pass. She looked apprehensive and I believed that she feared our arrival meant her departure. I smiled at her and she returned my smile. She seemed to read my thoughts and to thank me for them.

Louise was enchanting. She reminded me a little of Fleur, which was not surprising, as they were half sisters. She had fair, curly hair and delightful blue eyes; her nose was small and pretty, but she lacked the tigerish look which I had noticed when I first saw Lavinia, who at that time would have been very little older than Louise. She was a pretty child, but she had missed her mother's great beauty. She was a little shy and stayed close to the Indian woman, to whom she was clearly attached. The boy was not quite two years old. He was taking his first steps and was a little uncertain of his balance.

When Alice picked him up he studied her intently and seemed to find her not unpleasing.

"Louise will be your pupil, Drusilla," said Lavinia.

"Hello, Louise," I said. "We are going to learn some wonderful things together."

She regarded me solemnly and when I smiled she returned my smile. I thought we should get on well together. I had always been attracted by children and although I had had little contact with them I seemed to have a natural empathy with them.

Lavinia watched us a little impatiently. I felt sad for her children. Their affection for the ayah was obvious, but Lavinia appeared to be almost a stranger to them. I wondered how Dougal was with them.

Lavinia did not want to linger in the nursery. She insisted on taking me away.

"There is so much to arrange," she said. She turned a dazzling smile on Alice. "I can see you are going to manage everything perfectly."

Alice looked gratified and I guessed she was assuming—correctly—that there would be no—or very little—interference in the nursery.

I went to my room to unpack and I was aware of a feeling of exhilaration such as I had not felt for a long time.

Each day was a new adventure. I had decided that at first two hours' tuition for Louise would be enough, and Lavinia was ready to agree with anything I suggested. I went riding with her in a carriage through the town, past the burial place of the Parsees, where their bodies were left in the dry, hot air that the vultures might leave nothing but their bones. I was fascinated by so much that I saw and I wanted to savour it to the full. Everything was so new and exotic.

Occasionally Alice and I ventured out together. We liked to walk through the streets, which were a continual fascination to us. We were assailed on all sides by the beggars, whose conditions appalled and distressed us. The deformed children worried me more even than the emaciated-looking men and women who exposed their infirmities to win one's sympathy and cash. Alice and I used to take a certain amount of money out with us, which we would give to what we considered to be the worst cases, but we had been warned many times that when we were seen to give we should be pestered unmercifully. We accepted this and eased our consciences.

There seemed to be a plague of flies which ascended on the goods for display, on the white garments of the veiled women, on the pink and yellow turbans of the dignified gentlemen and, most disconcertingly, on the faces of the people, who apparently were so accustomed to them that they ignored them.

We watched the snake charmer piping his rather dismal tunes; we strolled through street after narrow street, past coolies, past water carriers with their brass pots on their shoulders, past donkeys laden with goods. Sometimes we heard the strains of unfamiliar music mingling with the shouts of the people. Most of the shops were frontless and we could see the wares spread out before us, presided over by their owners, who would do their best to lure us to pause and examine. There were foodstuffs, copper ware, silks and jewellry. Presiding over these last was a plump man in a glorious pink turban smoking a hookah. Cattle often lumbered through the streets. Small boys ran among us, often naked except for a grubby loincloth, like mischievous gnats darting around seeking the right moment to rob the vulnerable.

Alice and I bought some Bokhara silk, which we thought amazingly cheap and which was very beautiful. Mine was blue and pale mauve, Alice's biscuit colour. Lavinia had said that my clothes were awful and that there was a very good *darzi* who made up materials with speed and efficiency at a very low price. She would help me to choose a style that would suit me and he would be only too pleased to come to the house. All the Europeans used him; all one had to do was tell him what was wanted. He could be paid the price he asked without the usual native haggle. Praise meant as much to him as the money.

Lavinia took quite an interest in my appearance; she was enthusiastic about my clothes. I felt she had some motive. Lavinia, I believed, would always have a motive.

She moved in an Army and Company set, for these two appeared to work closely together. The Company was more than just a trading company. It was part of the government of the country, it seemed, and the Army was there to support it. It stood for British interests in India.

Lavinia was contented, and that meant something. I was

certain she had a lover. I had come to realize that Lavinia was the sort of woman who must always have a lover. Admiration and what she would call love were essential to her. She attracted men without even trying and when she did try the effect was great. I had intercepted glances between her and a certain Major Pennington Brown. He was a man in his early forties with a mouse of a wife who, I imagined, at one time had thought him wonderful. Perhaps she no longer did. I thought him rather foppish and affected, but he certainly was handsome.

I tackled Lavinia about him. She said, "Oh, spying already, are you?"

"No great effort was needed. I just assumed there was an intrigue in progress. I know the signs. They haven't changed much since your French Comte put in his untimely appearance."

"Garry is rather sweet and he absolutely dotes on me."

So Major Pennington Brown was Garry!

"I am sure his wife agrees with you."

"She's a poor little thing."

"Evidently he didn't think so once. He must have found her attractive to have married her."

"Her fortune was very attractive."

"I see. And you find such conduct 'rather sweet'?"

"Now please don't take up that tone. Remember . . ."

"I am the servant. Very well . . ."

"Hush! Hush! I shall certainly not allow you to go home in high dudgeon . . . whatever that is. I like Garry if you don't, and why shouldn't he find *me* attractive?"

"As he is looking for just a light love affair, I suppose he would."

"Just a light love affair! Don't speak so slightingly of such a delightful occupation. What do you know of light love affairs?"

"Nothing, and never want to."

"Oh, we are so virtuous, are we?"

"We are not stupid, if that's what you mean."

"Well, I think you are if you refuse to indulge in what is really a great pleasure." Her eyes narrowed. "I'll make you change your mind one day . . . you see."

Now I knew what she was planning for me. She wanted

261

me to find someone among that social circle of hers, someone with whom I should have a light love affair. She wanted someone to giggle with, to share chat of our experiences. I could not really think why Lavinia would be so eager to have me here when she could find so many Army or Company wives who would much more suitably fill her need for companionship.

I did not like her circle of friends; they seemed to me superficial and not very interesting. But I enjoyed my sessions with Louise, who was a delightful child, interested in the picture books I had brought with me. She liked me to tell her simple stories, and when I came into the nursery she would hurry to me and bury her head in my skirts in enthusiastic welcome. Already I loved the child.

The ayah would sometimes sit watching us, nodding her head and smiling. Our love for Louise had made a bond between us.

It was in the gardens that I came upon her on one occasion. I had a feeling that she had followed me from the house and had chosen a suitable moment to speak to me.

There was a gazebo in the gardens—a favourite spot of mine. It looked over a beautiful lawn, in the centre of which was a spreading banyan tree.

She approached me and said, "Please . . . may I talk?"

"Of course," I replied. "Do sit down. Isn't it beautiful here? How lovely that tree is . . . and the grass is so green."

"Much rain make it so."

"Do you want to talk about Louise?"

She nodded.

"She loves to learn," I said. "It is a joy to teach her. I think she is an enchanting little girl."

"She is to me . . . my own baby."

"Yes," I said. "I know."

"And now . . ."

"Are you afraid that now the nanny is here you will be sent away?"

She looked at me with wide, piteous eyes. "Louise . . ." she said, "is like my baby . . . I do not want to lose."

I took her hand and pressed it. "I understand," I told her.

"Missie Alice . . . she new nanny. Poor ayah . . . no more."

"The children love you," I said.

A smile spread across her face, but the sorrow returned.

"I will be told," she said. "I will be told . . . go."

"And that would make you very sad."

"Very sad," she repeated.

"Why do you tell me? Do you think I could change this?"
She nodded.

"Memsahib Countess like you very much. She listen. She is very happy you come. All the time say, 'Where is Missie Drusilla?' " She pointed at me. "You listen . . . but she not listen. I think she will say Go."

"I tell you what I'll do. I will speak to her. I will tell her how the children love you. I will say it is best that you stay."

Her smile was dazzling. She stood up, put her hands together and bowed her head as though in prayer. Then she moved gracefully away, leaving me staring at the banyan tree but seeing nothing but the ayah coming to the house, taking over the care of Louise, growing to love the child, being excited at the prospect of another child, and in due course giving the same devotion to Alan. And then all this love and care was to be terminated because of Lady Harriet's whim. Lady Harriet knew nothing of the true circumstances here and would not understand the love that could exist between an Indian nurse and her English charges.

I took the first opportunity to speak to Lavinia. She was taking a rest before preparing for the evening, which would be a gathering of friends before dinner. I had been present on several of these occasions, where she graciously introduced me as her friend from England. I had been quizzed by the men, who might have thought I would be an easy conquest, but the effort of attempting my seduction must have seemed hardly worthwhile to them; and when it was discovered that I was the governess, brought into contact with them through the generosity of Lavinia, I was more or less politely ignored. These sessions had become ones which I wanted to avoid whenever possible.

She was lying on her bed, pads of cotton wool over her eyes.

"Lavinia," I said, "I want to have a word with you."

"Didn't they tell you I was resting?"

"Yes, but I came all the same."

"Something important?" She lifted the cotton wool from her right eye and looked at me.

"Very important."

"Do tell me. You've changed your mind and want to come to the party? All right. Wear the mauve Bokhara. It's the best thing you have."

"It is not that. How many servants do you employ here?"

"What a question to ask me! Ask Khansamah. He's the one who would know."

"So many that one makes little or no difference."

"I suppose you are right."

"I wanted to speak to you about the ayah."

"What about her? She'll be going soon."

"I don't think she should go."

"Well, Nanny Philwright will want to be rid of her, I'm sure."

"She doesn't want to."

"She has told you so?"

"Yes. You see, Louise loves her."

"Oh, children love everybody."

"That's not true. Listen, Lavinia. That ayah has been with those children since Louise was born. She represents something to the child. Security, stability. Can't you see that?"

Lavinia was beginning to look bored. She wanted to talk to me about a certain Captain Ferryman who was making Major Pennington Brown decidedly jealous.

But I was determined. "Lavinia, it won't make any difference to you whether the ayah is here or not."

"Then why bother me with it?"

"Because you can change everything for her. She is a most unhappy woman."

"Is she?"

"Listen, Lavinia, I want you to do something for *me*."

"Unto half of my kingdom, as they say in the fairy stories."

"Oh, not as much as that."

"Then it is yours."

"Be serious. I want you to let the ayah stay."

"Is that all?"

"It's a great deal to her."

"And what is it to you?"

"I care, Lavinia. I want her to be happy. I want Louise to be happy. If she goes away they will both be miserable."

"Look here, Drusilla. Why are you so intense about it? Why should I care whether the woman goes or stays?"

"I know you don't care about these things, but I do."

She laughed at me. "You're such an odd creature, Drusilla. You have the most queer obsessions. I don't care what you do. Keep the ayah if you want to, as long as Nanny Philwright doesn't mind. I don't want trouble there. She mustn't be upset. Mama would be cross, because she is her choice."

"I can assure you that Alice Philwright will agree with me. She has the welfare of Louise at heart. Alan already loves her, too."

"Pass me the mirror. Do you think I am getting too plump?"

"As far as your looks go you are beautiful."

"So it is only my soul that is black?"

"Not exactly black."

"Not shining white either."

"No. But I think you are not entirely beyond redemption."

"And if I grant your wish will you plead for me when you reap the rewards of your virtue and I am consigned to the flames?"

"I promise."

"All right then. Request granted."

"I may tell ayah that you wish her to stay on?"

"Tell her what you want to."

I went to the bed and kissed the top of her head. "Thank you, Lavinia. You don't know how happy you've made me."

"Then stop and talk to me till it is time for them to come and dress me. I want to tell you about Captain Ferryman, who is really very good looking. He's quite clever, too. They say he has wit."

So I listened and made the comments she expected until the maid came in to help prepare her.

It was a small price to pay for victory.

When I told the ayah that there was no question of her being sent away, she took my hand and kissed it reverently.

I drew it away, murmuring, "It was nothing . . . it is right that you should stay."

But she continued to regard me with her soulful eyes.

Alice said to me afterwards, "The ayah looks upon you as a kind of all-powerful goddess."

I told her what had happened.

"I think you have earned her eternal gratitude," she said.

Louise was changing. She was now a very happy child. She was ready to love anyone who showed her affection. She had her ayah and along we had come: Nanny and myself. Alice was strict but loving; she was completely fitted for the job and she filled it with efficiency. Alan loved her, too. Young as he was, I was teaching him. He liked the pictures in the books I had brought and could already pick out certain animals which I had pointed out to him.

Louise liked to sing. She loved the nursery rhymes I taught her and the strains of "Ba, Ba, Black Sheep" and "Ring a Ring of Roses" could often be heard.

It was a happy nursery. I was delighted with my task and so was Alice. But I had, though, a strong feeling of transience. This was ephemeral.

There was talk of our going to Delhi, which we must do sooner or later.

"We shall leave the Army personnel here, I expect," said Lavinia ruefully. She was enjoying the rivalry between her captain and her major. She had repeatedly tried to bring me into her circle of friends, but my reception of them was as lukewarm as theirs of me.

Lavinia was irritated. "You make me angry," she said. "You take no pains. You make no effort."

"Do you want me to roll my eyes and flutter my fan as you do?"

"You'll never get anyone with that 'keep off' air of yours. You might just as well write it on a board and carry it round your neck."

"It's in contrast to your 'come hither' approach."

That made her laugh. "Drusilla, you'll be the death of me. I shall die of laughing at you."

"What I say is true."

" 'Come hither' anyway is more friendly than 'keep off.' "

"It helps to maintain that devastating attraction of yours. Your way of going on is tantamount to an invitation to all and sundry. 'Lover wanted. No lengthy courtship necessary.' "

"I wonder why I put up with you."

"There is an alternative."

"Oh, are we back at the dreary subject? I give in. You amuse me too much for me to let you go. I shall just ignore you and put on my 'come hither' look whenever I wish."

"I didn't expect anything else."

And so we continued to banter and there was no doubt that Lavinia was happy to have me here. One of the things she enjoyed most was shocking me.

One day when I went to the schoolroom the ayah was there with a young girl who must have been about eleven or twelve years old. She was a strikingly lovely child. Her long black hair was tied back with a silver ribbon and she wore a pale-pink sari which set off the smoothness of dark skin. Her eyes were large and luminous.

"This, Missie, my niece."

I said I was very pleased to make her acquaintance.

"She . . . Roshanara."

"Roshanara," I repeated. "What a lovely name."

The ayah smiled and nodded.

"Is she visiting you?"

The ayah nodded. "Missie let her stay . . . listen to Missie Louise."

"But, of course," I said.

And as I sat with Louise over the books, Roshanara watched and listened intently.

Roshanara was exceptionally beautiful, even for an Indian girl. Her natural grace was delightful to watch. She already spoke English tolerably well. She loved learning and it was delightful to see her rather solemn little face break into a smile when she mastered some unfamiliar word. Louise loved having her with us, and those two hours teaching were some of the most enjoyable of my days.

I learned a little about Roshanara. She was the ayah's niece, her father being a prosperous tradesman, and she was heiress to a little money, which meant that her marriage prospects were good. She was already betrothed to a young man a year older than herself. He was the son of the Great Khansamah, who presided over the house in Delhi.

"The house," Ayah told me, "where live the great sahibs . . . Memsahib Countess's sahib and her sahib brother."

I found out more about this house from Lavinia. It was a Company house, as most of the houses were, and they were kept up for the convenience of important directors of the Company. The house in Delhi was grander than this one in Bombay, but Lavinia found this more cosy. I think she meant that here she was free of her husband and the censorious eye of her brother.

According to Roshanara, the house in Delhi was under the command of the Great Khansamah, who was a very important gentleman indeed. He was employed by the Company, as the Khansamah in Bombay was, and it was their duty to look after the comforts of important gentlemen sent out from England—I presumed such as Fabian and Dougal.

The man in Delhi was known as Great Khansamah Nana. Later I wondered whether this was his real name or one given to him for his authoritative attitude to all those who came under his sway. I had not heard then of Nana Sahib, the revolutionary leader who was obsessed by his hatred of the British. It seems strange, looking back. that we should have been completely unaware of the gathering storm.

The Great Khansamah Nana had a son, and it was to this son that Roshanara was betrothed. When the household moved to Delhi, which would be before long, the marriage would be celebrated.

"You are looking forward to it?" I asked Roshanara.

I looked into those limpid eyes and saw a hint of fear overshadowed by resignation.

"It is what must be," she said.

"You are too young to be married."

"It is the age to be married."

"And you have never seen your bridegroom!"

"No. I shall not until we are married."

Poor child! I thought, and I felt very tender towards her. We were becoming good friends. I talked to her often and I fancied she found confidence, which grew out of our friendship.

As for the ayah, she looked on with contentment. She was happy. She was to remain with her beloved children and her beloved niece was with her—learning, as she said, from a very clever lady.

I had been apprehensive as to my skill as a governess, but I really was beginning to congratulate myself that I was rather good at it.

In two years' time we were to return to England. Then, of course, Louise, probably under the guidance of Lady Harriet, would have a professional governess and be taught all the things an English young lady should know. In the meantime I would suffice.

Lavinia sent for me. It was afternoon, when a silence lay over the house. There was no sound but that of the creaking punkahs as the sleepy boys worked the pulleys.

Lavinia was lying on her bed, looking languid in a green peignoir, which contrasted charmingly with the tawny shades of her hair.

I sat on the edge of the bed.

"We're going to Delhi," she said. "Orders from above."

"Oh?" I said. "Are you pleased?"

She grimaced. "Not really. It was getting quite interesting here."

"You mean the rivalry between the handsome major and the ambitious captain?"

"Oh, is he ambitious?"

"To enjoy your obvious charms."

"Oh, thank you. A compliment from you means a good deal, because you don't give them often. You're one of the dreadful honest people who have to tell the truth at all costs. You're the sort who'd go through fire and torment rather than tell one little white lie."

"And you would tell them without compunction."

269

"I knew you couldn't continue to praise me. Seriously, Drusilla. We have to depart next week."

"That's short notice surely."

"They think it rather long, and I'm only getting it because of the children. Otherwise it would be up and away with twenty-four hours' notice. Someone is coming out to Bombay . . . Papa, Mama and three children. They want the house so we have to go to Delhi . . . where we should be in any case."

"So we set out next week?"

She nodded.

"It will be interesting to see Delhi."

"Dougal will be there and, I expect . . . Fabian."

"You will be delighted to see your husband and your brother again."

She pursed her voluptuous lips with faint distaste.

"Oh," I said, "I suppose it will mean you have to behave with a little more decorum than you usually display."

"Can you see me acting with decorum? I shall be myself. No one is going to change me. It's quite a business moving the nursery. It's a good thing Ayah is here. We have to ride in those wretched *dâk-gharis,* as they call the awful things. I can tell you, it will be most uncomfortable."

"Well, I did survive that journey across the desert, which is not exactly the most comfortable I have undertaken."

"You wait till you see our *dâk.* It's a long journey and there are the children."

"I don't suppose you will worry much about them."

"They will have Nanny Philwright and the ayah . . . not to mention their resourceful governess."

"What about Roshanara?" I asked.

"Oh, that young girl who is going to marry Great Khan-samah's son. She'll go with us. We can't afford to offend G.K."

"G.K.?"

"Oh, come. Where are your wits? Great Khansamah, of course. He rules the household, I gather, with a rod of iron. You need someone of Mama's calibre to stand up to him. Dougal could never do it. Fabian could, of course. But he would consider it a waste of time."

"So," I said, "we in the nursery shall be making tracks for Delhi?"

"Exactly so . . . with the rest of us."

"I shall look forward to seeing more of India," I said. And I was thinking: Fabian will be there. I wonder what he will be like now.

Preparation went on apace. Ayah was delighted that she was accompanying us. She told me she owed her happiness to me. She knew that it was my word with Memsahib Countess that had made it possible for her to stay.

"This I never forget," she told me earnestly.

"It was nothing," I assured her; but she would not have it so. She told me she was happy because she would see her niece married. She loved Roshanara dearly and she was delighted that she would make a grand marriage.

Roshanara was less content, and as the days passed she grew more and more apprehensive.

"You see . . . I do not know him," she confided in me.

"It seems wrong to marry you to someone whom you have never seen."

She turned her sad, fatalistic eyes on me. "It happens all girls," she said. "Sometimes happy . . . sometimes not."

"I heard he is an important young man."

"Son of Great Khansamah in Delhi," she told me, not without pride. "Grand Khansamah is very great gentleman. It is an honour, they say, for me to marry his son."

"He is about your age. You'll grow up together. That might be good."

She shivered a little. I could see she was trying to comfort herself by painting a rosy picture in which she could not believe.

In due course we were ready to leave. Baggage had already gone off in horsedrawn carriages, all cleverly packed by the servants on the instructions of the Khansamah—not the great one, of course, but a very impressive gentleman for all that. Now it was our turn.

It was a long journey and, having travelled before, I was prepared for acute discomfort.

I was, perhaps, on the whole, a little too pessimistic.

Our *dâk-ghari* was a badly constructed carriage drawn by a wild-looking horse. There were several of these vehicles for our party. I was with Lavinia and a certain Captain Cranly who, I suppose, was there to protect us. The children travelled in a *dâk* that they shared with Alice, the ayah and Roshanara, with the small amount of luggage that we would need for the journey. In another *dâk* we had our brass pots, which we would use for washing, and mattresses on which we could sleep if there were no beds in the rest houses where we would stay during the journey.

And so we set off.

It was, as India always would be, interesting, stimulating and intensely exciting, but so intent were we on keeping our balance as the *dâk* lurched along that we could not give our full attention to the scenery.

Lavinia was sighing for a palanquin, which would have made the journey so much more comfortable. A palanquin, she told me, was a kind of litter, with bedding inside on which the occupant could recline in comfort. They were suspended on poles, which four men carried.

"Rather hard on the men," I commented.

"They are used to it. I think I shall refuse to travel any more without a palanquin."

The journey seemed long. We stopped at several of the *dâk*-bungalows, which bore a striking resemblance to the caravan-serai that we had discovered in the desert on the way from Cairo to Suez. We were usually given chicken and oatmeal bread there, and we had tea, too, with goat's milk, which I did not like very much. Still, hunger seasons all dishes, they say; and it certainly did on that journey to Delhi.

Every time we stopped the children greeted us as though they had not seen us for months, which amused us very much.

And in due course we saw in the distance the red stone walls of beautiful Delhi.

To ride through that city was an exhilarating experience. My first impressions filled me with excited anticipation. I wished that I had a guide with me to answer my eager questions and explain what these impressive buildings were.

The walled city stands on high ground, with a commanding view over verdant woods. Domes, minarets and gardens gave it a touch of mystery that enthralled me. I saw the red walls of the Fort, the old palace of Shah Jehan. I yearned to know more of its history. I thought suddenly: How Dougal must enjoy this.

We went through the city past Jama Masjid, the great mosque, which was surely one of the finest structures in India. I caught a glimpse of the imperial tombs. I did not know what the future held, but I did know I would always be glad that I had seen India.

And so we came to Delhi.

The house was much grander than the one in Bombay.

We were met by the Great Khansamah, a middle-aged man with more dignity than I have ever seen in any other person. The house might have been his and we distinguished guests, but not quite of his high caste.

He clapped his hands and servants came running. He cast an eye on Roshanara and his expression was censorious. I remembered that this was her future father-in-law; and I hoped for her sake he would not live too close to the married couple.

"Welcome to Delhi," he said, as though he owned the city.

We found ourselves talking to him deferentially. Watching him, I saw his eyes linger on Lavinia with a certain gleam in them which I had noticed in the eyes of others when they looked at her. She was aware of it and did not resent it.

We were taken to the rooms that had been assigned to us. There were punkahs everywhere and I noticed there was no surreptitious idling here.

I kept thinking of one thing: I shall soon meet Dougal . . . and Fabian.

Alice, with the ayah, took the children to their quarters. I was shown to my room, which looked down across the veranda to the stately pipal tree with its abundant green foliage. The garden onto which I gazed was beautiful. In the pond, water lilies and lotus flowers floated under a tall, feathery tamarind tree.

There was a feeling of serenity and peaceful beauty. Later I tried to tell myself that it was a brooding calm before the storm, but I believe that did not occur to me at the time.

After a while I went along to see how Alice was settling the children in. Their quarters were more spacious then those

in Bombay. Roshanara was there. I noticed she shivered inter-
mittently.

I said, "All will be well."

She looked at me pleadingly, as if I had the power to help
her.

"I feel it in my bones," I added with a smile.

"My bones tell different."

I believed it was the overbearing Great Khansamah who
had struck fear into her heart.

I said, "Stern fathers often have gentle sons. You see, they
have been brought up strictly and perhaps suffered. It makes
them kind and understanding."

She listened attentively. I thought: Poor child! What a sad
fate to be given in marriage to a stranger. I, who had successfully evaded the efforts of Lady Harriet to marry me off to
Colin Brady, could feel especially sorry for frail Roshanara.

Alice was delighted with the new nursery. She, too, was
finding life strange and exhilarating; but sometimes I detected
a wistfulness in her eyes and I guessed then that she was thinking of Tom Keeping. A thought struck me: He had come to
Delhi; he worked for the Company. Perhaps we should see him
again soon. That thought delighted me. Alice was such a good
sort. She should have children of her own rather than lavish
affection on those of other people who, as the ayah had stressed,
could so easily be snatched from her.

After leaving the children I went back to my room. Lavinia was there, sprawling in one of the armchairs.

"Where have you been?" she demanded.

"Just giving them a hand in the nursery."

"I've been waiting for you."

I did not apologise. I was a little irritated by her lack of
interest in the children's welfare.

"You will dine with us tonight?"

"Oh, should I?"

"Dougal will be there. So will Fabian, I expect . . . unless
they are dining somewhere else, which they often have to do.
Company business crops up."

"I see. But I am here as the governess."

"Don't talk nonsense. They know you. Dougal rather well,

I fancy. There would be an outcry if you were put in the category of servant . . . even higher servant."

"I don't suppose they would notice."

"Don't you fish for compliments from me. That's my province. I want you there. There'll be lots of boring conversation about the Company, of course. You and I can chatter on the side."

"Well, if I shall serve a useful purpose . . ."

She laughed at me. "I wish we'd stayed in Bombay. Those awful *dâk* things. They were horrible. I shall reprimand Dougal for not sending palanquins for us to ride in. I shall say it is an insult to the Company to have Company people's memsahibs riding around in those awful things. They might take some notice if I put it that way. Why couldn't we have stayed?"

"I know you hate to leave the romantic major and the aspiring captain behind."

She snapped her fingers. "Oh, they'll have a regiment here. They'll have to. This is, after all, the important place, where most of the business is done. Here and Calcutta . . . I'd rather Delhi than there . . . I must say."

"So there will be replacements for the gallant pair."

"There is no need for you to worry on that account. What shall I wear tonight? That's what I wanted to ask you."

She chattered on about her clothes and I listened halfheartedly, my mind on what it would be like to see Dougal and Fabian again.

I was soon to find out.

I saw Dougal first. I had found my way to the room that was a kind of anteroom to the dining room. Dougal was already there. I had a notion that he would have heard that we had arrived and was waiting for me.

He came forward and took both my hands.

"Drusilla! What a great pleasure."

He had aged quite a bit. He had lost that air of looking out on the world and finding it full of interest. There was a faint furrow between his eyes.

"How are you, Dougal?" I asked.

He hesitated just for a second. "Oh, well, thank you. And you?"

"The same," I said.

"I was delighted when I heard you were coming . . . and so sorry to hear of your father."

"Yes. It was a great sadness."

"I shall always remember those days when we talked together." A wistful look came into his eyes. It had always been easy to read Dougal's thoughts . . . though perhaps not always, for had I not believed at one time that he was growing fond of me? Fond of me he was. But not in the way I had thought.

And then Fabian came into the room and my attention was all for him.

He stood still, legs apart, studying me. But I was not able to read him as I did Dougal. I did see his mouth turn up a little at the corners as though he found something amusing in the fact that I was here.

"Well," he said. "Miss Drusilla Delany. Welcome to India."

"Thank you," I said.

He had advanced, and he took my hands, looking intently into my face as he did so.

"Ah . . . still the same Miss Delany."

"Did you expect someone different?"

"I was hoping I would find no change. And now I am content." He spoke lightly. "What did you think of the journey?"

"Tremendously interesting. A trifle uncomfortable, but a stimulating experience."

"You take a philosophical view, I see. I knew you would, of course. And I do hope the interest and stimulation outweighed the discomfort."

Lavinia had come into the room. Both men turned to her. She looked beautiful, with her hair dressed high on her head and her somewhat diaphanous gown clinging to her superb figure.

I immediately felt like an insignificant wren in the presence of a peacock.

Dougal went to her and they kissed perfunctorily. It was not what one would have expected from a husband and wife deprived of each other's company for some months. I noticed the change in Dougal. He seemed apprehensive.

She turned to Fabian.

"Well, sister," he was saying, "you seem to look better than ever. I guess you are delighted that Miss Drusilla has joined you."

Lavinia pouted. "Oh, she disapproves of me, don't you, Drusilla?"

"I expect with reason," said Fabian.

"Drusilla would always be reasonable," added Dougal with an air of resignation.

"Of course, Drusilla is a paragon of virtue," said Lavinia mockingly.

"Well, let us hope that you profit from her example," added Fabian.

"We had better go in to dinner," said Dougal. "Great Khansamah will be annoyed if we do not."

"Then let us delay," said Fabian. "I believe that we should make the rules."

"He can be very difficult in many ways," Dougal reminded him. He turned to me. "He has complete control over the servants."

"All the same," protested Fabian, "I don't intend to let him govern my life. But I suppose the food will be spoiled if we don't go in. So perhaps Great Khansamah has reason on his side. We don't want to give Miss Drusilla a bad impression, do we?"

It was cool in the dining room—a large, salon-like place with French windows looking out onto a beautiful lawn with a pond, on which floated the familiar water lilies and lotus flowers. There was a faint hum in the air from the countless insects and I already knew that when the lamps were lighted the curtains would have to be drawn to prevent certain obnoxious creatures invading the room.

"You must tell us all about your journey," said Fabian.

I told them and mentioned our hazardous progress across the desert.

"Did you become friendly with any of your fellow passengers?" asked Fabian. "One does on ships."

"Well, there was a Frenchman. He was very helpful to us, but he was taken ill on the journey through the desert and we didn't see him again. We met someone from the Company. You will know him, I expect. A Mr. Tom Keeping."

Fabian nodded. "I trust he was helpful."

"Oh, very."

"And what do you think of India?" asked Dougal.

"I feel I have seen very little of it so far."

"Everything is different here from in England," he said a little ruefully.

"That is what I expected."

The Great Khansamah had come into the room. He was dressed in a pale blue shirt over baggy white trousers; his puggaree was white and he wore a pair of dark red shoes of which, I discovered, he was very proud. He wore them with an air that was meant to imply that they were a sign of his great position.

"Everything is to the satisfaction," he said in a voice daring us to say that it was not.

Lavinia smiled at him warmly. "It is very good," she told him. "Thank you."

"And the sahibs . . . ?" he said.

Fabian and Dougal told him that it was very satisfactory. Then he bowed and retired.

"He really has a great opinion of himself," murmured Dougal.

"The trouble is," replied Fabian, "so has the rest of the household."

"Why is he so important?" I asked.

"He is employed by the Company. This is for him a permanent post. He regards the house as his and those of us who use it are merely his passing guests. That is how he sees it. Of course, he is very efficient. I suppose that is why he is tolerated."

"I think he will be easy to get along with," said Lavinia.

"He will if he gets complete subservience," Fabian told her.

"Which you resent," I said.

"I won't have my life ruled by servants."

"I don't think he sees himself as that," said Dougal. "To himself he is the great Nabob, the ruler of us all."

"There is something about him that makes me wary," said

Fabian. "If he becomes too arrogant I shall do my best to get him replaced. Now what news from home?"

"You know the war is over," I asked.

"It is about time, too."

"They have brought the men home from the Crimea and the nurses are looking after them. They did a wonderful job."

"Thanks to the redoubtable Miss Nightingale."

"Yes," I said. "It took a great deal of hard work to make people listen to her."

"Well, the war is over," said Fabian. "And it ended in victory for us—a Pyrrhic victory, I fear. The losses were tremendous and the French and Russians suffered more than we did, I believe. But our losses were great."

"Thank Heaven it is all over," said Dougal.

"It took us a long time," commented Fabian. "And . . . I don't think it has done us much good here."

"You mean in India?" I asked.

"They watch closely what the British are doing and I have come to the conclusion that attitudes have changed a little since it started."

He was frowning as he looked into his glass.

Lavinia yawned. She said, "I believe the shops here are very much like those in Bombay."

Fabian laughed. "And that is a matter of the utmost importance, which you will no doubt quickly investigate."

"Why should the attitude change because of a war far away?" I asked.

Fabian leaned his arms on the table and looked intently at me. "The Company has brought great good to India . . . so we think. But it is never easy for one country to impose its customs on another. Even though the changes in some cases may be for the better, there is necessarily a certain resentment."

"There is undoubtedly resentment here," agreed Dougal.

"And it alarms you?" I asked.

"Not exactly," replied Fabian. "But I think we have to be watchful."

"Is that one of the reasons why the despotic rule of the Great Khansamah is tolerated?"

"I see you have grasped the situation very quickly."

"Oh, Drusilla is so clever," said Lavinia. "Far cleverer than I could ever be."

"You do show a certain perception, since you are able to see it," said her brother. "Although I must say it is rather obvious."

"Fabian is always beastly to me," said Lavinia, pouting.

"I am truthful, dear sister." He turned to me. "Things have changed a little in the last year or so. And I think it may have something to do with the war. There were accounts in the papers of the suffering endured by our men and of the long siege of Sebastopol. I sensed that some were regarding that with a certain satisfaction."

"But surely our prosperity helps *them.*"

"It does, but all people are not so logical as you and I. There is something such as cutting off one's nose to spite one's face. I fancy there are many here who would be ready to do just that . . . to let their own prosperity suffer for the sake of seeing us humiliated."

"It sounds rather a senseless attitude to take up."

"There is a strong sense of national pride in us all," put in Dougal. "Independence is dear to most of us, and some fear to lose it, even if retaining it means dispensing with certain comforts."

"What would be the result of this feeling?" I asked.

"Nothing we shouldn't be able to handle," said Fabian. "But it shows itself now and then. The Khansamah of this house is a man of overweening pride, as you have seen."

"I think he is rather fun," said Lavinia.

"If you recognize that he is the head of the household, all will be well,"said Fabian. "I believe he is not a man whom it would be wise to cross."

"What could he do?"

"Make things uncomfortable in a hundred ways. The servants would obey him. They daren't do anything else. If there is a growing restlessness in the country, it is probably due to the way we have brought in new laws. They are afraid we are going to impose our ways on them to such an extent that their native institutions will be stifled out of existence."

"Is it right to do that?" I asked.

Fabian looked at me and nodded. "Thuggery. Suttee . . .

they are evils which have been suppressed by the British. You looked surprised. I see you are unaware of these matters. Both are pernicious, wicked, cruel customs long overdue for suppression. We have made the performance of them against the law. There were many Indians who lived in fear of these practices, but at the same time they resent our coming here and making them criminal acts. Dougal, of course, has made a study of all this."

"He would," said Lavinia.

Dougal did not glance at her. He turned to me. "It is the Hindustani Thaga. We have called it thuggery. It is a worship of the goddess Kali, who must be the most bloodthirsty of all gods and goddesses ever thought of. She demands perpetual blood. Those who take the oath to her are by profession murderers. It is considered an honourable profession . . . to murder."

"Surely everyone agrees that it is good to stop that," I said.

"Everyone . . . except the Thugs themselves. But it is interference by foreigners with the customs of the country."

"People must have been terrified."

"It was a religious community. Those people who took the oath lived by murder. It was not important whom they murdered, as long as they killed. They lived on the plunder they took from their victims, but the motive was not robbery, but to placate their goddess. They banded together in groups, falling in with travellers, seeking their confidences and choosing the appropriate moment to murder them."

"How . . . diabolical!"

"They usually killed by strangulation."

"Quite a number of them made use of the thorn apple," said Fabian.

"Oh, that's a special sort of drug," said Dougal. "It grows profusely here. The leaves and seeds are used in medicine. When the leaves are dry they have a narcotic smell. You'd recognize this plant when you see it. The name is actually datura, but they call it thorn apple. You can see the tubular five-cleft calyx with a large carolla, shaped rather like a funnel. It has a prickly sort of capsule."

"Trust Dougal to get the scientific description," said Lavinia mockingly.

"There's nothing scientific about that," said Dougal. "It is just easy for anyone to see."

"I fancy I wouldn't recognize it if I saw it," said Lavinia. "Would you, Drusilla?"

"I don't think so for a moment."

"There you are, Dougal. You're boring us with your description. I want to hear more about the poison."

"It's deadly," said Dougal. "A peculiar alkaloid called daturina can be distilled from it. Some of the natives use it as a drug. When they do, they become wildly excited. The world seems a beautiful place and they are almost delirious."

"And they like that?" I asked.

"Oh yes, indeed," said Dougal. "It makes them feel wonderful . . . while it lasts. But I believe it is followed by acute depression, which is usual in the case of these substances. Moreover, it can be very dangerous and in the end fatal."

"You were saying that these thugs used it to kill their victims."

"It was one of their methods," replied Fabian, "but I believe the more usual was strangulation."

"I should have thought most people would have been greatly relieved that these thugs had been put out of action by the law."

Fabian lifted his shoulders and looked at the ceiling.

"It is a matter of what we were saying . . . independence or better rule. There are those who will always want the former. It is the same with suttee."

"That was abolished about the same time as thuggery," Dougal told me. "They really have a great deal to be thankful for to Lord William Bentinck. He was the governor of Madras for twenty years and then he became Governor General from 1828 to '35. You know what happens in suttee. A husband dies and his wife leaps into his funeral pyre and is burned to death with his body."

"How terrible!"

"So thought we all, and Lord William brought in the laws condemning suttee and thuggery," added Fabian.

"It was a great step forward," commented Dougal.

"Do you know?" put in Fabian. "I believe both are still practised in some remote places. It is a defiance of British rule."

Lavinia yawned again and said, "Really, this is getting like a history lesson!"

"A fascinating one," I said.

"Drusilla, don't be such a prig! You infuriate me. You just encourage them. I know what she's going to say. 'If you don't like it, I'll go back home.' She's always threatening me with going back home."

"That," said Fabian gravely, "is something we must persuade her not to do."

I was happy suddenly. It was the experience I had known before. It was like coming alive.

For the rest of the evening we talked of India, of the various castes and religions. Looking out on the lawn, I thought it was one of the most peaceful scenes I had ever encountered.

When I retired that night, it was long before I slept. I kept thinking about the evening, the old cruel customs of the country and the fact that I was living under the same roof as the two men—I had to admit it—who had been most important in my life: Dougal and Fabian. How different they were! I was a little alarmed by the wistfulness I saw in Dougal's eyes. He was sad and regretful. It was not difficult to see that his marriage had brought disillusionment to him; and he seemed, even in the brief time we had been together, to be turning to me for solace. I thought I would have to be careful. As for Fabian, he had changed little. I must not allow myself to become too impressed by him. I must remember that he was a Framling and they did not change. They would always believe that the world was made for them, and all the people in it made to suit their purpose. Moreover, I must not forget that Lady Geraldine might soon be coming out to marry him.

Almost immediately Roshanara was married. We did not attend the ceremony, which was carried out in accordance with the ancient Indian custom. Asraf, the young bridegroom, I heard from the ayah, was about a year older than Roshanara.

"Poor children," said Alice. "I pray that life will not be too difficult for little Roshanara and her husband."

We saw the decorated carriages, for it was a grand occasion presided over by the Great Khansamah, who looked very magnificent. I saw the glitter of jewels in his puggaree.

I did not see Roshanara after her wedding. She was leaving
with her husband for the tea plantation where he worked for
his uncle, and it was some distance away. I wondered whether
the uncle was as grand as Asraf's father; but it was difficult to
imagine that anyone could be that.

We had settled into a routine. We had made a schoolroom
in the nursery and there I taught the children. We all missed
Roshanara. Alan was becoming quite a little person now.

They were happy. The change of scene had affected them
very little, because they had those they loved and relied on
about them. It was sad, Alice said, that their mother was not
very interested in them, but I replied that she never had been,
so they would not notice. True, she was their mother, but titles
were not important and they were content with Alice, Ayah
and me. We represented their close little world and they asked
for nothing more.

Lavinia was somewhat pleased with the move now that she
was settling in. Delhi was more fashionable than Bombay;
there was more going on and naturally there was a greater
military presence here, which pleased her.

"More handsome officers to choose from," I told her sardonically.

She put her tongue out at me.

"Jealous?" she asked.

"Not in the least."

"Liar."

I shrugged my shoulders. "Have it your way."

"Poor Drusilla, if you'd only *pretend* to think they're marvellous they would like you."

"I leave all that to you."

She laughed secretly.

As usual she was very preoccupied with her appearance
and what clothes she should wear to enhance it. She had found
some exotic perfume, which pleased her. I was amazed how
little her experiences had changed her. The sordid affair with
the mock Comte had passed her, leaving her unrepentant and
able to forget Fleur as though she did not exist. Others had
taken care of that misdemeanour. I think she must have imagined that there would always be those around her to do that.
But in her way she was fond of me. She enjoyed shocking me;

she liked my veiled criticism. If ever I suggested going she was alarmed. That gave me the weapon I needed against her now and then. She realized this and accepted it. And in spite of everything I had a fondness for her, too, though often I thought her behaviour outrageous.

She had followed the custom of the ladies of the household by interviewing the Khansamah each morning to discuss the day's menu. This surprised me, for in Bombay, where it had also been her duty, she had shirked it. But now she did it regularly. I was to discover why.

The Great Khansamah would come with his usual pomp to the upper part of the house and Lavinia would receive him in the little boudoir-type room close to her bedroom. She would be wearing a beribboned peignoir or some equally feminine garment, which I thought unwise.

She did not seem to be aware that this was a ceremony—a ritual almost. The lady of the house should sit at a table, dignified and precise, listen attentively to the suggestions made by the Khansamah, sometimes query them and make a suggestion herself, and then give way or insist, whichever etiquette demanded.

The procedure was quite different with Lavinia. I knew why she bothered. It was because the dignified Khansamah emerged sufficiently from his regal aura to imply that he considered her beautiful.

Dougal and Fabian were away for most of the day. Sometimes they dined at the house; at others they did so elsewhere. Dougal came more often than Fabian, who seemed to be more closely involved with the Company.

I took my meals with them. I had wondered how Alice felt about this, because she had hers in the nursery or in her own room. I tried to explain to her. "I think it's because I'm supposed to be here as a sort of companion to the Countess. I knew her from my childhood . . . you see . . . living close. She seems to want me there at the moment. Of course, she could change. She is very unpredictable."

"I'm happier this way," said Alice. "It suits me."

"I hope you don't mind . . . really."

"My dear Drusilla, why should I? I'm sorry for you sometimes . . . having to spend so much time with the Countess."

"I know her well. I don't let her bully me."

"She seems to be a very reckless woman."

"She has always been that."

"I guessed that, but I thought it would be different here than in England."

I agreed; and I often had uneasy twinges about Lavinia. Well, if there were scrapes here she had a husband and a brother to look after her.

We had dined. Fabian was not with us; there were just Dougal, Lavinia and myself. We had talked generally about things and as soon as the meal was over, Lavinia said that she was going to bed.

Thus Dougal and I were left alone together.

We were in the drawing room. The heat of the day was gone and the cool of the evening was delightful.

"The gardens are so beautiful in the moonlight," said Dougal. "If we put out the lamps we could draw the curtains and enjoy the scene."

This he did, drawing back the curtains. He was right. The scene was breathtakingly beautiful. I could see the pond with the blooms floating on its surface, and the banyan tree looked mysterious in the pale light.

Dougal said, "It isn't often that we get an opportunity to talk alone. It's a rare luxury, Drusilla."

"I know you are a little homesick, Dougal."

"Each day brings Home a little nearer."

"Are you determined to break away when your two years are up?"

He nodded. "I think so. People must live their own lives as they want to, don't you agree?"

"Yes, I think you are right . . . providing they don't hurt anyone in doing so."

"I was never meant for this."

"No. You were meant to live quietly surrounded by your books in the shades of academe."

"I think you know me well, Drusilla."

"One wouldn't have to, to realize what you want from life."

"I would like to be reading . . . learning all the time. There is nothing so exciting as discovering facts about the world we live in. I wonder more people don't realize it. It seems to me that most of them are chasing shadows."

"Perhaps they think you are doing the same. All people view life differently. What is excitement to one is boredom to another."

"How right you are."

"It is something we have to remember."

"I want very much to go home. I don't feel happy here. There is a brooding sense of evil in the air, I fancy."

"Do you really feel that?"

"It seems to me that these people watch us . . . purposefully. It seems they are saying, 'You don't belong here. Get out.' "

"Have you told Fabian?"

"My brother-in-law is a practical man. As they say, his feet are firmly on the ground. To be in authority here suits him as it would never suit me. So you see why I plan definitely to go home when the two years are up and stay there."

"If you feel that, why do you not go before?"

"I have to give a good warning. So far I have hinted. I have certain commitments at home, I tell them. The trouble is, the family has been connected with the Company for years. If one comes from such a family one is expected to uphold tradition."

"Poor Dougal!"

"Oh, I deserve my fate. I have made one mistake after another."

"I think that is not uncommon with most of us."

"You have made none."

I raised my eyebrows and laughed. "I am sure I have."

"No major ones. Drusilla, there is no sense in trying to cover up what is obvious. I have made just about the most ghastly mistake a man can make."

"Are you sure you want to talk to me about this, Dougal?"

"To whom else should I talk?"

"Fabian, perhaps."

"Fabian? These Framlings are too self-centred to concern themselves very much with other people's problems."

"I'm sure Fabian would be sympathetic." He did not answer and I went on, "Is it your marriage?"

"Lavinia and I have absolutely nothing in common."

A sudden wave of anger swept over me. I thought: Why do you realize this only now? It must have been obvious from the first, and why tell *me?*

"I used to enjoy our times at the rectory," he went on wistfully.

"My father did, too."

"I got the impression that we all did."

"Oh yes. We talked of interesting things."

"You always took up any subject with enthusiasm. If only . . ."

"That must be one of the most used phrases in the language."

"Do you never use it?"

"I suppose so. But it is always ineffectual. Nothing that has ever gone before can be changed."

"That doesn't prevent my saying . . . if only . . ."

"You will not be here always, and if you have made up your mind to go back and study when you get home . . . well, that is something to look forward to."

"Lavinia would never agree to live the kind of life I would want."

"That seems very likely, but why did you not think of that before?"

"I was bemused."

"Ah yes, I know."

Silence fell on us. It was broken only by the sound of an enormous flying insect passing the open door.

"He would have been in the room if we had had the lamp burning," said Dougal.

"He looked very beautiful."

"There is so much beauty here," said Dougal. "Look at the garden. Is it not exquisite . . . the trees, the pond, the flowers. There is a feeling of deep peace . . . but it is quite false, in fact. Everything in this country is mysterious. It seems to me that nothing is what it appears to be."

"Does that apply here particularly?"

"I think so. These servants who come to do our bidding . . . I often wonder what is going on in their minds. They seem almost accusing sometimes, as though they harbour resentment and blame us for it. Look at that garden. Where could you see a more peaceful-looking spot, and yet out there among the grass lurk Russelian snakes. You could even come face to face with a cobra lurking in the undergrowth."

"You make it sound like the garden of Eden with the serpent lurking," I said with a laugh.

"It is not dissimilar. You must be careful in the garden, Drusilla. These snakes are everywhere."

"I have seen one or two. Are they the pale yellowish kind?"

"Yes . . . the variegated ones. They have big oval spots, brown with a white edge to them. Avoid them. Their bite could be fatal."

"I have seen them in the bazaar emerging from the snake charmers' baskets."

"Ah yes, but those have had their poisonous fangs removed. The ones you find in the garden have not."

"It makes me shiver to think of the peaceful aspect of this place and all that danger lurking beneath it."

"It is like a mirror to life. Often great beauty will disguise emptiness . . . and sometimes evil."

In the half light I saw his sad smile. I knew he was thinking of Lavinia and I wanted to comfort him.

We sat in silence for a few moments and it was thus that Fabian found us.

He came into the room suddenly.

"Ah," he said. "Forgive me. I did not know that anyone was here. So you are sitting in the dark."

"We wanted the air but not the insects," I said.

"Well, I daresay a few of them have found their way in."

He sat down near me.

"You have had a tiring day?" I asked.

He shrugged his shoulders. "No more than usual." He stretched his long legs. "You are right," he went on. "It seems very peaceful here sitting in the dark. Tell me, have I interrupted some interesting conversation?"

"We were talking of the contrasts here. The beauty and the ugliness beneath the surface. The beautiful flowers, the green grass and the Russelian snakes out of sight and ready to strike the fatal blow."

"Danger lurking everywhere," said Fabian lightly. "But isn't that what makes it exciting?"

"I suppose most people would say yes," said Dougal.

"And what of you?" asked Fabian of me.

"I am not sure. I suppose it would depend on the lurking danger."

"And whether, having met it, you could escape it?" suggested Fabian.

"I suppose so." I stood up. "I daresay you have business to talk of. I will say good night."

"Oh, you mustn't let my coming break up this pleasant tête-à-tête."

"We were just talking idly," I said. "And I will go now."

Fabian accompanied me to the door.

"Good night," he said, and there was a quizzical expression in his eyes.

I was reminded of that conversation a few days later. I was in the garden with Alice and the children. The ayah was with us. I was talking to her about Roshanara and asking if she had heard anything of her.

She shook her head. "No . . . no. She go far away. Perhaps I never see her again."

"Oh, but she will come and see you!" I protested. "She can't be so very far."

The ayah lifted her hands and gently rocked from side to side. There was something fatalistic in her attitude.

Louise came running up to us. She was holding something in her hand.

"What is it?" I asked.

"I picked it for you," she said and handed a plant to me. I stared at it. I had never seen anything like it before.

The ayah had taken it. Her face had turned pale. She said in a frightened voice, "Thorn apple."

Memory stirred in me. What had I heard about the thorn apple? Snatches of conversation came back. It was the thorn apple from which drugs were distilled. The thugs had used it in the past to poison their victims when they did not despatch them by strangulation.

And here was Louise . . . picking it in the garden.

I could see that the ayah knew about it.

I said: "I . . . I have heard something of this plant."

She nodded.

"Where did Louise find it?"

She shook her head. "Not here. It could not be. It would not be permitted . . ."

Louise was watching us with some dismay. She was a bright child and would understand immediately that something was wrong.

"Thank you, Louise," I said. "It was kind of you to bring me the flower." I kissed her. "Tell me. Where did you find it?"

She spread her arms and waved them as though to embrace the whole of the garden.

"Here?" I said. "In the garden?"

She nodded.

I looked at the ayah. "Show us," I said.

I was holding the thing gingerly. I could smell a faint narcotic odour.

Louise was leading the way to a small gate. It was locked, but possible for one of Louise's size to crawl under it, which she proceeded to do.

"This Great Khansamah's garden," said Ayah, shaking her head.

"Come back, Louise," I called.

She stood on the other side of the gate looking at us wonderingly.

"It was in here I found your flower," she said, pointing. "Over there."

"This Great Khansamah's garden," repeated Ayah. "You must not go there. Great Khansamah . . . he be very angry."

Louise scrambled back looking alarmed.

"Never go there again," said Ayah. "It is not good."

Louise gripped her sari as though for protection. Everyone had heard of the power of the Great Khansamah.

I took the sprig into the house and burned it. Then I realized that I should have kept it and shown it to Dougal or Fabian.

I saw Dougal soon after that and told him what had happened.

"Are you sure?" he said.

291

"The ayah called it thorn apple and I remembered what you had said."

"Could you recognize it from my description?"

"Well, no . . . not exactly, but it could have been. But the ayah knew it. She would surely know and she recognized it at once."

He was silent. Then he said, "The Great Khansamah's garden is his own property and we cannot tell him what he can and cannot grow there."

"But if he is growing this drug . . ."

"He is a law unto himself."

"But he is employed by the Company and if he breaks the law . . ."

"I think it wiser to say nothing abut this just yet. After all, we have to have proof, and it could cause a great deal of trouble if we tried to prevent his growing what he wants to, in that patch of land that the Company has decided shall be for his sole use."

I wished that I had spoken to Fabian about it. I was sure his reaction would have been different.

On the other hand, I had only the ayah's word for it that it was the dreaded datura. She could so easily have been wrong, and I could imagine the outcry there would have been if we had tried to interfere with the Great Khansamah's right to grow what he wanted to in his own garden.

That very day we had a great surprise and perhaps that is why I was not more concerned at the time with the discovery of the deadly plant in the garden.

Tom Keeping came to the house.

He came face to face with us as Alice and I were preparing to take the children into the garden.

"Miss Philwright, Miss Delany," he cried, his face breaking into a delighted smile.

I was aware of Alice, a little tense beside me.

"I knew you were here," he went on. "It is a great pleasure to see you again. Are you well? Are you enjoying being here?"

I said we were and Alice agreed with me.

"I knew we should meet again sometime, and urgent business has brought me here."

"Shall you be staying?"

"That depends on many things. However, we shall be able to meet at times." He was looking at Alice. "You find it congenial?"

"Yes," she said. "I get on well with the children. Don't we?" she said, looking at Louise.

Louise nodded vigorously, staring up at Tom Keeping with interest.

"Me too," said Alan.

"Yes," said Alice, ruffling his hair. "You too, darling."

"I want to see Sir Fabian urgently," said Tom. "I am told he will be here this afternoon."

"We never know when he will be here," I told him.

"We should be getting along into the garden," said Alice.

Tom Keeping smiled. "We shall meet again soon. *Au revoir,*" he said.

Dougal had appeared. He said, "Sir Fabian will be here very soon. In the meantime, come into the study and we can talk things over."

They left us and we went into the garden.

"What a surprise!" I said.

"Yes, but I suppose as he is employed by the Company . . ." Alice's voice trailed off.

"He is such a nice man."

Alice was silent. She looked pink and flushed and younger; I noticed, too, that she was rather absentminded. I thought: It would be wonderful if he cared for her, but if he does not it would have been better if he had not come back.

Fabian returned later that day. He was closeted in his study with Dougal and Tom Keeping. They did not appear at dinner, but had something sent to the study.

Lavinia and I were alone.

"Thank goodness," she said. "I can't bear all this Company talk. You'd think there was nothing else in the world."

She chattered on about a certain young captain whom she had met the previous evening.

"So handsome, and married to the plainest girl . . . I expect it was for her money. She doesn't even know how to make the best of herself. Fancy anyone with her dark skin wearing brown."

I could not give much attention to such matters. I was thinking about Alice and Tom Keeping.

The next day we took the children into the gardens. Tom Keeping joined us. I made an excuse and left him and Alice together. Alice looked a little alarmed, but I was firm. There was something I had to do for the Countess, I lied.

I could not help feeling that Tom Keeping was rather pleased.

On the way into the house I came face to face with Fabian. He said, "Hello. Are you busy?"

"Not particularly."

"I'd like to have a talk."

"What about?" I asked.

"Things," he said.

"Where?"

"I think in my study."

I must have shown some apprehension. I had never forgotten that occasion when he had made some sort of advance when he had been under the impression that I was Fleur's mother. I could never be alone with him without wondering whether he was going to do the same again. He knew now that I was not a woman of easy virtue, but I fancied that would not prevent his belief that as a Framling and so much above me in the social scale, it would be in order to amuse himself with me for a while. Perhaps that was why I always seemed to be on the defensive. He was aware of this, I was sure. That was what was so disconcerting. He seemed to read my thoughts with ease. I had always felt that he was faintly attracted by me—not for my good looks, which were nonexistent, not for my feminine appeal, but because I was, as Lavinia had pointed out many times, prim, and a man such as he was would find it diverting to break through my armour and to see me submit to him.

I was determined not to show him that I felt excited as well as apprehensive.

He shut the door, his lips turning up at the corners. He held the chair for me and as I sat down his hand touched my shoulder. He took a chair by the table, which was between us.

"You know Tom Keeping is here," he said.

"Yes, he is in the garden with Miss Philwright and the children."

"I noticed the little charade. You discreetly left them together. Is there some relationship between Keeping and the nanny?"

"That is something you should ask them."

I saw the amused look in his eyes. It faded suddenly. "Drusilla," he said seriously, "you are a sensible girl. I wish I could say the same for my sister." He hesitated. "We are a little alarmed."

"About what?"

He waved his hands. "Everything," he said.

"I don't understand."

"I wish we did . . . more fully. Tom Keeping has a special position in the Company. He travels around a great deal. He keeps an eye . . . on things."

"You mean he is a sort of Company spy?"

"That is hardly the description I would use. You see the position we are in here. It is, after all, an alien country. Their customs are so different from ours. There are bound to be clashes. We think we could help improve conditions here. They are thinking we are an imperialistic conqueror. That is not so. We want the best for them . . . providing it is also the best for ourselves. We have made good laws for them . . . but they are our laws . . . not theirs, and they often resent them."

"I know. You have told us."

"They act in defiance to us. That is the trouble. That is what Tom is here to talk about. There has been a rather bad outbreak of thuggery some thirty miles from here. A group of four travellers have been murdered. We recognize the methods. They had no enemies . . . four innocuous men, travelling together for company. They have all been found dead in the forest near a certain inn. The innkeeper admits they stayed there. There were two men at the inn who dined with them. A few hours later the four travellers were found dead in the forest. They had died of poison, which must have been administered in some drink just before they left the inn. There was no reason for the deaths . . . except to placate the bloodthirsty Kali. It seems to me that in defiance of our law there is a return to this old barbaric custom."

"How dreadful! Innocent travellers . . . murdered by strangers!"

"That is the way of the Thagi. It makes me very uneasy. There have not been many cases lately and we were beginning to think we had wiped the whole thing out. It's a return to it . . . a defiance . . . That is what is so upsetting. Tom is investigating. If we could find the source of the trouble . . . if we could find the murderers and where they come from we might be able to stamp it out, and we must stamp it out quickly. To allow it to go on would not only bring terror to countless Indians, but, worse still, it is an open defiance of British law."

"What are you going to do about it?"

"No doubt there is some sort of central control. These people have their meetings, you know. Wild ceremonies with blood offerings to Kali—strange oaths and so on. If we could find the leaders and root them out, we'd stop the whole thing. No sensible Indian would want to continue with that."

"But Dougal was saying that people value their independence more than anything. They don't want improvements if they are going to interfere with that."

"Oh, Dougal. He's a dreamer. We've got to find out what this means and root it out."

"Perhaps it could be explained to the people."

He looked at me in exasperation. "Drusilla, you are a child in these matters. The sentimental view will only make matters worse. We have to stamp out these evils if we are going to have a reasonable country here where we can live and work and bring benefits to them as well as to ourselves. If they won't accept this, we have to make them."

"Do you think you will ever do that?"

"We have to try."

"What would you do if you found the murderers?"

"Hang them."

"Would that be wise? They are following what seems to be a religion with them. It is the worship of the goddess Kali that makes them do such things."

"You are a clever young lady, my dear Drusilla, but in these matters you are . . . infantile."

"Then why do you bother to tell me of them?"

"Because I think we should all be warned. Keeping doesn't

like the way things are going. He says he is aware of an under-
current. He has detected insolence in certain people. He is
trained to recognize these moods. He is a very experienced
man, and he is disturbed."

"What should one do about it?"

"Take great care. Watch the way the wind blows. It is no
use talking to Lavinia."

"No use at all. But why do you talk to me?"

"Because I expect you to be . . . sensible."

"In what way?"

"Be watchful. Tell one of us if you see anything that may
seem strange. We are going through an uneasy patch. We have
them from time to time. We must be careful not to offend . . .
not to show arrogance . . . to respect their customs."

"Except thuggery."

"That is true. But we are hoping that this is an isolated
outbreak. If we could track it down and put an end to it there
might be no more. If it goes undetected it might grow."

"I understand your anxiety. Thank you for telling me."

"I daresay Tom Keeping will tell Miss Philwright. In fact,
I am sure he will. He has a great respect for her intelligence.
He seems to be very interested in her."

"It was obvious when we travelled with him."

"And she . . . what are her feelings?"

"I am not sure. She is not one to betray them."

"There are some like that," he said, smiling at me.

"It is often wise."

"I am sure anything Miss Philwright—and you also—
would do would be wise. Tom Keeping is a good fellow . . . a
very faithful member of the Company. I owe him a good deal."

"Yes, he is clearly very efficient."

"You owe him something, too."

"You mean because he looked after us during the latter
part of our voyage?"

"He looked after you very well. I don't think you are
aware of how well."

I waited.

He went on, "Do you know he rescued you from a rather
tricky situation?"

I looked at him in surprise. "I know he was very kind and helpful."

"How good a student of human nature are you, Miss Drusilla?"

"Do you mean can I judge people? Oh, tolerably well, I believe."

"I imagine that might be so . . . among ordinary people with whom you come into contact. The lady helpers at the church and the garden bazaar and so on; who must arrange the flowers in the church for Easter; who must be given that best stall at the sale of work; who is a little jealous because someone had too friendly a smile from the delectable Reverend Brady . . . By the way, Brady is married. He married the doctor's daughter."

He was watching me intently.

"A very suitable match," I said. "I trust it satisfies Lady Harriet?"

"There might not have been a marriage if it had not."

"I suppose not. Colin Brady is a very docile subject."

"You were less so."

"I like to manage my own life, don't you?"

"Precisely. But we stray from the point, which was an assessment of your ability to judge human nature. I can tell you this, Miss Drusilla, you may be an expert in your narrow field, but when you stray outside that you are an utter ignoramus."

"Indeed."

"Indeed yes. You were completely taken in by the charming Lasseur."

I was startled.

"He was attractive, was he not? The attentive Frenchman. Were you just a little impressed by him? Did you find him quite attractive?"

"Monsieur Lasseur . . ." I murmured.

"The very same. He was not really a Frenchman, you know."

"But . . ."

He laughed at me. "You were an innocent . . . a sheep among wolves. I think it would always be well to know when one is out of one's depth."

"You are talking in riddles."

"Always an amusing way to talk, don't you think?"

"No. I would like plain speaking."

"Then I will speak plainly. Monsieur Lasseur, no French-man but a gentleman of obscure origins, was playing a part. The gallant gentleman was out to deceive unsuspecting ladies who believe they have such a good understanding of life and its little vicissitudes that they are ready to fall into his trap. Your Monsieur Lasseur . . ."

"Mine?"

"Monsieur Lasseur is what is known in certain quarters as a procurer for a very wealthy employer, an oriental gentleman who has his own country's traditional ideas about the uses of women . . . with which a young lady such as yourself would never agree. In other words, Monsieur Lasseur had selected you as an interesting addition to his master's harem."

I felt myself blushing scarlet and I could see this amused him very much.

"I don't believe it," I said.

"Nevertheless, he is known to some of us. English young ladies are very desirable in certain circumstances. First, they belong to that proud country which sees itself as master of the world. They have had a different upbringing from the women of eastern countries. They have had more independence; they have not all been brought up to believe that their mission in life is to serve men in any way in which they are called on to do so. I am sorry if this conversation shocks you, but you see, if you are going adventuring through the world you must be made aware of the facts of life. Lasseur travelled with the ship from England. He was there on his master's more legitimate busi-ness; but if he could find someone delectable enough to titillate his master's somewhat jaded palate and bring her back in tri-umph he would win the great man's approval and gratitude. He would have done more than merely complete his master's business, which he had been sent to England to do. Well, he saw you."

"I really don't believe a word of this."

"You can ask Keeping. He saw what was happening. It would not have been exactly the first time a young woman had disappeared in the desert with him and been heard of no more. By the way, you owe a little gratitude to me. I sent word to him to look out for you when you left the ship at Alexandria. He did. He made you his concern, for he knew that was what I would wish. You look stunned."

I was. I was remembering it all. The meeting with Monsieur Lasseur . . . the conversations . . . the coming of Tom Keeping. And Monsieur Lasseur had intended to arrange that we travel without the rest of the party. Good heavens! I thought. It is feasible.

Fabian was smiling, reading my thoughts.

"I hope you are not disappointed to have been snatched from a sultan's harem."

"I am sure the sultan would have been, but I would have thought I was hardly worth the trouble."

"You underestimate yourself," he said. "I believe that you are worth a great deal of trouble."

He rose from his chair and came over to me. I rose too. He put his hands on my shoulders.

"I'm glad Keeping rescued you and brought you safely to us," he said seriously.

"Thank you."

"You still look bewildered."

"I have been astonished by what you have told me. I really find it hard to believe."

"That is because you have lived most of your life in a rectory where cunning eastern gentlemen are unheard of."

"There are predatory creatures the whole world over, I suppose."

"Yes," he said with a smile, "but their methods would be different."

"I must tell Mr. Keeping how grateful I am to him."

"He will tell you he was doing it all as a matter of duty . . . obeying orders."

"The Company's orders?"

"The Company is only those who work for it. Shall we say, my orders. I am the one to whom you should show gratitude."

"Then if that is so, I thank you."

He inclined his head. "I might ask your help one day."

"I can't imagine my feeble efforts would be of any use to you."

"You underestimate yourself again. You mustn't, you know. There is a belief that people take you at your own valuation. You see, for all his faults, the discerning Monsieur Lasseur recognized your worth. Others might too . . . if you let them."

"I think I should join the children. I am usually with them at this time."

"And spoil the tête-à-tête between Miss Philwright and Tom Keeping?"

"Perhaps I should take the children off her hands. They would be able to talk more easily then."

"Drusilla . . ."

"Yes?"

"Are you a little grateful to me?"

I hesitated. I still found the story incredible.

"I . . . I suppose so," I said.

"You suppose! That is a very hesitant comment from a young lady who is usually so determined."

"I am grateful to Mr. Keeping, of course. What did he do to the man?"

"He will tell you. There was a stop at one of those places."

"Yes. It was where he was taken ill."

"Helped by Tom, of course."

"It must have been something he put in the wine. I remember there was wine."

"Of course. He did tell me. He slipped it into the fellow's glass, knowing the effect would be quick. He went in with him to the men's rest room so that he was handy when Lasseur began to feel strange. He looked after him, called the manager of the place and arranged for him to stay there until he was fit to travel. By the time he had recovered, the ship would be sailing from Suez, with you out of harm's way."

"It was very cleverly done. What did he give him?"

"Something to get the desired effect. In the course of his business Tom has learned of such things."

"Perhaps it was datura," I said. "The thorn apple."

"Oh, that . . . Dougal was talking about it, wasn't he?"

"Yes. He explained what it looked like. I could hardly recognize it from his description."

"You have seen it, then?"

I said, "It seems the Khansamah grows it in his garden."

Fabian dropped his bantering manner. "G.K.," he said. "In his garden. But . . . the cultivation is forbidden . . . except in certain cases."

"Perhaps he is one of the certain cases."

"I should not think so. How did you know of this?"

I told him how Louise had brought the sprig to me.

"Good God!" he said. "He is growing it in his garden!"

"Shall you speak to him? Ayah was very upset. You see, Louise crawled under the fence and thought she was bringing me a nice flower."

"The child took it . . ." he murmured. "You have said nothing of this to the Khansamah?"

"No. You know how important he is."

"I do indeed," said Fabian grimly. "Did you tell anyone about this?"

"I told Dougal, but foolishly I had burned the thing, so I couldn't show him. I am sure he thought I had been mistaken and I think he felt it was not possible to question the Khansamah."

"H'm," said Fabian slowly. "That would be difficult, I admit. Perhaps it is one of those pieces of information best hidden . . . for a while. I want to see Tom Keeping. Perhaps you could go out there and tell him I'm in my study. Would you do that?"

"Of course."

I could see that the possibility of the Khansamah's growing the thorn apple in his garden had driven all frivolous thoughts from his mind.

I sat on in the garden, talking to Alice. Tom Keeping had immediately gone in to Fabian when I had told him where he was.

Alice was different. There was a lilt in her voice. I thought to myself: This is Alice in love.

She said how strange it was that Tom Keeping had come to the house.

"It's not strange at all," I said. "He is the Company's servant, as they all are. Sir Fabian has just told me the strangest thing. I don't know whether to believe him or not."

I explained.

She stared at me in amazement. "It was all rather odd, wasn't it?" she said. "The way in which he was so suddenly taken ill."

"It fits," I agreed. "But it does seem a rather wild story to me."

"Well, we were in a wild country. Things are different there . . . and here . . . from what they are at home. It just seems improbable because you are putting it into an English setting. I think Tom acted splendidly—so quickly . . . so efficiently."

"Yes, I shall have to thank him."

"What would have happened if he hadn't been there!" She shivered. "It is too awful to contemplate."

"Sir Fabian says that Tom was acting on his orders."

"He would, wouldn't he?"

"It sounds . . . possible."

Alice lifted her shoulders. "I think Tom was wonderful," she said.

I could see that she was obsessed by Tom and I wondered what the outcome would be.

We chatted in the nursery together when the children had gone to bed. Alice was more talkative than usual.

"Tom is apparently a wonderful man," I said. "They all seem to think highly of him."

"His life is very adventurous. I don't suppose he'll stay here long. He is always on the move. He was delighted to see us."

"He was delighted to see *you.*"

"He did say that he was. Then . . . he said a strange thing . . . how glad he was to have met us, but he did not think it was a good time for us to be here. I asked him what he meant by that, but he was rather noncommittal."

"I told Sir Fabian about the discovery of that plant in the Khansamah's garden. He was rather disturbed."

"There is a strange feeling in the air. This matter of the Thugs . . . I think it is causing them a great deal of concern."

"Naturally it would. It's rebelling against the law."

"Tom says he expects to be here only a few days and he never knows where he will go next." She was silent for a while;

then she went on, "It was really wonderful what he did in the desert."

She smiled proudly. I hoped everything would turn out well for her. She deserved some good fortune.

As soon as I saw Tom Keeping I told him I now knew what he had done and I thanked him.

"It was a pleasure," he said. "I only wish I could have had that man arrested. But it is not easy in such places. I recognized him at once, for he had tried the same tactics before. There was a young girl who was going out to be married. Lasseur was one of the party and they disappeared together on the journey across the desert. He had procured a small carriage at the stables, persuaded the girl that they would take the last stage of the journey in greater comfort and . . . she was never seen again."

"I don't know what to say to you. It is so bewildering. When I try to think of what might have been . . ."

He laid a hand on my arm. "Well, it didn't happen. Sir Fabian did not like the idea of you two ladies travelling unaccompanied and he told me to look out for you, as I was in the neighbourhood and would be making the last part of the journey back to India with you. I saw at once that he was trying the same trick again. I thoroughly enjoyed foiling the loathsome creature."

"He will probably do it again."

"Doubtless he will. I should have liked to expose him, but it is a tricky thing to do. His employer is, I believe, a man of great wealth and power. Heaven knows what the consequences would be if anyone interfered with one of his men. It could be an international incident! Discretion had to be the better part of valour on that occasion and I had to content myself with bringing you safely to your destination."

"Well, thank you."

"You should thank Sir Fabian. Your safe arrival was a matter of the utmost importance to him."

I felt a glow of pleasure which, ridiculously, seemed to make the dangers through which I had passed worthwhile.

Then something disturbing did occur. It was afternoon, that time when the day was at its hottest and the household was quiet.

Lavinia had asked me to go to her. She wanted to chat and ask my opinion about a new dress she was having made up. Not that she would take my advice on such a matter; but she wanted to talk.

I thought this would be a good time. She usually rested at this hour, though she did not sleep, so I guessed I would find her alone.

As I approached her door I heard the sound of voices. Lavinia's was high pitched. She sounded alarmed.

I ran to the door and opened it. For a few seconds I stared in blank amazement. She was standing by the bed; her peignoir had fallen from her shoulders. She looked startled and afraid— and with her was the Great Khansamah. He was there beside her, his puggaree awry . . . his face distorted. It seemed to me that he was attacking Lavinia. His eyes were glazed and there was something odd about him.

As for Lavinia, her hair was loose about her bare shoulders. She was very flushed. When she looked at me I saw the fear fade from her face and an almost smug expression cross her features.

"I think," she said to the Khansamah, "that it would be better if you left now."

I could see that he was desperately trying to recover his dignity. His hand went to his half-opened shirt. He looked at me and said haltingly, "Missie come to see Memsahib Countess. I will go."

"Yes, Khansamah," said Lavinia, a trifle imperiously. "You should go now."

He bowed and throwing a look of dislike in my direction, he departed.

I said, "What was that all about?"

"My dear Drusilla, I was most surprised. The fellow thought I might allow him to make love to me."

"Lavinia!"

"Don't look so surprised. He thinks he is better than any of us."

"How could you allow it!"

"I didn't allow it. I protested vigorously."

"Why should he have thought it would be possible?"

"I tell you, he has a high opinion of himself."

"You must have given him some encouragement."

She pouted. "That's right. Blame me . . . as you always do."

"Don't you see how dangerous this is?"

"Dangerous? I could have handled him."

"You looked rather alarmed when I came in."

"In the nick of time!" she said dramatically.

"You should never have received him the way you have. You should have seen him downstairs for your daily consultations."

"What nonsense! I was only doing what all the women do. They see their khansamahs every morning."

"This one is different. You have behaved foolishly. You have flirted with him. You must have made him think that he might be successful with you. It would never have entered his mind if you had behaved with decorum as the others do. Who else would dream of encouraging the servants to have such ideas?"

"I did nothing of the sort."

"You did. I have seen you. Receiving him in your negligée . . . smiling at him, accepting his compliments. Naturally he thought he was making headway with you."

"But he is a servant here. He should remember that."

"Not when you behave like a slut."

"Be careful, Drusilla."

"It is you who have to be careful. If you do not want plain speaking there is no point in our going on talking."

"I thought you would be sympathetic."

"Lavinia, don't you realize the situation here? Tom Keeping is here because of it. There is unease . . . unrest . . . and you create this situation with that man!"

"I didn't make it. He did. I didn't ask him to come to my room."

"No. But you have implied your interest in him."

"I have never said a word."

"Looks speak as loud as words. You are just as bad as you were at school."

"Oh, you are going to bring all that up, are you?"

"Yes, I am . . . as an example of one piece of folly. This is almost as bad."

She raised her eyebrows. "Really, Drusilla, you do give yourself airs . . . just because I have been friendly towards you."

"If you don't like my manner . . ."

"I know. You'll go home. You would go back to that boring old rectory . . . so you think. But you can't. You can't marry Colin Brady, because he's already married."

"I never intended to marry him. And I don't want to be where I am not wanted."

"Fabian would never let you go."

I flushed slightly. She saw it and laughed. "He's quite interested in you . . . but don't deceive yourself. He'd never marry *you*. Fabian is no better than I am, really. But . . . you shouldn't be so standoffish with him, you know."

I prepared to go, but she cried piteously, "Drusilla, wait a minute. I'm so glad you came in when you did. I think the Khansamah would be very determined. I was really getting just a little scared that he might rape me."

"I don't want to hear any more, Lavinia. What happened was largely your fault. I think you ought to be a little more responsible. I believe he was drugged. I know he grows datura in his garden. This would account for his indiscretion, for I cannot believe that even he would dare presume so much in the normal way."

"So what are you going to do now? Tell Dougal what a terrible wife he has? Don't bother. He knows already. Tell him he's such a bore and that is why I have to find a little *divertissement*."

"Of course I shall not tell Dougal."

"I know. You'll tell Fabian. Drusilla, for Heaven's sake don't do that."

"I think perhaps it ought to be mentioned. It's intolerable . . . his coming to your bedroom like that."

"Well, I am rather irresistible."

"And full of implied promises."

"Drusilla, please don't tell Fabian."

I paused. Then I said, "I think it might be important in view of . . ."

"Oh, don't be so profound! He's a man like any other. They are all the same if you give them half an inch."

"Then stop giving away inches . . . though in your case it must go into yards."

"I promise . . . Drusilla, I promise. I'll behave . . . only don't tell Fabian."

At length I agreed, but somewhat uneasily, for I felt that the fact that a member of the Indian household should contemplate such a relationship with the lady of the house was significant.

It was about two days later when the news was brought to the house.

I had seen the Khansamah once during that time. He was his old dignified self. He bowed his head in the customary greeting and made no sign that he remembered that scene in Lavinia's bedroom and the part I played in it.

Lavinia said that when he came to pay his daily call she received him in her sitting room and she was dressed for the day. It had gone off in a calm manner—much as many such meetings must be going on in houses in the British quarter, where matrons were discussing the day's menus with their khansamahs. There had been no reference to what had happened.

"You should have seen me," said Lavinia. "You would have been proud of me. Yes, even you, Drusilla. I just discussed the food and he made suggestions as to what would be suitable. I said, 'Yes, Khansamah, I will leave that to you,' just as I am sure the most dignified ladies do it. Then . . . it was over."

"He will understand that he behaved in a way that will not be tolerated," I said. "He wouldn't apologise, of course. That would be asking too much. Besides, the fault was largely yours. He has decided to ignore the whole thing, which after all is the best way of dealing with it."

A young man came to the house. He had ridden from afar. He was quite exhausted and wanted to be taken to the Great Khansamah without delay.

In due course we learned that the message that had been

brought was from the Khansamah's brother, and that the Khansamah's son, Asraf, who had recently been married to Roshanara, was dead. He had been murdered.

The Khansamah shut himself into his room in mourning. A pall of gloom fell over the house. Fabian was deeply disturbed. Tom Keeping and Dougal were in the study with Fabian for a long time. They did not emerge for dinner and, as on other occasions, trays were sent to the study.

Lavinia and I met over dinner alone. We talked, as the whole household was talking, about Asraf's death.

"He was so young," I said. "He and Roshanara have only just been married. Who could have wanted to kill him?"

Even Lavinia was shocked.

"Poor Khansamah. It is such a blow to him. His only son!"

"It is terrible," I said, and felt sorry for the man in spite of the fact that he was fast becoming a sinister figure in my imagination.

Lavinia said she would retire early and she went to her room. I was in no mood for sleep. I felt very disturbed. I wondered what would happen to Roshanara. Poor child, she was so young.

I sat in the drawing room in the dark, with the curtains drawn back so that I could look out on the beauty of the moonlit garden.

Just as I was thinking I would retire, the door opened and Fabian came in.

"Hello," he said. "Still up? Where is Lavinia?"

"She has gone to bed."

"And you are sitting here alone?"

"Yes. All this is so disturbing."

He shut the door and advanced into the room. "I agree," he said. "Very disturbing."

"What does it mean?" I asked.

"It means that for some reason Asraf has been murdered."

"Perhaps it is one of those thugs. They murder without reason."

He was silent for a while. Then he said, "No . . . I do not think it was the thugs this time . . . though it might be connected with them."

"You think that someone murdered . . . not just for the sake of killing . . . but for a definite reason?"

He sat down opposite me. "It is imperative that we find out what is going on."

"I understand that."

"It could be of the utmost importance to us. I don't like the way things look. I have been discussing with Dougal and Tom the possibility of getting Lavinia and you away with the children."

"Away! You mean . . ."

"I should feel happier." He smiled at me a little sardonically. "I don't mean happier . . . exactly . . . I mean relieved."

"I don't think Lavinia would go."

"Lavinia? She will go where and when she is told to go."

"She has a will of her own."

"It's a pity she hasn't some sense to go with it."

"I don't think I would like to be sent here and there . . . like a parcel."

"Please don't be difficult. Things are hard enough to decide, so don't make them worse."

"It is just that one wants to have a little say in what happens to one."

"You have no idea what is going on and yet you want to make decisions. Women and children should not be here."

"You raised no objections to Lavinia's coming out here. The children were born out here."

"She came with her husband. I could not arrange where the children were born. I am just stating that it is unfortunate that she and they and you are here. But all that came about naturally enough. I blame myself for bringing you and Miss Philwright out."

"*You* did not bring us out."

"It was my suggestion that you come."

"Why?"

"I thought perhaps you would have some influence on Lavinia. You did in the past and, as I believe I told you . . . or implied at least . . . I also considered the benefits your presence here would give me."

"Because you think with your mother that it is necessary

for the children to have an English governess and an English nanny."

"But of course . . ."

"And now you regret it."

"For one reason only. I don't like the situation here and I think it would be better not to have too many women and children around."

"I think your concern does you credit."

He said with a touch of sarcasm, "You know the real reason why I manoeuvered your visit. It was because I wanted a little pleasure for myself."

"I am surprised that you should think I could provide it."

"You can't be. You know, for one thing, how I enjoy these spirited conversations . . . also, I wanted to get you away from the odious Colin Brady."

"I thought he was regarded as a devoted Framling subject."

"All the more reason why I should dislike him. I wanted to see you . . . so I arranged it. Besides, what would you have done at home? You couldn't stay at the rectory without marrying Brady. Where would you have gone?"

"Where I did go. To my old nurse."

"Ah yes, that good woman. I wanted you here, that was all. In spite of your indifference to me, I am fond of you, Drusilla."

I hoped I did not show the pleasure I felt. He was irrepressible. He must know that I would never indulge in a light love affair with him; but he never gave up.

I changed the subject. "Why are you so disturbed now?"

"This Asraf business."

"The murder?"

"Exactly. Why was he killed? He was little more than a boy. Why? It is something we have to find out . . . quickly. If it were the Thugs, I think I would feel easier. But this was an isolated killing. Thugs deal in numbers. The blood of one innocent boy would not placate Kali for long. As much as I would deplore further outbreaks, I feel that would be more understandable than this mystery. You see, this comes back to our own household. I have a feeling that that is significant."

"Can you question the Khansamah?"

He shook his head. "It might be dangerous. We have to

find out what is going on. Why was Asraf murdered? We must know whether it was a ritual killing or for some other reason. Tom has left at once for the tea plantation. We may have some news when he gets back."

"It is all very mysterious."

"There are many mysteries in this country. Drusilla, I think I should warn you. I may decide that you would have to go at a moment's notice. I should have sent you off before now, but travelling is so difficult and the journey might prove more dangerous than staying here. It might be necessary to move you to another town here in India. But we have to understand what this murder means first. So much depends on what is behind it."

There was silence for a few moments. Then he said, "How peaceful it seems out there . . ." He did not go on. I stood up suddenly. I wondered what Lavinia would think if she came down and found me in this darkened room with her brother.

I said, "I will say good night."

I heard him laugh. "You think being here alone with me . . . is a little improper?"

Again he was reading my thoughts, which surprised and disconcerted me every time I discovered it.

"Oh . . . certainly not."

"No? Perhaps you are not quite so conventional as I sometimes think. Well, you came on a very hazardous journey. You came with great risk across the desert . . . so it is hardly likely that you can be afraid of me just because we are alone and in a darkened room."

"What an idea!" I said lightly.

"Yes, it is, isn't it? Stay awhile, Drusilla."

"Oh, I am very tired. I think I should go to bed."

"Don't worry too much about what I have told you. I may be wrong. There could be a logical answer to all these things . . . chains of coincidence and that sort of thing. But one must find out and be prepared."

"Of course."

"I would be most unhappy if you had to go."

"It is kind of you to say so."

"It is merely truthful. I wish you were not so afraid."

"I am not afraid of you, you know."

"Afraid of yourself, perhaps?"

"I assure you I am by no means overawed or in terror of myself."

"I didn't mean in that way."

"I must go."

He took my hand and kissed it.

"Drusilla, you know I am very fond of you."

"Thank you."

"Don't thank me for what I can't help. Stay awhile. Let's talk. Let's stop hedging, shall we?"

"I was not aware of hedging."

"It's built up between us. You planted the seeds and they grow like weeds . . . of the most prolific kind. I know what started it. It was that business in France. It had more effect on you than it had on Lavinia. You decided that all men are liars and deceivers and you have made up your mind never to be lied to or deceived."

"I think you are talking about something of which you are quite ignorant."

"Well, give me a chance to learn. I shall be your humble pupil."

"I am sure you would never be humble . . . nor take instruction from me. So I'll say good night. I will remember what you told me and hold myself in readiness for departure at any moment."

"I hope it doesn't come to that."

"Nevertheless I shall be prepared."

"Do you insist on going?"

"I must," I said. "Good night."

I went upstairs in a mood of exhilaration. I wished that I could believe it when I told myself I was indifferent to him.

Alice showed me a letter Tom Keeping had left for her to read after he had gone. He was expecting to return before long and then perhaps she would have an answer for him. He was asking her to marry him. He knew that she would not want to give a hasty reply and would need time to think. They had known each other such a short time, but he himself was certain that he wanted to marry her.

"The times are somewhat uneasy," he wrote. "I shall be

here for some years, I imagine. You would be travelling with
me. It could be dangerous at times and there would be occasions when we would be apart. I do want you to consider all
this. I thought it better to write, for I did not want my feelings
to carry me away to such an extent that I glossed over the
difficulties. Everything will be different from what you have
known. But I love you, Alice, and if you care for me I should be
the happiest man on Earth."

I was deeply moved when I read it. It might not have been
an effusive love letter, but it conveyed a deep sincerity.

I looked at Alice and I did not have to ask what her answer
would be.

"I would not have believed such a thing could happen to
me," she said. "I never thought for one moment that any man
would want to marry me . . . and a man like Tom. I feel I
must be dreaming."

Dear Alice! She did look bemused, but incredibly happy.

"Oh, Alice," I said. "It's wonderful. It's a beautiful romance."

"That it should happen to me! I can't believe it. Do you
think he really means it?"

"Of course he means it. I'm so happy for you."

"I couldn't marry him yet."

"Why not?"

"What about my job here? The Countess . . ."

"The Countess wouldn't care about you if it suited her. Of
course, you must marry him. You must begin this wonderful
life as soon as you can."

"What about the children?"

"They have a good nurse in Ayah and an excellent governess in me."

"Oh, Drusilla, we have been such friends!"

"Why the past tense? We *are* good friends. We always shall
be."

It was wonderful to see the change in Alice. She was like a
different person. She had never thought to meet someone like
Tom Keeping who would love her and whom she loved. She
was very fond of children and wanted to have her own; but she
had long thought that it would be her mission in life to look
after other people's.

A wonderful vista was opening out before her. An adventurous life . . . travelling through India with a man who had a most unusual and exciting job—and she would be with him forevermore.

She looked at me rather wistfully, and I guessed that, like many people in love—unselfish ones like Alice, that is—she wanted to see others in the same state, and especially me.

"I wish . . ." she said rather sadly.

I knew what she was going to say and added quickly, "You wish that Tom would come back quickly and you are wondering when you can be married. It will be quite simple, I imagine. Think of all the girls who come out to be married. They must be quite used to it by now."

"I was wishing that you could find someone . . ."

"Oh," I said lightly, "there aren't enough of Tom Keeping's kind to go round. Only the fortunate ones get them."

She was frowning. "I shan't like leaving you."

"My dear Alice, I shall be perfectly all right."

"I shall worry about you."

"Oh, come, Alice. You know I'm not a wilting blossom. I shall manage the children perfectly with Ayah's help."

"I wasn't thinking of that, Drusilla. We have been very close. Oh, I feel I can talk to you. How do you feel about Fabian Framling?"

"Oh . . . an interesting man. Very much aware of his own importance."

"How important is he to you?"

"I suppose the same as he is to everyone else. He seems to be quite a power around here."

"That isn't quite what I meant."

"Then what did you mean?"

"I think he is not indifferent to you."

"He is not indifferent to anything that goes on around here."

"You know what I mean. He's interested . . ."

"In seduction?"

"Well . . . I did think of something like that."

"And I think it might enter his mind . . . as it would where any youngish woman was concerned."

"That is what I'm afraid of. It wouldn't be wise to feel too strongly."

"Don't worry. I know him very well."

"Isn't that Lady Somebody coming out to marry him?"

"I should imagine all that is shelved because of the uneasiness here."

"But eventually the marriage will take place."

"I think it is Lady Harriet's will . . . and that is usually obeyed by all."

"I see. I wish you could come away with me when I go."

"I don't think Tom would want a third person to share his honeymoon."

"I do hope you will be all right. Of course, you are very sensible. I don't like your being here . . . with the Countess, who is very reckless and selfish . . . and as for her husband . . . I think he is half in love with you."

"Don't worry, I tell you. Dougal would always be half in love . . . never wholly so."

"I don't like the situation at all. You must never let anyone take you off your guard."

"Thank you. I suppose you feel that as an about-to-be-married woman you should look after your less experienced and fragile sisters. Oh, Alice, just concentrate on being happy. For I am happy for you."

Lavinia was amused when she heard that Tom and Alice were to be married.

"Who would have thought it of her! She seems a born old maid. Frankly, I can't understand what he sees in her. She's very *plain*."

"There is more to people than waving tendrils and tigerish looks, you know. She's highly intelligent."

"Which, you imply, I'm not."

"Nobody could call you plain."

"Nor intelligent either?"

"Well, the way in which you behave does rather suggest a scarcity of that valuable asset."

"Oh, shut up. Anyway, I think it's funny. Nanny Alice and Tom Keeping. And what about the children? Mama will be furious. She sent Alice Philwright out to look after the children, not to get married."

"The matter will be passed out of your mother's jurisdiction. She may rule Framling, but not all India."

"She'll be extremely put out. I wonder if she will send out another English nanny."

"I wouldn't think so. After all, your time out here is not very long, is it?"

"Thank you for reminding me of that blessed fact."

"You might not enjoy such male adoration on the Carruthers country estate as you do here."

"No. That is a point. And Mama will not be so far off. I shall have to reconsider. Perhaps I shall persuade Dougal to stay after all."

"I think he longs to get home."

"To those dry old books, which he can't get here. Serve him right."

"Such a dutiful spouse," I murmured; and she was laughing.

Fabian's reaction to the news was one of surprise.

We were at dinner when the matter was brought up.

"I thought Keeping was a confirmed bachelor," he said.

"Some men are until they meet someone they really care about," I replied.

He threw me an amused glance.

"Nobody could be more surprised than I," said Lavinia. "I thought people like Nanny Philwright never got married. They're supposed to be devoted to their charges all their lives and in the end live in a little house bought for them by some grateful one who visits Nanny every Christmas and on her birthday and makes sure she is comfortable for the rest of her days."

"I am not surprised at all," I said. "They are a delightful couple. I could see there was a rapport between them from the moment they met."

"On the road across the desert," said Fabian, smiling at me significantly and reminding me how Tom Keeping, at his command, had saved me from a fate too horrible to contemplate.

"It means we are losing our nanny," said Lavinia. "That is a bore."

"The ayah is very good," I reminded her. "I shall help to look after them, as I always have done. But we shall all be very sad to see her go."

"She will visit the house with Tom from time to time, I daresay," said Dougal.

"Then there can be a joyous reunion," added Fabian.

"I am very happy for Alice," I said. "She is one of the best people I have ever known."

"Then," said Fabian, "let us drink to them." He lifted his glass. "To lovers . . . wherever they may be."

Mutiny

Asraf's body was brought to his father. It was kept in state in the little house in the grounds that was the Great Khansamah's home. There was to be a traditional burial, which meant that Asraf's body would be placed in a wooden cart and taken to a certain spot, where it would be burned.

Roshanara had come back. She was staying under the protection of her father-in-law, the Great Khansamah. I wished that we could see her again. I should have liked to talk to her. I wanted to know what her future would be.

I was soon to learn.

Ayah came to me; she plucked my sleeve, implying that she wished to see me alone.

I said, "Is anything wrong?"

She did not answer that. Instead she said, "Missie . . . come . . ."

She took me out to the garden and to the gazebo, there among the tall grasses and shrubs. Few people went there. We were told that snakes abounded in the long grass. The Russelian snake had been seen there, and on one or two occasions the dreaded cobra.

I drew back a little as we approached the gazebo. The ayah noticed. She said, "We take care . . . great care. Follow where I go, please."

I followed her, and in the gazebo I came face to face with Roshanara. We looked at each other for a few seconds and then she was in my arms.

"Oh, Missie . . . Missie . . ." she said. "So good . . . so kind."

I held her at arms' length. I was a little shocked by her appearance. She was no longer the child who had sat down with Louise and listened to my lessons.

She looked older, thinner and what alarmed me was her expression of apprehension, which was immediately noticeable. I realized that here was a very frightened girl.

"So you are a widow now, Roshanara," I said.

She gave me a sorrowful look.

"I am so sorry," I said. "It was terrible. You have been so briefly married. How sad to lose your husband."

She shook her head and said nothing, but her big, frightened eyes never left my face.

"He was murdered," I went on. "It was so senseless. Was it some enemy?"

"He did nothing, Missie. He just frightened little boy. He die because of what was done . . . by another."

"Do you want to talk about it?"

She shook her head. Then suddenly she was kneeling at my feet, clutching at my skirt.

"Help me, Missie," she said. "Do not let me burn."

I looked at the ayah, who nodded. She said, "Tell. Tell, Roshanara. Tell Missie."

Roshanara looked up at me. "There will be the funeral . . . the funeral pyre. I must throw myself into the flames."

"No!" I said.

"Great Khansamah say 'Yes.' He say it is the widow's duty."

"No, no," I said. "That is suttee. It is no longer permitted under British rule."

"Great Khansamah, he say this our way. He will not have the foreigners' way."

"It is simply forbidden," I told her. "You just have to refuse. No one can make you. You have the law on your side."

"Great Khansamah, he say . . ."

"This is nothing to do with Great Khansamah."

"Asraf was his son."

"That is of no account. It is against the law."

"Missie will know," said Ayah.

Roshanara nodded.

"It is not going to happen," I said. "We shall see to that. Leave it to me. I shall see that it does not happen."

Roshanara's terrified look was replaced by one of confidence. I was a little shaken that she put so much reliance on my powers.

I wanted to act quickly and I was not sure how to go about it. This was too big a matter for me to deal with alone. I must consult Fabian and Dougal. It would have to be Fabian. Dougal would be all sympathy, but he was a little ineffectual. Fabian would know what was the best thing to do.

I must find him quickly and talk to him.

I said, "Leave this to me. Now I must go. What will you do, Roshanara?"

"She will go back to Great Khansamah's house," said Ayah. "He must not know she come and tell you this. I take her back."

I said, "I am sure I shall soon be ready to tell you what you must do."

I went at once to Fabian's study. By good fortune he was there.

He rose and showed his pleasure at the sight of me. I was annoyed with myself for feeling so elated when I had this terrible situation to face.

I said, "I have to talk to you."

"I'm glad of that. What is it?"

"It's Roshanara. She's here. I've just seen her. The poor child is terrified. The Great Khansamah is going to force her to leap into Asraf's funeral pyre."

"What?"

"It is what she has been told she must do."

"It's impossible."

"It's the Great Khansamah's orders. What do we do about it?"

"I'd say we'd stop the proceedings."

"That would not be difficult in view of the law, would it?"

"It wouldn't be difficult, but it might be dangerously provocative. We have made a few alarming discoveries and it is my opinion that the situation is becoming explosive. I believe we have to act with the utmost caution."

"But in a case of lawbreaking . . ."

"Drusilla," he said seriously, "I can trust your discretion."

"Of course."

"Don't speak of this to my sister, or anyone. When Tom Keeping returns I daresay he will put Miss Philwright in the picture . . . but she is a sensible girl. Tom wouldn't have fallen in love with her otherwise."

"I have promised Roshanara that something will be done."

"Something shall be done. This atrocious thing will not be allowed to take place. Rest assured of that. But we have discovered certain things. There is a rebellion in the air. It would take very little to set a spark to the smouldering fires, and when it comes—if it comes—the conflagration will be great. We've gone wrong somewhere . . . or perhaps it has all come about naturally. The Company has never wanted to make a subject race of the Indians. We have improved their lot in so many ways, but there are bound to be mistakes. Perhaps we have made a few. I think our influence has been too rapidly felt. These people may believe that their civilization is threatened and that their native institutions are being squeezed out to make way for others."

"But surely they must realize that they are better off without such evil practices as suttee and thuggery."

"Perhaps. But still there will be some who object. You see, under Lord Dalhousie we have annexed the Punjab and Oudh. But the real trouble at the moment is that a certain unrest is growing up here in Delhi round the deposed King Bahadur Shah and Dalhousie is now threatening to send the old Mogul family from their seat in Delhi."

"Why?"

Fabian lifted his shoulders. "We are watchful of the leader Nana Sahib, who will seize the first opportunity to rouse the people to revolt against us. We are in a difficult position. I am telling you this so that you will see that we have to act with the utmost care."

"What about Roshanara?"

"This must be stopped. There is no doubt of that. But we shall have to be careful how we act. We have made discoveries about the Great Khansamah and it seems we have trouble in our own household."

"That does not surprise me. Can you not denounce him?"

"Certainly not. That would start the rebellion at once and Heaven knows where it would end. He is not only a khansamah. He has taken this position because this is a house frequented by officials of the Company."

"You mean . . . in a way . . . he is a spy?"

"Oh, more than that. G.K. is a leader. He hates the intruders. I am sure of that. He is a follower of Nana Sahib, who wants us out of the country."

"He is Nana, too. Great Nana. I have heard him called that."

"Whether he took the name after the leader or whether it is his by right, I do not know. All I do know is that we have made discoveries about him and because of what he is we must act with the greatest caution."

"What discoveries?"

"He is growing datura in the garden. Because thuggery has been abolished by our law, he wants to defy the law. Keeping suspected . . . and he has now found evidence to prove that he was right and that G.K. was helping his friends to go back to thuggery. The travellers who were found in the forest had been poisoned, and we believe that the poison came through G.K. This seems likely for a relative of one of the travellers who died took his revenge by murdering Asraf."

"Oh, poor Asraf, to be the victim of someone's revenge on someone else!"

"His own father, of course. Asraf is G.K.'s only son. It would have been hard to inflict a greater injury. So, you see, we have the seeds of deception in our own household."

"But what can we do about Roshanara?"

"We shall stop it . . . but subtly and in secret. To make a scene at the funeral pyre would be the utmost folly and could start an instant revolt. I feel certain that if we did there would be an immediate uprising in this very house. We must avoid that. When Keeping comes back I shall discuss with him the urgency of getting you, with Lavinia and the children, out of Delhi."

"You expect trouble in Delhi?"

"Delhi is an important city. When there is trouble it is likely to be at the heart of it."

"Tell me what you propose to do about Roshanara."

"I shall have to give the matter some thought, but at the moment it seems to me that what we must do is smuggle her out of the city."

"The Great Khansamah would never allow that."

"I will do it without his knowledge, of course."

"Is it possible?"

"We must make it possible. The Company owns several houses in various places. There it is possible for people to live in secret for a little while. I do believe this is the best way to act. We must be very, very careful, though. Tom should return tonight. He comes and goes with frequency, so it will not arouse much comment if he leaves again. When is the funeral to be?"

"Very soon, I believe. I think in two days' time."

"Then prompt action is necessary. Be ready. I may need your help. And remember, not a word to anyone."

"I'll remember," I said.

He smiled at me and leaned towards me. I thought he was going to kiss me, but he did not. I think he must have seen the alarm leap into my eyes. I must disguise my feelings. Alice had noticed something. I must be sure no one else did . . . especially Fabian.

The events of that day stay clearly in my mind.

As soon as I could I saw the ayah, which happened almost immediately, because she was as eager to see me as I was to see her.

I said to her, "It is all right. It is going to be stopped, but we have to be careful. There must be no betrayal of what we are going to do."

She nodded gravely.

"Sir Fabian is going to see that it is all right. You must do exactly what you are told and not whisper a word to anyone."

She nodded again. "Now?" she asked.

"When we are ready I will tell you. In the meantime you must behave as though nothing has happened."

I knew she would. She was terrified of what would happen to her if the Great Khansamah ever discovered she had been involved in a plot to undermine his authority.

Later that day Tom Keeping arrived.

Fabian summoned Dougal and me to the study and said that Miss Philwright must come, too, for her help might be needed and now that she was engaged to Tom she would work with us.

It was obvious that Tom already knew that Alice had accepted him. His look of contentment mingled with one of apprehension, for which the situation was responsible.

"Sit down," said Fabian. "You too, Miss Philwright. You have heard what is happening?" He looked questioningly at Alice.

Alice said she did know.

"Well, we have to get this girl out of the house. Tom is seeing to that. There are several small houses owned by the Company to which many of its members can go if ever there is the need to hide. They are run as little inns in the country. There anyone who has to hide for a while can pass as a traveller and little notice is taken of them. Tom, tell your plan."

"We are going to get the Indian girl out of danger," said Tom. "We could, of course, forbid the ceremony and call in the law. That is what I would suggest normally. But we think that would not be wise in view of the explosive state of affairs at present."

Fabian said, "I believe that both Miss Delany and Miss Philwright are aware of the growing tension among the people here. Our enemies are spreading rumours among the sepoys that the bullets they use have been greased with the fat of beef and pork, which they consider unclean. They think that we are trying to suppress their old customs by treating them with contempt. Several fires have been started in Barrackpur. I'm sorry, Tom. I digress, but I do think it is important for the young ladies to understand the gravity of the situation and why we have to act in this devious manner. There have been outbursts of rebellion which we have suppressed, but rumours are running through Oudh and Bundelkhand, which are under-mining our prestige. Now, carry on, Tom."

"We're highly suspicious of the Khansamah. He is a man who seems able to lead people. It is because of his presence in this household that we have to proceed with the greatest cau-tion, and Sir Fabian and I have come to the conclusion that until we are more sure of his intentions, we must concentrate —for the moment—more on saving the life of this girl than on seeing justice done. Our plan, therefore, is to get Roshanara out of harm's way."

"How?" asked Dougal.

"By taking her away from here."

"You will be seen leaving," said Dougal.

"Not if we do it this way. She will not leave until after dark."

"She will be missed from the Khansamah's house," I said.

"We hope that she is supposed to remain alone in her room, prostrate with grief for the loss of her husband. Accord-ing to tradition, she should be spending what they believe will be her last night on Earth in meditation and prayer. They will leave her in solitude to do this. What she must do is slip out of his house, but not come into this one. She will go to the ga-zebo."

"The grass around it is infested with snakes," said Dougal. "I can tell you that some of them are . . . lethal."

"I know how interested you are in the various species, Dougal," said Fabian impatiently, "but there is not time to dis-cuss them now."

"I merely thought the approach to the place is dangerous."

"The danger is minor compared with what we would have to face if we did not take this action. Go on, Tom."

"Well," said Tom, "we must disguise Roshanara. This is where you ladies will help. I have a wig here, which will trans-form her appearance." He opened a small bag and brought out the wig. It was made of human hair and looked quite realistic. It was light brown in colour.

"It will make a good deal of difference to her appearance," I commented.

"A little face powder might lighten her skin," said Alice.

"I am sure it would," I said. "Lavinia has lots of pots and bottles on her dressing table. I'll ask her."

"No," said Fabian. "Don't ask her. Take what you want."

"She may miss them."

"You must make sure that she does not. You will only need them briefly and they can be replaced before she notices they have been taken away. So you really think you could alter her appearance . . . make her look . . . European?"

"I think we might," I said. "We can try."

"But you must not tell Lavinia a word."

"It will mean purloining these things."

"Then purloin."

"The plan is," went on Tom, "to get Roshanara here at midnight. She must in no circumstances come into this house. Servants have sharp ears and eyes and are always on the alert, but particularly so now. She should make her way to the gazebo."

"In spite of possible snakes," added Fabian, throwing a glance at Dougal.

"There," went on Tom, "she will be dressed in some garments which you will find for her . . . European style. Her appearance should be entirely changed. She and I will leave at once. I shall get her to a house on the fringe of the city. Mr. and Mrs. Sheldrake will arrive. Sheldrake is one of the Company's men. His wife will be a help. Roshanara will pose as their daughter. Mrs. Sheldrake and the girl can travel in a palanquin . . . the girl being ill, we shall say. That will insure against too many questions being asked, for no one will want to go too near her for fear of catching some infectious disease. Thus we will get her to a house of safety, where she will remain until we can review the situation."

Fabian looked at me. "You are thinking this a little melodramatic. Why do we not simply stop the proceedings? Believe me, it is what I should prefer to do."

"I do understand," I assured him. "It must be done as you have arranged. Alice and I will do our best to disguise her."

"The thing is to find something to fit her," said Alice. "She is so young and slight."

"Any garment will do," said Fabian. "She will be in the palanquin most of the time . . . except at first, of course."

"And that, I should imagine, is the most dangerous part," I said. I turned to Alice. "Where shall we find the clothes?"

Alice studied me for a few seconds. "You are very slim, though much taller than the girl. We could cut off the bottom of one of your dresses."

"That's the answer," said Tom, looking proudly at Alice, who had produced it.

"And don't forget," said Fabian, "my sister must not be in the secret. She would be unable to stop herself blurting out something about it."

"We must first get the message to Roshanara," said Tom.

"I will speak to the ayah at once," I told him.

"I don't like a native being involved," said Fabian.

I looked at him with exasperation. "Don't you see, Ayah wants this to succeed as much as any of us. She is her aunt. She brought her up. She will do everything she can to save her. I know."

"It doesn't do to get emotionally involved," said Fabian. "It leads to misjudgement. Impress on the ayah . . ."

"Of course I will, but she will understand that without telling. We can trust her discretion absolutely."

"It is a mistake to trust absolutely."

Why was it, I asked myself, that I could never be with him without this argumentative mood overtaking me? This was no time for it. We had to concentrate all our efforts on making the plan work.

As soon as I left the house I saw the ayah. I suggested she go to the gazebo, where we could talk. Fabian was right. One should not be too trusting, and although I was sure there must be many of the servants who would be sad to see Roshanara burned to death, they would never know where the wrath of the Khansamah would end, and some might feel a patriotic desire to drive the British out of India and defy their laws.

I told Ayah what we planned. Roshanara would hear what she had to do when she arrived at the gazebo. We would tell her while we dressed her. It was pathetic to see the hope in her eyes. She believed Roshanara's chances of survival had come through my goddess-like power. I wanted to tell her that it was

Fabian and Tom Keeping who had formulated the plan between them.

She listened carefully to what I said. Roshanara would come to the gazebo at midnight, when the house of the Great Khansamah was quiet and all in it were sleeping. It could be done, she knew, because the whole family would be in their rooms praying the night before the funeral.

Alice and I would go to the gazebo during the day, taking certain of the things we would need to change the appearance of Roshanara. Our great fear was that we might betray in some way that we were acting in an unusual manner.

Apparently we did not, for all went smoothly.

Alice and I dressed Roshanara. The poor child was trembling with fright. She could not believe that anyone could challenge the orders of the Great Khansamah, but at the same time she had great confidence in me.

There was no need to warn either Indian of the consequences to themselves if the plan went wrong. They were as aware of that as we were.

So in due course Roshanara was ready. She did not look in the least like her old self. The cut-down dress hung on her a little, but it was not entirely ill-fitting, and the wig of light brown hair completely transformed her. She looked like a Eurasian. Her graceful movements and her striking dark eyes could not be disguised.

I knew how successful our plan had been when, a few days later, a note was delivered from Tom Keeping.

"All is well," he wrote. "Cargo will be safely delivered from the city tonight."

That seemed satisfactory. We had saved Roshanara.

There was a great outcry the next day when the news of Roshanara's absence became known.

The Khansamah said nothing, but I knew he was in a murderous rage. He had wanted the old custom of suttee to be carried out to the letter. He wished to defy the British, which was apparently a sentiment gaining ground throughout the country.

The ayah told me that many questions had been asked. He had interrogated her particularly. What did she know? She

must have an idea. Had the girl gone off on her own? They
would find her, never fear. She would die in the fire if she were
found, and she would not have the honour of making a sacrifice
for her husband and her country. But die she would, for defy-
ing the orders of the Great Khansamah and for being a traitor
to her country.

Poor Roshanara! I hoped she had escaped from her formidable father-in-law forever.

Lavinia had been kept in ignorance of all this on Fabian's
orders, but now she was aware of Roshanara's escape. The reason for it had seeped out and everyone was talking of it.

"Poor girl," she said. "Did you know they wanted her to
jump into the funeral pyre?"

"Well, it was an old custom at one time."

"But it isn't now."

"No. Thank goodness it has stopped."

"But they still do it. The Great Khansamah wanted it done
this time. It was out of respect for his son. He seems a little
annoyed that his wishes were disobeyed."

"Serve him right."

"He's only following the old custom."

"I wonder if he would be prepared to jump into a fire for
the sake of an old custom."

"Of course he wouldn't. Roshanara's well out of it. I wonder how she managed it. I wouldn't have thought she would
have had the spirit."

"When one is faced with death one finds the power to do
all sorts of things."

"How do you know? You've never faced death."

"You're right. We none of us know how we would behave
in certain circumstances if we have never faced them."

"Philosophising again! Trust old Drusilla. G.K. has been
questioning them all. He is trying to find out who disobeyed
his orders."

"Has he been telling you?"

"Not he! He's very dignified now . . . since that time I
sent him off with a flea in his ear."

"As I remember, you did nothing of the sort. The encounter was brought to an end when I came in and rescued you."

"Drusilla to the rescue! Because you did it once over that boring old Comte, you think you do it all the time."

"I am glad he has become that boring old Comte. He was so wonderful at one time."

"Well, Khansamah has been behaving very well lately."

"Very well! Trying to force his daughter-in-law to burn herself to death."

"I was referring to his way with me."

"Of course. You never give a thought to anything that does not concern you."

Lavinia laughed. "Stay with me. I love the way you treat me. I don't know why. Mama would have dismissed you long ago for insolence."

"But you are not Mama, and if I am dismissed I will take myself off without delay."

"Huffy again! Of course I want you to stay. You're my best friend, Drusilla. What a name! It suits you. You look like a Drusilla."

"Prim? Disapproving of all the fun?"

"That's right."

"It's not true. I only disapprove of the so-called fun you like to have with the opposite sex, which has once had dire consequences, which you should remember."

"Are we back to that?"

"Yes . . . and be careful of the Khansamah. He may not be what you think."

"Oh, he's polite to me always. He's quite humble now."

"I wouldn't trust him."

"You wouldn't trust your maiden aunt who goes to church four times a day and prays for an hour kneeling by her bedside every night."

"I have no such maiden aunt."

"You ought to be one yourself—only you haven't any family to be aunt to. That's why you impress your prim propriety on me."

"I tell you . . ."

"I'm going home!" she mimicked. "Oh, no you won't. What was I telling you? Oh, I know. How G.K. is with me. He is rather sweet really. Do you know he brought me a present the other day. I know what it is for. He's asking for forgiveness

331

for that outburst. Of course I forgive him. He just admired me so much."

"I believe you would have surrendered if I hadn't come in."

"Give up my virtue! What an experience it would have been!"

"You have so little virtue that you would hardly be aware of its loss. As to experience . . . so is jumping into the sea and drowning yourself, but I don't suggest you try that for the sake of sweet experience."

"Oh, shut up and look at the present G.K. brought to me."

She went to a drawer and took out a case.

"You mean you accepted a gift . . . from him!"

"Of course I accepted it. One has to accept gifts in the spirit in which they are given. It's extremely impolite not to do so."

She opened the box and drew out its contents. She held it to her face, peering over the top coquettishly.

I was staring in horror at a peacock-feather fan.

The weeks that followed were marked by increasing tension. In certain parts of the country open rebellion had broken out, but so far it had been kept under control.

At the beginning of March of that year, 1857, Alice and Tom Keeping were married. It was a simple ceremony, which I attended with Dougal, Lavinia and Fabian, who had made a flying visit to Delhi for the occasion and left immediately afterwards. He did say that he had urgent Company business and must keep in touch with the Army. He was going to the Punjab, where, so far, everything was quiet.

Dougal remained in Delhi and I had several opportunities of talking to him.

He said he would very much like to get out of the country and Fabian had agreed with him on this. Undercurrents of rebellion were springing up everywhere and the journey to the coast might prove very hazardous. But for the children, he thought it would be advisable to attempt to leave. Both he and Fabian agreed that Delhi might perhaps be the safest place for us to be after all, for the biggest concentration of Army personnel was stationed there.

I had thought a great deal about the Khansamah's gift of the peacock-feather fan to Lavinia. I could not help feeling that there was some sinister implication in this. I chided myself. It was a small matter compared with the cloud of uncertainty that hung over us. Fans made of peacock feathers were common enough in the bazaars and marketplaces. True, they were mostly bought by foreigners who would not know of their reputation . . . whatever that was. But what was the significance of Khansamah's gift of one to Lavinia?

She believed it was a form of apology for his behaviour; but then Lavinia would always believe what she wanted to.

I did ask Dougal about peacock feathers. He was very interested in old customs and he had probably heard that they were considered to be unlucky. He had not, but being Dougal, he set himself the task of finding out.

As he had known that one day he would have to visit India, he had made it his duty to find out all he could about that country, and in his possession were several books which he had brought out with him from England. There was not much that he could tell me, however, but he did discover that there were suspicions regarding peacocks' feathers and one or two sources stated that in some quarters they were considered to be bringers of ill luck.

I told him that I had one in my possession, which had been given to me by Miss Lucille Framling, who had certainly believed in its evil influence.

"Odd that she should wish to pass it on to you," he said.

I told him of the incident when I had taken the fan. He smiled and said, "I believe she was a little unbalanced."

"Yes, she had a great tragedy. Her lover was murdered and it seemed to her that it was all due to the fan."

"Well, that's a lot of nonsense."

I did not tell him that the Khansamah had presented Lavinia with one. I wondered what he would say if he knew that she had carried on a mild flirtation with the man. Sometimes I thought he did not care what Lavinia did.

"It goes back to the legend of Argus, whose eyes went to the peacock's tail. Some believe that Argus wants revenge and that the spots are eyes which see everything that is going on . . . not only what is visible, but what is in the mind. There

333

are quite a number of people in this country who never have peacock feathers in their houses."

"They don't all feel like that, I suppose. Some might think the fans made pleasant gifts. They are really very beautiful."

"It might be that the fact that they are would make them more evil in the eyes of the superstitious."

I tried to forget that the Khansamah had given Lavinia the fan. Heaven knew there were far more important matters to concern me.

I received a letter from Alice. She was very happy. She wrote: "Tom is wonderful and we often marvel at the fortuitous way in which we met. Tom is wondering what is going to happen next. I think he realizes the danger of the situation more than most, for his work takes him all over the country. His work is so exciting and it is marvellous to be able to help him. You will be happy to know that the cargo is settled and being taken care of. I look forward to meeting you some time. Perhaps we shall come back to Delhi. Tom is never sure where his work will take him and things are a little uncertain now. It would be wonderful to have a real talk about everything."

I was so pleased to read her letter. How wonderfully life had turned out for Alice!

Meanwhile, as the uneasy weeks passed, rumour intensified. April had passed and May was with us. Lord Canning made a proclamation assuring the sepoy troops that the cartridges they used were not greased with pork or beef, but it was, I believed, received with scepticism.

Dougal was called away. He went reluctantly.

"I don't like leaving you here alone," he said. "Major Cummings will keep an eye on the house. You must do whatever he tells you."

Lavinia was rather pleased. She was developing a fondness for Major Cummings.

The day Dougal left, Fabian returned.

He asked me to go to his study. When I arrived, I saw how serious he was.

He said, "I can't talk to Lavinia. She has no sense of responsibility. I can't tell you how worrying this is, Drusilla. It seems to me you are the only sensible one here, now that Alice Philwright has gone. A pity. She is a practical young woman."

"What has happened?"

"God knows. There is a terrible feeling of uneasiness throughout the Company and the Army. It was a mistake to depose the King of Delhi—old Bahadur Shah was quite harmless—and an even greater one to try to turn them out of the family mansion. You see, Drusilla, we have won many a battle with the sepoy troops. Now they say to themselves: Who won these battles? It is the soldier who wins the battles . . . not those in command. What we could do for the British we could do for ourselves. They are against us, Drusilla . . . and they are part of the Army."

"Do you really think they would revolt?"

"Some would. The Sikhs are loyal . . . so far. I think they can see what benefits have come through us and they care enough for the country to want us to continue. But this headlong nationalism . . . we can't stop it. What worries me is you and Lavinia and the children. I do wish I could get you home."

"I don't think that would be easy, would it?"

"Far from easy . . . but just possible. You see, if we got you out of Delhi, where would you go? One doesn't know from one hour to the next where revolt will break out. We might be sending you into disaster . . . whereas here in Delhi . . . at least we are well represented and we know where we are."

"There must be more important things to worry about than us."

"That is not the case," he said. "I wish to God you had never come. I wish I could stay here. I want to keep my eyes on things . . . here. But I can't. Drusilla, you will have to think for yourself and Lavinia."

"Have you talked to Lavinia?"

"I have tried to. It doesn't make much impression. She doesn't really see danger. I don't like leaving you here with the Khansamah. I wish I could get rid of him. I am certain that he was responsible for that outbreak of thuggery. He would regard it as a gesture of defiance . . . against us, you see. He is at variance with the laws because *we* have imposed them. But someone took revenge on *him*, for the murder of young Asraf was revenge by the family of one of the victims. Now he may suspect that we were involved in the plot to spirit Roshanara away. I want you to be ready to leave at a moment's notice."

"I will be."

"There may not be much warning. I wish I could stay in Delhi, but I have to leave tonight."

"Don't worry about us. I will be prepared."

"The children . . ."

"I shall manage that. I shall tell them it is a new game. They will be easy to handle then."

"I'm sure you'll manage. Sometimes I thank God you are here and at others I curse myself for having brought you."

I smiled at him. "Please don't do that," I said. "It has been . . . illuminating."

He looked at me steadily for a moment and then suddenly he put his arms round me and held me tightly against him.

Then I felt that everything was worthwhile.

When he had gone I felt a frightening loneliness. There seemed to be a special stillness in the air . . . a tension, as if something terrible were lurking, ready to spring out on us and destroy us.

It was early evening. The children were in bed. The ayah's cousin had joined her to help her look after the children. She was a quiet, gentle girl and both Louise and Alan were already fond of her.

I heard a gentle knock at the door. I went to it and there was the ayah.

"Is anything wrong?" I cried in alarm.

She put her fingers to her lips and came into the room.

"I want you to come . . . see my brother. He must see you."

"Why does he want to see me?"

"He want to say thank you." She lowered her voice. "For saving Roshanara."

"There is no need for that."

"Yes . . . great need."

I knew how easily susceptibilities could be wounded, so I said, "I shall be home tomorrow. Perhaps he would call then."

"He not come. He say you go to him."

"When?"

336

"Now."

"The children . . ."

"They are in good care."

I knew that she had set her little cousin to watch over them.

"Very important," she said and added mysteriously, "for plan."

I was very puzzled and she went on, "Come. Go to gazebo. Wait there."

I was very curious, but I did sense an urgency in her manner, and because I knew that I must be prepared for any extraordinary occurrence I fell in at once with her suggestion.

I looked in at the children. They were sleeping peacefully and the ayah's cousin was seated by Alan's bed.

"I watch," she said.

I went with all speed to the gazebo. The ayah was already there. She opened a box and took out a blue sari, which she asked me to put on. It seemed to become more and more mysterious, but remembering Fabian's warnings and the dangers in which we were living, I complied. She gave me a piece of material rather like a shawl to put round my head.

"We go," she said.

We left the garden, avoiding coming in view of the house, and we were soon hurrying along the streets.

I knew the way well. It was near the bazaar.

We came to a house. I had noticed it before, because it had a magnificent mango tree in front of it. Now it was full of blossom.

"This is my brother's house," said the ayah.

The brother came out to greet us. He bowed twice and took us into the house. He drew aside a beaded curtain and invited us into a room which seemed full of carved wooden furniture.

"Salar very happy," he said. "He want thank for Roshanara . . ." He shook his head and there were tears in his eyes. "She safe now . . . she well. She happy. Missie Drusilla, she say, she one great lady."

"Oh, it was nothing," I told him. "Naturally we wouldn't have allowed it to happen. It is against the law."

"Salar . . . he wish to do service. He wish to say not good in big house. Not good stay."

"Yes," I said, "there is trouble everywhere."

"Not good," he went on, nodding. "Salar want to say big thank."

"Well, you must not think any more of it. We were fond of Roshanara. We could not allow her to do as they wanted her to. Naturally we did what we could."

The ayah said, "My brother does not understand. He say you must leave big house. It not good."

"I know," I said. "We shall go when we can."

"My brother say best go back across sea."

"Tell him we shall when the opportunity comes."

They talked together, Salar shaking his head and the ayah nodding with him.

"He say will help," she told me.

"Will you thank him very, very much and say that I shall not forget his kindness."

"He owe debt. He like not to owe. He like to pay."

"I am sure he does and I do appreciate it. Tell him that if I need his help I will ask."

In due course we were ushered out of the house.

Salar evidently felt relieved, for he had made his gratitude known to me.

It was a few days later when I heard that incendiary fires were springing up all over Meerut and that mutiny had broken out there.

The tension in the household increased. The Great Khansamah had grown in importance over the past weeks. He strutted about the house as though he were indeed master of us all. I was very much afraid of what he might do.

I talked to Lavinia about it.

I said, "Lavinia, aren't you afraid?"

"What of?"

"Are you completely oblivious to what is going on around you?"

"Oh, all this talk, you mean? There's always talk."

"You know that Fabian and Dougal are worried about us?"

"There is no need to. Major Cummings is here to protect us. He says he will make sure that I am all right."

"What about the children?"

"They are all right. They are only children. They know nothing of all this whispering. Besides, you'll look after them . . . and Ayah, of course."

"Lavinia, you don't seem to have an inkling of what is going on. This is an explosive situation."

"I tell you we shall be all right. Khansamah will make sure of that."

"He is against us."

"He's not against me. We understand each other . . . besides, he's one of my great admirers."

"I marvel at you, Lavinia."

"All right. Marvel away. It is what I expect."

I knew it was no use trying to impress on her the gravity of the situation.

It was only a day or so later when, in the evening, the ayah came to my room.

She said, "We must go . . . go now. I will take the children to the gazebo. Come there . . . as quick as you can. I take children . . . now."

I could see that she was aware of some impending danger and that it was very close. The urgency of her voice convinced me that I must obey at once without question.

"I will go and bring the Countess."

"Quick. No time to lose."

"The children are in bed."

"No matter. I tell them new game. I keep them quiet. We will bring them. Must be quick. No time."

"Why . . . ?"

"Not now. Just come. I tell . . ."

I ran to Lavinia's room. Fortunately she was alone. She was seated by the mirror, combing her hair.

I said, "Lavinia. We have to go at once."

"Where?"

"Down to the gazebo."

"What for?"

"Look. There is no time to explain. I don't know myself

yet. Just come. I know it is important. The children will be
there."

"But whatever for?"

"Don't argue. Come."

"I'm not dressed."

"Never mind."

"I won't be ordered like this."

"Lavinia. Ayah will be frantic. Promise me you'll come at
once. And come quickly. Don't let anyone know where you are
going."

"Really, Drusilla."

"Look, you must have some idea of the danger we're in."
She did look slightly alarmed. Even she must have been aware
of the changing atmosphere.

She said, "All right . . . I'll come."

"I'll go on ahead. I must tell Ayah. She'll be wondering
why I'm so long. Don't forget. Don't tell anyone . . . *not anyone* where you are going, and try not to let anyone see you. It's
very important."

I went down by means of a back staircase. I reached the
garden without seeing anyone, and sped across the grass to the
gazebo.

Ayah was there with the children. I could see the panic in
her eyes.

"We must go . . . quick . . . ," she whispered. "It is dangerous to wait."

Louise said, "It's a new game, Drusilla. It is hide and seek,
isn't it, Ayah?"

"Yes, yes . . . we now hide and seek. Come."

"I must wait for the Countess," I said.

"No wait."

"She will come down here and not know what to do."

"We must take the children now. You come, too."

I said, "I have to wait."

"We cannot. No wait."

"Where are you going?"

"To my brother house."

"To Salar!"

She nodded.

"This what he say. When time come you must be here

. . . with Missie . . . with children . . . Time come. We must go."

"Take the children. I will bring the Countess there. I have told her I will wait for her here. I must stay for her."

The ayah shook her head. "No. Bad. Bad . . . not good."

She had wrapped the children in cloaks so that I could hardly see them. She put the box she had brought to the gazebo into my hands. "You wear," she said. "Cover head. You look Indian woman . . . a little then. Come. Do not wait."

I put on the sari and the shawl over my head.

"Drusilla, you do look funny," said Louise.

"Now we go. I take children. You come to brother. We want do this for you."

"As soon as the Countess arrives I will bring her. She can't be long. I think she is realizing the danger at last."

"Tell her cover head. Wear shawl . . ."

I was dismayed, but I knew I must deal with such problems when they came.

Taking Alan's hand and commanding Louise to keep close, Ayah hurried out of the gazebo.

The stillness was broken only by the sound of insects, with which I had now become familiar. I could hear the beating of my own heart. I was aware the ayah was better informed of danger than I could be and I could see that it had become more acute.

I felt alone and helpless. As soon as I had let the children go I believed I should have gone with them. They were in my charge, but how could I have left Lavinia? The folly of Lavinia had once before had a great effect on my life. I now believed that it was about to do so again.

If only she had come with me at once. It might well be that there was no need for the flight from the house, but Ayah believed so. I went to the door of the arbour and looked towards the house. And then . . . suddenly I heard shouting. I saw dark figures at the windows. It seemed that the entire household was invading the upper rooms.

My heart was thundering, my throat parched. I kept whispering, "Lavinia . . . Lavinia, where are you? Why don't you come?"

There was nothing I wanted so much as to see her stealthily creeping across the grass to the gazebo.

But she did not come.

Instinctively I knew that I should go, that I should find my way to the house with the mango tree. I knew my way there. I had passed it many times.

Go! Go! said my common sense. But I could not go without Lavinia.

What if she came to the gazebo and found me gone? Where would she go? What would she do? She did not know that there would be sanctuary in that house.

I must wait for Lavinia.

I did not know how long I waited. I could see Lavinia's window from where I was. Some of the lamps had been lighted. And as I watched I saw the Khansamah at her window. So he was in her room! He was gone in a second and I wondered if I had been mistaken.

I stood there shivering. I did not know what to do. I prayed for guidance.

Go . . . go now, said the voice within me. But I could not go while Lavinia was in the house.

It must have been an hour later. The night was hot, but I was shivering. I heard the far-off sound of singing . . . drunken singing. It was coming from the lower part of the house.

I hesitated. Then I ventured across the grass. I knew it was folly. Something dreadful had happened in the house. I should run from it as quickly as I could. I should find my way to Salar's house, where Ayah and the children would be waiting for me.

But still I could not do it.

"Lavinia," I heard myself whispering. "Where are you? Why don't you come?"

The waiting was unbearable. I could not endure it. I knew I had to go into the house and find her.

It was folly, of course. The ayah had known that it was imperative for us to get away. She had saved us just in time. But how could I leave Lavinia there?

I told myself that my duty lay with the children. They would need me now. But they were safe with the ayah. If she had reached her brother's house they would be there waiting for me now.

I knew what I had to do. I had to find Lavinia. I could not leave without her. She should have come with me, of course; she was foolish. She always had been foolish. But still I was fond of her. It seemed to me that my life was somehow bound up in hers and I could not desert her now.

I was outside the house. I stood leaning against the wall, listening. The sounds of revelry were coming from the servants' quarters. I pictured the Khansamah there. But where was Lavinia?

She had said she would come. What was she waiting for?

The door was open. I stepped into the hall. I could hear the shouts and laughter more distinctly now. They were very merry . . . the merriment of intoxication, I was sure.

Silently, fearing the Khansamah would appear at any moment, I crept up the stairs. Fortunately that part of the house seemed to be deserted.

The door of Lavinia's room was wide open. I crept along the corridor and paused there.

The sight that met my eyes was one that will be forever imprinted on my mind. Disorder . . . and horror. The walls of the room were splashed with blood. And there, spreadeagled across the bed, was Lavinia's nude body. Something about its posture was obscene, and I knew it had been placed deliberately so. Her eyes were wide and staring with horror. Her glorious hair was matted with blood, and spread out at her feet was the blood-spattered peacock-feather fan. I knew then that the Khansamah had done this.

I felt sick and faint, for I saw that her throat had been cut.

Lavinia was dead. That beauty which had been her pride, which had obsessed her and made her what she was, had in the end destroyed her.

Instinctively I knew that the Khansamah had taken his revenge in his own way, because she had encouraged him and then rejected him. She had committed the great crime in his eyes of insulting his dignity. He had been waiting to avenge his lost prestige; the gift of the peacock-feather fan had been a warning.

For some moments I could see nothing but the horror of this.

Lavinia . . . Lavinia . . . why did you not come? Why did you hesitate? You have destroyed yourself.

How can I tell the children? I asked myself, as if that were the most important thing in the world.

The children! I must get back to them. I should be looking after them. I would have to plan for them as I had planned for Fleur.

I must get out of this house of death immediately. If I were discovered my fate would be that of Lavinia. I was needed. I must look after the children.

I turned away from that scene of horror. I crept down the stairs. Luck was with me, for no one appeared. I was out through the open door, speeding across the grass.

The night air sobered me. I went inside the gazebo and allowed myself a few seconds to regain my breath. I must get to the children. To do so I had to pass through the streets. I could guess what was happening in every house where Europeans were living. The Mutiny had started in earnest. What we had feared for all these weeks had erupted, and it was far worse than anything I had imagined.

There were few people in the streets. I was glad of the shawl and the sari. Ayah had been wise to provide them. I stooped a little, for I was tall and my height might betray me.

That journey through the streets seemed to take a long time. I saw several bloodied bodies lying in the roads. They were all Europeans. I guessed what was happening and as I turned each corner I expected to come face to face with someone who would recognize me as belonging to the race they hated.

My good fortune was great that night. I realized how great later.

I reached the house.

Ayah embraced me when she saw me.

"I have been worried."

"Ayah," I stammered. "They've killed her. She's dead."

She nodded. "She should have come."

"Oh yes . . . yes . . . She wouldn't believe it. It was awful. Blood . . . blood all over the room."

"Remember the children," she said.

"Where are they?"

"Asleep now. You have been long."

"Ayah . . . what are we going to do?"

She said resignedly, "We wait. We see. You rest now. Safe for a while. My brother, he happy. He pay debt."

She took me into the workshop. Carved wooden objects were scattered about the place. There was a smell of wood in the air. I noticed a window that looked out onto a courtyard.

"All right," she said. "Out there courtyard. Salar's courtyard. No one see."

She took me into a small room which led from the workroom. There was no window in this room. The children lay on a pallet on the floor, fast asleep. There was another pallet beside them.

"You here," said the ayah, pointing to it. "You rest now. You feel very bad."

Feel bad? Indeed I did. I was desperately trying to shut out of my mind that scene, which I knew I would never be able to forget.

I lay on the pallet. I was seeing it all again. That once-pleasant room transformed into a scene from some hellish horror . . . something I could never have imagined. Blood . . . blood . . . everywhere, and Lavinia's body placed across the bed, her once-flaunted beauty degraded and gone forever.

I lay there thinking of the first time we had met, of going away to school . . . Lavinia, who had been so much a part of my life almost always . . .

And now . . . no more.

What could I have done to save her? I should have impressed on her more urgently the need to go. I should have made her understand the danger. But who could make Lavinia do what she did not want to?

My face was wet. I was weeping. It helped a little. It soothed me somehow.

Oh, Lavinia . . . Lavinia . . . dead.

One of the children stirred in sleep as though to remind me that it was my duty to calm myself, not to give way to grief, to cherish them, to make them as my own.

I often wondered how the woodcarver Salar managed to keep us hidden in his house for all those weeks. It was an amazing feat.

The house was not big. He lived alone, for he was unmarried. He carved his wooden objects and took them along to the shops that bought them from him. He had always lived a lonely life, so this was a help.

I learned a little about him from Ayah, who told me that his niece Roshanara had meant a great deal to him. He loved the girl more than he had ever loved anyone else and he would never forget that we had saved her life. One day he would visit her; perhaps he would live close to her; and he owed that to us. He was happy now, for he was paying his debt . . . more than paying it. Three lives for one. He was pleased about that. But he had not yet saved us. Only the first part of the operation had been carried out. The debt would not be wiped out until we could walk freely in the streets again.

On the very night of our escape Ayah went back to the house. She did not want suspicion to fall on her, for that could lead the Khansamah to Salar's house, and if he came that would be the end of us all. Salar would not be able to protect us then; and whatever happened, Salar must pay his debt.

This was a blessing, for she could keep me informed of what was happening there; also, she could walk the streets and get an idea of the general situation.

It was very difficult to keep the children amused and to answer their questions. The little courtyard which I had seen from the window was shut in by very high walls; but at least it was open to the sky, and this was the only fresh air that the children could have. We dared not let them be seen. Ayah brought some little trousers and tunics so that they were dressed like the natives, but their fair hair betrayed them. We toyed with the idea of dyeing it black, but we doubted whether we could do this satisfactorily. In any case, we would be afraid to let them venture out. We could not keep up the pretence that this was merely a game of hide and seek. Louise was too intelligent for that.

I said to her, "We have to hide here for a little while, because there are some bad men who are trying to find us."

Her eyes widened. "What bad men?" she asked.

"Just . . . bad men."

"Great Khansamah?" she asked.

How much does she know? I wondered. I had often been startled by the mingling of innocence and shrewdness displayed by children.

I decided to tell her the truth. "Yes," I said.

She regarded me seriously. "He does not like us," she said. "I know."

"How did you know?" I asked.

She merely nodded. "I know," she said.

"So we have to stay here for a little while until . . ."

"Until he has gone away?"

"Yes," I said.

"Where is my mama?" asked Alan.

Louise was regarding me intently and I knew I had to tell them. I made up my mind quickly. "Your mama has gone away."

"When is she coming back?" asked Louise.

"Well . . . she has gone a long way."

"Home to England?" asked Louise.

"Well . . . not exactly. She has gone farther than that."

"There isn't farther than that," said Louise gravely.

"Yes, there is. There's Heaven."

"Is that where she's gone?"

"Yes."

"How long will she stay?" asked Alan.

"Well, when people go to Heaven it is usually for a long time."

"Will she be with the angels?" asked Louise.

"I'm an angel," said Alan.

"You're not an angel," said Louise. "You haven't got any wings. You're only a little boy."

"I'm Drusilla's angel," he said. "Aren't I, Drusilla?"

I hugged him and said he was.

I was near to tears and Louise was watching me intently. She was a very serious little girl and I think she did not entirely accept my stories of what was happening.

"*You* won't go away, will you?" she said.

I shook my head and said that if I had my way I would never go.

Days passed. Each morning I awoke and wondered whether this would be my last day on Earth, and each night when I lay on my pallet I wondered whether I would live through to the next day.

I tried to carry on with lessons. I invented games that we could play. We had guessing games and I was continually trying to devise new versions of old ones. Alan was often fretful. He wanted to go out into the garden. It was difficult to explain to him. Louise understood, I think, that we were in real danger; she was a sensible and clever little girl.

Ayah visited us often. It was quite natural that she should call on her brother. She brought news of what was happening.

The sepoys who had murdered their officers were now the Army, and they were in Delhi. Moreover, Bahadur Shah had been restored. Everyone must do homage to the King. The British had been driven out of Delhi. Any found on the streets would be instantly despatched. India was now for the Indians. The great Nana Sahib, who bore the same name as our Great Khansamah, was marching through Oudh to the North West Provinces preaching rebellion and the need to throw off the foreigners' yoke. Risings had taken place in Lahore and Peshawur. Soon the British would be driven out of India, said Salar.

I did not believe my countrymen would allow themselves to be so easily dismissed and it seemed that I might be right in this, for soon after we heard that Sir John Lawrence had armed the Sikhs and with their help had curbed the power of the sepoys. The Punjab remained faithful to the British and rumour had it that Sir John Lawrence was sending an army to the relief of Delhi.

I knew that we were in acute danger and that if any man, woman or child of European origin were found in the streets they would be instantly killed.

I gave myself entirely up to the care of the children. I had to keep them happy and myself occupied. I gave my entire attention to them; it was one way of shutting out that fearful memory.

I wished that I had never seen it. To have heard vaguely that Lavinia had been killed, as had thousands of others, would have shocked me deeply, but that I should have seen the manner in which she died, seemed more than I could bear to think of.

The children were a blessing. They were very good in the circumstances. At least we were not so much in the dark as we had been. Louise had a strong sense of danger. Sometimes she would come and stand beside me for no apparent reason. I understood. She was old enough to realize that we were living through dangerous times. She clung to both me and the ayah. I knew she was very disturbed when the ayah was not with us.

They were wonderful, those two . . . the ayah and her brother. I had complete trust in them; the fidelity of Ayah and the integrity of Salar were an example to us all.

All the time I was wondering about Fabian and Dougal. Where were they? How had they fared in this holocaust? I guessed that Fabian, at least, would be somewhere in the heart of the trouble. I longed for news of him. Lying on my pallet at night I would think of him, and because I felt life was so uncertain and death was hovering all the time behind any door, I faced my true feelings for him.

I longed to be with him. The times I had spent with him had been the highlights of my life. I liked to brood on the childish episode when he had seen me as a baby and taken me for his own. He might have kept me there always. What a difference that would have made to my life! I thought of him as he had been, stretched out on the settee . . . with Lavinia kneeling before him with a chalice of wine while I fanned him with Miss Lucille's peacock-feather fan.

Then my mind switched to that terrible scene . . . the sight of the bloodstained feathers of the fan that the Khansamah had given to Lavinia. How strange that there should be yet another feather fan to haunt me. When he had given that fan to Lavinia she had believed it meant contrition on his part. How little she understood. It meant disaster was coming to her . . . revenge because she had slighted him.

I must cling to something to blot out the memory. Fabian would save us, I told myself. I prayed that he might still be alive and that I should soon see him again.

I must face the truth. He was more important to me than I dared admit; but what was the point of deceiving myself now? Why did I not admit to my obsession with him? It had been there ever since we had been children. I supposed I was in love with him. I had always been what was called a sensible girl. Even Lady Harriet had admitted to that. Had she not sent me to the finishing school in France—which my father could never have afforded—for the purpose of looking after Lavinia?

And I *had* looked after her. I had brought her through a difficult situation which, had we not been successful, would have ruined her prospects for a grand marriage. That was something of which Lady Harriet was ignorant, but I was sure she would have approved of my action had she known.

I was a sensible girl. I must go on being sensible. Just because I was overwrought . . . just because I had witnessed something more terrible than I could ever have imagined, I must not allow it to unnerve me.

The ayah came in to tell me the news. Something was happening. The British were advancing on Delhi and there was great consternation throughout the city.

"Take great care," said Salar. "They must not find you."

We waited. Could this life be going to change? The weeks were passing. Surely something must happen soon?

It was a hot June day when an attempt was made to blow open the gates of the city. Perhaps Delhi would be taken. Then perhaps I might see Fabian.

However, this was not to be. The people rose in their determination to hold the city. The sepoys were well trained and they were brave soldiers; and they did not fight the less boldly and skilfully because they were fighting for India.

It was a bitter disappointment when the attempt failed, but of course that was not the end. There followed more long weeks of waiting and speculation, wondering if each day would be our last. We had come to Salar's house in May, and it was not until September that the city of Delhi was taken by the Sikhs and the British.

It was still unsafe to venture out. Fighting was going on in the streets and anyone not of the Indian race would be shot on sight.

But hope had returned. Something must happen soon. Louise was aware of this.

"Will my mother come back now?" she asked.

"No, Louise. She can't come back."

"Will my father?"

"Perhaps."

"And my uncle?"

"I don't know. They will come if they can. They will want to make sure that we are all safe."

"Shall we go away from here then?"

"Yes, we shall go away."

"On a big ship? Home?"

It was pleasant to hear her speak of England as home, for she had never seen it, yet it meant home to her.

"Yes," I told her. "One day . . ."

"Soon?"

"Perhaps that may well be."

She nodded, smiling. She knew that if she asked some questions she would get evasive answers and her instinct told her that they might not be true.

And so we waited.

One day the ayah came to me. It was in the late afternoon. I thought this was simply one of her periodic visits, but it was quite different.

She said, "We all leave house. Khansamah say it is not safe. He says enemy come. Soldiers in all houses, British soldiers now. He say they blame us . . . kill us."

"They wouldn't kill you."

"Khansamah, he say . . ."

"Where is the Khansamah?"

"I do not know. He say all go. They all go different places."

She stayed in her brother's house all that day and the next night. We waited eagerly for news.

The following day she went out. She still thought it might be unsafe for me to venture into the streets with the children. People were still being killed, and even though the British Army had taken over the town there were still pockets of resistance.

When she came back she said, "I see Fabian Sahib. He is at house."

I was speechless, but I think she must have been aware of the joy that was surging through me.

"Did you see him? Did you speak to him?"

She nodded. "I go to him. He say, 'Where Missie Drusilla and children? Where Memsahib Countess?' "

"You . . . you told him?"

She shook her head. "I fear Khansamah. He watch me. I think he know." She began to tremble. "I think he watch me."

"But where is he?"

She hesitated. "I didn't see . . . but I think he watch. I think he follow me. I did not see, but I know."

"Well," I said. "He won't be able to do any harm now. He is no longer at the house. What did you tell Sir Fabian?"

"I tell him Countess dead, children safe with you."

"So you did tell him that?"

She nodded. "He say, 'Where? Where?' But I did not tell. I fear Khansamah come here. I fear he watch. I say, 'I bring Missie Drusilla to you.' He say, 'Yes, yes.' And then I run away."

"I must go to him," I said.

"Not in day. Wait for night."

How did I live through that day? I felt lightheaded. An exultation had taken hold of me. Then I experienced guilty feelings. There was death and destruction all around me. How could I feel this joy when I was still mourning Lavinia's death and that of all the others who had died with her?

At last it was evening.

"Wear sari," said Ayah. "Cover up head best. Then come."

I went through the streets with Ayah, hurrying along, being able to think of nothing but the possibility of seeing him, yet fearing that I never should. I imagined an assassin at every turn.

I had an uneasy feeling that we were being followed. A light footfall . . . a hasty glance over my shoulder. Nothing. Only imagination stretched beyond belief because of all the terrible things that had happened in the last months of my life.

I must live through the next moments. I must see Fabian again.

And there was the house.

"I wait for you in the gazebo," said Ayah.

I went swiftly across the grass. There were lights in several of the windows. I wanted to call out: Fabian. I'm here, Fabian.

There was a clump of flowering shrubs near the house. As I passed this I heard a movement behind me. I turned sharply and as I did so, terror swept over me. I was looking into the murderous eyes of the Khansamah.

"Missie Drusilla," he said softly.

"What . . . what are you doing here?"

"My home," he said.

"No more. You have betrayed those who trusted you."

"You very bold, Missie Drusilla," he said. "You go . . . you take children . . . you hide. I know now where. I kill Ayah . . . but you first."

I screamed for help as he sprang towards me. I saw the knife in his upraised hand. I called out again and with all my strength pushed him from me.

It was a feeble effort, but it did cause him to reel back a little. He regained his balance immediately and was coming nearer. Those seconds seemed to go on for a long time. It amazes me, thinking back, how much can pass through the mind at such a moment. My first thought was: Has Ayah betrayed me? Is it for this she brought me here? No. She would never do that. She loved the children. She was fond of me for what I had done for Roshanara. It was an unworthy thought. I believed in that fearful moment that this was the end. I shall never see Fabian again, I thought. And who will look after the children?

Then there was a shattering explosion. The Khansamah threw up his hands. I heard the knife fall to the ground; he reeled drunkenly before he collapsed in a heap at my feet.

Fabian was coming towards me, a pistol in his hand.

"Drusilla!" he said.

I felt faint with shock. I thought I must be dead and dreaming.

His arms were round me. He was holding me tightly against him. I was trembling.

I heard him mutter, "Are you all right? Thank God you are safe . . ."

"Fabian," I whispered. "Fabian . . ." Repeating his name seemed to relieve me.

"Let's get inside . . . away from that."

"He's dead," I murmured.

"Yes, he's dead."

"You . . . saved me."

"Just in time. The old villain. It's his just deserts. Tell me . . . I've wondered so much . . . such nightmare thoughts. You're shivering. Come into the house. Don't be afraid. They've all gone . . . none of them stayed when we came in. The house is safe now. There's so much to say . . ."

He put his arm round me and led me into the house. It was quiet.

"I'll find some brandy or something," he said.

A soldier in uniform came into the hall.

"Can you find some brandy, Jim?" said Fabian. "There's been a nasty accident out there. Get rid of the body, will you? It's an old rascal who used to work here. He tried to kill Miss Delany."

"Yes, sir," said the man. He was clearly no more moved by one request than the other.

We went into the drawing room, which no longer looked familiar, and after a few moments the man returned with the brandy and two glasses.

Fabian poured it out. "Drink this," he said. "You'll feel better."

I took the glass with trembling hands.

"That man . . ." I began.

"Stop thinking of him. It was you or him. So he had to go. Moreover, he has caused a lot of trouble. He's had that coming to him for a long time."

"Lavinia . . ." I said. And I told him.

He was deeply shocked. "My poor foolish sister . . . she never learned, did she?" He took a sip of brandy and stared ahead of him. He had cared for her, I knew, although he had deplored her conduct and had usually treated her with an affectionate contempt. He had done what he could for Fleur's future. It was a terrible blow to him that she was dead.

"It was that man . . ." I said, and I heard myself blurting out what I had seen. "The peacock-feather fan was at her feet. It was spattered with blood. He must have put it there."

Fabian put an arm round me and held me close to him. I fancied we comforted each other.

"I have avenged her, then," he said at length. "I am glad I was the one. We have been looking for him for some time. He was one of the leaders. Fancied himself a Nana Sahib. Thank God we've got him now. It will be over in a little time, Drusilla. But there's a good deal to do yet. We'll get away from it all . . . we'll be able to put all this behind us . . . once we are out of this mess."

I started to talk about the children . . . about Salar and his workshop and the way in which he had sheltered us all this time.

"Good man. He shall be rewarded."

"He doesn't want rewards," I said. "He wants to pay his debt for what we did for Roshanara."

"Yes," he said. "I understand that."

"What was the Khansamah doing here?" I asked.

"Probably trying to get me. He was lurking in the grounds, I suspect. So that must have been his idea. We have some of the military here and I daresay there were attempts at sniping. We'll have to take the greatest care."

"And Dougal?" I asked. "Where is Dougal?"

"I haven't heard from him for some time. I think he may be in Lucknow. Alice and Tom will be there, too."

I shivered. "If only this were over."

"It will be," he assured me. "But there is plenty of danger yet. You must go back to Salar's shop. You've been safe there so far. The children must stay there. How are they?"

"Restive . . . but otherwise all right. I can't tell you what I owe to the ayah and her brother. It's really all because of Roshanara."

"Well, we foiled the old devil over that little matter. It is comforting to know he is beyond seeking revenge now. You have been constantly in my thoughts, Drusilla . . . all of you."

"And you have been in mine . . . with Dougal . . . Alice and Tom."

"I know the children will be as safe as it is possible to be with you. The thing is, where do we go from here? I wouldn't want you to come to the house . . . yet. I feel that would be

355

unsafe. I am going to move heaven and earth to get you all home as soon as possible."

"You said the trouble was dying down."

"It will be a slow death, I fear. Although we are here in force there is going to be trouble yet. I'd be so much easier in my mind if I thought that you and the children were out of it. A pity we're not in Bombay. Then it might be possible to get you away. But here . . . you'd have to travel across country and heaven knows what you might run into. Now what you have to do is get back to Salar's. Stay there as you were for a few days and then we'll see how things are. I shall know where you are . . . and I am going to concentrate on getting you out of the country and home."

I could not think clearly. It was all-important that he was alive . . . that we had met again . . . that he was so moved and delighted to see me, that he was the one who had saved my life when I was on the brink of death. Perhaps in such circumstances one thinks more lightly of death than one does normally. This night I had seen a man shot dead before my eyes and I could only feel a numbed sense of shock, which was overpowered by a tremendous happiness.

He took me back to the gazebo, where the ayah was waiting. She had heard the shot and had crept out to see what had happened. She had thought at first that I might have been killed. I think she must have been relieved when she saw the dead man, for she herself had lived in fear of him for a very long time. There was no doubt that he had been arrogant, cruel and sadistic. I suppose I should not feel so disturbed because he had been treated as he had treated so many. But death is shocking and I could not throw off the effects of that shock.

Ayah was delighted to see me safe, but she was a little worried to see Fabian, and more so when he told us that he was going to see us safely to her brother's house, where I was to stay for a while longer. She was very disturbed. He must not be seen with us. Who knew who would watch?

She was really frightened, and Fabian saw reason in her fear, so it was arranged that she and I should walk ahead of him, with Fabian watchful of us but keeping his distance, his pistol ready, in case he should have to come to our assistance.

And so I went back to Salar's house.

I lay on my pallet in a bemused state for the rest of that night.

Life had changed. The streets of Delhi were safer now, though there were periodic outbreaks of violence. Nana Sahib had been defeated, but the Mutiny was by no means quelled, though the British were gaining success after success, and it was becoming clear that, although it might take time, order would eventually be restored. I could go out, but I never went far. Fabian was still at the house and I saw him now and then.

We talked a great deal about the position here. He never discussed the future. Later I thought that was because he did not believe then that there would be one for us.

Death had receded a little. It was no longer lurking beside us, but it was still not very far away.

Fabian's great concern was to get us out of the country. He was continually making enquiries as to how safe it would be for us to travel to the coast. There were big British successes at Rajpootana, Malwa, Berar and some remote places.

It was safe for me to go to the house now, but Fabian did not wish me to go there too often. He thought that some of the Khansamah's men might be around and take it into their heads to avenge his death, and they would shoot anyone connected with the house for that purpose. I was to stay at Salar's house until something could be arranged to get us out of the country.

Fabian did not leave Delhi.

He told me that this would probably be the end of the Company as such. It was being realized, he had heard, that a trading company was not fitted to govern a country; it could be said that the Company had done that, with the aid of the Army. It was not very satisfactory, and he believed that some other form of government would take its place when all this was settled.

"You mean we shall still keep our interests in India?"

"Most certainly, yes. There is no question of that. But there will be new legislation, I am convinced."

I loved those sessions with him. We seemed to grow very close. I was greatly soothed, for the terrible things that I had witnessed had changed me forever. I would never forget the sight of Lavinia, spreadeagled across that bed. I should never be rid of the memory of the peacock-feather fan. I would always remember the look of startled horror on her face. I thought so often of her . . . she who had lived in a world of dreams where she was always the beautiful siren, adored by gallant knights. What had she thought when she had found herself face to face with horrific reality? Perhaps the answer was in those wild, staring eyes.

I often spoke her name aloud. "Lavinia . . . Lavinia, why would you not come with me when I begged you to? Why did you delay? Could you really have believed that the Khansamah was your devoted slave, that no harm would come to you while he was there?" Oh, poor deluded Lavinia!

Fabian had been deeply shocked by what had occurred, but he was a realist. She was dead. Nothing could bring her back. Her death was in a way due to her folly. What we had to do now was think of the children.

The coming of the new year saw the end of rebellion in Bengal, and in most of Central India. Bahadur Shah, the last of the Moguls, had been tried and convicted of treason and sent to Burmah. Order was slowly being restored. I still thought a good deal about Dougal, Alice and Tom. It seemed they must still be in Lucknow, for we had heard no news of them. I was desperately afraid of what might have happened.

Life was more tolerable. We were still living at Salar's house, but we were freer now and there was no need for us to keep our identity secret. Our own people were back in command in Delhi. We had nothing to fear from the Sikhs, who had always been loyal to British rule and had realized the benefits it brought to them.

I did not take the children to the house, for I feared it would bring back memories and start them asking questions about their mother; but Fabian came to Salar's house. They were pleased to see him and showed some rather restrained affection towards him, for they were still a little in awe of him.

He had changed somewhat. He was more serious now. What had happened to Lavinia had affected him more deeply than I realized. Moreover, he had lost several friends and colleagues in the debacle. I supposed no one who had lived through all that could ever be the same carefree person again.

One must take life seriously when one could never be sure when one could be plunged into horror.

Our conversation was very sober now and we talked a great deal about what was happening in this country. Those verbal battles between us were no more. I felt that our relationship—however deep it was now—must change when we returned to more normal circumstances. Perhaps we had been drawn together closely but superficially. I had a sense of transience.

I thought often: I shall never be the same person again. I told myself often that I must not attach too much importance to my new relationship with Fabian, for neither of us was living a normal life.

The year was advancing. At any moment I was prepared to hear that I must make ready to go.

Then it came. I was to prepare to set out for Bombay in two days' time, taking the children with me. The ayah would remain behind in her brother's household. I would travel in the company of a party of women and children. For a long time plans had been in progress to get them home.

"So," I said blankly, "I shall travel alone."

"I shall accompany you as far as Bombay," said Fabian. "I cannot contemplate your making that journey, which may be highly dangerous . . . without me."

I felt my heart leap with joy while I chided myself for my folly.

How sad it was to say goodbye to the ayah. Salar was triumphant. He had successfully paid his debt. Ayah was calm; the children were quiet. It was a great wrench for them—perhaps their first real sorrow.

I said, "Dear Ayah, it may be that we shall meet again."

She gave me that infinitely sad smile of hers, and told me of her deep unhappiness, but that she must accept her fate.

That journey to Bombay seems unreal to me even now.

We set out in a *dâk-ghari* type of vehicle, in which I had travelled before. I knew that in those rough carts drawn by one unkempt-looking horse we must prepare for a somewhat uncomfortable journey. The children, sad as they were to leave Ayah, were glad to escape from the confinement of Salar's house. They were going home, Louise told Alan, and the little boy so far forgot his sorrow at parting with his beloved ayah as to jump up and down and sing "Home, home."

There was a magic in that word.

We had set out from the house very early in the morning, I riding in the cart with the children, and Fabian on horseback beside us with half a dozen armed men. We did not have to wait long before more joined the party, and by the time we left Delhi our numbers had increased considerably. There were women and children in *dâk-gharis* like ours. More soldiers joined us. And the long trek began.

We knew that the Mutiny was by no means over and that it was possible that we could be attacked by hostile natives. The fact that we were women and children and elderly people would not save us. This was a war against a race, not against individual people. It was moving to see how everyone wanted to help each other. If anyone was sick or some minor accident occurred, everyone, without exception, wanted to give whatever possible. It amazed me how the sense of impending danger could have that effect on people.

Most of us had seen death in some form over the last months; we knew that its shadow still hung over us and that any moment could be our last: but for some reason we had lost our fear and awe of death. It had become an everyday occurrence. We had learned that life was transient. Perhaps we had become more spiritual, less materialistic. I did not know. But, looking back, I see that it was a strange and elevating experience to have lived through.

We stopped now and then at the *dâk*-bungalows for food and to rest or change horses. We did not sleep there. There was a sense of urgency among the company. Everyone knew that we must get on the ship before we would be safe.

The stops were a relief. It meant that we escaped for a spell the violent jolting of the *dâk-gharis*. We snatched a few hours sleep here and there. The children usually closed their eyes when the sun set and slept through the nights.

I was always aware of Fabian's presence and it comforted me. While he was there I felt assured that we should come safely through. In one way I did not want the journey to end, because I knew it would mean saying goodbye to him, and in spite of the discomfort I found his presence exhilarating.

When we reached Bombay, he would return to Delhi and we would sail away. We might be safe, but he would be going back into danger. Often I wondered what was happening to Tom, Alice and Dougal.

During our little halts Fabian and I would talk together. We would wander a little distance from the others.

He said, "Once you are on the ship all should be well. You will have the journey across land, of course, from Suez to Alexandria . . . but you know of the pitfalls now. You will be with a great number of people and you are not likely to get taken in by handsome strangers of the Lasseur breed."

"No," I answered. "I know better now."

"When you get home you will stay with the children."

"Lady Harriet will want to have them with her."

"Of course. But you will be there, too. You can't desert them. Think what that would mean to them. They have lost their mother and the ayah. They cling to you, I notice. You represent security to them. You must stay with them at Framling. I have written to my mother to tell her this."

"You think a letter will reach her?"

"I have already given it to one of our people who left two weeks ago. I have told her that you will be arriving with the children and I shall want you to remain with them until I come home."

"When will that be?"

He lifted his shoulders. "Who can say? But you must be with them. My mother might be a little . . . formidable . . . just at first. They will need you there to help them understand her. Poor children, they have suffered enough through their experiences."

"It does not seem to have affected them adversely. I believe children soon come to accept everything as normal. They are used now to this hole-and-corner existence. They had all those weeks at Salar's."

"And their mother?"

"They accept her death. They think she has gone to Heaven."

"They will still be wondering."

"So much has happened and Lavinia did not see very much of them. She was a rather remote person to them."

"Perhaps that is as well."

"They miss the ayah, of course."

"That has made them turn more to you. So, you see, Drusilla, you must not leave them. I've explained that to my mother."

"You want me to remain at Framling . . . as a sort of governess."

"You are a friend of the family. When I come home we can make arrangements. Until then, I want you to make sure they are all right. Promise me."

I promised.

"There is something else," he went on. "I have told my mother about . . . the other child."

"You mean Fleur?"

"Yes. I thought she should know."

"But Polly and her sister . . ."

"I know. They have looked after her . . . and very well, too. But what if anything should happen to them? It is right that Fleur should be with her family."

"So Lady Harriet knows at last."

"Well, she had to know sometime. I could not break it to her gently. Who knows what is going to happen here?"

"What do you think she will do?"

"She will probably try to get the child."

"Oh no!"

I could imagine the confrontation, with Polly and Eff on one side and Lady Harriet on the other. It would be the meeting of two formidable contingents. I wondered who would be the stronger.

"I do hope . . ." I began.

"My mother will make up her mind what should be done about the child. And in any case, whatever happens, we know that Fleur will have a home."

I heard myself say faintly, "I suppose you are right."

"I think so."

"Polly and her sister will never let Fleur go."

"I fancy there will be some sort of battle, but I am not sure which side will be victorious. My mother is a very determined lady."

"So are Eff and Polly."

"It will be a battle of the Titans."

He laughed and I found myself laughing with him.

I felt suddenly secure, unafraid.

I shall never forget that night . . . that line of vehicles, the grazing horses . . . the warm balmy air, the hum of insects . . . and Fabian there beside me.

I wanted it to go on. It was absurd, but I was in no hurry to reach Bombay.

There were other pauses. We talked and sometimes were silent, but there was a great bond between us. More than ever I was sure that my life was bound up with the Framlings. Sometimes we talked of the past, and again of those days when he had captured me and made me his child, when he had pretended he was my father.

"You thought you could take what you wanted," I told him, "including other people's children."

"I suppose I did."

"Perhaps you still do."

"Old habits persist."

I thought of the peacock-feather fan, but I did not speak of it. To brood on it brought back the memory that I knew I would never entirely forget—Lavinia on the bloodied bed, with the fan at her feet.

I must put all that behind me. I must live for the future. I had a great task to do. I had to get the children home, to give my life to them . . . until Fabian returned.

At last we were in Bombay. There were the familiar buildings, their walls brilliant white in the dazzling sun, the sea—the gateway to India, as they called it. Now we were to pass through those gates . . . on our way home.

We had to wait a few days for the ship; at last it came. We were taken on board and Fabian came on to see us settled. There was a small cabin that I was to share with the children.

There was no time to be wasted. Soon after we were on board we were ready to sail.

Fabian took his farewells of the children, admonishing them to obey me in all things. They listened solemnly.

Then he took my hands.

"Goodbye, Drusilla," he said. "I'll come home as soon as it is possible." He smiled at me. "We'll have lots to talk about and plenty of time to do it in then," he said.

"Yes," I said.

He kissed me twice, once on either cheek.

"Take great care," he said.

"You, too," I told him.

And that was all. I sailed out of Bombay with the children, leaving Fabian behind in that strife-torn land.

ENGLAND

Homecoming

I remember little of the journey. I suppose it was eventful, as all such journeys are, but everything that happened seemed trivial after what had gone before.

There were the children to look after. There seemed to be children everywhere and they needed constant attention. A sailing ship is not the easiest of nurseries.

There was a certain tension among the older passengers. Many of them had left husbands and other relatives behind in India and were constantly wondering what had happened to them. We had no news; we were a little band of refugees from a strange land.

The children, of course, were excited by everything they saw, and the crew were happy to have them around. I saw Louise on deck, with others of her age, while seamen pointed out to them the dolphins and flying fish. I remember the great excitement when a whale was seen.

We had the inevitable storms, which kept us to our cabins, and the children shrieked with laughter when they could not stand up straight and small objects rolled about the cabin. Everything was new and exciting to them, and at the end of it they were going to that wonderful place called Home.

What they were expecting I could not imagine. I hoped they would not be disappointed.

So we reached Suez.

I was not looking forward to the ride across the desert, but it was of immense excitement to the children. They did not appear to notice the discomfort of the wagons and the wildness of the horses that carried them along. They were thrilled when we stopped at the caravanserais. I could hear Louise telling Alan all about it while he jumped up and down, as he always did to express excitement.

How it all came back to me! The journey with Alice, our acquaintance with Monsieur Lasseur, and then the arrival of Tom Keeping and the mysterious disappearance of the so-called Frenchman.

I shivered to contemplate where I might be now, but for the intervention of Tom on Fabian's orders.

All my thoughts led back to Fabian.

At last we arrived at Southampton.

"Is this home?" asked Louise.

"Yes," I said with emotion. "This is home."

How strange England seemed after that land of brilliant sunshine, often overpowering heat, lotus flowers, banyan trees and dark, silent-footed people with their soft, melodious voices.

It was April when we arrived—a lovely time of year to return to England, with the trees in bud and the spring flowers just beginning to show themselves, the gentle rain, the sun warm without being hot, no longer fierce, merely benign and a little coy, since it so often hid behind the clouds. I watched the children's eyes grow wide with excitement. I think they had long ago made up their minds that home was a kind of Mecca, the promised land, and in it everything would be wonderful.

We were taken to an inn, where we could make our arrangements to return to those who were waiting for us.

I had a message sent off at once to Framling to tell Lady Harriet that I had arrived with the children.

There we heard the news. Sir Colin Campbell had relieved Lucknow. There had been great rejoicing at home at this news. It was believed that the Mutiny was grinding to a halt.

Everyone in the inn wanted to make much of us. We had been through the terrible Mutiny and we had survived. They could not do enough for us.

I was thinking of those I had left behind. How was Fabian?

Had the relief of Lucknow come in time for Alice, Tom and Dougal? I could not bear to think that the love Alice had planned to share with Tom might have been snatched from her.

Lady Harriet was never one for delays. As soon as she received my note, a carriage was sent to take us to Framling. And there we were, riding through English country lanes, past fields like neat green squares, past woodland, streams and rivers. The children were entranced. Louise sat silent, while Alan could not curb his desire to jump up and down.

And there was the familiar village, the green, the rectory, the House, the scene of my childhood. How was Colin Brady? I wondered. Still the humble servant of Lady Harriet, I was sure.

I watched the children as we approached Framling. It looked splendid in the pale sunshine . . . arrogant, formidable and heartbreakingly beautiful.

"Is this home?" asked Louise.

"Yes," I said. "You will soon see your grandmother."

I had to restrain Alan, who was almost jumping out of the carriage.

Up the drive we went . . . so many memories crowding in. Lavinia . . . oh no. I could not bear to think of the last time I had seen her. Fabian . . . I dared not think of him either. Perhaps I had had wild dreams. Now, face to face with that magnificent pile of bricks and soon to see Lady Harriet, I knew how absurd my dreams had been.

He would come back and everything would be as it always had been, except that I was the plain girl from the rectory who would have a good post as governess to Lady Harriet's grandchildren: a good, sensible girl who would remember her place. That was what Lady Harriet would want and expect; and Lady Harriet always had what she wanted.

The carriage had pulled up. One of the servants appeared. Jane? Dolly? Bet? I couldn't remember; but I knew her and she knew me.

"Oh, Miss Delany, Lady Harriet said you're to go to her with the children as soon as you come."

The children could hardly wait to get out of the carriage.

Into the hall . . . the familiar hall with its high, vaulted roof and the weapons on the walls, weapons used by long-dead Framlings to protect the House against any who came against it. Up the staircase to the drawing room, where Lady Harriet would be sitting waiting.

"They're here, Lady Harriet."

She rose. She looked, as ever, stately and formidable. There was a faint colour in her cheeks and her eyes immediately alighted on the children.

I felt their grip on my hands tighten.

"This is your grandmother, children," I said.

They stared at her and she at them. I believed she was deeply touched by the sight of them and she would be thinking of Lavinia, of course. I was glad she did not know the nature of her dying. Fabian would never tell her; nor would I. So many people had died in the Mutiny. It was accepted that it might have been the fate of any one of us.

She looked at me. "Good day, Drusilla," she said. "Welcome home. Come along in. And this is Louise."

Louise nodded.

"I'm Alan," said the boy. "This is home, isn't it?"

Did I see the blink of the eyes, as though she feared she might betray her tears? I believed that was so. I heard the faint catch in her voice when she said, "Yes, my dear child, you have come home." Then she was immediately the familiar Lady Harriet. "How are you, Drusilla? You look well. Sir Fabian has written to me about you. I know you have been very sensible. You were always a sensible girl. Your room is next to the children's. Temporarily perhaps . . . but just at first . . . they would no doubt like that best. Sometime you must tell me of your adventures. Now, Louise, come here, my dear."

Louise released my hand reluctantly.

"My dear child," said Lady Harriet. "How tall you are! All the Framlings are tall. This will be your home now. I am your grandmama. I shall look after you now."

Louise turned to look up at me anxiously.

"Miss Delany . . . Drusilla . . . will be here, too. We shall all be here together. And then you shall have a nanny . . . an English one . . . like Miss Philwright." A faint look of criticism came into her eyes. How dared Nanny Philwright be so forgetful of her duties as to marry and leave the Framling children! She was still the old Lady Harriet. There was no change. I had thought there might be, as I had seen a little emotion. But of course that was merely for the Framling family. It did not extend to outsiders.

Both children watched her with a kind of wonder. I think the sight of them moved her deeply. Perhaps she feared she would show how much, and that made her brisk.

"I daresay the children would like something to eat," she said. "What about some broth . . . some milk, bread and butter? What do you think, Drusilla?"

I felt it was an indication of her emotion that she should ask my opinion.

"They will be having their luncheon soon," she said.

"Then I think a little milk and perhaps a slice of bread and butter would be best." I turned to the children. "Would you like that?" I asked.

Louise said, "Yes, please," and Alan nodded gravely.

"Good," said Lady Harriet. "It will be sent to your rooms. I shall show them to you myself. I have had the old nursery made ready. And, later, Drusilla, I will have a talk with you. You are in the room next to the night nursery for the time being. Later we shall have a nanny . . . but perhaps just at first . . ."

I said I thought that was an excellent arrangement.

We went up the stairs to the old nursery and on the way up Lady Harriet despatched one of the servants for the refreshments.

The rooms were light and airy. I remembered seeing them in the old days when I had come to play with Lavinia. Then I was seeing her again, just as I had that last time, and a terrible sense of doom descended on me. Here in these rooms Fabian had held autocratic sway over, so it was said, even his mother. He had been the pampered one whose slightest whim was to be indulged, even when it meant taking a child from her family.

There would be so many memories here, and in that moment I felt that I wanted to go right away, for I could never be anything but an outsider in this house . . . the rector's daughter, not quite good enough to mingle with Framling society except when she could be of some use to it.

"I will leave you to settle in," said Lady Harriet.

I had the feeling that she wanted to get away, that she could not bear to be in this room where her dead daughter had lived and played as a child, as these grandchildren of hers would now do. Could she really be overcome by emotion? I was sure it was something she would never admit.

At last she had gone and I was alone with the children.

"Is she the Queen?" asked Louise.

That was a strange day. I took the children round the house and the garden. They thought it was all wonderful. We met some of the servants, who could not hide their pleasure at the prospect of having children in the house.

I thought: They will be happy here in time. They clung to me with a little more intensity than before, which told me that they were a little uneasy about the change in their lives; and they were certainly in awe of their formidable grandmother.

My food was sent up on a tray.

Lady Harriet had intimated that she wished to talk to me that evening and I was invited to her sitting room after she had had her dinner.

"Sit down, Drusilla," she said. "There is so much I wish to say to you. I know you have endured a great deal. Sir Fabian has told me how you looked after the children and kept them safely during that dreadful time, for which we are both extremely grateful to you. Sir Fabian says you are to stay with the children, at least until his return, which he hopes will not be very long. He believes there will be changes in India because of this awful mutiny. Louise and Alan are now out of danger, but there is that other child. I know about that and your part in it. It was very unfortunate, but we will not dwell on that. I have had the whole story from my son and I have been to see those people who have the child. That dreadful place where they are living! I sent for them to come here, but they rudely ignored my request . . . and I went to them. What a pity they took the child."

"I must tell you, Lady Harriet, that they were wonderful to us. I don't know what we would have done without them."

"I am not blaming you, Drusilla. Your part in the affair was . . . commendable. That nursemaid of yours . . . she is a forthright woman." I fancied she conceded a grudging admiration for one not unlike herself. "I suppose what they did at the time was . . . admirable. But we have now to think of the child. However unfortunate her birth, she is *my* granddaughter and she must be brought up here at Framling."

"Lady Harriet, they have cared for her since she was a baby. They love her as they would their own. They will never let her go."

"We shall have to see about that," said Lady Harriet firmly. "Sir Fabian thinks she should be here with her half-sister and -brother."

"I know they will never give her up."

"She is a Framling and I am her grandmother. I have my rights."

"It would not be good for the child to take her away immediately."

"We shall in time make them see sense."

"But, Lady Harriet, sense to you might not be sense to them."

She looked at me in surprise that I could make such a suggestion. I did not flinch. I had made up my mind, as I had with Lavinia, that she should not dominate me. If they objected to my behaviour, I should simply have to make them understand that I was here only because I did not want to leave the children. I was more useful to Lady Harriet at this time than she was to me, and that gave me an advantage. My status was not that of an ordinary nursery governess.

"We shall see," she said ominously. Then she added, "I want you to go along and see these people."

"I intend to. Polly is very dear to me, and so are her sister and Fleur."

"Then I should like you to go as soon as possible."

"It is what I intend."

She nodded. "Explain to them the advantages the child would have here. In spite of her birth she is still my grandchild. I think they should be made to understand what that means."

"I think they will want to do what is best for the child."

"Ah. Then you can make them see good sense."

"I am not sure what their reaction will be, Lady Harriet."

"I have confidence in you, Drusilla." She bestowed a smile

on me—a reward in advance for bringing her ill-begotten grandchild back to the flock, I thought. But it was not going to be as easy as that. I knew Polly and I knew Eff. They would be as resolute as Lady Harriet herself. "Well," she went on, "now that Louise and Alan are here, their future is assured."

"What of their father?" I asked. "When he returns he may have plans for them."

"Oh no." She laughed. "He will do nothing. He will see that they are better with me."

"Is there news . . . ?"

"We have had very little. He was in Lucknow with that nanny and her husband." She sniffed to show distaste. "They were all safe. We did hear that. But, of course, those dreadful things are still going on. Those wicked people—to murder those who have done so much for them. *English* men, women and little children . . . murdered by natives! They will get their just deserts, never fear."

I said, "I am glad to hear they are safe."

Lady Harriet nodded. "Well, Drusilla, it has been a long day for you . . . and for me. I will say good night now. The children are sleeping, I suppose."

"Oh, yes, they are very tired."

"I have no doubt of that. I am sorry to impose the duties of nursery maid upon you. But they are used to you and it is best for the time being. I think too many changes would not be good for them at the moment. But I have a good nanny in mind."

"I certainly think that for the time being they are best with me. I have looked after them throughout the journey . . . and before. They very much miss their Indian nurse."

A look of disapproval crossed her face. "Well, we shall have a good English nanny . . . and that will be an end to all that. Good night, Drusilla."

"Good night, Lady Harriet."

How strange it was to be in this house once more . . . to be actually living under its roof!

I went to my room. The sheets seemed very clean and cold, and the room airy and a little austere. There were too many memories . . . beyond the gardens . . . the green, the old church . . . and the rectory . . . the scenes of my childhood.

I thought of my father. I could see him, walking from the rectory to the church, his prayer book under his arm, his fine hair blowing untidily in the wind . . . his thoughts far away . . . in ancient Greece, most likely.

So much had happened since I left.

I did not feel tired, and yet as soon as I lay between those cool, clean sheets I fell into a deep sleep, so exhausted was I both physically and emotionally.

The next day I spent with the children. I took them for a walk through the old churchyard. I saw Colin Brady and his wife. There was a young baby now.

Ellen Brady, the doctor's daughter, now Colin's wife, insisted that I come into the rectory, where she gave me a glass of her elderberry wine. Colin came and joined us. The children sat quietly by.

I thought that *I* might be sitting there by the tray dispensing glasses of *my* elderberry wine to visitors. No. I would never have settled for that, although I had no doubt that Lady Harriet still considered it foolish of me not to have done so.

"We thought of you when we heard the news, didn't we, Ellen?" said Colin.

Ellen said they had.

"All those terrible things. How could they? It must have been really frightening."

The children had been taken by the maid to look at the garden, so they could speak freely by this time.

"And Miss Lavinia . . . the Countess. What a terrible thing to die like that . . . and so young . . ."

I agreed, thinking: You have no idea how she died. You could never have imagined it.

When I went into the village people came to speak to me. Shopkeepers came out of their shops as I passed.

"Oh, I'm glad to see you back, Miss Drusilla. It must have been terrible. All those awful things . . ."

They were interested in the children.

"It will be nice to have little ones at Framling. Lady Harriet will be pleased."

There was no doubt that she was. She mourned Lavinia, I knew. It seemed outrageous to her that natives should attack the English, but that they should *murder* her daughter was even more outrageous. Perhaps I had never really understood her. One thing she did care for was children—and now her grandchildren. I knew there was going to be a great battle for Fleur.

I thought about that a good deal, and as soon as I was assured that the children were sufficiently settled to do without me for a few days, I decided to go to see Polly. So I wrote to her.

Lady Harriet visited the nursery. I encouraged the children to talk to her, but I noticed they kept close to me when she was around.

She did not force herself upon them. That would not be Lady Harriet's way. But I could see how pleased she was when Louise addressed her directly. Alan averted his eyes when she was near and refrained from jumping.

"The children seem to be very quiet," she said to me once when they had gone to bed.

"They have to get used to their surroundings," I told her. "They have lived through so many changes. But they will settle in time."

"They shall be taught to ride."

I said I thought that an excellent idea.

"I shall delay getting the nanny . . . just for a little while yet."

I told her I thought that was a good idea. "Let them get accustomed to new faces for a while."

She nodded with approval.

"The news is getting better," she said. "General Roberts is working wonders. He is showing those dreadful people who are the masters, and Sir John Lawrence, they seem to think, deserves great praise for the part he has played. It seems that soon things will be more or less normal out there . . . as normal as they can be in such a place. It may well be that we shall have Sir Fabian and the children's father home sooner than I had hoped."

"That will be a great relief for you, Lady Harriet."

"Indeed yes. Then, of course, we shall have wedding bells. Lady Geraldine has waited long enough."

I did not want to look at her. I thought I might betray something.

"There will be no delay," she went on, "not once Sir Fabian is home. It is the last thing he would want." She smiled indulgently. "He is rather impatient, I'm afraid. He always has been. When he wants something he wants it at once. So . . . I am sure there will be a wedding . . . soon."

It seemed so reasonable now. Everything was different at home. When we were in India, travelling from Delhi to Bombay, I had perhaps dreamed impossible dreams.

Here, I could realize how foolish I had been.

I had had a rapturously loving reply from Polly.

"I'm just singing all over the place. Eff says I'm driving her mad. It's just that I'm so happy you're safe and sound and back home. We'll be waiting, so come just as soon as you can."

The papers heralded the good news. The Mutiny was fast coming to an end and black headlines in the papers proclaimed victory. General Roberts and Sir John Lawrence were the heroes. There was a great deal written about the loyal Sikhs and the treacherous sepoys. But all would be well. The wicked had been shown the evil of their ways and the just were triumphant.

Old men sat by the pond and discussed the relief of Lucknow. Names like Bundelkhand and Jhansi were tossed about with abandon. They had all defeated the villainous Nana Sahib; they had triumphed over Tantia Topee. They had put the mutineers where they belonged.

There was peace in the air. The spring was with us; the faint hum of insects mingled with the sound of clipping shears as the garden hedges were cut.

This was home. And I set out to see Polly.

I told the children that I would be away only for a few days. They had taken a great fancy to Molly, one of the parlourmaids, and I knew they would be happy with her. She would take them down to the drawing room in the afternoons to spend an hour with Grandmama. This had become a ritual which they accepted, and they were indeed becoming less in awe of her. I felt I could leave them safely and in any case I did feel it was necessary for me to hear what Polly had to tell me.

She was waiting for me at the station. Her eyes filled with

tears when she saw me and for a few moments we clung together.

Then she became practical. "Eff stayed at home. She'll have the kettle boiling by the time we get back. My goodness, am I glad to see you! Let's have a look at you. Not bad. I've been that worried . . . you out there in all that. Enough to make your hair curl. When we heard you was back . . . you should have seen us . . . Eff and Fleur . . . Oh, she remembers you all right. To tell the truth, sometimes Eff's a bit jealous. She is like that. But it's good to see you. I've told you, I've been singing all over the place ever since . . . nearly driven Eff off her rocker. Well, here you are."

We said little in the cab going to the house. And there it was, so dear and familiar.

The door was flung open and there were Eff and Fleur—Eff the same as ever and Fleur grown far more than I had expected . . . a beautiful, dark-haired girl, who threw her arms round my neck and kissed me.

"Well, are we going to stand here all night?" demanded Eff. "I've got the kettle on the boil. And there's muffins for tea. Got to be toasted. Didn't dare start till you come. Didn't want them all dried up, did we?"

And there we were sitting in the kitchen, too emotional to say very much at first, but so happy to be together.

I had to meet the governess. "Mrs. Childers, a real lady," I was told. "Come down in the world," Polly added. "She's ever so particular, and glad to be here. No airs and graces . . . just fond of Fleur, and my goodness, is Fleur fond of her. Clever, she is. History, geography and French, would you believe? Fleur's a natural for that. You should hear 'em parleyvousing. Eff and me just curl up, don't we, Eff?"

"You do," said Eff. "I know French when I hear it, and it's not all that to laugh about. And it's right and proper that Fleur should speak French, because most ladies do, and that's what she's got to be."

Mrs. Childers turned out to be a very pleasant woman. She was in her late thirties, I imagined; she was a widow and very fond of children. She had obviously, as Eff told me, come down in the world, but—Eff again—there was "no side to her." She faced facts and, as Polly said, they might not be Lady High and

Mighty or Lady Muck, but they treated her like one of themselves and she could take it or leave it.

Mrs. Childers had obviously taken it, and she told me that she was happy in the house and fond of Fleur. So it seemed they had all come to an excellent arrangement.

Each morning Mrs. Childers took Fleur into the park. They looked at flowers and things, Eff told me. It was something called botany.

Eff went often to the market to shop, and this gave me an opportunity to be alone with Polly.

She very soon began to talk about Lady Harriet's visit.

"Sent for me, she did. 'Please come to Framling without delay.' Who does she think she is? 'You go and take a running jump at yourself,' I said, not to her . . . but to Eff. Then down she comes. You should have seen her. I would have took her into the kitchen, but Eff would have her in the parlour. She was going to take Fleur with her, she said. 'If you think that,' I said, 'you've got another think coming. This is Fleur's home and this is where she stays.' She started to tell us how much more she could do for her. So could we, I told her. Do you know we own this house now? Yes, we bought it, and we're on the way to getting next door. Eff talks about retiring to a little place in the country."

"The country! You, Polly! But you love London."

"Well, when you're getting on a bit it's different. Eff always liked a bit of green. Anyway, it's not for now. It's for later. But what I'm saying is we can look after Fleur without her ladyship's help. Now what about you? You're living there . . . with that woman."

"The children are there, Polly . . . Louise and Alan. You'd love them."

"If they're half as nice as their sister, I reckon I would. I reckon they're glad to have you, but it can't be much fun in that house with her ladyship."

"I manage. She is fond of the children and she realizes that they need me. I was with them all through that terrible time in India, remember."

Polly nodded. "You know, if you couldn't stand her you could always come here. I reckon we'd manage all right the way we're getting on. Rents are coming in regular and now

379

that we've got our own house . . . it's good. Mind you, we had a struggle to get it and we were a bit short at one time. That reminds me. I ought to have told you before. Well, I had to do it. You'll understand, I know."

"I expect so, Polly. What is it?"

"Fleur's been ill."

"You didn't tell me."

"There wasn't no sense in worrying you when you were so far away. There was nothing you could have done. There was one time when it was touch and go."

"Oh, Polly! Do you mean that?"

"H'm. If that old grandmother had been there then, I reckon Fleur would have been with her by now. We'd have had to let her go. Something in her throat it was. It could have been the end of her if she hadn't had this operation."

"This is terrible, Polly. And I didn't know it."

"There was this man . . . a clever surgeon or something. Dr. Clement told us about him. He thought he was about the only man who could save her. Mind you, he was one of the Harley Street men . . . and it was fancy prices to get him to work. We had to find the money. We'd just bought the house. If it had been earlier we could have used that money and let the house go. But there we were . . . not much we could lay our hands on. Well, we'd got the house now, but that wouldn't have meant much to us if we'd lost Fleur."

I looked at her in horror, but she shook her head and smiled at me. "It's all right now. He did the job . . . it was a complete cure. I'll tell you what we did. Remember that fan you'd got . . . the one the old lady gave you?"

I nodded.

"There was a bit of jewellry in it."

"Yes, Polly, yes."

"I took it to the jeweller and he said that piece of glitter was worth quite a lot of money." She looked at me apologetically. "I said to Eff, 'This is what Drusilla would want if she was here.' She agreed with me. We had to have that money quick. I had to make up my mind there and then. And there were the jewels and there was dear little Fleur . . . so I took the fan to the jeweller and he bought the jewels . . . took them out he did . . . ever so careful . . . It saved Fleur's life.

There was even some over, so we took her to the seaside with that . . . Eff and me. A rare old time we had. You should have seen the colour come back into that little one's cheeks. You see . . ."

"Of course I see, Polly. I'm glad . . . I'm so glad."

"I knew you would be. What's a bit of stone compared with a child's life, eh? That's what I said to Eff. And I tell you this. He's made a good job of the fan, that jeweller. It looks just like it did before. I've kept it very special here. Just a minute."

I sat still, feeling shaken, while she went away to get it. I could never think of peacock feathers without seeing that terrible bloodstained fan lying at Lavinia's feet.

Polly stood before me and proudly opened the fan. It looked scarcely different from when I had last seen it; the place where the jewels had been was neatly covered.

"There!" said Polly. "A pretty thing it is. I'll never forget what it's done for Fleur."

As soon as I returned Lady Harriet wanted to know what had happened.

"They are adamant," I told her. "They will never give Fleur up."

"But didn't you point out the advantages I could give her?"

"They think she is better with them. They have a governess, you know."

"I did know. What any *good* governess would be doing in a place like that, I cannot imagine."

"She seems to be a very intelligent woman and she is very fond of Fleur."

"Rubbish!" said Lady Harriet. "They must be brought to their senses. I can assert my rights, you know."

"The circumstances are rather extraordinary."

"What do you mean? Fleur is my grandchild."

"But you have only just learned of her existence."

"What of that? I know she is my grandchild. I have a right."

"You mean you would go to law?"

"I will do anything that is necessary to get possession of my grandchild."

"It would mean bringing out the facts of the child's birth."

"Well?"

"Would you care for that?"

"If it is necessary it will have to be done."

"But if you took this matter to law there would be publicity. That would not be good for Fleur."

She hesitated for a moment. Then she said, "I am determined to get the child."

I felt it was a little ironical that when Fleur had been born she was unwanted by her mother and we had been at great pains to find a home for her. Now there were two strong factions—one determined to get her, the other to keep her.

I wondered who would win.

Time was slipping by. Louise and Alan were growing up into Framling children. They were given riding lessons, which delighted them, and each morning they spent half an hour in the paddock with a Framling groom. Lady Harriet used to watch them from her window with great satisfaction.

The nanny arrived. She was in her mid-forties, I thought, and had been looking after children for more than twenty-five years. Lady Harriet was pleased with her. She had worked in a ducal family, Lady Harriet told me—only a younger son, but still ducal.

"She will relieve you of the more onerous duties," she said. "You can confine yourself to the schoolroom now."

The children accepted Nanny Morton, and as she was in full possession of that nanny-like gift of keeping a firm hand and at the same time conveying the impression that she was one of those omniscient beings who would protect them against the world, she soon became part of the daily routine and she helped them gain a strong hold on that state which is all-important to the young: security.

Now and then they referred to their mother and the ayah, but these occasions were becoming more rare. Framling was now their home. They loved the spaciousness of that mysterious and yet now-familiar house; they loved their riding; and although they were in awe of their formidable grandmother, they had a certain affection for her and were gratified on those rare occasions when she expressed approval of something they had done; then they had Nanny Morton and myself.

Those weeks that they had spent cooped up in Salar's house and the general feeling of unease that they must have experienced made them appreciate the peace of Framling, the glorious gardens, the exciting riding and the general feeling of well being.

Lady Harriet often talked of Lady Geraldine.

"There is some restoration to be done in the west wing," she told me. "But I am doing nothing. Lady Geraldine may want to change it all when she comes." And then, "Lady Geraldine is a great horsewoman. I daresay she will want to improve the stables."

Lady Geraldine had a habit of cropping up in the conversation, and as time passed she did so more frequently.

"Surely there is nothing now to keep Sir Fabian in India," she said. "I am sure he will be home soon. I shall invite Lady Geraldine over so that she is here when he comes. That will be a nice surprise for him. Louise and Alan had better make the most of the nursery. They may have to be sharing it before long."

"You mean Fleur . . ."

"Yes. Fleur, and when Sir Fabian marries." She gave a little giggle. "Lady Geraldine's family are noted for their fertility. They all have large families."

She was getting more and more excited, because she could not believe he would be away much longer.

Then Dougal came home.

We were at lessons in the schoolroom when he arrived. There was no warning.

Lady Harriet came in with him. I heard her say before she appeared, "They are having their lessons with Drusilla. You remember Drusilla . . . that nice sensible girl from the rectory."

As if he needed reminding! We had been good friends. I had seen him in India, and he knew I had looked after the children there. But Lady Harriet was never very clear about the relationships of menials.

He came in and stood still, smiling, his eyes on me, before they went to the children.

I stood up.

Lady Harriet said, "Children, your papa is here."

Louise said, "Hello, Papa."

Alan was silent.

"How are you?" said Dougal. "And you, Drusilla?"

"Very well," I answered. "And you?"

He nodded, still looking at me. "It has been so long."

"We heard about Lucknow. That must have been terrible."

"Terrible for us all," said Dougal.

"I think the children might finish with their lesson," said Lady Harriet, "and as it is rather a special occasion, we will all go to my sitting room."

They left their books and I paused to shut them and put them away.

"You will want to be with your papa, children," said Lady Harriet.

"Yes, Grandmama," said Louise meekly.

Dougal looked at me. "We'll talk later," he said.

I was alone in the schoolroom, reminding myself that, in spite of all that had gone before, I was only the governess.

The children did not seem to be particularly excited to see their father, but Lady Harriet was delighted; the reason was that he brought news that Fabian would soon be coming home.

"This is good news from India," she told me. "My son will soon be on his way home. The wedding will take place almost immediately. They would have been married now, but for those wicked natives. I have started thinking about what dress I shall wear. As the bridegroom's mother I shall have my part to play, and Lizzie Carter, although a good worker, is rather slow. Louise will make a charming bridesmaid and Alan will be quite a stalwart little page. I always enjoy planning weddings. I remember Lavinia . . ."

Her animated expression faded. "Poor Dougal," she went on briskly. "He is a lost soul without her."

I had never noticed his reliance on her, but I did not imply this. The mention of Lavinia was as painful to me as it was to Lady Harriet.

Dougal was staying for a few days at Framling; then he was going to his estates. He took an early opportunity of talking to me.

"It was wonderful to see you, Drusilla," he said. "There

384

were times when I thought I should never see anyone again. What experiences we passed through."

"We did . . . among thousands of others."

"Sometimes I feel I shall never be the same again."

"I think we all feel like that."

"I am leaving the Company. I intended to in any case. Indeed, I think there will be changes. The feeling is that this will be the end of the Company as such. It will be passed over to the State. I intend to hand over my interests to a cousin."

"What shall you do?"

"What I always wanted to. Study."

"And the children?"

He looked surprised. "Oh, they will be with their grandmother."

"That is what she wants, of course."

"It seems the most sensible thing. She has the big house . . . the nurseries . . . everything the children need and . . . er . . . she is determined to keep them. I was telling Louise about some of the newest discoveries in archaeology and she was quite interested."

"Louise is very intelligent . . . the sort of child who is interested in everything she hears."

"Yes. It's fascinating to study a child's mind . . . to watch the dawning of intelligence. They have perfect brains . . . uncluttered . . . and quick to learn."

"They have to be, to grasp what is necessary in life. It has often occurred to me that they think logically and clearly. All they lack is experience, and therefore they have to learn how to deal with triumph and disaster."

"It is good to be with you, Drusilla. I have missed you. I often think of the old days at the rectory. Do you remember them?"

"Of course."

"Your father was such an interesting man."

We were watching the children on their ponies and at that moment Alan passed. He was riding without holding the reins. The groom was beside him.

"Look at me, Drusilla," he cried. "Look. No reins."

I clapped my hands and he laughed joyously.

"They are so fond of you," said Dougal.

"We grew close while we were in hiding. Both of them were aware of the danger, I think."

"How fortunate that you came through all that."

"You were with Tom and Alice."

"Yes, they were in Lucknow. That was a time of real terror. We never knew, from one moment to the next, what was going to happen. I can't explain to you what it was like when Campbell's troops took the city. It was a hard struggle. They fought like demons."

"Will Tom and Alice come home?"

"Not for some time, I imagine. Things are in upheaval over there. Everyone is anticipating great change. Tom will be needed and is sure to be there some time yet. But he has Alice with him. They get along very well together. Fabian will be home quite soon. I don't know how it is all going to work out. He will want to see people in London. Everything is in a state of flux. There will be great changes in the Company and I don't know how this will affect Fabian."

"Nor Tom Keeping, I suppose."

"Tom will be all right. He is a lucky man. Alice is a fine person." He looked a little wistful. "Just imagine. They had known each other such a short time . . . and there it was. They seem as though they were just made for each other."

"I suppose it happens like that sometimes."

"To the lucky ones. To the rest of us . . ." He lapsed into silence and then went on, "There should be no pretence between us, should there? We know each other too well. Drusilla, I have made a mess of things."

"I suppose we all feel that about ourselves at some time."

"I hope you don't. Here am I . . . adrift. A man with two children to whom sometimes I fancy I am a stranger."

"That could soon be remedied."

"They are so fond of you, Drusilla."

"I have been with them for a long time. They were my charges when I came to India and have been ever since. Then we went through that fearful time together. They weren't aware of the enormity of the dangers, but even young children can't live through a time like that without being affected. I represent a sort of rock to them, security, I suppose."

"I understand that. It is how they would see you. There is

a strength about you, Drusilla. I often think of the old days. We were very good friends then. I can't tell you how much I used to look forward to those sessions with you and your father."

"Yes, we all enjoyed them."

"We talked of interesting things . . . important things . . . and because we shared our pleasure we enjoyed it the more. Do you ever wish you could go back in time . . . to act differently . . . to change things?"

"I think everyone does that now and then."

"Mine was not a happy marriage. Well . . . it was disastrous really. You see, she was so beautiful."

"I don't think I ever saw anyone as beautiful as Lavinia."

"It was a blinding sort of beauty. I thought she was like Venus rising from the sea."

"You worship beauty, I know. I have seen your eyes when they rest on certain pieces of statuary or great paintings."

"I thought she was quite the most beautiful creature I had ever seen. She seemed to be fond of me, and Lady Harriet was determined . . ."

"Ah yes," I said. "You became very eligible overnight."

"That should never have happened to me. Well, she is dead now, and there are the children."

"They will be your chief concern."

"They will be brought up here, I suppose. They are well and happy here. I am not sure about the influence of the Framlings. I worry about them a little. I feel they might take their values from Lady Harriet. I am glad that you are with them, Drusilla."

"I love them very much."

"I can see that. But when Fabian returns . . . I believe he will soon get married. I gather there is already some understanding with Lady Geraldine Fitzbrock. Not an official engagement yet . . . but that will come, and Lady Harriet wants a quick marriage, so . . ."

"Yes, I too have gathered that from her."

"Well, it will be a little time before Fabian has children, I suppose. But the nursery will be theirs, and if his children are anything like him they will soon be dominating mine."

The subject of Fabian's marriage filled me with deep depression, which I hoped I did not show.

He went on, "I wish I could take them away . . . have a place of my own."

"You have, haven't you?"

"A rambling old place . . . more like a fortress than a home. It came along with the inheritance. It would not be much of a home for children, Drusilla."

"Perhaps it could be made so."

"With a family . . . children perhaps . . ."

"Well, it is all before you."

"Yes. It's not too late, is it?"

"Some say it is never too late."

"Drusilla . . ." He was smiling at me.

I thought in panic: He is going to ask me to marry him, as my father thought he might all those years ago. He is thinking it could be a solution. I have already been a surrogate mother to his children and he knows that I will be interested in whatever he takes up. I am not beautiful . . . hardly like Venus rising from the sea . . . but I have other qualities. As Lady Harriet would say, I am a sensible girl.

Just at that moment the children ran up. Their riding lesson was over. I was glad of the diversion.

Louise said, not looking at her father, "Drusilla, I did the jump today. Did you see?"

"Yes," I told her. "You did it beautifully."

"Did I? Jim said it's going to get higher and higher."

"Right up to the sky," said Alan. "Did you see *me*?"

"Yes," I assured him. "We both watched . . . your father and I."

"You were very good," Dougal told him.

Alan smiled at him and jumped.

"Stop, Alan," said Louise. She looked apologetically at Dougal. "He's always jumping," she added.

"It shows he's happy," I said.

"You wait until *I* do the jumps with my horse," Alan cried.

"We will," I told him. I turned to Dougal. "Won't we?"

"You too?" said Alan, looking doubtfully at his father. "*You* and Drusilla?"

"We shall be there," I replied.

Alan jumped again and we all laughed.

Then we walked back, Alan running on ahead and turning

to look back at us every few seconds while Louise walked rather soberly between us.

Fabian was coming home. He was on the high seas and in a week or so he would be with us.

Lady Harriet was more excited than I had ever seen her. She was quite talkative to me.

"I have decided that I won't ask Lady Geraldine just at first. He will pay too much attention to her and as I have not seen my son for a long time I want him to myself. Besides, it will be more romantic for him to go down to her. He should propose in her father's house. Everything will be different when he comes. There will be no nonsense about the child from those two women. Fleur will be brought to her rightful home."

"I daresay she will want to have some say in her future herself."

"A mere child! What are you thinking of, Drusilla?"

"I was thinking that perhaps I should consider my position."

"Your position! What do you mean?"

"I thought Lady Geraldine might want to make changes."

"In the nursery. I am mistress of this house, as I was when I came here as a bride, and I intend to remain so. Moreover, you teach the children very well and *I* am satisfied with their progress. Louise is getting on admirably. You have a gift for teaching. *My* governess was with me from my earliest days to the time when I had my season."

That was an end of the matter . . . for her. But not for me. I could not stay. I certainly would not remain when Fabian was married to Lady Geraldine. I knew I had had ridiculous dreams. I suppose those days in India, which now seemed part of an unreal nightmare, had had their effect on me. Back in Framling I realized how impossible those dreams had been.

The Framlings were Framlings. They would never change. They looked upon the rest of us as pawns in a game, to be moved around as benefitted them. We were of no importance except in our usefulness.

During that week, while Lady Harriet went around in a state of happiness which I had never seen her in before, I was getting more and more depressed. I did not want to be here when he came home. I could not join the general rejoicing because of the suitable marriage he was making. Fabian *would* marry suitably, I was sure. He was as much aware of family obligations as his mother was. He had been brought up to regard them as all-important. I had not been mistaken when I had thought there was an attraction between us. There always had been . . . with him as well as with me. I knew that he wanted to make love to me; but the question of marriage would never arise. I had heard whispers of past Framlings . . . the vivid lives they had led, the romantic adventures which had nothing to do with marriage. They married suitably and that was all that was expected of them.

But that was not the life for me. I was too seriousminded, as Lady Harriet would have said, "too sensible."

I saw Dougal often. He did not ask me to marry him, but I knew it was in his mind. He was afraid to ask me outright, for fear I should refuse. I realized that Dougal was not the man to take quick decisions. He would always waver; others would have to make up his mind for him.

If I gave him that little bit of encouragement for which he looked, he would have asked me. Why did he want me? I asked myself. It was because I represented a certain security to him, as I did to his children. I would be the surrogate mother, for which post I had already qualified.

It would be convenient, wise no doubt. I could look to a peaceful life ahead with Dougal, quiet, pleasant, with a husband who would be considerate and caring . . . and the children growing up with us. We would study together. I would learn a great deal. Our excitement would be in the antiquities of the world . . . books, art . . . they would give us our interest.

Perhaps I should grow like him.

He was seeing me as the antithesis of Lavinia, but he would never forget that outstanding beauty, which I believed he had marvelled at when he saw her.

Everyone would say I should be glad of the opportunity. "What is your life?" they would say. "Are you going to spend it serving the Framlings?" And what about Lady Geraldine?

Would she sense her husband's feelings towards me? It could develop into an explosive, impossible situation.

I should have to go. Where? I had a little money, just about enough to keep me in a rather dreary, comfortless style. What a fool I was to turn away from all that Dougal was offering me.

And Fabian would be home in a day or so.

I could not bear to be there when he came.

I said to Lady Harriet, "I would like to go to see Polly again."

"Well," replied Lady Harriet, "that is not a bad idea. You can tell them that Sir Fabian will soon be home and he will put a stop to their nonsense. They might as well give up Fleur with a good grace. Tell them we shall not be forgetful and shall reward them for what they have done."

I did not remark that that was the very way to stiffen their resolve, if it needed stiffening—which it did not. But how could one explain such things to Lady Harriet?

I was happy to be with Polly again. I was taken back to my childhood, when she was there to soothe away my little problems.

It was not long before she sensed there was something on my mind. She managed in that skilful way of hers that we would be alone together.

"Let's sit in the parlour," she said. "Eff won't know. Besides, you're a visitor and parlours are for visitors."

So we sat there on the stiff, unused chairs with their prim antimacassars on the backs and the aspidistra on the wicker table in the window and the clock, which her father had thought such a lot of, ticking away on the mantelshelf.

"Now, what's on your mind?"

"Oh, I'm all right, Polly."

"Don't give me that. I know when something's wrong with you and that's now."

"Sir Fabian is coming home," I said.

"Well, it's about time, I should think."

I was silent.

"Here," she said. "Tell me. You know you can tell your old Polly anything."

"I feel rather foolish. I've been so stupid."

"Ain't we all?"

"You see, Polly, if you can imagine what it was like in India . . . From one minute to the next we never knew whether it was going to be our last. That does something to you."

"You tell me what it does to you."

"Well . . . he was there and all those other people were, too, but it was like being with him alone. He'd saved my life, Polly. I had seen him shoot a man who was going to kill me." She nodded slowly.

"I know," she said. "He seemed like some sort of hero to you, didn't he? You had this fancy for him. You'd always had it, really. You can't fool me."

"Perhaps," I said. "It was silly of me."

"I never thought he'd be any good to you. There was that other one." She looked at me. "And he goes and marries that Lavinia. I reckon you're better off without the both. Men . . . they're chancy things . . . Better none at all than the wrong one . . . and, my, my goodness, the good ones don't grow on trees, I can tell you."

"There *was* your Tom."

"Ah . . . my Tom. Not many like him in this world, I can tell you, and he goes and gets himself drowned. I said to him, 'You ought to get a job ashore, that's what.' But would he listen? Oh no. No sense, men, that's about it."

"Polly," I said. "I had to get away. You see, he's coming home and he is going to be married."

"What?"

"Lady Harriet is making preparations. She is Lady Geraldine Fitzbrock."

"What a name to go to bed with!"

"She will be Lady Geraldine Framling. I couldn't stay there. She wouldn't want me."

"Not when she sees he's got a fancy for you."

"It was only a passing fancy, Polly. He'd forget all about me if I was not there."

"You'd better get out of that place, I can see. There's always a home for you here."

"That's another thing, Polly. Lady Harriet says he will do something about Fleur."

"What about her?"

"She says they will stand by their rights. She's the grand-mother, you see."

"Grandmother, me foot! Fleur's ours. We brought her up. We had her since she was a few weeks old. Nobody's going to take her away from us now. I tell you straight."

"If she took it to court . . . all their money and the fact that Fleur is their flesh and blood . . ."

"I won't have it. Eff won't either. They wouldn't want all that dragged through the courts . . . all about Madam Lavinia's affairs in France. Course they wouldn't."

"Nor would you, Polly. You wouldn't want Fleur to be faced with all that."

Polly was silent for once.

"Oh . . . it won't get to that," she said at length.

"They are very determined and accustomed to having their own way."

"Here's someone who's not letting them. But we're talking about you. You know you want to get that Fabian out of your mind. That other one . . . well, it mightn't be such a bad idea."

"You mean Dougal?"

"Yes, him. He's a bit of a ninny, but there are the children, and you know how fond you are of them."

"We were great friends really. I liked him very much. But then Lavinia appeared. She was so beautiful, Polly. I think it ruined her life in a way. She couldn't resist admiration. She had to have it from everyone and in the end . . . she died."

I found myself telling the story. It all came back to me so vividly. Roshanara . . . the Khansamah . . . his meetings with Lavinia in her boudoir . . . to that last terrible scene.

"She was lying on the bed, Polly. I knew what had happened. She had insulted his dignity and she paid for it in a special way. He gave her a peacock-feather fan. She thought it was because he was contrite and so enamoured of her beauty. But it was the sign of death. That's what it meant. And there she lay with the bloodstained fan at her feet."

"Well, I never."

"You see, Polly, there is a legend about peacocks' feathers.

They are bringers of ill fortune. You remember Miss Lucille and her fan."

"I do indeed. And reason to be thankful for it. I reckon it saved our Fleur's life."

"But getting the jewel cost her lover his."

"I reckon them men would have got him at any time."

"But it was when he was taking the fan to have the jewels set in that it happened. Lucille believed it was the ill luck of the fan."

"Well, she was off her rocker."

"I know she was unbalanced . . . but it was due to what happened to her."

"You want to get rid of all them fancy ideas about fans."

"But it means something to them, Polly. They are a strange people. They are not like us. What seems plain common sense here is different there. Dougal found there was a legend about peacocks' feathers. The Khansamah must have believed it, for he gave Lavinia the fan and when he killed her he laid it at her feet. It was a sort of ritual."

"Well, let them think what they like. A bundle of feathers is a bundle of feathers to me, and I can't see anything to frighten yourself about that."

"Polly, I have the fan. At one time my father . . . and others . . . thought Dougal would ask me to marry him. They all thought it would be good for me."

"He'd have shown a lot more sense if he had asked you, and I'm not sure you wouldn't have shown some if you'd said yes. He might not be all that you'd want . . . not one of them dashing heroes . . . he might be just a timid little man . . . but he's not so bad, and you can't have everything in life. Sometimes it's best to take what you can get . . . providing it's all right in the main."

"He didn't want me when he saw Lavinia. It was as though he were bewitched. He didn't *see* me after that. I was interested in what interested him, as my father was. He enjoyed being with us . . . talking to us . . . and then he saw Lavinia. He had seen her before, of course, but she was grown up and he saw her afresh. He forgot any feeling he might have had for me. You see, it's a sort of pattern."

"I shall begin to think you're going wrong in the head. What's all this got to do with fans?"

"I think, Polly, that I shall never be happy in love because I took the fan. It was in my possession for a while. That is what Miss Lucille believed . . . and it seems as if . . . you see."

"No, I don't see," said Polly. "This isn't like you. I always thought you had some sense."

"Strange things happen in India."

"Well, you're not there now. You're in plain, sensible England, where fans are just fans and nothing else."

"I know you're right."

"Of course I'm right. So don't let's have any more of this nonsense about fans. I reckon that fan done us all a good turn. When you look at young Fleur now and think what she was like at that time . . . it makes me tremble all over now to think of it. So you're not going to marry this Dougal?"

"He hasn't asked me yet, Polly."

"Looks like he's just waiting for a shove in the right direction."

"I shall not do the shoving."

"Well, you'd have a grand title, wouldn't you? I never thought much of them myself, but there's plenty as do."

"I wouldn't want to marry for that, Polly."

"Course you wouldn't. But he seems a nice enough fellow. All he needs is a bit of pushing and you'd be rather good at that. And there's the children, too. They're fond of you and they'd have you as their mum. I reckon that's what *they*'d like."

"They probably would, but one doesn't marry for that reason."

"You're still thinking of that old fan. You're thinking it's going to be bad luck and nothing will go right while you have it. Here. Wait a minute. Come into the kitchen. I want to show you something. Just a minute. I'll go and get it."

I went into the kitchen. It was warm, for the fire was burning. It always was, for it heated the oven and the kettle was always on the hob.

Within a few minutes Polly came in; she was carrying the case that contained the peacock-feather fan.

She took it out and unfurled it.

"Pretty thing," she said.

Then she went to the fire and put the fan into the heart of it. The feathers were immediately alight—their deep blues mingling with the red of the flames. I gasped as I watched it disintegrate.

Nothing was left of it but the blackened frame.

I turned to her in dismay. She was looking at me half fearfully, half triumphantly. I knew she felt unsure of what my reaction would be.

"Polly!" I stammered.

She looked a little truculent. "There," she said. "It's gone. There's no need to worry about that any more. You was getting worked up about that fan. I could see it was beginning to get a hold of you. You was expecting things to go wrong . . . and somehow that's often a way of making them. It's gone now . . . that's the end of it. We make our own lives you know. It's got nothing to do with a bunch of feathers."

I had been in the park with Mrs. Childers and Fleur, and as soon as we returned Polly came hurrying into the hall, Eff just behind her. Polly looked anxious. Eff excited.

Eff called, "A visitor for you, Drusilla." And then, in a high-pitched, overawed sort of manner, she added, "In the parlour."

"Who . . . ?" I began.

"You go and see," said Polly.

I went in. He was standing there, smiling, making the parlour look smaller and less prim than it usually did.

"Drusilla!" He came to me and took my hands. He looked at me for a second or so and then he held me to him tightly. After a moment he released me, holding me slightly away from him, looking at me intently.

"Why did you go?" he demanded. "Just when I was coming home."

"I . . . I thought you would want to be with your family."

He laughed, a happy, derisive sort of laughter.

"You knew I wanted to be with you more than anyone."

I thought then: It is wonderful. I don't care what happens afterwards . . . this is wonderful *now*.

I began, "I was not sure . . ."

"I did not know you could be so foolish, Drusilla. You knew I was coming and you went away."

I tried to calm myself. "You've come here because of . . . Fleur. You've come to try to take her away."

"What on Earth is the matter with you? Have you forgotten? Remember the last time we were together . . . all those people around, when we wanted to be alone. The first thing I said when I came home was, 'Where is Drusilla? Why isn't she here with the children?' And my mother told me you had come here. I said, 'But I said she was to be here.' I expected to find you at Framling as soon as I got back."

"I didn't know you would want to see *me.*"

He looked at me incredulously.

"Drusilla, what's happened to you?" he demanded.

I said slowly, "I've come home. Everything is different here. It seems to me now that in India I was living in a different world, where anything could happen. Here it is . . . as it always was."

"What difference does it make where we are? We are *us*, aren't we? We know what we want. At least I do. And I want you."

"Have you thought . . . ?"

"I don't have to think. Why are you being so aloof? It wasn't like this when we were last together."

"I tell you it is different now. How was it in India?"

"Chaotic."

"Alice and Tom?"

"In a state of bliss . . . a most wonderful example of the joys of married life."

I smiled. "Ah," he said. "Now you are more like yourself. What is the matter? We're talking like strangers. Here am I come home to marry you and you behave as though we have just been introduced."

"To marry *me!* But . . ."

"You are not going to raise objections, are you? You know my nature. I just ignore them."

"What of Lady Geraldine?"

"She is well, I believe."

"But your mother was arranging . . ."

"Arranging what?"

"The wedding."

"*Our* wedding."

"Your marriage to Lady Geraldine. Your mother has been arranging it."

"I arrange my own wedding."

"But Lady Geraldine . . ."

"What has my mother said to you?"

"That you were coming home to marry her."

He laughed. "Oh, she has had that in mind for some time. She forgot to consult me, that's all."

"But she will be . . . furious."

"My mother will agree with me. She always does. Though I believe I am the only one whose opinion she considers. Stop thinking about my mother and think of me. You're not marrying her."

"I can't believe all this."

"You're not going to say, 'This is so sudden, sir,' as so many well-brought-up ladies are supposed to."

"But, Fabian, it *is* sudden . . ."

"I should have thought it was obvious. The way we were in India . . . have you forgotten?"

"I forget nothing of what happened there."

"We went through all that together, didn't we? I blamed myself for bringing you out there. But now we're here . . . together . . . I think those times taught us a great deal about each other. It taught us that there was a special bond between us and it grows stronger every day. It's never going to break, Drusilla. We're together . . . forever."

"Fabian, I think you go too fast."

"I think I have gone unforgivably slowly. You are not going to refuse me, are you? You should know by now that I never take refusals. I would immediately abduct you and drag you to the altar."

"Do you really mean that you want to marry *me?*"

"Good Heavens! Haven't I made that clear?"

"You do realize it is most unsuitable."

"If it suits me it has to suit everyone else."

"Lady Harriet would never allow it."

"Lady Harriet will accept what I want. She already knows. I was enraged when I came back and found you weren't there. I said, 'I am going to marry Drusilla and there will be no delay about it.' "

"She must have been outraged."

"Only mildly surprised."

I shook my head.

He said, "I am disappointed in you, Drusilla. Have you forgotten everything? That night you came to the house . . ." I shook my head and he went on, "That dreadful moment when I feared I might miss . . . that I might be too late. You've no idea what I went through. I lived a lifetime in those few seconds. Have you forgotten that trek to Bombay? I was desolate when you sailed away and I promised myself that the moment I was free of all that, we would be together . . . and never part again. Drusilla, have you forgotten? Didn't I choose you when you were a baby? 'That's mine,' I said, and it has been like that ever since."

I felt numb with happiness, which I could not accept as real. He was holding me tightly. I felt protected against the fury of Lady Harriet, the disappointment of Lady Geraldine and the terrible fear that I would wake up and find I had been dreaming. Don't think of what's to come, I admonished myself. Live in the moment. This is the greatest happiness you could ever know.

He felt no such qualms. I knew, of course, that he would never have any doubts that he could have what he wanted.

"So," he said, "we'll go back. No delays. It will be the quickest wedding in Framling history. No more protests . . . please."

"If it is true. If you mean it . . . if you really mean it, then . . ."

"Then what?"

"Then life is wonderful."

We called in Polly and Eff and told them the news.

"So you are getting married," said Polly. She was a trifle bellicose, I must admit. I saw the glint in her eyes. She was still a little uncertain whether her little ewe lamb was going to be devoured by the big, bad wolf.

He knew how she regarded him and I saw the glint of amusement in his eyes.

"Soon," he told her, "you shall dance at our wedding."

"My dancing days are over," said Polly tersely.

"But on such an occasion they might be revived, perhaps," he suggested.

Eff's eyes glistened. I could see her choosing her dress. "It's for a wedding, a rather special one. *Sir* Fabian Framling. He's marrying a special friend of ours." I could hear her explaining to the tenants. "Well, I suppose you'd call it one of them grand weddings. Polly and me, we've had our invitations. Such an old friend."

Polly was less euphoric. She didn't trust any man except her Tom, and her suspicion of Fabian was too deeply rooted to be dispersed by an offer of marriage.

I could smile at her fears and be happy.

Fabian wanted to stay on in London for a few days, and then we would go back together. He had booked a room in a hotel. Eff was relieved. She had had an idea that she might have to 'put him up,' but she did not really think there was a vacant room in any of the houses that would be worthy of a titled gentleman, although the prestige that would come from being able to say, "When *Sir* Fabian was in one of my rooms . . ." would be great.

Later that day Fabian and I went to a jewellers to buy a ring. It was beautiful—an emerald set in diamonds. When it was on my finger I felt happier than I ever had been in my life . . . for the ring seemed to seal the bond and to proclaim to the world that I was to marry Fabian.

I believed I would be happy. I believed I could forget the horrible sights I had witnessed during the Mutiny. I was loved by Fabian, more deeply, more tenderly than I had ever believed possible; and somehow at the back of my mind I linked my happiness with the destruction of the peacock-feather fan.

It was ridiculous, I knew—a flight of fancy. Perhaps I had been too long in India, where mysticism seemed to flourish more than it could in the prosaic air of England. No blame could attach to me. I had not destroyed it. Polly had done that for me and she had never owned it, so it could not involve her. I closed my eyes and could see those beautiful blue feathers curling up in the flames. It was ridiculously fanciful. I had allowed the fan to take hold of my imagination: subconsciously

I had endowed it with magical qualities and so it had seemed to influence my life.

But no more. I felt free. I wanted to live every moment ahead of me to the full. There would be difficulties to face. I could leave those for the future and live in this moment . . . this wonderful moment . . . with the joy of loving and being loved.

Fabian and I sat in the gardens opposite the house and talked.

He said suddenly, "There is the question of the child."

"They will never give her up," I told him.

"She can't stay in this place."

"Fabian, you can't use people when they are useful and when you think they have served their purpose cast them aside."

"I have an idea. They should bring her down to Framling."

"Polly and Eff!"

"This is what I think. There are a couple of vacant houses on the estate. They could have one of these and the child would be there . . . near Framling. She could live between the two houses for a while. Then the time will come when she will go away to school. And she can think of both the house with those two in it *and* Framling as her home."

"They have their houses. They wouldn't want to go to the country."

"They'd want what was best for Fleur, and they'd be near you. I think they could be persuaded and you are the one to persuade."

"I am not sure they will accept it . . . or even consider it."

"You'll do it. You'll persuade them."

"They are independent."

"They own that house, don't they? They could sell it and buy this place."

"What about the price?"

"It could be anything that fitted. They could have the place for nothing."

"They would never accept that. They'd call it being beholden."

"Then let them buy it . . . at whatever price will fit. It's quite simple."

"You don't know Polly and Eff."

"No, but I know you and I am sure you can make it work out."

I talked to Polly first.

"Well, I never!" she said. "Give up this house. Take the one they've got empty. We want no charity from them."

"It wouldn't be charity. You'd be absolutely independent of them. You could sell this house and buy the other with the proceeds."

"Not on your life."

"You'd be near me, Polly. That would be lovely."

She nodded.

"And Fleur would have all that the Framlings could give her."

"I know that. It's worried me at times. I've talked to Eff."

"You gave her a home when she needed it. You gave her love. That was wonderful, Polly. But she will have to go to school. Framling will be a good background."

"You don't think Eff and me haven't thought of that."

"Why not speak to Eff?"

Polly was weighing the advantages. Most certainly she and Eff wanted the best for Fleur. It was more important to them than anything; and I could see Polly was liking the idea of being near me. She was thinking I might need a bit of advice, married to that one.

She was wavering. Eff had said she was getting tired of some of the tenants. She had had a lot of trouble with Second Floor No. 28.

I said, "Polly, it would be wonderful for me."

"I'll speak to Eff," said Polly. "She won't, though."

"You might persuade her."

"Oh, I know she wants the best for Fleur, and I can see it would be a bit different there than here . . ."

"Think about it, Polly . . . seriously."

Later I said to Fabian, "I think it might work."

Fabian and I travelled back to Framling together. I was bracing myself for facing Lady Harriet.

I was amazed at how graciously she received me. There was a difference in her attitude. I had left the house as the governess to her grandchildren; I returned as the fiancée of her beloved son.

I wondered if she were asking herself what Fabian was doing, throwing himself away on the plain girl from the rectory—particularly when *her* choice had fallen on someone else.

I remembered that long-ago incident when he had brought me as a baby to his house and proclaimed that I was his child. Lady Harriet had insisted that her son's whim should be gratified. Now perhaps it was a similar situation.

Smiling, she discussed the wedding.

"There is no point in delay," she said. "I have thought for long, Fabian, that it was time you were married. You can't be married from here, Drusilla, that would be quite irregular. Brides should not be living under the same roofs as their bridegrooms the day before their marriages. So you can go to the rectory. That will be the most appropriate, because it was your old home. It's a pity Colin Brady can't give you away. He would have been the best person for that. But he will have to officiate in the church . . . so it will have to be the doctor. That will be an excellent alternative, as his daughter is at the rectory now. The next best thing to Colin Brady himself."

Lady Geraldine was mentioned only once. "A nice girl . . . a little too fond of riding. She spent most of the day in the saddle. I believe that broadens the figure and can mean a lack of other interests."

She gave no hint that she was disappointed. Here was a new side to Lady Harriet. Her love for her son went as deep as did that she had for Lavinia . . . and perhaps deeper, for Fabian was perfect in her eyes. The fact that she rarely mentioned her daughter did not mean that she had forgotten her. She often went to Lavinia's old room and stayed there for a long time and she would be noticeably subdued when she emerged. As for Fabian, he could do no wrong in her eyes. He was *her* son and therefore the perfect man. Fabian had chosen me and, because I was his choice, miraculously I had become hers.

I could not believe in such a *volte-face* until I began to understand Lady Harriet. She must, of course, always be right, so wisely she promptly adjusted her views to the inevitable and made herself believe that it was what she had wanted all the time. I felt warmer towards her because we both loved the same person and he was more important than any other to us. She recognized this and it made an instant bond between us.

History did seem to be repeating itself. I overheard a conversation and shamelessly I listened, as I had on another occasion.

It was in this very garden that I had overheard her remark that I was the plain child from the rectory. It had affected me more deeply than I had realized at the time.

Lady Harriet was in the drawing room with the doctor and his wife. The doctor was receiving his instructions, as he had been chosen by her to play his part at the ceremony.

Her voice, resonant and authoritative, floated out to me.

"I had always meant Drusilla for Fabian and I am so happy that it has all turned out as I planned. She is so good with the children . . . and such a *sensible* girl."

The sun was shining on the pool; the water lilies were enchanting. A white butterfly paused and alighted on one of them. It rested a moment and was gone.

I was happier than I had believed possible.

Fabian loved me. Polly and Eff, I was sure, would soon be close at hand, and Fleur with them. The qualms that my formidable mother-in-law might have aroused in me were stilled. Moreover, I felt an understanding of her which could develop into fondness.

Fabian would be beside me and life would be good.

About the Author

Victoria Holt is one of the world's most popular and beloved authors. Her previous bestsellers include *The Silk Vendetta*, *The Demon Lover*, and *The Judas Kiss*. She lives in London.